the ART *of* SPIES

PRODIGAL SON

A NOVEL

Robert E. O'Connell III

OIA

PRAISE FOR THE ART OF SPIES: PRODIGAL SON

"My favorite novels are sophisticated espionage thrillers by authors like John Le Carre and Frederick Forsyth. I'm an expert on art crime and I'm always curious to see how authors integrated the dark side of the art world into their fiction. Robert E. O'Connell's work recalls the great authors of espionage but brings in the shadow realm of crimes involving art and museums. A winning combination that steals the show!"

-Dr Noah Charney Best-selling author of The Art Thief and The Art of Forgery

"In The Art of Spies, O'Connell captures the specialized complexity and psychological intensity of international art fraud investigation with incredible accuracy and nuance, as only one who lives and breathes that world can. This prequel to his riveting debut thriller amplifies that intensity into one wild ride!"

-John M. Griswold, Art Conservator

"As an art world specialist, I read The Art of Spies and found it not only completely intoxicating, but full of incredibly realistic detail. Now, we have been gifted with a prequel, The Art of Spies: Prodigal Son. Readers will be transported to 1945 following the end of World War II. Focusing on Okie's young adult life, including his recruitment into the newly formed C.I.A. Readers are sure to be swept up into the times of the Nixon White House as history and politics converge into another page turner you won't be able to put down. I highly recommend."

-Gary F. Metzner, Sotheby's Senior Vice President: Head of Office, Chicago

"Robert E. O'Connell's "The Art of Spies" coupled a riveting swirl of intrigue with a fascinating reveal of the high-end art world—I thought it couldn't be topped. But now comes the prequel: "The Art of Spies: Prodigal Son" in which O'Connell has somehow managed to outdo himself with a stunning mix of CIA manipulations, Nixonian conspiracies, and international fraud in the art world. Once you begin this post-World War II account, the story will consume you until you complete the novel."

-Anthony R. Licata, Author of Hannibal's Niece and Caesar Obsessed

The Art of Spies: Prodigal Son/OIA Productions, Inc.
Printed in the United States of America

Front Cover:
Emmett
Acrylic on Canvas
by Robert E. O'Connell Jr.
Collection of the Author

The Art of Spies: Prodigal Son/ Robert E. O'Connell III. -- 1st ed.

ISBN 978-1-7357858-4-4 Print Edition
ISBN 978-1-7357858-5-1 Ebook Edition

For the Wolfhound and the Sly Fox …

"If You Can Meet with Triumph and Disaster and Treat Those Two Imposters Just the Same"

-Rudyard Kipling

ACKNOWLEDGMENTS

Writing has always provided an escape for me, as well as a safe place to hide. A place to hide and exorcise demons. An isolated escape from my environment and a creative outlet for my right-brain, ambidextrous nature. The love of the written word and the spoken word has apparently been a gift received from my father. My love of art and my evolving professional career has been dedicated to art, insurance, and creativity. *Ars gratia artis.*

Thank you to my editors, Travis Heermann and Christopher Short, as well as my designer Colin Graham for their enduring patience and constant creativity. We have created a collaborative team to bring to fruition my life stories. You have challenged me and pointed me in directions that now make sense. We have collaborated on my vision and created another masterpiece. You have helped me to bring my life to the pages, and for this I am grateful in perpetuity. *Grātiās vōbīs agō.*

Joel Surnow entered my life serendipitously while playing golf in Palm Desert, California. We discovered that we share a profound interest in the Kennedys, the CIA, and the conspiracies. Thank you for your interest in my life story and your constant encouragement and mentoring. Yes, there is tremendous truth in a memoir.

Sandra Dijkstra, I have now completed my second novel in a conceived triptych. Works of art to be admired and treasured for posterity's sake. Thank you for your eternal support and muse.

Mark Fedota is alive and well, thank God, even though we killed him in the first book. Our friendship has been an inspiration and extremely beneficial for me and my storytelling. Mark is a lawyer, raised by Jesuits, and a Brother in the traditions of Saint Barnabas. *Qui dormit non peccat.*

William Conrad Tosch (19 January 1934 to 12 March 2022) is my father-in-law and an enormous influence on my life. His legacy has been part of my life story since 1978 when we first met in Littleton, Colorado. He evolved into an involved father, grandfather, and mentor. He is loved by his immediate family, extended family and countless friends and colleagues. Forever in our lives.

Thank you to our three children, Billy, Matt, and Finnian, who bring tremendous joy to our lives. Accept no limits and few boundaries. Live your life to tell your stories. For our family, my hope is my novels create a family legacy and documented history for future generations.

Thank you to my Aunt Ann and her husband John Buckreis including their children and my cousins. We are family and yet we are still getting to know each other. This is our family history and hopefully some of your questions have been addressed and gaps in the family history are closing.

My Buffalo family, including the Griffins, Reedys, and McGillicuddys, have been so generous with their time and sharing their genealogy so we may benefit from our gaps in family history. Your hospitality, your love and your inclusion for my family is greatly appreciated and will never be forgotten and always reciprocated.

O'Connell is a last name of Irish origin with a family motto of Reason and Power. It is an Anglicization of the Irish Ó Conaill (meaning "descendant of Conall"). The personal name Conall is composed of the elements con (from cú meaning "hound" or "wolf") and gal (meaning "valour"). Remember The Wolfhound!

Thank you, Hotel Bramante, for your inspiration. I love you, I miss you and we will visit soonest. *Un paradiso nel cuore di San Pietro.*

There are so many people to thank, and I fear that I may, once again, forget someone. You know who you are, and I thank you for your support. Remember, "*semper ubi sub ubi*" as Okie once taught me.

Mostly and profoundly, I wish to thank my wife, Darci Marie Tosch O'Connell. She is my guiding light, my saving grace, my entirety. She constantly inspires me and challenges me to improve the quality of my life. I want to be the best version of myself, and you are my encouragement and my reward. I love you completely and always without hesitation.

"I preach there are all kinds of truth, your truth and somebody else's. But behind all of them there is only one truth and that is that there's no truth."

-Flannery O'Connor

PREFACE

I always wished that my father had written his memoir before he died in early February 2019. He could have answered an accumulation of lingering questions and resolved most of the conspiracy theories that have haunted me for multiple decades. Now he has left me with the challenge to expose the mysteries surrounding his untimely death and expose the strangers in the shadows during his final days.

My father was born ten years before the end of World War II, known as the Good War. He grew up in a post-war environment in the United States that became known as the Cold War. His early years were defined by war and propaganda. Okie may seem like a Zelig or Forrest Gump character; however, he was real, and his life in service to his country and his faith was real. He intersected history and was part of the inner circles, the shadows, and the truth.

His life story reveals a man who was, in fact, "in the room" when many historical events happened, surrounded by many twentieth-century icons. He was recruited into the CIA when the Company was created after the Second World War, replacing the OSS.

He was proficient at many languages, and he always loved the written word. He loved the intellectual challenges of chess and the improvisations of jazz. However, he was not necessarily the best communicator as a father. A man of few words. He was most intimidating when he was silent and overshadowing the shared space, sucking up the oxygen in the room. He never gave credibility to the recurring Patsy Theory of John F. Kennedy's assassination that was fed to the American citizens by their own government.

You never knew what he was thinking or how he was going to react. He was always assessing the situation, reading the room, formulating a plan, and always at least two moves ahead of everyone. A Grand Mastermind at playing chess with his fool's mate strategy.

My father's life was a mystery. He was estranged from his father and only sibling. He never discussed his past, leaving us to speculate about The Truth. My siblings and I were left to accept only superficial truths. We were cut off from family and estranged from the city of Buffalo, where my grandfather and father were born and educated. During my father's lifetime, he never took our family to Buffalo to meet our extended family with its rich immigrant history.

My first visit to Buffalo was in 2018, with my wife and our children. I was hoping to exorcise the past and hopefully find answers to my father's anguished childhood, which was filled with the death of his mother and his perceived abandonment by his own father. We visited the cemetery where my grandfather and my grandmother are buried next to each other. We made a pilgrimage to Canisius High School where both my grandfather and my father excelled in academics and athletics. Their deep faith and parochial indoctrinations, primarily ingrained by Jesuit priests, shaped their convictions and their blind-faith defense of the Catholic Church.

We never understood what he did for a living. He was "self-employed," primarily in his own advertising business. We grew up middle class, but we never understood the source of the money. My parents installed a tennis court and separate half-court basketball court in our back yard. No one else had this setup within a thirty-mile radius. My father had a rotary dial cellular phone installed in his car in 1968. We moved multiple times, following our arrival in Littleton, Colorado, because people kept breaking into our homes searching for God knows what. Who were we? Were we living a lie, significantly above our means, or were we hiding from something? Maybe hiding in plain sight under witness protection?

My father's sister, Ann, always asked me why my father begged her to move her family from Buffalo to Northern Virginia so "all of the children" could grow up together as family, only to subsequently abandon her there. In 1968, after Ann moved her family to Annandale, Virginia, we apparently "upped and moved" from Kings Park, Virginia to Littleton, Colorado "in the middle of the night" without saying goodbye to Ann and her husband and our cousins. My siblings and I have zero recollection of this move across the country either by airplane or automobile.

I must now write my father's memoir fused with my memoir. My series of novels now represents these memoirs and the researched documentation of our collective family history. In the words of Constantine, "In hoc signo vinces."

-Robert E. O'Connell III, July 2022

"Practice any art, music, singing, dancing, acting, drawing, painting, sculpting, poetry, fiction, essays, reportage, no matter how well or badly, not to get money and fame, but to experience becoming, to find out what's inside you, to make your soul grow.

Seriously! I mean starting right now, do art and do it for the rest of your lives."

-Kurt Vonnegut (2006)

PROLOGUE - 1946

OKIE SAT ON THE PARLOR floor at the coffee table, sketching in his notebook, trying to tune out the drone of the Philco radio. His parents sat before the fireplace on this chilly autumn night. Cradling her needlepoint, his mother snickered at verbal sparring between the Bickersons, while his father remained oblivious behind a wall of *Buffalo Courier-Express*.

Okie didn't like *The Bickersons*, but his mother listened to the show all the time. All that arguing—that's all the program was, really—just annoyed him, so he tried to concentrate on his drawing, a line-by-line homage to the Captain America illustration from the cover of the comic book his mother had bought him this week. Something inspired him about the image of Captain America and his friend Bucky striding giant-sized over a crowd of panicked evildoers. Throughout the war years, almost half of Okie's life, he'd loved the stories of Captain America punching Nazis and Japs and bouncing his shield off their heads and trying to bring down the Axis. With the end of the war a year behind the world now, the ration books and war bond drives all seemed like ancient history.

But then *The Bickersons* paused for the chime of a news broadcast.

"This is NBC News for Tuesday, October first," intoned the announcer's voice. "Judgment at Nuremberg!"

His father's newspaper pages crinkled and tipped downward.

But Okie tried to plug his ears and concentrate on getting the curve of the shield just right. The news was *boring.*

"Twelve Nazi war criminals were found guilty today..."

Okie tucked his tongue into the corner of his mouth, concentrating on the wings on Cap's head.

"...sentenced to hang in two weeks' time..."

He couldn't quite get the eyes right. They either looked too kitten-eyed or too mean.

"...Grand Admiral Karl Dönitz, sometimes called the Last Führer, was sentenced to ten years in Spandau Prison..."

This caught Okie's attention. "Hey, Pops, why do they call him 'the Last Führer'? I thought Hitler was the Führer."

His father lowered his newspaper enough to peer over it. Okie could see only his pale eyes, forehead, and slicked-back hair. "The Third Reich didn't end with Hitler, at least not immediately. Right before he killed himself, he anointed a successor, this Grand Admiral Dönitz. Dönitz carried on the war effort for three weeks until the Reich finally surrendered."

Okie snickered. "Sounds like 'donuts.'"

"Do you suppose he liked Bavarian creme?" Okie's mother asked with a restrained smile.

Okie sensed a joke, but didn't get it; then, "Oh, because Bavaria is in Germany." He laughed.

His father shook his head and rolled his eyes.

Mom poked his shin with her foot. "Oh, come on. That was funny."

His father grunted and raised his paper again.

She asked, "Why this Dönitz? Why not Goering or Himmler? Goebbels."

"Goebbels was already dead, and Hitler had lost faith in Goering and Himmler."

"Well, it seems strange not to execute *him,* of all people. I mean, Goering was just sentenced to execution," Okie's mother said.

"Allied admirals vouched for him, Admiral Nimitz in particular. They convinced the tribunal Dönitz was just doing his job, sinking Allied shipping with his U-boats."

The flutter of a skirt and creak of the sofa behind Okie announced Ann's arrival. "Whatcha drawing?"

He edged around his drawing. "It's not ready yet."

"Mickey Mouse? Bugs Bunny?" Her voice took on a teasing tone. "Flash Gordon!"

"Nope." He leaned over the paper so she couldn't see.

"Oh, come on, show me?" she said, elbowing him. Big sisters were the most annoying creatures on God's green earth. "Betty Boop." She leaned in.

"No."

"Batman!"

"No! Cripes!"

"Watch your language!" his father snapped.

Okie's ears heated, and the unspoken threat in his father's voice sent a chill down his spine. Then he sighed and scooted the picture so that Ann could see it.

"Hey!" she said. "I don't know what you're talking about, but that's really good."

Okie blinked. "You think so?"

"I think it's really swell, Okie."

"Thanks."

"Who is it?"

He gasped at her, and she laughed. "Of course I know who Superman is." As his mouth fell the rest of the way open, she laughed harder. "Gotcha."

He elbowed her knee in feigned outrage. "Dork."

She grabbed the paper and handed it to Mom.

"Hey!" he protested. "It's not done!"

Mom gave him a kindly smile, then, as she took a look, her eyes widened in surprise and pride. "Your sister's right, this is really good."

Okie's face warmed and he couldn't help grinning.

The corner of the newspaper tipped down as his father took a look, too. Mom tipped it toward him. His father *hmphed.* "Comic books are not real art any more than Captain America is a real person. Captain America didn't stop the Nazis, real people did. Real people saved the art that the Nazis looted, all across Europe."

"The Moments Men, right?" Okie said. He'd heard these stories before. Apparently, his father knew some of them personally, but Okie couldn't remember which one, guys who'd looked all over Europe, even during the war, for all the stuff the Nazis had stolen.

"The *Monuments* Men," his father said distractedly from behind his newspaper.

Mom nudged Pops' leg with her foot. "Well, tell him about it, Emmett. He wants to know."

His father cleared his throat. "Well, they're still looking for all sorts of things. Paintings, sculptures, rare books, all sorts of things are still missing. Art is the highest expression of the divine. God's majesty shining through the inspired hands of Man."

"Is that why we have all the pictures and stuff, Pops?" Okie asked. His father had decorated their new, bigger house with artworks. A miniature version of Michelangelo's *Pietà*, about the size of a cinder block, rested on the mantelpiece beneath a table-sized print of da Vinci's *The Last Supper*. The *Pietà,* which depicted Mary holding her dead son in her lap, made Okie sad. His heart went out to her whenever he paused to look at it. In the kitchen was a painting of Jesus, with His infinitely kind face. Except for the long hair, Okie thought He looked like one of his elder cousins on his mother's side. His father often went on about art, as if Okie was supposed to remember all those big words. He still wasn't sure what a "renaissance" was. Nevertheless, in the study, his father had a print of a painting by somebody named Raphael called *The Transfiguration*, which showed Jesus ascending to heaven, surrounded by Moses and Elijah on either side and his disciples down below, who all looked like they were arguing or stricken with surprise. It was his father's favorite painting. Okie occasionally found himself looking at all the faces, trying to emulate them with a pencil and paper. He thought it all made their house feel like church, which made him a little uncomfortable, afraid the Virgin Mary was watching him whenever he was naughty.

"That is why," his father said.

Ann turned to their mother. "Hey, Mom. Can I make some cookies?"

"They'll make you fat," their father said.

Ann flinched as if she had just been slapped, and suddenly the air in the room thickened, becoming difficult to breathe. Okie saw the tears form in her eyes, and she wiped them quickly. Then she noticed Okie staring at her and forced a wan smile.

"You know what?" their mother said. "I believe there's a church bake sale this weekend. I was planning to make some cookies for that." It was as if the air in the room returned to its normal consistency.

"Peanut butter?" Okie said. He liked the crisscrosses on them, and he was reasonably certain he could purloin one or two during the baking process.

"Peanut butter and ginger snaps," Mom said definitively.

The two females and Okie all traded smiles while Pops wasn't looking.

"The proper function of man is to live, not to exist. I shall not waste my days in trying to prolong them. I shall use my time."

-Jack London (1916)

PART I

Mundus vult decipi, ergo decipiatur.

"The world wants to be deceived, so let it be deceived."

I

***"BLESS ME, FATHER,** for I have sinned. It's been three days since my last confession. I've been having a lot of anger the last few days, and I can't control it. It feels very much like the day my mother died, when I was fifteen. Or the first time I killed a man...just this raw explosion of cold rage."*

"Is there something that caused this anger, my son?"

"Trey is a nosy little fuck. I caught him snooping around in my office papers, after I told him not to a hundred times. He's too clever for his own good."

"The apple doesn't fall far from the tree."

"There he was, just about to find some things I couldn't let him see, and I just... Well, he'll be okay. He's a tough kid. Or at least, he will be someday, if I have anything to say about it."

"Spare the rod and spoil the child?"

"Oh, he got a whipping, all right. Then I made him write, 'Honor thy father and mother' ten thousand times, like my father did to me. Honey still isn't speaking to me. She thought I was too hard on him. But that's a joke. She was already half a bottle of chardonnay into the evening and wasn't paying attention. I told her to mind her place. 'Wives, be subject to your husbands, as to the Lord.' Right, Father?"

"That is the Scripture."

"So, my sin is wrath."

❁❁❁

1951

It was a bright sunny day in Buffalo, New York, the day Okie's previous life was delivered its death blow.

He was walking home from school with his friend John, tired from basketball tryouts, duffel bag over one shoulder, school bag over the other, pondering whether he'd make varsity this year. His Canisius High School blue and gold uniform blazer was perfect for keeping the fall chill at bay.

John was saying, "There ain't no question you're gonna make varsity. You're better than half the seniors—oh, hey, dollies at eleven o'clock." He pulled out a comb and raked it through his thick black hair.

Okie followed John's glance to three high school girls walking the opposite direction across the street. There wasn't much combing to be done with Okie's tow-headed flat-top, but John's luxuriant Italian coiffure went heavy on the pomade.

As six pretty eyes fell upon him, Okie's cheeks heated, and his feet lost their will to move. The breeze carried their scent on the wind, flowers and vanilla and Ivory soap. The middle one was a blonde almost as tall as he was, long and lithe with curves in all the right places, her honey-gold ponytail bouncing along behind her. Perfect cheekbones and alabaster skin, long legs under a turquoise-print skirt. She met Okie's stare with a steady emerald gaze. In an unexpected revision of Romeo's words from English class earlier that day, the thought came to him of how he would love to be a glove upon those hands that he might touch that body. His skin tingled from crown to crotch and settled there.

John whistled and hooted at them, but they hurried along. A delivery truck passed between them, breaking the spell. The stench of exhaust erased the girls' intoxicating scents, and the growing stiffness in Okie's tweed trousers relaxed. Then he chided himself. Lustful thoughts would have to go into his confession on Saturday.

"Good grief, John, did you see that?" Okie's mouth was dry, his voice raspy. He'd never seen them before, and the need to know *who that girl was* exploded in his mind and wouldn't allow anything else.

"Three of them, two of us, I'd call that a triple-decker sandwich with extra bacon and mayo," John said. "Can you imagine!"

"I don't think I'll be able to imagine anything else for a while."

"Go home and rub one out, you'll be fine," John said with a snort.

"You're filthy," Okie said, resuming his course toward home.

"Don't give me that shit, Mister Holier-Than-Father-McSweeney. That's exactly what you're gonna do."

"Shut up, that's a venial sin," Okie said, walking faster. What annoyed him the most was that John was right.

John guffawed. "I'm just jerking your chain, buddy." He laid a hand on Okie's shoulder, and his face went deadly serious.

"What is it?" Okie asked.

"You want I should go and catch her and tell her what your plans are?"

Okie stared in mortified horror until John could no longer suppress another laugh. John slapped him on the back, hooting with fresh guffaws. "All right, this is where I get off this train." He thumbed down the street in a perpendicular direction. "Farewell, brave Romeo!"

"Buzz off, Mercutio," Okie said.

"See you tomorrow, anon and shit," John said, walking backwards.

Okie smiled, waved, and continued toward home. He passed Busby's Soda Fountain and caught the strains of Nat King Cole's "Too Young" drifting out on a scent of orange, and he imagined himself sitting inside sharing a soda with that honey-blonde goddess.

He went inside and bought a few pieces of licorice taffy for his mother. It was her favorite, and she needed some cheering up, still recovering from heart surgery a few weeks ago. The last few days, her normally energetic self had been flagging. Even smiling seemed to exhaust her, and she was spending a lot of time in the bathroom. "Oh, don't worry about me, boyo, I'll be right as rain soon," she would say to his worried inquiries, carrying threads of the Irish lilt inherited from her working-class family in South Buffalo.

The sidewalks of North Buffalo were clean, the nearby houses resplendent and full of character, the yards and hedges well-manicured, so different from the area Okie and his family had lived in just a few years ago, when his dad had been just an assistant coach for Shel Hecker at Niagara University. His father's success as a businessman had meant a bigger house across town and a spot for Okie in the most prestigious Catholic school in western New York. He sometimes missed his cousins who still lived in South Buffalo, though.

After a block or two, his mind returned to rehashing the basketball tryouts. If he didn't make varsity, he would have some explaining to do to his father, who fully expected his sophomore son to take over the Canisius basketball team and lead it to another state championship. Would he ever be able to fill the shoes expected of him? His backside burned with the recollection of the whipping his father had given him for bombing his algebra mid-term. Okie didn't much care for the math teacher.

Okie's father, Emmett Hansen Sr., had been the most recruited high school athlete east of the Mississippi, an All-American at Holy Cross in basketball, football, *and* baseball. Emmett even turned down a full ride to Harvard. Okie had read the newspaper articles his grandmother had kept in a scrapbook, seen the newspaper and magazine photos of his father in action, even his brief stint as a pitcher for the Buffalo Bisons, out-dueling Warren Spahn. He hadn't gone on to the major leagues for reasons Little Okie didn't know, but Emmett's athletic prowess had carried him on its shoulders into Buffalo's newspapers and restaurants. Everyone knew Okie Sr. To the Buffalonians, he was *their* Emmett.

From the time Okie Jr. was a little boy, everybody called him Little Okie, after his father. He wasn't even sure where the nickname came from, and his taciturn father would never tell him. "Just work to be worthy of it," Emmett Sr. said. It was never black and white but always shades of gray with his father.

He turned the corner onto his street, North Bailey Avenue, and a chill hit him like a dash of ice water. Half a block ahead, an ambulance and a police car were parked out front of his house. He burst into a run, his bags pounding heavily against his back. A policeman came out of the house, spotted Okie, and his expression went blank as a mask.

Okie's breath wouldn't cooperate. "What happened?" he tried to say, but couldn't be sure he managed it.

"Sorry, kid," the policeman said, passing down the steps.

Okie leaped up the steps three at a time and through the front door.

In the sitting room, his father rested on his favorite wingback chair, head in his hands, his face pale and stricken.

A strange woman stood next to him, hand on his shoulder. At the sight of Okie, the woman slowly withdrew her hand, and wouldn't meet his gaze. She might have been pretty if her face hadn't been made of hard, angular planes and flinty blue-gray eyes. A hair net contained her frizzy blonde hair and a dark-gray hat sat atop her hair like a limp, burnt pancake. Her lips were too red.

"What's going on?" he demanded.

His father's mouth worked but no sound came out, his eyes haunted, shocked.

"Where's Mom?" Okie asked.

His father said, "She..." He took a deep shuddering breath. "I came home, and she was lying on the kitchen floor. It was too late. There was nothing..."

The woman squeezed his shoulder, but it wasn't a gesture of comfort; it was a gesture of controlled possession. In that moment, Okie hated her like he'd never hated another human being. Who was this woman?

His father stood and shoved his hands in his trouser pockets, stretching up to his full five foot eleven, a sturdy, athletic frame of broad shoulders and strong hands. Little Okie would be wearing a similar frame very soon, his mother often told him.

"Where is she?" Okie said.

The engine of the ambulance outside started up and it began to move.

"I want to see her!" Okie said.

"That's not a good idea," his father replied.

The air inside the house was filled with a strange smell, sickly sweet and cloying, like finding a freshly dead animal along the riverbank.

"You do not vant to remember your mutter zat vay," the woman said in her thick, German accent.

"Who the hell are you?" Okie asked.

At the utterance of foul language, his father stiffened and started forward, but the woman stopped him. "You can call me Marge."

In a split second, Okie's mind connected several disparate threads into a knot of incredulous pain. "You're his *secretary?*" His father had occasionally mentioned her by name, the new secretary at Watson Safety Equipment. "What are you doing here?"

"I vas just passing by, I live near here, and saw ze ambulance..."

His hands were shaking, clenching and unclenching as if with a will of their own. His ears pounded with heat at the speed of a racehorse's hooves.

"Calm down, son. You're not helping the situation. Show some respect to your elders."

"*Respect!*" Okie roared. "Her body's not even cold and there's another woman here!"

Storm clouds rolled over his father's face, and Okie threw down his bags, squaring himself for a beating.

A female voice, gasping in desperation came from behind him. "Dad? Okie?" Okie's sister Ann came running through the front door. "I came as soon as I could!" Her glance flicked once toward Marge, but then she threw her arms around Okie.

As he succumbed to his sister's embrace, a whirlwind of emotions and words swirled around him. But none of it made any sense. "It's Mom," he sobbed into his sister's hair.

"I know," she said, sniffling. "This must be so hard for you, kiddo." Her body shuddered with restrained sobs.

His father's mouth was working now. "I tried to call the school to have them send you home, Okie, but you'd already left..."

His sister's closeness squelched Okie's white-hot rage, but he knew it would only work temporarily. She cupped his face in her hands and looked desperately into his eyes and gave him words he couldn't remember, because he was standing in the rubble of his life as if it were the ruins of a bombed-out Berlin.

All of it, every chunk of brick and mortar, was a lie.

His devoutly Catholic father, who professed to so love Okie's mother; who beat Okie soundly for the slightest infraction; who sent Okie to his room to write the Fifth Commandment, "Honor thy father and mother" ten thousand times; who had been the darling of the sports pages and was now a captain of industry; who walked the halls of power in Buffalo; was an adulterer. With his goddamn secretary.

When Okie was finally allowed to retreat to his room, he pulled his knees up to his chest and stared at the handful of licorice taffy.

II

"BLESS ME, FATHER, *for I have sinned. It's been two days since my last confession..."*

"Please, continue, my son."

"I...I've been having hateful thoughts, Father, wrathful thoughts. The Fifth Commandment says to honor thy father and mother, but what if my father was committing adultery while my mom was still alive?"

"What kind of thoughts are you having?"

"I'm so angry sometimes I want to kill him. That's some serious wrath, right? Would God forgive me for that?"

"You must first beg forgiveness and repent."

"But is it wrong to kill a known adulterer, Father?"

"It is still murder, my son. Besides, you are too young for such thoughts. Take heed of your soul. Grief can twist our minds in terrible ways, allow the Devil inside our hearts. We mustn't open the door for evil this way."

"What kinds of killing are okay?"

"Our duty as children of Christ is to love our fellow men, even adulterers."

"But what about all those Communist gooks in Korea?"

"The Lord makes allowances for those who fight on behalf of the leaders God has put above them. Romans 13, 'Let every soul be

subject unto the higher powers. For there is no power but of God: the powers that be are ordained of God. Whosoever therefore resisteth the power, resisteth the ordinance of God: and they that resist shall receive to themselves damnation. For rulers are not a terror to good works, but to the evil. Wilt thou then not be afraid of the power? Do that which is good, and thou shalt have praise of the same: For he is the minister of God to thee for good. But if thou do that which is evil, be afraid; for he beareth not the sword in vain: for he is the minister of God, a revenger to execute wrath upon him that doeth evil.' Battle is not murder, my son. God will always give victory to the righteous, provided that the war is just, and the cause is noble."

"The funeral is tomorrow. How am I supposed to grieve for her when my father is spitting on her grave?"

"Your father has his own cross to bear, Okie. Take an inventory with your own heart. What lies in your father's heart is between him and the Lord."

The primary cause of death was listed as gangrene of the bowel and secondarily, hardening of the arteries. She was never going to recover from her heart surgery. She was only 39.

These facts felt like they should be happening to someone else. They were just simple words that didn't convey the truth that Okie would never see his mother again.

As Okie stood beside the casket on a cold, drizzly autumn morning, Father Stehly's intonements droned in Okie's head. Beside him stood Ann, who was wearing a black ankle-length dress and proper black veil, and beyond her, his father, in a dark suit, surrounded by a large throng of other mourners. Across the casket stood Okie's friend John, and his father, John Sr., and a great many aunts and uncles and cousins from South Buffalo on the McGillicuddy, Reedy, and Griffin side, plus a wider circle of friends from the community. The plethora of floral wreaths and casket sprays were apparently from his father's customer, Stefano Magaddino, and his family.

Okie's insides were an empty, sizzling cavern. He hadn't slept in days. He'd locked himself in his room during the wake. The conflicting aromas of all the food people brought made him sick. The smells of liquor and beer heightened his queasiness, until he wondered if getting stone drunk might help. So he sneaked downstairs, stole a half-empty bottle of Irish whiskey when no one was looking, and then guzzled it in his room. *That* made him throw up and feel even worse.

So much for that idea.

At least he was able to shut his eyes without visions of Marge and his father there in the living room, pretending to grieve over his mother's still-warm corpse. He liked most of his McGillicuddy, Reedy, and Griffin relatives, and it warmed him slightly to see them so broken up by his mother's death. Everybody loved her. Okie took heart in that.

Except for the one person who should have the most, and that he could not let go.

Fortunately, the secretary slut was nowhere to be seen, or else Okie might have made a point to throw up on her.

Ann hung close to their father, giving Okie the opportunity to stay as far away as he could. He prayed when prayers were expected, mumbling through empty words and rote phrases that had no meaning in a world where his mother didn't exist. What part of God's plan could his mother's death possibly serve?

His attention clicked back into the moment when he heard, "Ashes to ashes, dust to dust." He took a deep, shuddering breath as cold, autumn raindrops splatted onto the surface of the casket.

SPLOT...SPLOT-SPLOT. An arrhythmic tattoo from a sky that didn't care.

Umbrellas opened and went up.

As mourners shuffled away from the gravesite in the Tonawanda Mount Olivet Cemetery, Okie walked alone. He saw John Montana Sr. approach his father, dressed in an Enzo Carlino tweed wool topcoat and a broad-brimmed Selco silver beaver fur fedora. He clasped Emmett's hand in ring-encrusted fingers, leaned in, kissing him once on each cheek, and offered solemn words.

John Jr. spotted Okie and came over. "Hey, buddy," John said, "I'm real sorry about your mom."

Okie made a noncommittal sound and thrust his hands deeper in his pockets. "Thanks."

"You coming back to school soon?"

"Monday."

"Say, you want to come over and play some pool sometime?"

Okie shrugged. "That would be swell." Then he added, half-joking, "Got anything in the liquor cabinet?"

"Are you kidding? My father has the best liquor cabinet in the city. He's got a bottle of scotch he says is worth more than my whole life." John chuckled. "So of course I drank a bunch of it and replaced it with cheap stuff."

Okie couldn't help but crack a smile.

John glanced over his shoulder at his father, who was walking toward a long four-door, black-and-silver Bentley Mark IV Streamlined Sports Saloon. "Gotta go. I'll see you at school."

Both Johns sat in the back seat escorted by two very large Italian-looking drivers in dark pinstripe suits.

Okie nodded. "'Bye."

He resumed his trek to the car. Along the way, an arm slipped lightly over his shoulders, and Ann's flowery perfume crept into his nostrils, the same perfume his mother had worn, and for the first time that day, tears blurred his vision.

"How are you doing, kiddo?" she asked.

He just wrapped his arm around her waist and said nothing.

She said, "I'm going to come back home and stay for a while, I think. How would that be?"

"That would be okay I guess."

"Don't sound so enthusiastic!" She squeezed him playfully. "Don't you miss me?"

He nodded.

"You need someone to take care of you for a while," she said.

"Who's going to take care of you?" he asked.

"Well, you, I suppose. Dad isn't going to be much good for either of us for a while."

Okie scoffed.

"No, he's really broken up, even though he doesn't show it."

"So broken up he's already got another girlfriend." Saying the words made Okie want to either throw up again or punch something.

"Shhh, not so loud!" she said.

"Well, it's true!"

"She's just his secretary, and she lives nearby and—"

"There aren't any secretaries can afford to live in our neighborhood. Open your eyes."

She sighed deeply and guided him around a patch of muddy sod. "No more of that. We're all hurting. Let's just let it be. Can you do that?"

No.

"I'll try," he said.

"Good boy."

Okie couldn't wait to get back into school.

When he received word that he'd made the varsity basketball team, he wished he could have been more excited, but at least practice gave him something else to think about, someplace to go that wasn't inside the scalding boil of his own head.

Ann moved back into her old room, taking a longer commute to secretarial school. Okie enjoyed having her around again. The female presence helped assuage the gaping wound in his heart, and she tried hard. Okie could see that, but she couldn't cook like Mom, and there was still the specter of Marge lurking in the corners of the house. Okie hadn't seen her since that day, but his father often went on long "walks," and given that she lived only a few minutes' walk away, it could be no mystery where he was going.

His father took on a wan, haunted look, and Okie comforted himself with the knowledge that a poisoned soul would soon be manifest in the flesh. Emmett was an unknowable man with a great penchant for secrecy. Stoic, silent and damaged only began to explain why he would disappear for periods of time.

Maybe it was the sense of temporariness that Ann was waiting to get back to her own life, that made Okie feel like it wasn't real. When she had left for secretarial school, he'd been happy for her. She wasn't supposed to have to come home for *him*.

The Canisius Crusaders ended their football season undefeated, winning the Western New York Catholic League for the third time in four years. They outscored their opponents 240-22. The basketball season was proving to be almost as good. Their only loss so far was to Timon. Okie should have been happier about being part of powerhouse teams that mostly dominated their opponents. It made him more popular than he'd likely have been on his own. But every day was a slog. Basketball became his religion. The culture taught him how to be a man when his father was not available.

After a sullen, tense Christmas break, at the beginning of the spring semester, two new boys appeared at Canisius High School, fair, blue-eyed boys, brothers. The elder one, Gerhardt, showed up in Okie's history class, speaking with a slight German accent, and constantly giving Okie measuring looks, until by the time class was over, Okie simmered with anger.

In the hallway between classes, Okie lay in wait for him. He grabbed the new kid by the jacket and spun him around. Gerhardt was a handsome boy in that chiseled Nordic ideal, with eyes like gray flint that went from surprise to amusement.

"You got a problem?" Okie said.

"Why would I have a problem?" Gerhardt said. "Do you?" He smiled at Okie, but it was a smile of arrogant condescension. Okie instantly wanted to punch him in the teeth. Gerhardt turned and walked away into the tide of uniformed boys.

By the end of the day, Okie had learned the brothers' identities. Their last name was Hall. The same last name as Marge the Slut. Could they be related? Were they *her* sons? She was about the same age as Okie's mother. If they were her sons, that would explain why they seemed to know him. Maybe they knew Emmett. If he was spending so much time at Marge's house, how could they not?

The question so burned in him that he couldn't concentrate for the rest of the day. Both brothers even joined the basketball team; the younger one, a freshman named Kurt, practiced with the junior varsity, but Gerhardt practiced with the varsity. Okie was infuriated when Coach MacKinnon switched Gerhardt and Okie in and out of the same forward position.

But Gerhardt smiled handsomely, and everyone seemed to like him.

Walking home that afternoon with John, Okie felt ready to explode. The winter air chilled his wet hair and bit through his trousers.

"So, what's up with you?" John asked. "You've had a jack up your ass all day."

"Those new guys." Okie shoved his hands deeper into his pockets so hard he strained the stitches.

"They seem like they're all right, for krauts."

"They have the same last name as my dad's secretary."

"So you're saying... Wow, no shit. They're *her* kids?"

"I'm going to find out for sure." More troubling was that Canisius High School was one of the top private schools in New York State. No secretary could afford tuition at Canisius. So that suggested she had other sources of money, such as Emmett. That possibility lodged in Okie's chest like a toothpick under a fingernail.

"You want me to help you make their life hell?" John asked.

Okie smiled at that. John Montana Jr. had a diabolic knack for hazing and retribution—and the will to follow through with it. No one at Canisius messed with him. That his father was one of the most powerful men in Buffalo no doubt augmented his aura of untouchability. "Let me find out first."

When Okie got home, Ann was preparing a pot roast for dinner. He asked her if Marge had any kids.

She shrugged. "I made some peanut butter cookies. Your favorite with the fork-tine marks."

Seeing the array of them cooling on the kitchen table brightened his spirits. He hugged her on the shoulder, took three of them, thanked her, and hurried away before she could protest.

When his father came home, the three of them sat at the dinner table. Okie said, "So I met Marge's sons at school today."

His father chewed on a pot roast that was too gristly, keeping his voice even. "Oh, did you?"

As the silence stretched, punctuated by the sounds of mastication, Ann said, "I got an 'A' on my stenography test today."

Their father nodded. "Well, done, Ann. You have always made your mother proud."

But Okie just stewed in the vague confirmation of his suspicions. There was no denial, no surprise.

"Son, congratulate your sister on her success," his father said sternly.

"Good job, sis," Okie said, trying to put some heart into it.

She gave an ashen smile. "Thanks. My teacher said I'd make a great court reporter."

"An admirable vocation," their father said, still chewing. "If you like, I could ask around some of the local law firms."

Ann clapped her hands. "Oh, that would be so keen, Daddy!"

He patted Ann's hand. "Whatever you need, pumpkin."

Okie wanted to flip the table onto his father's head, smash the plate over his face. His hands trembled with the yearning of it. "May I be excused?"

Ann said, "Don't you like the pot roast?"

"It's great," Okie said. "I'm just not feeling well. I need to go do some homework and then go to bed."

"You're excused," his father said, "*after* you do the dishes."

Okie nodded, then sat quietly stewing.

He did the dishes in an exasperated stupor and didn't speak to his father for the rest of the night. His father sat alone before the fireplace with the newspaper, drinking a snifter of Bénédictine and brandy and listening to some radio drama, and when Okie went to bed, no one paid the slightest attention.

III

"BLESS ME, FATHER, *for I have sinned. It's been one day since my last confession. I know it was a long time ago, but I can't help wondering why my father started a relationship with Marge Hall. She wasn't a particularly pretty woman. On one hand, I'm glad he never married her, but he was so concerned about appearances that I'm surprised he didn't. Having an adulterer for a father, and not even careful about hiding it, just eats at me. I've tried for years to let it go. But I can't. And you want to hear the really messed-up part?"*

"You have not yet confessed your sin."

"Well, here's the stupid, twisted sin. Her sons tried so hard to become his sons, that they succeeded. When he took them on that camping trip upstate, I wanted to just die. And I had to stay home and work because I 'didn't have any time off.' I covet, Father. I covet their importance in his life. I *was his son! Not those two assholes. He treated them like princes and me like a bastard."*

"Curious that you used past tense 'was.'"

"Good point. Am I his son? And why do I still chew on this? I have kids of my own now. So much has happened since then—I mean, wow, Berlin, Mexico, the Bay of Pigs—it feels like somebody else's life. But that I can't let go."

"His sins are against God, between him and the Lord. Those aren't for you to forgive. You must forgive him for the wrongs done to your family. A lifetime journey of truth for a damaged father who appears to be lost. It is the only way for you to heal."

"The truth is, I still miss my mother. I always wonder how my life would have been different if she'd lived. It makes me sad that it's getting hard to remember her face. But I'll always remember her smell, like cookies and fresh linen, and the way she stroked my hair when I was sick, and the way she saved me from a few beatings with that special way she had with him, this gentle deflection. Plus, she had an Irish temper. When she got mad, look out. My father seemed to respect that..."

"Your memories of her are indeed precious."

"Maybe I don't want to heal. Maybe I need not to."

1952

"Okie, look who's here!" Ann called from the foyer.

From his room, Okie peeled himself away from his theology homework, in which he was wrestling with the idea of free will, and went downstairs. A tall, fair-haired man in a dark coat shook off the early spring rain and tucked his umbrella into the rack near the coat tree at the front door. Okie was 5'11" but this man outstretched him by three inches.

Okie recognized the man as Cornelius McGillicuddy, his mother's cousin. Unlike the last time Okie had seen him, he now wore a priest's collar.

Cornelius and Ann exchanged greetings as she took his coat and hat. Okie came down the stairs, welcoming the visitor. Okie had always admired Cornelius, a few years older, one of the profusion of relatives on the prolific Irish Catholic side of the family.

Cornelius smiled at him. "Oh, goodness, Okie! You've become a man in my absence." The Irish lilt in his accent had not been entirely erased by Jesuit university.

Okie caught a genuine smile on his face as he crossed the foyer to shake his cousin's hand.

Ann said, "To what do we owe the pleasure?"

"I wished to come and pay my respects," Cornelius said. "It has been a great burden to me that I couldn't come to the funeral. Your mother was a special person, and she was called home too soon for the rest of us."

Okie had been too caught up in his own blackness to notice Cornelius's absence from the funeral.

"Thank you," Okie said. "Where were you?"

Cornelius offered an ingratiating mix of regret and amiability in his smile. "Direct as always. I was offered a special, sequestered course of study at the Holy See, which took me away from Holy Cross. I only received word of her passing a week after the funeral was over. I came as soon as I was able." It struck Okie then how much Cornelius reminded him of his mother. They were both McGillicuddys through and through. The same nose, the same cheekbones, same spoken mannerisms and phrases.

"Come, let's sit by the fire. Something to drink?" Ann said, leading them into the living room, where a fire crackled warmly in the fireplace, offering a pleasant respite from the cold and wet outside. "I made a chocolate cream pie."

Cornelius gave a nod of approval. "That sounds awfully decadent."

"Coffee?"

"Water will be fine. Early to bed, early to rise, and all that."

When she had gone, Okie gestured Cornelius toward his father's wing-backed chair and said, "So tell me about Holy Cross. I think that's where I'm going to go."

"A chip off the old block, eh?" Cornelius said. "Where is your father anyway?"

Okie looked at the floor and tried to keep his voice even. "I don't know. I was busy studying." But he was on one of his "walks," from which he often came home late at night. Good riddance.

Cornelius's kindly blue eyes studied Okie for a moment. "A busy man, your father. You've some mighty big shoes to fill at Holy Cross. Football, basketball, baseball, academics. No doubt they'll be delighted to have you joining them, especially coming from Canisius. You really had great football and basketball seasons."

"I have another year of school." Okie shrugged, trying not to sound too excited about getting the hell out of this house.

Cornelius studied Okie for a moment that stretched longer and longer. There was so much Okie wanted to say but couldn't. His thoughts about his father had started to sound like a broken record, even to himself sometimes. So, he just sat there, tongue-tied, trying to ignore the grief and sympathy on his cousin's face. He didn't want kindness. He wanted someone to be as angry as he was, and he wanted to know why his mother had to die, and his father, the adulterer, got to live.

Just then, Ann saved him from an unseemly display of emotion with a tray laden with slices of chocolate cream pie. Cornelius took one look at the slab of pie slathered in whipped cream and his eyes brightened. “That looks wonderful, Ann.”

After distributing the pie, she sat beside Okie on the sofa and folded her hands. Okie could hardly wait to dig in, but Cornelius said, “Let us give thanks, shall we?”

The three of them bowed their heads, and Cornelius said grace, then appended, “Lord, please give comfort to this family in their time of profound grief. No doubt they are still in agonizing pain from their mother’s sudden departure from this life to the communion of saints. Bring them strength, comfort, and love in your divine mercy. In Christ’s name we pray. Amen.”

“Amen,” Okie and Ann said.

For a while they chatted about relatives, and Cornelius made a point of asking how Okie was doing in school. His grades were slipping, and fears of a ritual beating kept him from telling his father. Then again, he’d often fantasized some altercation with his father in which he stood up to him once and for all. No more belt whippings, no more toilet cleaning with a toothbrush, no more biblical lines of “Honor thy father and mother” scrawled in a notebook until his hands cramped. Sometimes he imagined living on his own, getting a room in some boarding house just long enough to finish high school. Then he would be gone from this place forever.

“You haven’t told me about Holy Cross yet,” Okie said.

"Well, it's like many colleges I suspect. You have to study hard. It is, of course, the Jesuit Way."

"And practice hard," Okie said. His father had often bored him with endless stories of how hard he'd practiced to become the legendary college athlete. Until he'd discovered his father was an adulterer, he had tried hard to emulate him. But since then, his heart wasn't in it.

"I suppose that's true," Cornelius said, "but athletics is not for me. My gifts are more cerebral. The real question is, what do you want from your life, Okie? Many students at Holy Cross go on to serve the Church, a higher calling, even join the priesthood."

Okie thought for a moment how Cornelius's words seemed laden with meaning he wasn't privy to. "I love the Church. I go to confession a lot. It helps."

Cornelius nodded sagely. "Confession can be a great balm for a soul, a way of unburdening yourself."

"But I don't think I could be a priest." Okie's face heated. The question of why hung in the air, with two sets of eyes on him, until he blurted, "I think I like girls too much for that."

Ann and Cornelius shared a chuckle.

Cornelius said, "Just mind the lustful thoughts until the proper season."

Okie nodded.

"So, if not the priesthood, what then?"

Okie shrugged. "The family business, I suppose, except..."

Cornelius waited for Okie to finish his sentence. Okie glanced at Ann, who looked away, wringing her hands. She'd heard him say this before.

But he wanted Cornelius to know the extent of the shame his father was putting the family through. He wanted his cousin to intervene somehow, to convince his father to end the relationship with Marge, beg forgiveness and forget her sons.

"I don't want to work there because I'd have to look at my father's mistress every day."

"Okie!" Ann gasped. "That's enough."

Cornelius straightened, looking surprised. The same way his mother used to when she heard unwelcome news. Suddenly Okie felt a compulsion to confide everything in Cornelius McGillicuddy.

"Well, somebody should be talking about it!" Okie said with less vehemence than he felt. Maybe if he didn't yell about it, somebody would listen to him. "She was here in the house the day Mom died. I knew instantly something was going on. Who the hell was this woman?" Okie rubbed his face, feeling ready to explode with frustration. Since the funeral, he'd become prone to heated outbursts over little things.

"Okie, language!" Ann said.

"Right," Okie said, "yell at *me* about language." He let the rest of that sentiment hang silently between them, and she turned away, biting her lip.

Cornelius said, "Judging by your level of anger, I needn't ask you if you're sure—"

"Where do you think he is right now, Ann?" Okie said. "He's not at work! He's at *her* house. And every day at school, I get to see Kurt and Gerhardt in the halls or at basketball practice. Those are her kraut butthead sons. And he takes care of *them!* He doesn't care about us!"

The front door opened with a cold, wet gust, and Emmett stood there like a pillar of iron turning red with heat.

All three of them jumped to their feet. Okie squared to face his father. Would this be the moment he and his father threw down once and for all? He clenched and unclenched his fists. How much had Emmett heard?

The Nordic side of Okie's heritage was the sanguine, taciturn side, but this stood in diametric contrast to the McGillicuddy side, where certain uncles and cousins could be counted on at family gatherings to get drunk, start fist fights over something stupid like politics, not speak to each other for the rest of the day, then come back at the next family gathering as if it had never happened. The McGillicuddys got drunk, punched it out, and everything was fine again. The Hansen side, however, held lifelong grudges.

"Cornelius, what a surprise," Emmett said. The flint in his eyes suggested he'd heard plenty, but by the time he hung up his coat, the emotion had been stifled, sequestered. Somehow, that frightened Okie worse.

The two men crossed the room to shake hands and exchange tense pleasantries while Okie, his heart hammering like a fist inside his chest, stood stiff as a lump of wood. Ann looked mortified.

"Would you like a slice of chocolate pie, Daddy?" Ann asked.

"No, thank you. I'm...not hungry." Their father approached the fireplace with Cornelius, pointedly averting his gaze from Okie. As his father warmed himself, it was the calm silence that terrified Okie, like a girder falling from a thirty-story building. All was silence until...

"I take it my son has been bearing false witness in my absence," his father said into the tense silence.

Okie's blood turned to half-slush, half-lava. He lurched forward. "An adulterer calls *me* a liar!"

Cornelius stepped between them, placing a strong arm against Okie's chest.

Emmett turned placidly, his eyes full of solemn resignation and implacable will.

Okie surged against his cousin's surprisingly powerful restraint.

"Do you have the spine, boy?" his father said.

Ann stepped in and grabbed Okie's arm with both hands.

Cornelius shouted in a booming voice suitable for a cathedral pulpit, "Gentlemen! Do you think she would want this?"

"She would want to know what he's doing!" Okie yelled, his eyes tearing up. "She *deserved* to know!"

"Keep your mouth shut about things you know nothing about," his father said. He turned to Cornelius. "All of this is quite regrettable, Cornelius. I'm so sorry you had to witness any of it."

Cornelius said, "We are all God's children, Emmett. We are all in pain. We all cannot understand why the Lord took her from us."

"I think it is time for you to go, Cornelius," Emmett said.

Cornelius gave Okie a glance. "I am a man of the cloth. Perhaps I can help—"

"I hope to see you again soon," Emmett said. He headed toward the front door and took down Cornelius's coat and hat from their hooks. "Perhaps when the time is more suitable."

Cornelius nodded and gave Okie a glance of regret. He leaned in and said, "The Lord knows of your pain, Okie. He'll send comfort."

Then he shook hands with Ann. "The pie was exquisite. Thank you." In the foyer, he accepted his coat and hat from Emmett Sr. "Please accept my condolences on your loss, Emmett. And please go easy on Okie. He's just a teenage boy, and he misses his mother."

"Thank you for coming, Cornelius."

With a sigh and a last forlorn look at Okie, Cornelius departed.

Emmett closed the door after him, then turned and approached Okie, his eyes a stone wall. Okie clenched his fists and braced himself.

But his father stopped and calmly regarded him.

Okie was expecting a harsh reprimand or orders for penitence. But his father, the youngest of nine with six brothers, just regarded him as if Okie were some sort of Martian.

Then, with a speed that belied reaction, he buried his right fist in Okie's stomach. Okie's breath exploded out of him in a blaze of pain. He doubled around the ball of hot agony in his belly. The left fist, in true Jimmy "Slats" Slattery style, slammed into his cheek like a sledgehammer and put his lights out.

IV

*"**BLESS ME, FATHER,** for I have been sinned against by my own father. Ow."*

"What is it, my son? Are you all right?"

"It hurts to talk."

"Do you need a doctor?"

"No. I have to tell someone. My father... He has violated me, for the last time, and I will not allow this abuse to continue. I'll put him down if necessary."

"Please tell me what has transpired since we last spoke. Why such anger? This is so out of character for you, Okie."

"He cannot handle the truth. He is lost in his blind lust with Marge Hall. She is trying to replace my mother and control my father. I don't even recognize him. He's a pawn in her chess game."

"Please tell me what happened and why you are so upset. Did he strike you, my son?"

"He punched me. Twice. I got to hand it to him, it was a great one-two combo. He used to train with 'Slats' Slattery. They're buddies."

"The World Light Heavyweight Champion."

"Once in the breadbasket and a knockout to my jaw. I woke up in my room ten minutes ago. My sister might have helped me to bed,

but I can't remember for sure. But I didn't want to be late to confession, so I jogged here from home. I've got a splitting headache—"

"What did you do to provoke your father? Did you dishonor him?"

"Why do I have to provoke him? His actions speak louder than his few words. He always tells me that the world does not revolve around me! Well, this must apply to him. What does he care about me? He's got a whole other family now."

"I'll see what I can do for you, Okie. In the meantime, seek comfort in Christ. He will never let you down."

"Where was Christ when I was getting knocked out by my own father?"

"Do not blaspheme, Okie. It was our Lord who helped you up. The Lord works in mysterious ways. He may be preparing you for great things. Meantime, I will see what I can do."

It was a quiet Saturday in the warehouse of Watson Safety Equipment. The enormous brick factory with its high transom windows had made munitions during the war. When Emmett purchased the building in early 1950, he had installed new fiberglass-molding machines, but left much of the previous assembly line and machining equipment.

Okie was still fuming at having to work on a glorious summer afternoon. He'd had plans to go with John to a Bisons game; they were playing a double-header against the Rochester Redwings today, but his father had commandeered those plans. He often questioned why in the hell he agreed to work for a man he hated, but he didn't know anything else, and his goal was to save up enough money that he could, if shove came to punches, run away and start up somewhere else. There was a certain irony in making Emmett pay for that.

"You want to keep this job?" Emmett had said. "You're cleaning the warehouse on Saturday. And if you can't eat off every square inch of the floor, you're going to do it again without pay. Put some elbow grease into it. Cleanliness is next to Godliness."

So, Okie bit back a scathing retort about breathtaking hypocrisy, then went and swept and mopped and dusted until his hands ached all the way to his shoulders, his shoulders all the way to his waist, and left the proof in his blisters. His father had hauled him here at 7:00 a.m., and it was now sometime after 4:00 p.m. He hadn't seen a soul in several hours, although he was pretty sure Emmett was still working in his office. The production floor was quiet today, its fiberglass-molding machines, riveters, and assembly lines quiescent. Before noon, he maintained illusions that he might finish in time to make the second baseball game, but by now they had drained away like sand from an hourglass. His fantasies turned toward counting the days until he graduated from Canisius and went on to Holy Cross. By the end of the school year, Okie had managed to rally his grades sufficiently to avoid another beating.

Watson Safety Equipment had risen to success thanks to a combination of Emmett's natural salesmanship and the careful management of his cachet as Buffalo's athletic Golden Boy. His early fame had gotten him meetings with city officials, even though they weren't initially interested in Watson's new, fiberglass firefighter helmets and other protective gear. University coaches and even the

NCAA were happy to meet with the former three-sport Academic All-American and consider his innovative football helmets and pads.

Okie would admit it only grudgingly, but the factory was a pretty swell place, and its success had given him a pleasant life. Going to Canisius made him feel special. Now that he was working here, he was making his own money, which gave him freedom he'd never felt before, at least when Emmett wasn't watching him.

In the month since he'd started work, he'd learned a great deal about how the business ran. He envisioned himself someday doing what his father did, wearing snappy suits and schmoozing, and making a good living in so doing. In spite of his feelings about Emmett, he recognized what made his father a success, and he wanted to emulate those traits. The American Dream was all his to be claimed. His father handled the sales duties, traveled extensively, forever on the telephone. The more he saw his father in action, the more he thought he could never measure up.

Somewhere he'd read the words: *We are damned to measure ourselves against our fathers*. It was one of the truest things he'd ever read.

But then there was Marge, the hatchet-faced harpy. She handled the day-to-day operations of the factory, ostensibly reporting to Emmett but with more autonomy than any mere "secretary" should possess. It made him sick to his stomach that she wielded so much power, more than Okie's mother ever had, and she ran roughshod over everyone in that severe, clipped German accent. What a Nazi she was. All the employees respected Emmett, many admired him, but all of them hated Marge Hall. They said she had a more German spelling of her name originally but had Anglicized it when her family came from Germany after the war. She often enlisted Okie to muscle heavy boxes around the warehouse, constantly arranging and rearranging shipments and receivables. He never spoke to her except to say, "Yes, ma'am," and "No, ma'am." It never failed to rankle him, but it was better than a beating or being forced to miss dinner in his room writing, "Thou shalt not..." Okie's hostility-tinged reticence toward her seemed to amuse her more than anything.

The bologna sandwich Ann had made him for lunch had long since vacated his stomach, and he still had an entire aisle to mop. But it was time for some clean mop water. He hefted his bucket of brown sludge toward the janitorial closet, his home away from home, where a drain and water hose awaited him.

As he walked gingerly along the edge of the production floor, careful not to spill a drop, he glimpsed a presence on the catwalk above that led to the executive offices. A young, blond man in a tailored suit leaned on the catwalk railing, watching him, smoking a cigarette. It was Gerhardt Hall.

Their eyes met. The distance was too great for Okie to see the smirk, but he sensed it, nonetheless. What was Gerhardt doing here, dressed so snazzy on a Saturday afternoon? Why wasn't he down here helping Okie? Didn't Gerhardt need a summer job?

In the months since Gerhardt's arrival at Canisius, he'd ensconced himself well with most members of the basketball team. He was handsome, clean cut, had charisma to burn, and was respectful to everyone but Okie. The teachers all liked him.

Beyond Gerhardt, Okie could see Marge and Emmett conversing in his office. He looked for evidence of their lustful entanglement, but their behavior looked serious, businesslike.

What the hell did they talk about anyway?

In the janitorial closet, he dumped his bucket and turned on the faucet to refill it.

As he waited, a mouse scuttled between shadows along the wall, disappearing under a steel shelving unit before Okie could react, so quickly he wasn't sure what he'd seen at first. Then an idea struck him.

As a general lackey and indentured slave, he'd garnered great knowledge about the interior of this building and its spaces. Suppressing a devious smile, he shut off the faucet to his bucket, then stole out of the janitor's closet. Gerhardt was no longer in sight.

Like the mouse, Okie darted from cover to cover, machine to machine, knowing almost instinctively where he might pass into view of the catwalk. Reaching the wall on the production floor below the offices, he stole up the corrugated steel steps toward the catwalk, keeping low.

Keeping below the windows, he crept toward Emmett's office. Through an open transom window, he heard Marge's voice.

"Gerhardt would love to go with you on sales trips this summer, wouldn't you, *Liebchen.*"

"I'll do whatever you need me to, sir," Gerhardt said. "It's an honor to help out." Gerhardt's German accent had shifted to more American over the last six months, harder to notice without listening for it.

Pausing beside the door, Okie suppressed a sneer. What an ass-kisser! *Nobody* was that nice. Nobody. Nevertheless, the thought made him feel petty, small. Since he'd started working here, a flicker of approval had come Okie's way from his father on a couple of occasions, and it angered him how proud it made him feel. Maybe he and his father didn't have to hate each other. Then the hope had quickly disappeared amid drudgery and resentments.

Emmett grunted noncommittally. "I'll think about it. Meantime, are we meeting production on the fire helmets for Cincinnati? The fire chief called me personally yesterday."

"On schedule," Marge said with satisfaction. She pronounced it in the British way, *shed-yule*.

"Good," Emmett said, with more genuine appreciation than had ever been directed toward Okie in the sum of his entire life. His stomach twisted into square knots.

He hurried away before he might be discovered. He had to finish his job and get the hell out of here. Hurrying back to the janitorial closet, he chided himself for foolishness. What had he been hoping to achieve anyway? On the other hand, he felt like a Sioux counting coup against the enemy. He had stolen into a hostile camp and gotten away again, undetected. Maybe he wasn't so useless after all.

After Okie had finished his job and obtained his father's surprisingly perfunctory seal of approval, he headed for home on his own. Emmett seemed unconcerned about giving him a ride home in the new Packard, saying, "I have more work to finish tonight. You know the way home, don't you?"

On his four-mile walk home that night, hungry, weary, and alone, he paused at Busby's Soda Fountain to see how the double-header was going. Joe Busby was a fan and always had the games playing on the radio. The Buffalo Bisons had lost the first one 6-4, but it was tied 2-2 going into the seventh inning stretch.

Okie sat alone at the counter and sipped a cream soda, trying not to stare at the two achingly cute blonde girls chattering in a corner booth, wishing he had Gerhardt's charisma and John's chutzpah. All he could manage was to sneak glances at them in the mirror behind the counter.

During the seventh inning stretch, the announcer gave a list of box scores for the day. The Boston Braves had just beat the Cincinnati Reds, and lefty pitcher Warren Spahn had given up just one run. It was the name Warren Spahn that dragged Okie out of his own thoughts for a moment. Spahn was a friend of Emmett's, and Okie had met him several times, even had dinner once with Spahn and his father Ed, a local wallpaper salesman, when Mom was alive.

A folded newspaper rested on the counter nearby, the *Buffalo Evening News*. Below a story about stalled armistice talks in Korea, a headline caught his attention: "Hitler's Pope." He frowned. What kind of lies were the newspapers spouting about the Church again? It was always some kind of anti-Catholic bullshit. According to the article, Pope Pius XII denied that the Vatican Bank had received 200 million Swiss francs from Nazi Germany, along with millions more in loot and artworks stolen from the Jews. Local

Catholic spokesman Father Cornelius McGillicuddy denied the story, saying that the Church would never have cooperated with so heinously evil a regime. "It would be like cooperating with the Devil himself," McGillicuddy said.

Okie smiled at that. Next time they were together, he would have to ask Cornelius about being interviewed by some hack reporter looking for a cheap scoop.

He flipped to the sports page. It was pretty swell to know a real major league pitcher, so he always paid attention to Spahn's stats. The Braves weren't doing well so far this year, but they could still turn their season around.

Back on opening day, the baseball season's prospects were the most common topic of conversation around Canisius High School. After track and field practice, Gerhardt had been among several boys extolling the virtues of their favorite pitchers as Okie and John came into earshot. A lefty himself, sophomore Andy Rogers idolized Warren Spahn, but before he could really get rolling, Gerhardt shut him down.

"Spahn is a bum, and the Braves couldn't win a game if they paid off the other team," Gerhardt had said. "Look at that nose. He's a Jew bastard."

"Shut up, he's not Jewish," Andy had said.

"Then he's got a kike in the woodpile," Gerhardt said with a sneer.

Okie stiffened at the epithet, realizing that he didn't know whether Warren was, in fact, Jewish. He didn't feel like he was friends with a real major league pitcher, but it was swell to know one, and Okie admired him, too.

Andy had laughed it off uncomfortably, by which point Okie and John had moved past.

Okie paused to consider whether today would be the day he beat Gerhardt Hall like a red-headed stepchild, but John bumped Okie's arm in a signal to move on, that this wasn't worth a fist fight. "Once a Nazi, always a Nazi," John said.

They moved on down the sidewalk.

"Then what is he doing here?" Okie said. "Why the hell didn't he stay in Germany?"

"Oh, didn't you hear?" John said. "He's starting a new chapter of the Aryan Sisterhood."

Okie snickered. As the war had drawn to a close, he had been horrified when news of the concentration camps emerged, even though at the time he was too young to grasp the enormity of what came to be called the Holocaust.

At home nowadays, he only brought up the Halls at great personal peril, but at the dinner table that night, he had made a point of mentioning Gerhardt's comments about Warren.

"Just forget about it," Emmett said.

"Dad, are they Nazis?"

Across the table, Ann tensed and stared at her plate of roast chicken.

"I said, forget about it," Emmett said.

"I thought Warren was your friend."

Emmett's fists clenched and unclenched on either side of his plate.

Okie shut his mouth, but he didn't forget about it. Not at all.

At school, the only time he and the Hall boys were in the same building, he found himself listening more to their conversations, which were never with him. To them, Okie seemed not to exist at all. But he noticed they never mentioned their father, and in that void of knowledge, all sorts of speculation played. He fantasized about hiring some Sam Spade-like private detective to bloodhound the Hall family's doubtless sordid past, discovering that their father was a Nazi rocket scientist, or a concentration camp *kommandant*.

As play resumed in the seventh inning, the Bisons sent three batters to the plate and three batters back to the dugout with two strikeouts and a pop fly. Okie took another sip of his cream soda and sighed. The pretty girls in the corner got up and left. So much for the scenery.

His stomach growled, driving him off his stool and back out into the night, turning his feet toward home.

V

***"TODAY IN SCHOOL**, we learned about a Jewish girl who died during World War II. Her book called* The Diary of Anne Frank *just came out. She inspired me. Father McNamee is requiring we all prepare to stand in front of the class tomorrow and recite our favorite quote.*

"She says, 'I know quite well what I want, I know who is right and who is wrong. I have my opinions, my own ideas and principles, and although it may sound pretty mad from an adolescent, I feel more of a person than a child. I feel quite independent of anyone.'"

"You're getting somewhat far afield of confession, Okie."

"She was a prisoner in somebody else's house. I feel the same way she did! The Nazis were coming to get her, and my father is consorting with a Nazi sexpot."

"You're hardly in physical danger—language!"

"I'm not? You can't see the bruises over there."

"Okie—"

"For the first time in my life I found a kindred soul, and she was dead before I ever met her. Are you telling me it doesn't matter?"

"Anne Frank was a Jew."

"Why does that matter? Are you saying she's in hell now? She didn't do anything wrong."

"We need to focus, Okie. Remember what Saint Bernard taught us. God removes the sin of the one who makes humble confession, and thereby the Devil loses sovereignty over the human heart."

"Emmett is an embarrassment to me and my sister. He is dead to me..."

"Get hold of yourself. Other people are waiting."

"I no longer have a father, and the Lord absconded with my mother. I'm an orphan of God."

"Okie, you have offended God with your anger. You must atone for it now. What would Bishop Burke think about now?"

"O my God, I am heartily sorry for having offended Thee, and I detest all my sins because of Thy just punishments, but most of all because they offend Thee, my God, Who art all good and deserving of all my love."

"That is much better. Now go home and obey your father and pray for God to reveal his intentions to you and for you. May almighty God have mercy on you, and having forgiven your sins, lead you to eternal life. Amen."

"I am just trying to be honest with myself and listen to my own conscience, Father."

It was September 27 when the Russians dropped the A-bomb on Buffalo. Funny, Okie thought he would have heard the noise.

Nevertheless, seeing the headline at a corner newsstand brought him to a dead stop on his walk home from the factory.

A-BOMB DESTROYS DOWNTOWN BUFFALO, 40,000 KILLED

His mind swam through a pudding of confusion and alarm.

"What is this?" he asked the newsie.

"Read it and find out," the newsie said with a smirk, a middle-aged man clenching a stub of well-chewed cigar in his teeth.

Okie paid for the paper and started reading. *Thousands of Buffalonians are dead. Thousands of frightened men, women, and children are injured.*

He shuffled off down the sidewalk, and between every horrific sentence of the article, he stared for a moment at the perfectly lovely autumn afternoon. No mushroom clouds filled the air. Birds sang in the trees. A junk man driving a decrepit Model A truck puttered along, businesslike as ever. Puffy clouds drifted across Lake Erie. Sixty degrees. A pleasant breeze ruffled his jacket collar, and the sun warmed his face.

Then he saw the disclaimer next to the article—in much smaller print—that this was a Civil Defense exercise. The world's axis righted itself and relief flooded him. Nevertheless, he read the entire article with a growing sense of alarm.

The Russkies were, in fact, out to burn the U.S.A. to the ground. Everybody knew it. How long before the fighting in Korea spread and communism took over the entire globe? Visions of faceless hordes of totalitarian gestapo sifting through the ruins of a surprise atomic attack, kicking down doors and summarily executing anyone who resisted, sent chills up and down his arms.

How many air-raid drills had he undergone at school? Every few months, he and his classmates would hear the alarm sirens and crawl under their desks, hunkering down and covering their heads. In an atomic attack by the Soviet Union, the U.S.'s major cities would probably be destroyed, but outlying areas and less strategic cities would likely be spared. There had been survivors in Nagasaki and Hiroshima after all.

When he grew up, he wanted to devote his life to fighting the godless Commies. It was his patriotic duty. But how? Join the military? He'd been so focused on getting out of his father's house and the expectations that he would attend the College of the Holy Cross that he hadn't thought much about what he would do with his life. How could he best serve God *and* serve his country? He certainly wouldn't be making a name for himself at Watson Safety Equipment. He was beneath the full-time janitor on that totem pole. Marge was the queen, and Gerhardt was her Golden Boy.

Okie and Gerhardt had entered their senior year with their athletic rivalry at full steam. Being on the same football team with Gerhardt left Okie with a habitual frown, but he wasn't about to let some kraut drive him out. Gerhardt was winning the popularity contest, claiming he had fifty-six college scholarship offers, but Okie was the better football player, and enough people knew it. John was the team clown who had found his place firmly in the second string. Coach Barnes was wise enough to put Okie on offense and Gerhardt on defense, where their mutual animosity would cause the least disruption. Plus, Okie had better hands, and he was well on his way to a banner year as a wide receiver.

In fairness, Gerhardt was a natural athlete. On Okie's most charitable days, he had to admit that Gerhardt's prestige was not completely unearned. In another situation, they might have accepted each other as teammates, maybe even friends.

But not in this life.

By the end of the season, Okie had made a new school record in pass completions, which led to a winning season and a place in the state playoffs. Everyone called him a "chip off the old block." He did his best to accept such words as the compliments they were intended, but inside he was thinking *Never!*

Ann still stayed and took care of the house, and he appreciated her presence, even as he felt sorry for how she'd put her life on hold for him. Without her tempering influence, though, things at home would have been much worse. She often told him he needed to get himself a girlfriend, but he didn't know how to meet any girls. Girls were simply aloof goddesses that a mere mortal like him could not hope to impress. In the presence of any given beautiful girl, he felt like a chimpanzee, reduced to hoots and grunts, and scratching his armpits.

His father he seldom saw, and when he did, their interactions were tense at best. Mostly they just stayed out of each other's way. He spent weekends working at the factory, saving all the money he could for the day he would bolt.

He marked the change of seasons by the sport he was playing—football season, basketball season, baseball season—ticking off the days until graduation.

Christmas was the most joyless holiday Okie could remember. His father gave him a safety razor as a gift, as his whiskers were "turning him into a man." Okie had bought one for himself a year earlier. He gave Ann a copy of *The Diary of Anne Frank*. The two of them discussed it often. She gave him a popular new novel called *Casino Royale*, about a British spy. He read it three times and yearned for a different name for himself. "Hansen, Emmett

Hansen," did not roll off the tongue like James Bond. Implacable in the face of danger, cold and calculating as a man of action, suave and debonair with the ladies, now there was a man to be admired. A man like Bond knew what to do in all circumstances. How did you learn how to do that?

1953

The most happiness Okie had seen Emmett express in years was the day in late spring that the letter arrived from the College of the Holy Cross, offering a full-ride football scholarship.

"*Your talent and discipline both on and off the field have shone through...*"

Okie read the letter with a strange mix of excitement and disappointment, without being able to put his finger on exactly why. His father's reaction was pure pride and elation, and it made Okie wonder who this man was. He could almost believe his old man gave a damn about him.

On the day he graduated from Canisius High School, Ann threw a party for him at the church parish hall, having organized it all herself, complete with streamers, confetti, and a big angel food cake. All the McGillicuddys came, as well as a number of his father's friends and business associates. Even a city councilman came, more to pay respects to Emmett than to congratulate Okie. Watching his father press the flesh, Okie couldn't look away from the way Emmett made everyone smile and feel like they were the most important person in the room. Everyone wanted to be friends with this luminary of Buffalo society.

When the Montanas came, with John still wearing his mortarboard, John gave Okie a peek at the flask of Irish whiskey in his jacket pocket, and the two of them sneaked off behind the church to put on a buzz.

"To the rest of our lives," John said.

"To the end of my sentence," Okie said.

For months, they'd been talking about the future. John always said he was going into the family taxi-cab business, rather than going to college, but whenever Okie asked exactly what that meant, John would say, "Oh, this and that. You know, business." Then he would change the subject.

But today, the two of them and two-hundred-odd other young men had graduated high school, all expected to carry on and do great things. Canisius was one of the top college-preparatory high schools in all the northeast. Many of his classmates were going on to Ivy League schools, others to join the clergy and serve the Church. All the speeches today had talked about how privileged they all were, how blessed by God, and how God expected them all to go on and do great things.

These sentiments lodged so deeply in Okie's heart he could almost forget his family's shame, and the pain they still suffered at his father's philandering. He could almost look across the sea of mortarboards to Gerhardt Hall and not despise him. He felt enough pride he could almost ignore Marge sitting next to Emmett in the audience, cheering when her son's name was called, and the way Emmett applauded with pride. Okie couldn't bring himself to look at them when his name was called only three names prior. He simply focused on putting one foot after the other, climbing onto the stage, every step taking him closer to freedom from the shame. When he landed on the Holy Cross campus this fall, he would never look back toward his family home. On holiday visits, he would stay in hotels, or with Ann, who was planning to move out and go back to secretarial school in the fall. Emmett and Marge could shack up and live in sin for all he cared. They could hardly stain their immortal souls more deeply than they already had.

The burn of John's whiskey helped to shake these thoughts away and bring him back to the moment and consider his friend. John's family went through the motions of Catholicism, but they could hardly be called devout. Okie's adherence to the Church had opened a schism between them. John was a drinking, smoking, skirt-chasing, pool hall kind of guy, and Okie simply wasn't allowed those sorts of vices. His father paid just enough attention to threaten a beating if he caught the whiff of hooch or tobacco on Okie's breath. A beautiful girl could still stop him in his tracks, but he lived in such constant fear for his immortal soul, that he hardly dared to give in to the lust he felt. Emmett repeatedly admonished Okie, "If you get some girl in trouble, it will ruin the rest of your life. Keep that loaded gun in your pants." On top of his own failings, how much of Emmett's sin would burden Okie all the way to meet his Maker?

On the other hand, he admired John for his worldliness. No one knew more about how to handle the fairer sex, so much so that he'd actually been to third base. Okie had never even made it to first. John's accounts of his female encounters fascinated Okie, even though he was pretty sure about half of it had undergone significant exaggeration.

"So, what's on your mind?" John asked, leaning against the ancient brick of the parish hall and taking another swig.

"Everything," Okie said.

"You know what your problem is?" John said. "You just need to get laid."

Okie's face heated. "That wouldn't be right—"

"Okay, bend over and let me get a flashlight so I can find the broom handle up your ass. Here you are on the verge of your greatest adventure yet—the summer before you go off to college—and you're worried about sin. Jesus Christ, Okie, this is our time! Kissing a girl ain't a goddamn sin!"

"Yeah, but—" What he did afterward would be, whether with her, or at home by himself.

"I ain't about to have a theological debate with you, my friend. You need to dip your wick, and there ain't no bones about it. Pun intended." He shoved the flask into Okie's hand. "Drink up and open your ears."

Okie did, however reluctantly.

"Listen, this girl I've been seeing, Third Base Jenny, she's got a friend named Emily, a real cute number. You like redheads?"

"Who doesn't?"

"Yeah, thought you might. You probably don't like big tits."

Okie's face heated again.

John cracked an infectious grin. "So, *Shane* is playing in a double feature at the drive-in tomorrow night. I heard it's pretty good. Why don't you come along with me and Jenny, meet Emily?"

"Is she pretty?" He didn't want to find himself saddled with some snaggle-toothed dough ball.

"Jenny says so."

❁❁❁

John picked up Okie the following night in the black and silver Bentley.

With a devilish grin, John said, "Old man is in New York City for a business meeting, doesn't know I'm taking this baby for a spin."

Okie had never ridden in such a fancy car before, with its brilliant white sidewall tires and ostentatious, chrome hood ornament.

John sniffed. "You smell like a French whorehouse at low tide. You raid your old man's cologne cabinet?"

Okie stomped on his rising panic. "Is it too much?"

"I think it'll air out before we get there. Roll your window down. At least it's the good stuff. You can tell the difference between good cologne and cheap drugstore shit. What is it?"

"It was French. Cologne-something."

"At least your old man has good taste in something."

"Yeah, like yours." He gestured toward the polished wooden dashboard with its elegant gauges. "Feels like we're royalty or something."

"Don't you know it. The girls are going to lose their pretty little minds. There's whiskey in the glove box. Sloe gin is for the girls."

As they passed down the pre-dusk streets of Buffalo toward Jenny's house, heads turned to stare, and Okie's chest puffed up, straightening him in his seat.

Jenny's house lay on the Abbott McKinley side of Buffalo, neighborhoods Okie knew well.

"What the hell is with the street signs?" John asked as he drove down narrow, lower-class streets. "What language is that?" He was referring to the bilingual street signs.

"Gaelic," Okie said. "Lots of Irish in these neighborhoods. We used to live here."

John grumbled, "Nobody ever did that for the Italians."

They passed by one of the McGillicuddy residences on the way, then within a few blocks of the Hayden Street house he'd lived in during happier times, when his mother was alive and they'd all been a family. It stuck like a piece of gristle between his teeth, until they pulled up outside a brownstone where two girls in sweaters, skirts, bobby socks, and ponytails waited on the front stoop.

Their mouths dropped open at the sight of the Bentley, and Okie's mouth dropped open in return. The luster of Emily's hair shone like liquid sunset. She had a round face and pert nose peppered with freckles, wide green eyes, and a big, friendly smile. Her sweater accented an ample bosom and curvy hips. Together they smelled like a whole bed of fresh flowers and fruits.

As soon as Emily saw Okie, her eyes turned demurely toward the ground, and she clasped her hands, upper arms squeezing her breasts together, accentuating those wondrous mounds.

He managed introductions without sounding like a caveman, and soon the four of them were off to the movies. In a moment of awkward hesitation, he wasn't sure where he was supposed to sit. John gave him a pointed look that said, *Back seat, you idiot!*

So he slid into the back seat with Emily, his heart hammering, hugging the opposite door. Fortunately, Emily was good with small talk, putting him at ease quickly enough. She had a pretty smile, and her face grew on him quickly, especially when she started touching his arm. She had graduated from high school the year before and had started waitressing at Chef's on Seneca in South Buffalo and he should come there to visit her because the cannoli were to *die* for. He soon found himself on the verge of telling her all his secrets, wanting to, but he held back.

She popped her Juicy Fruit gum and sidled up close to him, sending his heart to a faster rhythm. She smelled like the breath of heaven, warm and soft, and her hair was beautiful.

By the time they reached the drive-in, the whiskey and sloe gin had made a few rounds of the car, lending the tang of alcohol to the sweetness of cologne, perfume, and shampoo.

The Transit Drive-in in Lockport, which lay a few miles north of Buffalo proper, had just opened the previous year, far from city lights, and it had fancy new speakers. The new movie *Shane* was showing in a double feature with an older John Wayne picture called *Rio Grande*. He found himself admiring Alan Ladd's stoic gunfighter, but found it difficult to keep his attention on the screen as Emily kept sidling closer and closer, popping her gum, and looking up at him with glimmering eyes.

For about twenty minutes, he agonized about whether to put his arm around her while dreading rejection. When he finally did, she snuggled closer. By that time, John and Jenny were no longer watching the movie. Their faces had fused at the lips. For half an hour after that, watching John and Jenny play tonsil hockey, Okie agonized about whether he should kiss Emily, but he also kind of wanted to watch the movie. Shane was the kind of hero Okie yearned to be. Strong, stoic, and deadly, with a tortured past, and like James Bond, beholden to none.

Only when Emily crossed her arms and sighed, popping her gum louder and louder, did he recognize his opportunity slipping away. The villains had been dispatched, the hero, triumphant. As Shane dwindled toward the horizon and little Joey called after him, "Shane? Shane! Come back!", Okie screwed down his rattling courage, took Emily's chin with one finger and turned her to look at him. Instantly her lips parted and plunged against his with an eagerness that pushed him against the window. But he quickly righted himself and returned the pressure.

"Wait, hold on a sec," she said. She took out her gum and stuck it to the rear of the front seat. Then her arm snaked around his neck and pulled him close again for a longer, deeper kiss, soft, warm, with the pressure of her teeth behind it. Then her probing tongue darted between his lips, further startling him.

But he was a quick learner, and she tasted like Juicy Fruit gum and sloe gin.

At some point, he vaguely heard John's voice, "Hey, you want any popcorn?"

But then Jenny giggled. "I think they're busy."

He squirmed at the stiffness in his trousers. Emily's breath was hot, and suddenly their bodies couldn't get close enough. Her breasts were two luscious pillows squeezing against him, and her fingers crawled through his hair, sending explosive tingles through him. The pressure against his zipper became a throbbing ache of need.

The front seat began to rock, and he caught a glimpse of Jenny's shoe braced high against the side window with no skirt in sight.

But then he submerged into the sea of his own sensations. His hands and Emily's roved over each other until she took one of his and guided it to her breast. Soft sweater became warm skin under his touch, then stiffly textured bra, then softly textured nipple. The stiffness in his pants raged for release. She panted warm, moist breaths against his neck, sighing with want. Her hand found its way into his shirt and played across his chest. His brain filled with hopes and fantasies, crowding out all other thoughts. Conscious thought went away. It was like his body knew exactly what it needed so desperately to do. His world became his body and its contact with hers, yearning to join with hers. He pushed her down onto the seat and pressed himself against her, feeling the heat of her against his thigh, grinding against him.

Then she pulled away. "Wait, wait."

The sound of her voice brought him back for a moment. "What, what is it?"

"I—we can't. My friend is in town." There was disappointment in her voice.

Confusion and intense guilt turned his brain to mush. His crotch throbbed against her thigh. "What the hell does that mean? Who's that?" How could a friend who wasn't here interfere with what was about to happen?

Her hand cupped his cheek. She whispered, "My period, silly!"

He blinked a couple of times. Her words were making no sense to him. He straightened and pulled away. A period of what?

Somehow, they were already halfway through the second feature. John Wayne and the U.S. cavalry stampeded across the screen.

John and Jenny sat watching the movie, sharing a cigarette, placidly passing the whiskey back and forth. The air in the car had an unfamiliar, musky scent. The fogged rear window cast diffuse light from the concession building.

Emily righted herself, rearranging her clothing with a sheepish smile, and reclaimed her gum from the back of the front seat.

For the rest of the movie, she told him about how she wanted to live in a big house with lots of kids, kids everywhere, and she'd learn how to make them blackberry pies, and they'd play in the back yard, and she'd take the car to the beauty parlor once a week, and have bridge parties, and all her huge family could come over for dinner, except for her cousin Siobhan who'd once dated a Negro, and...

And Okie tuned out. All he could focus on was trying to figure out what had happened. Had he done something wrong? Was God punishing him? It was a mystery that plagued him until they dropped off the girls back at their brownstone at almost 2:00 a.m.

Upstairs in his silent bedroom, he spilled his seed twice, sinning against God, and felt his shame, even as the pleasure ebbed.

The next day, he consulted the *Encyclopedia Britannica* in the living room, with its illustrations and explanations. His fellow teenage boys often joked about girls being "on the rag," but he never really understood what that meant, so he just laughed along and didn't ask questions. Piece by piece, his mind assembled the facts of what had and had not happened, and he felt even dirtier.

Emily had given him her phone number and told him to call her, but when he did the next day, someone answered, "Chef's on Seneca," and Emily wasn't working that day. He called the next day, but she was too busy to talk to him for more than thirty seconds. He gave her his phone number, but she never called him. He tried again a couple of days later. Someone else picked up, but he heard Emily's voice in the background, exasperated. "Tell him I'm busy."

He never heard her voice again.

VI

***"BLESS ME, FATHER**, for I have sinned. It's been one week since my last confession..."*

"What is it, my son?"

"I feel like I'm losing my way."

"Have you sinned against God in thought or deed?"

"Thoughts, I suppose. The irony is that I'm in this place devoted to the Church and to learning, but...I feel like I'm caught up in worldly matters. This is my first time confessing to you, Father. Everything is new and different and fun and strange."

"What you're experiencing is common to all freshmen. It is easy to become overwhelmed by moving to a new place. Is this your first time away from home?"

"Yeah. Yes. And I'm excited about that. Things between me and my father have not been right since my mother died, two years ago. He went to college here, too. He was a star athlete and—"

"Oh? Who was your father?"

"Emmett Hansen."

"I remember him. He was a fine student, and a natural athlete—"

"Yeah, yeah, I know all that. And he's also an adulterer, but you probably didn't know that. He was cheating on my mom before she died. Frankly, I'm tired of hearing about how great he was. I couldn't

wait to get out of the house, but it's like he lives here, too. His picture is everywhere. Coach Anderson talks about him all the time. And you know, when I was little, I wondered if he was a mobster. He was violent, he was never home, and I had no idea where he went during the day."

"You owe your father your respect. He has given you a great legacy. His sins are between him and the Lord."

"Yeah, and I've heard that before, too. I was hoping I might get a different tune here."

"The Lord has a plan for all of this. You must trust in this."

"I do, Father. It's just...I was hoping to get away from it, but it's following me even here."

❁❁❁

In mid-July, Okie arrived in Worcester, Massachusetts, to report for football training camp, his insides on fire with anticipation.

On the entire nine-hour drive from Buffalo to Worcester, Emmett had chattered away like he and Okie were lifelong pals, waxing nostalgic for his own days as a star athlete at Holy Cross, including football, basketball, and baseball. Okie had heard all these stories so many times before, they were woven into the fabric of family history. He could repeat them in his head verbatim.

Emmett's favorite was the time he had been captain of the football team, the youngest captain ever at the School on the Hill, playing center, and led them to their first-ever victory over Harvard, 7-6.

"Harvard offered me a full-ride, you know," Emmett would say.

Okie knew.

In the forested hills of rural New York, Emmett fell silent for a while, the crease in his brow suggesting deep consideration. Then he spoke as if he'd just made a decision. "I hope you are lucky enough to find someone you can trust. Holy Cross boys stick together like glue. Forever." The way he said the last word suggested lifelong ties.

"Me, too, Pops," Okie said, but there was something in Emmett's expression that suggested Okie couldn't possibly grasp the full import of Emmett's cryptic statement, at least not yet.

Then they fell silent again.

Throughout the long car ride, across the mountains and forests and farmland of central New York and New England, he let his attention drift into the beauty of nature. His father's pride was so strong, it could almost erase Okie's long-standing grudge. Almost. He could imagine what it might be like having a father like the ones on TV, but he would never let this go, never forgive. At least he would never have to see the Halls again. There was a whole new world to explore, and he was ready to break the chains of family. Ann was moving out at the end of the month, returning to secretarial school.

As they drove onto campus for the first time, Okie stared and stared. The entrance to Fenwick Hall, the college's central building, sported a grand colonnade and three sharp spires, two flanking the entrance and the other atop an asymmetrical wing. He could feel the pull of history at these century-old structures, infused with a reverence for education and the Catholic Church and a staunch adherence to Jesuit traditions.

On the way here, he had read the undergraduate catalog cover to cover twice, planning out his courses, even discussing some of them with Emmett, who was only too happy to slather on his wisdom. Okie planned to major in Latin, having discovered at Canisius that he had some talent for it.

Fenwick Hall was not only the college's central building, dating back to the 1850s, it would also be Okie's new residence. His father seemed willing to hang around long enough to get Okie ensconced in his room, handing him off like a football. But when the time came to leave, Emmett hesitated, hands in his pockets.

Then he pulled out a leather clamshell case about the size of a fist and held it out. "A present."

Okie stared for a moment but took it. Opening it revealed a military-looking chronograph with two extra stopwatch dials and radium hands.

"That's a Heuer 'Baby' chronograph," Emmett said. "Most accurate timepiece there is. You'll never be late for class."

"But this is your watch."

"It's yours now." The look of pride on Emmett's face crossed several of Okie's internal wires.

Okie just stared at it, feeling more confusion than anything else. "Thank you," he said finally.

"You're welcome. I should go then." Emmett shoved his hands deeper into his pockets, then spun and left Okie there in his room.

For several minutes, Okie considered whether he would wear it. It was a mighty swell watch, and he had to confess to himself that when he was little, when his mother was still alive, he had often coveted that watch. Finally, he put it on and proceeded to unpack his things.

He soon discovered that, as a scholarship football recruit, he was a cut above the average student, and thus was blessed with a single-occupancy room. He spent the evening exploring the campus, wondering how he would ever come to know all these buildings, how he would ever be as cool as the smattering of upperclassmen he saw around campus—but he was a Legacy student.

Under the night sky, strolling around the campus's meticulously manicured grounds, he could feel the eye of God looking down on him with approval. He did not yet know his path, but he trusted that God had a plan for him. All the world was possibilities. What adventures would he undertake? What would it be like to be a college football player? He'd been running and doing calisthenics all summer to keep himself in shape, fearing he wouldn't be able to measure up to older, bigger players. It would be like being a 14-year-old freshman again playing against seniors.

The sight of the football stadium, dark and quiet tonight, made his chest swell. That was going to be *his* field. Tomorrow, he would *make it* his field.

Okie walked into the gymnasium building the next morning alongside a steady flow of other players, many of them sizing up each other for the first time, others getting reacquainted with ribbing and light roughhousing. He found himself measuring up his teammates as well, wondering about their abilities and the positions they played, sizing them up as too fat or too skinny. The thing about football was that there were players who were smart, clever, and could think on their feet. Others were knuckle-draggers, even at an academically focused school like Canisius. Tuition was the same for gifted students as it was for those on the slow side. Would it be the same for the college level? He wasn't seeing any cavemen among these players, however. Just smart, fit, well-groomed young men.

As he passed out of the morning sun into the gloom of the gymnasium entrance hall, his gaze found the trophy case. He stepped out of the flow of young men and approached the case, which covered an entire wall of the hallway, floor to ceiling.

Enshrined near the center was a patinated, chocolate-red pigskin resting on a stand, which bore gold lettering on the game ball. *Holy Cross 7 — 1925 — Harvard 6.*

Right above the football was a team photo, and there, unmistakable even without the key, was Emmett Hansen, captain of the team.

Was that a twinge of pride that just shot through Okie's heart? Or was it something else, maybe anxiety that he wouldn't measure up? He frowned and traced the old laces of the football with his gaze. Harvard had been a football powerhouse in those days, a dynasty, and that game had solidified Emmett Hansen's stardom.

It was time to go kick his father's legacy in the ass.

He turned back toward the flow of players filtering into the gymnasium and saw something that froze him in place and kicked him in the stomach so hard he choked.

Gerhardt Hall strode down the hallway as if he owned it, chatting amiably with an upperclassman as if they were long-lost friends.

"You've got to be kidding me!" Okie blurted to no one in particular, but his expostulation brought Gerhardt about.

Their eyes met, and in Gerhardt's was a look of smug amusement.

Okie said, "What are you doing here?"

"Okie," Gerhardt said with careful neutrality.

"I said, what are you doing here?"

"Same as you, I should think. Playing football. I presume you did not hear about my scholarship. It was in the newspaper."

Okie hadn't. His own scholarship hadn't made the newspaper at all. Maybe he needed his own public relations firm.

"Perhaps we should bury the hatchet," Gerhardt said, approaching. "This is a new dawn, yes?" He extended a hand. "We mustn't let past differences affect our future here before we even get started."

I'll bury a hatchet in your smug fucking face, Okie thought. He was already living in the shadow of his legendary father and now being shaded by his father's "other" son. He hesitated before accepting the shake, but there were too many new teammates watching for him to appear petty. Best to be magnanimous.

They shook hands, but Okie could almost see Gerhardt's fingers crossed behind his back—just like Okie's were.

Every day was a mix of the new and comfortingly familiar. All Okie knew for sure was that for the first time since he could remember, he felt like his life had finally begun. He met enough new friends that he could forget about Gerhardt. Nearly all of them were good Catholic boys, so they automatically had history as altar boys in common. He was so enjoying himself that he felt the urge to go to confession only a couple of times a week, rather than every day.

Football training was a similar mix of the familiar and the new, with mostly the same kinds of physical training, but also with new and grueling kinds of training, new plays to memorize, and the fact that he was playing with young men now, not boys, young men who were several years older than him. He congratulated himself on his foresight to keep up with calisthenics after graduation, because several of the recruits struggled for the first couple of weeks, pouring sweat and gasping for breath. Coach Anderson seemed to appreciate Okie's level of fitness, offering encouragement amid constant scrutiny.

By way of freshman initiation, Okie and the other freshmen were forced by the upperclassmen to carry all the gear from the locker room to the field. He took illegal hits whenever the coaches' backs were turned, a couple of times ringing his bell so hard he woke up to find himself flat on his back with coaches standing over him. After a day of scrimmage, he felt like the aftermath of a carpet-bombing run, a target for annihilation on every play. Bruises bloomed all over his body, and even some of those grew bruises in a strange layering effect like a watercolor painting. He endured the obligatory hazing with all the stoicism he could muster. He would *not* let them beat him. He would not show pain. He would not show weakness. His history of physical and emotional conditioning from Emmett had thickened his skin and put a callus over his heart.

For almost two months before classes began, he endured all this, while familiarizing himself with campus and establishing his place in the pecking order. He could run faster than most, had surer hands than almost anyone, with athleticism bequeathed him by his father that he could hold his own, even against many of the older boys. When the season began, however, the hazing ended. A couple of recruits had dropped out or been cut, but most of the freshmen toughed it out.

The week before school began, each incoming class had its own registration day, and they were greeted at the campus entrance by the Crusader mascot, a knight wearing a gleaming helmet with a purple plume and surcoat, emblazoned with the cross of a medieval crusader, carrying a spear and shield as well. Okie found the image inspiring. Some of his favorite stories were the tales of King Arthur, Hugues de Payens, and books like *Ivanhoe* and *Beowulf*.

After Mass on the Sunday afternoon before classes began, in the resplendence of St. Joseph's Chapel, under the gaze of God, the class of all incoming freshmen underwent the matriculation ceremony for College of the Holy Cross. Each freshman would introduce himself and shake hands with the president of the college, Father John A. O'Brien. A man who epitomized what a Jesuit professor should look like, tall and cultured, slicked-back salt-and-pepper hair. In his stately white collar and ceremonial frock, Father O'Brien greeted each new student with magnanimous words and solemn mien.

Amid more than two thousand fellow students and faculty, little Okie from Buffalo shook hands with this eminent Jesuit scholar.

Father O'Brien gave him an earnest smile, eyes full of wisdom and expectations. "You know, Mr. Hansen, your father was one of my students. He was a brilliant young man, and a gifted athlete."

"Yes, sir," Okie said, his mouth as dry as talcum powder.

"We expect great things of you."

Okie swallowed hard. "Yes, sir." And he sounded like an idiot as well, as if he had no other vocabulary.

Father O'Brien looked past him to the next student in the shuffling procession, and Okie took that as his cue to move along.

When the procession was complete, Father O'Brien climbed to the pulpit and addressed the student body in a long speech that extolled the virtues of the institution and its expectations of them all both during their attendance and afterward.

"As an alumnus of College of the Holy Cross, you will be expected to commit yourselves to a life of service," Father O'Brien said. "Service to God, service to your country, service to your fellow man."

As these words resonated through St. Joseph's Chapel, they resonated in Okie's heart as well. A life of service. That's what he wanted. He didn't want to just be a businessman and make money for its own sake. Serving God would edify his soul. Serving his country might be a possibility, but how? Going to college kept him from getting drafted and shipped to Korea. An armistice had just been put in place at the end of July, but who knew if that would hold or what new military schemes the Communists would enact on the world chessboard?

He saw the ROTC students marching around campus at various times, their uniforms smart and well-pressed. The Air Force had just opened a detachment at Holy Cross a year or two ago, and they were out there as well in their blues. Was he officer material? Was a career in the armed services in the cards for him?

So many considerations and uncertainties, so many things awaiting his discovery. His classes were challenging, but he felt Canisius had prepared him well for the transition into college. He was acing Latin, Greek, and Russian. Religion class was boring but tolerable, with little in it that he hadn't learned at Canisius. He would have enjoyed history class more if his professor didn't have the kind of voice and demeanor that could put a forest fire to sleep.

He found that he really loved studying foreign languages, especially if, like Greek and Russian, they used unfamiliar alphabets. Learning the new characters felt like unlocking a cipher to which he was slowly becoming privy. Discovering the differences in grammar and syntax felt like building blocks falling perfectly into place, igniting his hunger to know more. Even speaking the new tongues was easier for him than for some of his classmates. His professors sometimes mentioned the delay between the understanding of an utterance in a new language and being able to reproduce the utterance oneself. They all told him he had a talent for it, and the pride swelled in his chest.

On game days, he reveled in the cheers and the grandeur of it, the thunder of the marching band, the waves of emotion coming from the ten thousand fans. He even enjoyed the cartoonish antics of the Crusader mascot brandishing his wooden sword at the opposing side.

The only fly in the ointment was Gerhardt Hall. Once the football season began, Gerhardt's politicking and undermining began.

Okie wrote in a letter to Ann:

I've never seen anyone so good at ass-kissing. His lips must be feather-light, because Coach Anderson doesn't even seem to know they're attached.

But everything changed on the day the Holy Cross Crusaders played the Fordham Rams, the Saturday before Thanksgiving break.

❁❁❁

Holy Cross hammered the Fordham team 20-7. Okie even got to run a few plays at center. His chest swelled whenever Coach Anderson tapped him to go in. He loved the anticipation of hiking the ball and slamming himself as hard as he could into the opposing nose tackle. The close-in striving, the purely physical contest, put a huge grin on his face.

As the horn sounded to end the game, cheers reverberated through the stadium and the team celebrated on the field. Okie surfed the waves of jubilation with his teammates. With a 5-4 record, the Holy Cross players savored every victory.

On the way back to the locker room, Okie caught himself in the gaze of a short, balding man in a woolen trench coat. The man had the kind of nondescript appearance that willed the eyes to pass on by—until his gaze was fixed upon you, and then you were a rabbit in the headlights.

The man approached Okie and extended a hand. "Mr. Hansen, that was an impressive victory. My poor Rams are going home to cry in their pillows." He sized up Okie through thick glasses.

Okie shook his hand tentatively. "Uh, thanks, Mr..."

"Casey. William J. Casey." Something in Casey's smooth, precise demeanor implied recognition. He offered a crooked-toothed smile. "I'm acquainted with your father."

Okie suppressed an eyeroll. *Of course you are.* But he maintained his politeness.

"But I'm not here to talk about him. I'm here to talk to you, my boy." Surrounded as they were by cheers and celebration, Okie had difficulty hearing Casey's soft voice.

"Really?"

"Indeed, but this is not the place. Meet me outside Fenwick Hall at 8:00 p.m. There's something I wish to discuss with you."

Okie frowned. "What's this about?"

"Your future, my boy. What else?" Then he disappeared into the crowd of players and students as if he had never existed. Try as he might, Okie could not spot him among the crowd again.

VII

***"BLESS ME, FATHER,** for I have sinned. It's been three days since my last confession. My sin is pride. I think."*

"You sound uncertain, my son."

"Is it really a mortal sin to know what you're good at and be proud of it? I'm really good at languages. I love how Latin and Greek fit into modern English. It's like I can see the building blocks, the foundations. And I'm proud of that."

"Tell me more."

"I was in Latin class yesterday, and we were conjugating verbs in front of the class. There's a guy in the class, Humphries is his name, and he's just terrible, easily the worst student in the class. His pronunciation is awful, even after a semester and a half, and he couldn't form a coherent sentence to save his life, even a simple one. He's just an idiot who doesn't even belong here. How he passed first semester is beyond me. His clothes always look like he just dragged them out from under his bed. Go pump gas and wash cars if you're going to dress that way. So he was called to the front of the class, and I just knew he was going to bomb it. He had that look on his face, red as a beet the moment he heard his name. So he screwed it up, then screwed it up again, and again, and again. Professor Murphy was trying to be patient, but even he was getting frustrated. Everybody in

that room knew the answer but Humphries, standing there with his pudgy, sweaty face and wrinkled shirt and tie.

"All I could think was, 'It's not that hard! How could you be so stupid? You're wasting everyone's time! God put us here! You're supposed to be better than this.' Every time he messed up, people started snickering. More and more each time. Finally, I leaned over to Edwards and said, 'Stultus est sicut stultus facit.'"

"'Stupid is as stupid does.'"

"The whole room exploded with laughter. Humphries had no idea what I said, but his face got even redder. Professor Murphy told him to sit down and called me up to the front to do the conjugation. I did it perfectly and went back to my seat thinking, finally *we can move on. Humphries looked like he wanted to just die. He put his forehead on his desk, and it looked like he was crying. After class, Professor Murphy really let me have it."*

"Cruelty is unbecoming a child of God. Mr. Humphries has his own set of God-given gifts. He is your brother in Christ."

"I just couldn't abide the sheer stupidity—"

"And that is your sin. When pride becomes overweening and vainglorious, it becomes sin. Love of your own worth makes you forget that you, too, receive all your gifts from God, including your facility with Latin. Never forget that."

"Yeah, that's what Professor Murphy said."

From the football field to the showers and through dinner, Okie couldn't stop thinking about the oddly intense little man. Most of his teammates took off to celebrate their victory with a beer party off campus—one of the definite perks of being a football player. He had developed a real taste for Falstaff beer. But he couldn't shake the memory of Casey's eyes that seemed to drill into him, through him, as if Okie were a book to be read.

He paced around the colonnaded entrance of Fenwick Hall, breathing deep of this sense of intrigue. It had been a glorious autumn day for football, sunny and sixty-five, descending into a cool, clear evening. Autumn leaves crackled and fluttered on the breeze. When the campus bells struck eight o'clock, Casey emerged from behind a column like a ghost, as if he'd been there all along.

Casey smirked faintly at Okie's startled flinch. "Again, let me congratulate you on your performance today."

"Thanks," Okie said. "I still don't get to play much." Under the lights of the Fenwick Hall entrance, he caught the glint of gold, white, and crimson on Casey's lapel, peeking from within the trench coat. A gold and lacquer lapel pin, about the size of a thumbnail, emblazoned with a coat of arms, a white cross with eight points on a red oval, centered beneath a golden cloak and crown.

"Walk with me," Casey said, and took off to descend the steps leading away from the entrance, moving along the shadowed walk as if that were where he was most at home.

Okie hurried to catch up. "So how do you know my father?"

"From certain circles," Casey said. "He's one of the most famous college athletes in the country."

Okie jammed his hands deep in his pockets. "So, who are you?"

"Let's just say for now that I teach law at NYU. I've worked for the Senate on occasion—"

"The *U.S.* Senate?"

"Special counsel."

"What on earth do you want with me?"

"It's not what I want, Emmett, it's what you want."

"Please, call me Okie. Emmett is my father's name."

"As you wish. Let me preface this by saying that certain parties see great potential in you."

Okie's chest swelled. "What parties?"

"Have you given much thought to your future?"

"All the time."

"And your conclusions?"

"I want to be of service. My purpose is to serve God and serve my country, in that order. I'm still trying to figure out how. Military maybe."

Casey nodded. "Are you a fighter, Okie?"

"I like to think so."

"I've spoken with some of your professors. They say you have a tremendous facility with languages."

Okie felt his face warm. "That's nice of them."

"Don't be so modest. It's clear that you know it, too. Your hereditary athletic gifts and natural ability with languages put you in a unique class of individuals. You could go far in certain circles."

Okie wanted to ask, *What circles?* But he held his tongue and let Casey go on.

"I'm a man of faith, Okie, just like you. I believe God has a plan for us. I believe He has a plan for this country. I believe the United States must lead the world as a beacon of light, whether that means we must wield sword or shield."

"Like the knights of old, code of chivalry."

"But on the world stage. Evil must be defeated, the weak protected. The scourge of godless communism must be wiped from the face of the world. It is God's will." True conviction stirred in Casey's voice, a bedrock upon which every word rested. "I belong to an ancient order whose mission is to serve God, serve mankind. Have you heard of the Knights of Malta?"

Okie sifted through his memories. "It sounds familiar. Maybe? But I love medieval history, knights and chivalry and stuff. That's the coat of arms on your pin?"

Casey nodded. "The Order of Malta is the oldest surviving chivalric order in the world. The full name is the Sovereign Military Hospitaller Order of St. John of Jerusalem of Rhodes and of Malta. A mouthful, I know. We have gone by many names, but the Knights of St. John were a religious order of knights dating back to the Crusades, in Jerusalem in the eleventh century. It began as a hospitaller mission but grew to a more martial stance with defending the Holy Land from Mohammedan infidels." Casey waved a hand. "All that is to say, it has a long history of service to the Church and to mankind. The Order has seen empires rise and fall."

Questions proliferated in Okie's mind, but he let Casey talk.

"Our members come from all over Christendom. Until the last century or so, one had to be a member of the nobility, but the rise of democracy has had an egalitarian influence." He chuckled at a private joke. "But we are considered a sovereign entity under international law. We have our own diplomatic relations. Our headquarters is now near the Holy See in Rome."

The questions became too much. "So, this is all really interesting stuff, but what does it have to do with me? It's not like you want me for a recruit. I'm just a kid from Buffalo..." He trailed off as Casey's gaze fixed upon him. "Wait, that *is* what you're saying."

Casey nodded. "I'm a loyal, red-blooded American through and through, but I also serve a higher power. There is so much evil in world, Okie. Stalin's death last spring may have saved us from another shooting war, or worse, an atomic one, but the aim of the Soviets and their lackey states is nothing less than obliterating the West."

"The Church is actively working against communism?"

"My boy, the Catholic Church has been embroiled in politics since its inception. And why not? It represents the very Hand of God on Earth. One might say its very inception rose out of politics. One might say the Knights of Malta are the closest thing the Vatican has to a standing army. Publicly we're a humanitarian organization—that's the hospitaller side, but somewhat less publicly we're still an order of chivalric knights sworn to protect the Church and its adherents, to protect the weak and vulnerable. I lack armor, and I'm not much of a horseman, but the swords I can wield have a long reach." Casey paused and took a deep breath, and looked into Okie, through Okie. "We could do much with a man of your talents, Mr. Hansen."

Okie had never felt so much like a bug under a microscope, scrutinized, measured, probed. Nevertheless, visions of Ivanhoe and the Knights of the Round Table galloped through Okie's mind, jousting with the prior belief that the Age of Chivalry was long gone. But maybe it wasn't. Maybe it had just evolved. That was a sobering thought, an exciting one. Everything this small man was saying sounded like all of Okie's dreams come true. But it also sounded too good to be true. How could he know this guy was legitimate? "So what happens if I say yes?"

"Then you would be inducted in a private ceremony, wherein you'll swear fealty to the Order, and to the Church. You'll also be sworn to secrecy. Our complete membership is not public knowledge. The Grand Master and others like myself are the organization's public face, but there are far more who are tasked to work...out of the limelight, shall we say. Let us just say that there are a handful of Knights of Malta working within the U.S. intelligence community. Some like myself make this public knowledge, others..."

"You're talking about spies."

"Among other things, but yes. International intelligence, domestic counterintelligence."

"But I'm just a freshman in college."

"A very promising freshman at a college closely tied to the Church, and from an illustrious heritage. And somewhat older than when knights of old began their training. We do not hand out such invitations like cinema tickets." Casey faced him. "You need not decide this now. It is a big decision, a life-changing one, and if you join us, we will test how far you're willing to go for God and Country."

Okie nodded. "It's a lot to think about." Nevertheless, everything inside him was screaming *yes!* Best not to jump in rashly, though.

"I will be in touch soon. And one more thing, Okie. If you tell anyone of this meeting—anyone at all—the invitation will be rescinded. Understood?"

Okie nodded.

"Say the words."

"I understand."

Casey nodded his satisfaction. "I wish you a pleasant Thanksgiving."

On the Saturday after Thanksgiving, the Holy Cross Crusaders lost their final football game of the season to Boston College in a heartbreaker, 0-6, leaving them with a 5-5 record. But it was the biggest crowd Okie had ever played for, with thirty-five thousand in attendance at Fenway Park.

It was a great disappointment, but Holy Cross's football team lacked the depth of other schools. The season had started off with promise—Okie even got some playing time—but then, thanks to some injuries of key players, they had lost five of the next seven games, nearly all of them shutouts.

As the days passed, his attention to his classes began to slip because his thoughts often drifted to Mr. Casey and the Order of Malta. He looked up everything he could find in the college library and found a great deal of information dating back to the twelfth century, a proliferation of names and events, battles and grand masters. Every name and exploit he uncovered led him down more paths of investigation. The thought of joining such an organization set his imagination on fire, as he sensed greater, interconnected stories of the dramatic lives of these men lurking beneath the dry recitation of facts and dates. If Mr. Casey ever showed up again, Okie would give him an emphatic yes.

One day as Christmas break neared, Okie was passing through Social Hall, formerly the intramural gymnasium, when he spotted a handwritten sign reading:

LEARN HOW TO SHOOT, Everything provided, Just pay for ammunition, no experience necessary

He had only fired his father's gun once before, in an ordered execution of the family dog. And now if he were to be a Knight of Malta, he needed to properly learn the weapons of the modern age. He signed up immediately.

The class was held in the Social Hall rifle range, administered by two upperclassmen, Army ROTC cadets who supplied several M1 Garands just like those that infantrymen had used in World War II, and the .30-06 ammunition that went with them.

After an hour of instruction on safety protocols and how firearms functioned, his heart thumped like a rifle butt against the inside of his chest as he picked up the M1 for the first time. His fingers stroked the worn, pitted wood of the stock, wondering if this weapon had seen action in war. Despite its obvious wear and tear, the action was well-oiled, and moved with smooth precision. The cadet in charge barked orders like a drill sergeant, step by step, from loading to aiming to breathing to firing. Despite all that, the grin on his face wouldn't go away as he sighted down the barrel at the target with its concentric rings and blood-red bullseye.

The instant he squeezed the trigger, the stock kicked back against his shoulder with surprising force, like he'd just been punched, but the elation that erupted in him when he saw the little hole in the paper target—it was the purest moment of joy he could remember, so powerful that he was still thinking about it the next day. He could hardly wait for his next opportunity.

By the end of the course, he could put ten out of ten shots through the bullseye. The distance was a mere fifty feet, practically point blank for a rifle—it was an indoor practice range, after all—but it was intoxicating, nevertheless. In the second semester, he learned that fifty feet with a handgun was another matter entirely, but even at that range he could shoot a respectable pattern. The cadets introduced him to a variety of revolvers, even an M1911 Colt .45. It bucked like a bronco, but the feeling of such raw power at his fingertips was an explosive release like nothing he'd ever felt before.

By the end of his first semester, he was scoring as well as the students who'd been shooting for years. The Army cadets both suggested he consider joining the ROTC and entering the Army after graduation.

"You're a natural," they told him, and invited him to join their unofficial shooting club, which he happily did.

He hadn't been planning to go home for Christmas break, but a letter from Ann convinced him otherwise. The truth was, he missed her, and he could put up with seeing Emmett if it meant a big grin on his sister's face and a slice of her chocolate cream pie.

On the bus ride back to Buffalo, he felt like a different person than the one his father had dropped off outside Fenwick Hall, but exactly how, he couldn't put his finger on.

“You look particularly smug, Okie,” Emmett said across the Christmas dinner table. A Christmas goose, mashed potatoes and gravy, Brussels sprouts and carrots, cranberry sauce, and fresh-baked rolls filled the table between them.

Ann said, “Dad, I don’t think smug is the right word. He should be proud of himself, making the honor roll his first semester in college.”

Emmett’s eyes narrowed. “He looks like a boy a bit too full of himself.”

There were so many verbal shots Okie would have enjoyed taking, but remembering Casey’s admonishment, he said nothing, just met his father’s gaze with sheer defiance.

Since arriving home the day before after the bus trip from Massachusetts, Okie had noticed his father looked strangely smaller now, as if he had diminished in Okie’s absence. When Emmett came home from work on Christmas Eve, he looked tired, beleaguered, as if he had aged a decade in the six months Okie had been gone.

Okie hesitated to admit it but walking through the front door and seeing a Christmas tree—Ann’s handiwork—beside a crackling fireplace and smelling a batch of snickerdoodles baking gave him such a warm feeling, despite the tension that still existed. But Emmett seemed to revel in it, as if stepping back into a practiced role.

“And you look like the perfect example of how guilt eats at a person’s soul,” Okie said.

“Okie!” Ann gasped. “It’s Christmas.”

“He started it,” Okie said.

"Neither of you are six years old!" Her voice rose sharply. "Mom would be ashamed of you both."

Okie's anger deflated like a balloon. "You're right. Sorry."

Emmett chewed on something sour behind his lips but said nothing.

They continued the meal in silence. Okie showered Ann with praise for the meal. "You really outdid yourself. This is just like Mom would have made."

Ann gave him a genuine smile and squeezed his hand.

Emmett wiped his mouth. "The goose is a bit dry, but everything else is delicious, honey."

Ann deflated at that, her smile sliding away.

Okie couldn't hold back. He jumped up, toppling his chair. "You *asshole.*"

Emmett's eyes blazed, and he stood, too.

"You can't say one fucking thing that's nice, that's *decent*!" Okie said. "What is wrong with you?"

Ann turned white as spilled milk.

Emmett's voice was unpolished granite. "I see college has expanded your repertoire of profanity."

"Oh, fuck you! Ann made us this incredible meal, and you just punched her in the stomach!"

"How dare you. Get out of my house."

Okie's fists clenched at his sides. A thousand different attacks flashed through his mind, flying fists, mashed potatoes and roast goose in midair, an airborne chair. In football, he had flattened men larger than Emmett. Emmett's fists were clenched, too, his body squared.

Ann wept. Over and over she whispered, "Please, please stop."

They hadn't even exchanged gifts yet. Okie had brought her an antique copy of *Little Women*, one of her favorite books. It still sat under the tree where he had placed it. He'd even wrapped it himself. He said to her, "I'm sorry." Then he turned to his father and said, "You're a disgrace. And everyone knows it."

As he turned away, he kept vigilant, but Emmett did not move.

Okie went upstairs to retrieve his suitcase. Ann met him at the front door. Emmett was nowhere to be seen. Okie hugged her, kissed her on the cheek, and said, "It really was a spectacular Christmas dinner. Sorry about ruining everything."

"Don't forget to write me."

"Likewise."

"Where are you going?"

"I'll let you know when I get there."

Then he turned, shut the door behind him, and walked out into the chilly winter night.

VIII

***"BLESS ME, FATHER,** for I have sinned. It's been one day since my last confession. I got into a fight with my son last night over dinner. The little shit is as stubborn as his old man. My wife and I have been pushing Trey toward Holy Cross his whole life, and now he swears to me he will not go."*

"Perhaps a carrot would be appropriate, rather than a stick. Holy Cross is a fine institution."

"It must be. They kicked me *out, right? But seriously, I think he'd really find his path to God there. He's such a pain in the ass, he needs to be set straight."*

"One might suggest that pushing him to go to Holy Cross could be a way of correcting an old mistake."

"The thing is, I never really regretted leaving. I was so beyond everything they were trying to teach me. Most of my time there felt like being forced back into elementary school. Of course, now *I know that was just a nineteen-year-old's arrogance. I've since gotten some perspective. But it did lead me onto this path, which I've never once regretted. Once God's plan for me became clear, nothing could stop me."*

"Believing you know the mind of God ventures into vainglorious pride. Is that your sin?"

"No, my sin is wanting to screw a stripper last night. After dinner, I told my family I was going back to the office for some last-minute work. The strip club is on the way to my office, right across the railroad tracks."

"Did you?"

"I didn't have enough cash."

Okie took a bus back to Holy Cross, where he at least had a roof over his head. The campus was all but deserted as all the students had gone home for the holidays. Only the resident faculty and staff remained. They all cast him sympathetic looks. Cutting holiday vacation short did not speak well of a student's home life, and no doubt they'd seen it before. One of the housekeepers, Mrs. Hudson, brought him a sandwich for lunch every day until the school cafeteria resumed operation. He spent the time reading and researching the Order of Malta in the empty library.

The Sovereign Military Hospitaller Order of St. John of Jerusalem of Rhodes and of Malta had a tangled history that went back almost a millennium, and in fact could be confused with other organizations that claimed affiliation by taking a very similar name. It was an arcane-sounding organization with priories, sub-priories, Masters and a Grand Master and other high officers, but at the bottom line traced its allegiance straight to the Pope. The more Okie uncovered, the more he wanted to know. He could sense the vast and intricate interplay of history lurking behind the lines of facts, names, and dates, a history so deep and profound he could spend a lifetime studying it—that is, if any of it could be sufficiently uncovered. In learning about the Order, he was also fascinated by the Knights Templar, a similar chivalric order born during the Crusades, but it had been suppressed, its knights condemned as heretics by the Church. Had their fates been intertwined somehow? It was difficult to find information that didn't conflict.

When the spring semester kicked off, he found himself less interested in his classes and more engrossed in the way these medieval knights had served God in wars against Mohammedan infidels. He imagined their lives, trained from boyhood to the saddle and sword, sworn to God and the code of chivalry. Instead of reading his assignments, he read *Ivanhoe* again, and pulp magazines featuring true-life stories of World War II. Those made him wish he'd been just a few years older. He could have gone overseas and proved himself against the Nazis or the Nips.

It hit him out of the blue one day that the more time he spent in school, the less he felt like a scholar. He had come to College of the Holy Cross thinking he would be among pious young men committed to the Catholic Church, men who were prepared to give themselves to a life of service.

Okie was discovering, however, that many of his fellow students were an ungainly mob of hedonistic fools and listless losers, all Catholics to be sure, but far from the ideals that Father O'Brien espoused during his induction speech. There were even those who talked of steady girlfriends back home, even as they went carousing every weekend. Okie had expected men who were a cut above, but they weren't. To be fair, there was a handful of earnest, Godly young men, but for the most part, they were all hopelessly square. Was that how people saw him, hopelessly square? Maybe it was because they were all simply lust-crazed young men yearning to spew their seed in whatever field they could plow.

He confessed such base urges whenever he had them. Fortunately, the dearth of women around the Holy Cross campus limited them to weekends when he would venture off campus or drink beer with his teammates.

As the semester went on, his class attendance slackened, especially in English. Writing dry argumentative essays about things that mattered little lacked urgency in the life of the man of action he wanted to become. Shooting practice, he continued to pursue with great enthusiasm. Had there been any classes on medieval sword-fighting or jousting, he'd have jumped into those with both feet, but he was almost as happy to practice the weapons of the modern age. The Army ROTC cadets who oversaw the rifle range became good friends, and they often encouraged him to sign up and join the Army.

But he hesitated for reasons he couldn't quite grasp. Was he officer material? Did he want to be a leader of men?

In April, a few weeks before the end of the semester, he received a letter from the administration saying that if he didn't start coming to class, he'd be put on academic probation and maybe lose his scholarship. The notice had also been sent to Coach Anderson.

He stared at the letter, sensing its heft and consequences. Had he really missed that much class? His grades were all Cs, he thought, except for Latin, which was a solid A—he could handle that class without doing any work at all—and English, which was a D. Maybe it was worse than he thought.

But somehow, he couldn't bring himself to feel like it mattered. He found enjoyment in football, but his coursework bored him to catatonia.

By the semester's end, he managed to slap his grades back into shape sufficiently to retain his scholarship, but that left the question of where he was going to live until football training camp started in July. He had no plans of ever setting foot in his father's house again, except maybe to burn it down.

Ann had returned to secretarial school and was living with a roommate in a South Buffalo apartment. He wrote to her to ask if he could borrow her sofa for a few weeks until training camp started, and was greatly relieved when she agreed, promising to introduce him to her friend Niamh. They'd met in secretarial school and moved in together to have some independence and save room costs at the same time.

Ann was not a fancy or glamorous woman, he realized, never having considered his sister in such terms before. She was big-boned, sturdy, more like a draft horse than a thoroughbred. The moment he laid eyes on her roommate, Niamh, he knew he was in trouble. She was not just a thoroughbred but an Arabian.

As he stood there inside their door, facing the two women, stricken dumb, his suitcase slipped from his fingers and clunked hard on the floor.

Ann jumped in and hugged him with a huge grin, saving him from looking more like an idiot than he already did.

When she finally released him, he was granted the vision of dreams he didn't know he had. As he shook Niamh's hand, it was warm, petal soft, lightly freckled by her Irish heritage. He wanted to kiss it in the old aristocratic manner. Her raven hair tumbled around the shoulders of her ivory Aran sweater. Her steel-blue eyes flecked with deeper azure seized his gaze and wouldn't let go. His mouth and throat went dust-dry. She was almost as tall as him, willowy and buxom at the same time with a long neck and a musician's graceful hands. She was a swan who made Ann look like a chicken.

"Thanks a lot for letting me room with you for a while," he said to the air between Ann and Niamh.

"We're so happy to have you!" Ann said. "You have to tell us all about college."

"I'll chip in for rent and groceries. I'm no freeloader," Okie said. "I might have a job washing dishes at O'Shea's. I called Mom's cousin Caulan, and he said he might have something for me to do."

"That's swell," Ann said, "but you're a guest. Don't you worry about those kinds of things."

She gestured him toward the sofa, a brown, coarsely upholstered thing that resembled an old, swaybacked horse. "This is, uh, your room." She chuckled nervously at that.

Their apartment was the second floor of a Victorian-era house with creaky floors and sticky windows, situated about five blocks from the highest concentration of their McGillicuddy relatives, eight blocks from the house they'd lived in when Okie was little.

The place needed some plaster and paint, and the cockroaches hadn't yet formed a trade union, but somehow it felt homey.

The truth was, Okie would have been happy to cross waist-deep sewage if Niamh's lips were on the other side.

The first time he saw her in her nightgown and chenille bathrobe, his heart stopped for what seemed like ten seconds, then made it up with double-time for the next ten minutes.

She came out of her bedroom while Okie was telling Ann about Holy Cross, poured herself a cup of tea, and retreated to her room again, and his gaze couldn't help but follow her.

Ann sighed and squeezed his hand with sympathy. "Good luck, kiddo."

"What are you talking about?"

She rolled her eyes.

"It's that obvious?"

She nodded slowly.

He sighed again.

As the days passed, he often tried to talk to Niamh—it was easier when Ann was around—but no shred of her carried the slightest interest in him. She was an enigma so opaque she might have been a sealed bank vault, but he sensed riches beyond imagining inside, if only he could find the combination. He tested her with the kind of bravado he'd seen John use with women, but that received only indulgent smiles or indifference. She was always polite enough, but whenever he tried to probe deeper, she gently rebuffed him.

It took him three weeks to build up the courage to ask her out to a movie.

She said, "You're a nice boy, but you're a little young for me."

"How old are you?" he asked her.

"Twenty-four."

"That's only four years difference."

"Five," she said.

She knew how old he was! She had asked! Oddly, this both encouraged him and sent him spinning. To her, despite that he was a college football player, he was just a boy.

Did he have to commit mortal sins to become a man?

In the showers and locker rooms during football season, his teammates often bragged about their sexual exploits, throwing out the names of things called "sexual positions" and acts of sodomy that made his ears hot. Some of the terms sounded both funny and confusing. He wanted to know more but didn't dare ask. John had occasionally used such terms, but Okie had never had the courage to expose his ignorance by asking what they meant. Besides, where those guys were finding all these women with such loose morals, Okie could not fathom. It was yet another mystery to which the Lord had not made him privy.

It was a Monday after practice, near the end of his first season at Holy Cross, when he could no longer duck the raunchy, locker-room story time. His teammates were all passing in and out of the showers when the conversation turned to taunts and boasts about the exploits of the weekend.

Someone made what sounded like a joke about how Catholics spend their whole lives in "missionary position," so they should all go find Jewish or Protestant girls.

"Hey, Hansen!" Gerhardt called with a challenge, standing like an Aryan statue of David in the steam of the showers. "What's your favorite position? I'll bet you're a missionary guy all the way."

Okie's cheeks heated, and he said nothing, rinsing off quickly and hurrying back to his locker.

Gerhardt turned to Evans, the second-string quarterback, a garrulous, forthright young man Okie rather admired, and said, "What did I tell you?"

Okie's fists clenched, but he put his head down and started getting dressed. Coach Anderson wouldn't smile on a fist fight in the locker room.

Next to him, Bob Rosmario, the star running back, leaned in and muttered, "Don't let him get to you. He's an asshole."

"Thanks," Okie said under his voice. "I just don't know what missionary work has to do with women."

Rosmario clapped him on the shoulder and said earnestly, "Someday you will." Okie listened for condescension or sarcasm but heard none. That was the day he decided Rosmario was one of the good guys. But understanding the meaning of "missionary" still eluded him.

So, he asked Ann about it one day.

She laughed even as she clamped both hands over her mouth and turned red as beet stew.

"What's wrong?" he asked. "For the love of Pete, somebody tell me something useful!"

"I can't, but..." She couldn't look at him, embarrassed. "You know the newsstand in front of the pharmacy, by the bus stop?"

He nodded. He walked by it on the way to O'Shea's Tavern to bus tables and wash dishes.

"Ask the newsie what he has behind the counter. There's this new magazine called *Playboy* I've seen around. The one I saw has pictures of Marilyn Monroe in it."

"So?" He'd seen pictures of Marilyn Monroe in every magazine on every newsstand.

Her voice dropped to a whisper. "She's...naked!"

He blinked. "You're kidding."

She shook her head.

"Is that legal?"

She shrugged. "But maybe a magazine like that can tell you what you want to know. I surely cannot."

The next day, the newsie gave Okie a knowing smirk. "You got the last one. I can't keep 'em on the rack." He stuffed the magazine into a plain brown paper bag and folded the top.

He paused along the way to work as curiosity got the better of him. The cover of the May issue looked reasonably innocuous, with a smug-looking white rabbit in a bow tie and sport coat holding up a blue flower for a buxom redhead's watering can. It was when he started paging through it that his eyes bugged completely out of his head. Pages and pages of no doubt well-written text blurred and disappeared behind full-color spreads of a knockout brunette named Joanne Arnold.

Her face and body hit him like a punch in the crotch. She could have been Niamh's sister.

He stared.

A little old lady passing by knocked him out of his stupor. "You should be ashamed of yourself, young man!"

And he was. He kept the magazine at work in its paper bag, hiding it behind one of the industrial refrigerators. He didn't dare take it home on the chance Niamh would see it. Nevertheless, he read it cover-to-cover multiple times over the next week, the scope of his prior ignorance becoming clearer with every reading.

Niamh fascinated him. He dreamed about her. He fantasized about her almost every day when he was alone in the bathroom, and then confessed his sins in church at least twice a week. Father Leo O'Brien admonished him to keep his mind and body chaste, but it was a futile effort.

It was almost a mercy when time came for football training camp to start, and he could go back to Worcester.

Training camp passed with excitement growing about the new team lineup but plagued by dreams and fantasies of Niamh. Okie was a sophomore now, and he did well enough in training that he was expecting a first-string assignment at center.

But on the eve of the first game against Dartmouth, Gerhardt Hall got the first-string slot.

In a rage, Okie paced campus for days. He asked to talk to Coach Anderson personally, but the coach brushed him off, saying he didn't have time. They lost the game 26-27, and he couldn't help but think that if he'd been the center, the line might have held.

He was still fuming about it early Sunday morning after the game.

"What's troubling you, Okie?" Father Cornelius McGillicuddy looked at him over a plate of pancakes and eggs in Miss Worcester Diner about a mile from the Holy Cross campus. His cool eyes bored through Okie, straight to the bone. On Friday before the Dartmouth game, Okie had received the invitation to meet for breakfast before Mass on Sunday, a nice surprise.

"Goddamn it!" Okie said, restraining the urge to hammer the tabletop with his fist. "Coach Anderson told me I'd be starting center this year, but he gave it Gerhardt Hall! I'm *legacy*."

"I'm sure it's merely a test, a test of your commitment to the football program. Coaches love to create competition."

"This college shit is not for me." Okie sighed and leaned back against the booth's purple vinyl.

Cornelius wore the modest black slacks, black shirt, black jacket, and clerical collar of his office. Okie hadn't planned on talking about any of this, but somehow Cornelius's presence made the booth feel like a confessional. Maybe he just needed to vent.

"I'm sick and tired of living in Emmett's shadow." He pointed in every direction. "He's everywhere, all over Buffalo, even here. As soon as anyone knows who I am, they talk about Emmett. He's in photos all over campus."

"Why does that bother you so much?"

"Because *they* don't know who he really is." He sighed again and sipped his coffee. "Yeah, he was a great athlete, but I want to be more than that. I want to be a Crusader."

"But you already are. A purple one," Cornelius said with a smile.

Okie scoffed. "You know what I mean. This place is a sham. Holy Cross is not my home. Holy Cross is not my future. The thought of another whole year of taking more of the same mind-numbingly dull classes makes me want to check myself into the booby hatch. I hate feeling like I'm going through the motions. But I can't quit, or Emmett will hunt me down and shoot me."

"I hear you had a falling out with him."

"That's one way to put it. He can burn in hell."

"Okie, now—"

"Yeah, yeah, I know. I've heard it all ten times. But that doesn't make it any better."

Cornelius gave Okie a look so full of kindness and compassion it instantly dispelled his frustrations.

"What?" Okie said, his voice cracking with emotions he could not name.

"You so remind me of your mother. She could hold on to pain like you do."

"You say I *like* feeling this way?"

"You have not accepted the Lord's comfort, so yes. I think you're still holding on to her death."

Okie rankled at having his head shrunk by a priest, but maybe Cornelius was right. His mother was his universe, and his father was his prison. It was a prison of guilt and shame, and he wanted out, *needed* out. He needed a path out.

Cornelius said, "You need to make your own way, just as Saul did on the road to Damascus. There's no conversion without the journey."

"What are you saying?"

"You do not have to die for the sins of your father. You must find your path, your road, your journey to salvation. *He* has a plan for you. He will give you a sign. I'm merely His messenger."

Okie pondered this.

Cornelius said, "Constantine's truth was revealed to him on the banks of the Tiber, at the Battle of Milvian Bridge in 312 A.D. It was the beginning of his path to Christianity. A man could now be both a killer and a man of God. He could not retreat, only forge forward to meet his destiny. I have confidence you will do the same."

"You really think so?" Okie asked.

"*In hoc signo vinces.*" *In this symbol, victory.* The motto of the Knights Templar.

After the Fordham game, which Holy Cross squeaked out by one point, William J. Casey came to Okie again with a single question. "Have you given thought to my offer?"

They walked the same dimly lit route from Fenwick Hall toward the stadium that they had taken the year before. Sounds of revelry echoed from somewhere. After that game, a beer sounded pretty good.

Okie said, "It's almost all I can think about. Where do I sign?"

"I've been watching your progress, Okie. Your grades are suffering."

"This place is starting to feel like a waste of my time. I want to do something *real.* I want to be a Crusader, a real one."

"Joining the Order of Malta is not as simple as all that. There are steps, procedures. Some of them we can sidestep for what we have in mind for you—"

"And what's that?"

"Like the United States government or even the Church in Rome, the Order of Malta has both a public face and private activities. A great deal happens out of the public eye."

"You're still talking about spies. James Bond stuff."

Casey chuckled, "Hardly as glamorous as all that, but yes. One might describe the espionage game as a thousand parts tedium, punctuated by one part stark terror and one part mortal peril."

"I'm listening."

"What I need now is your verbal assent. There will be no written record of anything spoken between us. Do you swear to serve God, the Church, and the Order to the fullest extent of your mind, body, and soul, even at the peril to your own life?"

Okie did not hesitate, even for a second. "Yes."

"Very well, then," Casey said, extending a hand. "I'll be in touch." They shook. Then he walked off into the darkness, just as he had before.

IX

***"THIS WORLD IS SUCH** an ugly place. Bless me, Father, for I have sinned, it's been four days since my last confession."*

"Please continue, my son."

"I'm having trouble putting my finger on it. There was this thing that happened, and I feel bad about it. I didn't hurt anyone, but my friend did, and..."

"Did you try to stop him?"

"I couldn't really. I was there to back him up. That's why he asked me to come along."

"A lookout? Was this illegal activity?"

"Maybe. Probably. But I didn't know my friend was...that he could...that he had to... He's always been just my friend, you know? His father runs a taxi company. At least that's what I thought. That's what my *father led me to believe."*

"There is a reason the law would consider you an accomplice, and in the eyes of God as well. You saw injustice, you saw wrongdoing, and did nothing to stop it. You were there to aid the injustice. How badly was the victim hurt?"

"We didn't send him to the hospital or anything. Maybe almost. It was just a warning. But he was so helpless, just this fat old Polish guy who hadn't paid his debt, and his son saw us, a kid about eight or

nine. I'll never forget the look on that kid's face, watching his father get beaten. He actually cared about his old man. In a really messed-up way, I envied him."

1955

The letter Okie received halfway through his sophomore year was even more sternly worded than the first one. Coach Anderson was strongly considering pulling Okie's scholarship. His professors were unanimous. If he didn't return to classes by the end of the semester, he'd be invited to leave College of the Holy Cross.

He threw the letter in the trash can.

On the last day before Easter Recess, the Dean of Discipline came to his room and asked him to pack his things and not return. He hadn't been to class in a month. Instead, he'd spent the time poring over old books about the Crusades, the Knights Templar, and the Order of Malta, or else drifting through the chilly streets of Worcester, looking for something he couldn't name. He chided himself for a moron on those days when he recognized how lucky he was to be in college at all. Just a couple of years ago, boys his age were being drafted and shipped off to fight Chinese Communists. But more and more he felt like he didn't belong at Holy Cross. Where he did belong, however, he had no notion. He felt unmoored, adrift, tossed on waves he couldn't see. Every day he prayed for a sign from the Lord to lead him on his path. He prayed for Casey to return like a flashlight to illuminate his path.

Worcester was an old city, steeped in colonial history mixed with modern suburban quietude, so different than the insular, sometimes chaotic Irish slums of South Buffalo or the affluent facades of North Buffalo. One thing he knew for sure, he wanted to see the world. He sensed endless, unguessable wonders beyond anything he could conceive, but didn't know how to reach them. Off campus and around the city, he saw beautiful young women and thought of Niamh, to whom he would write letters, then throw them away.

He took a job busing tables at a modest Italian restaurant, trying to pocket enough scratch to pay for beer and food, and it sufficed as long as he didn't have to pay rent.

So, when the final eviction came, he wasn't surprised. It was like taking a punch he knew was coming. It still hurt, but at least the blow had landed. He could pick himself up and move on. His time at Holy Cross had granted him a sizable cadre of teammates and drinking buddies, but no close friends. He regretted that his abrupt departure might confuse or dismay them for a minute or two, but in a year they would have forgotten him. At least now he would be free of Gerhardt Hall, hopefully for good this time. Gerhardt and his whole vile family could walk into one of their own ovens and never come out, as far as Okie was concerned, and take Emmett with them.

With nowhere to live, nothing to eat, and only a few dollars wadded up in his pocket, he hopped on a Greyhound for Buffalo.

He showed up on Ann's doorstep with no notice, as she didn't have a telephone. The thought of seeing Niamh again made his belly do somersaults. He wanted to tell her about all the letters he didn't send, all the times she'd set his heart aflame. But now he was just a college dropout with no job and no prospects. What did he have to offer her? Nevertheless, on the twelve-hour bus ride across New York State, he rehearsed all the ways he would turn on the charm, the ways he had seen his teammates do, at least the ones who seemed to be wading in girls.

Once Ann recovered from the shock, she let him in. "What happened? This is terrible! Are you all right?"

He dropped his suitcase next to the sofa, looking around for Niamh. Then he shrugged. "That place is a hellhole. I'm lucky to be out of there."

She crossed her arms and gave him a long, concerned look that said she wasn't buying his simplistic explanation. "It seems like a such a shame after everything you went through to get there. Does Dad know?"

"I don't give a damn if he does. He can pay Gerhardt's tuition. I want zilch from him." He looked around the apartment again.

"Niamh's not here," Ann said. "She's got a boyfriend now. I don't see her much anymore."

"Oh." Okie suddenly couldn't breathe, clenching his teeth. Bitter heat bloomed in his stomach. A storm of self-recrimination exploded in his mind. He should have sent the letters. He should have told her how he felt. Why hadn't he been good enough? Was this other guy better looking? Did he have more money? A job? Did he treat her right? Okie wanted to find him and—

"Are you hungry?" Ann said. "I could make you a sandwich."

"Starving." He hadn't eaten anything since leaving Worcester this morning, and he'd spent most of his money on the ticket. Maybe a bologna sandwich would quench the fires of jealousy.

❁❁❁

The next morning, the familiar ache of unrequited want filling his torso, he called John from a pay phone down the street.

A maid answered the call. “The young master is still sleeping. Whom shall I say is calling?”

“Okie Hansen.”

“One moment.”

The stark reminder of the difference in their circumstances made Okie fidget. The elder John Montana owned a cab company with a lock on some exclusive city contracts that dripped with cash like sponges. He’d been a councilman both in Buffalo and Niagara Falls.

“Hello?” came the bleary voice over the phone.

“Hey, Sleeping Beauty.”

John’s voice brightened. “Well, look what the cat hacked up onto the phone line.”

“And here you are ready to lick it up. I’m back in town.”

“For how long? Thought you were in Massachusetts.”

Okie hunched his shoulders against a chill wind. “For good, I guess. Didn’t work out.”

“You sound like someone just shit in your cornflakes.”

“I’m fine.”

Silence hung on the line for a moment, then John said, “You know what you need? A pick-me-up. Let’s blow this town, go to Niagara Falls, find a couple broads, have some fun.”

“I’m a little short on cash—”

“Don’t worry, I know you’re good for it. Where you staying?”

"With my sister."

"She still got that knockout roommate?"

The bitter heat in Okie's belly surged like lava. "Theoretically, but Ann says she's got a boyfriend."

"Well, don't let that stop you. In the meantime, tonight is party time. I'll pick you up at six."

"That's a little early for you."

"Got something to do on the way. You okay with that?"

"Sure."

After hanging up, Okie picked up a newspaper to comb the want ads but had trouble focusing. Niagara Falls and Buffalo were close neighbors. The "Honeymoon Capital" had been cleaned up a lot since the war, people said, but it still had a reputation as a honky-tonk border town, where ladies of the evening outnumbered the respectable girls and betting the ponies was the number one pastime.

When John picked Okie up, he was driving a shiny new Chevy the color of a candied apple. John pulled a can of Falstaff from a paper bag behind the seat. "Priming the pump."

Okie took it, cracked it, and drank. "Thanks."

But Okie grew confused when John crossed the Peace Bridge into Fort Erie, Ontario. "I thought we were going to Niagara Falls."

"Like I said, I have a quick stop first. Won't take long." John downed his beer and tossed the can in the back seat. "I could use your help." He had a look in his eye that gave the impression he was holding back.

"Doing what?"

"Won't take five minutes," John said, but there was a nervous quaver in his voice.

The Canadian border guard took one look at their IDs and asked, “Business in Canada?”

“We’re going to the horse races,” John said.

“Anything to declare?” the guard asked.

“I declare that Canada is a mighty fine place,” John said.

The border guard gave a little sigh, then waved them past the customs office. They continued into Fort Erie.

Fort Erie, Ontario, was a small town, but boasted one of the most popular horseracing tracks in the area. Big names raced there. Okie had never been to one before. Emmett always said they were seedy, and gambling was a sin.

But John didn’t go to the track. He parked the Chevy outside a butcher shop called Tender Cuts Meats on a rundown stretch of street. The sign said CLOSED but a wispy-haired proprietor with a body like a pumpkin and a nose like an eggplant was still sweeping the floor under a couple of dim bulbs.

“We’re here,” John said, his hands on the wheel, shaking. The engine was still running.

“What are we doing? Picking up some pork chops?”

“I gotta go in and talk to this guy. I want you to stand outside and keep an eye out.”

The words sank in, and Okie’s legs went weak.

“You don’t gotta do nothing,” John said, “just keep an eye out.”

Okie took a deep breath. “Okay.”

They got out of the car and John went up to the door. He found the latch still unlocked and went inside.

The proprietor spun on him, startled. “Sorry, we’re closed.” His Eastern European accent was plain through the closed door.

Okie turned, thrust his hands in his pockets, and scanned the empty street, easing back into the shadows of the butcher shop entrance.

The conversation came through the door clearly.

"You know why I'm here, Mr. Stefanik. You're behind."

"Sorry, you have to go."

"I'm being polite, Mr. Stefanik. You don't get to play the ponies with other people's money and not pay them back."

"Get out!"

"Or what?"

"Please, my son is here."

Okie glanced through the window and spotted a dark-haired boy of about eight standing beyond the meat counter in the doorway to the back of the store.

A passing car drew Okie's attention to the street, but it was just a beat-up old Nash that looked like a rowboat flipped over onto four wheels and held together with bacon and poutine.

Then he heard a meaty smack from inside—and knew it wasn't from pork chops.

John kicked the man in the balls, then in the stomach, then in the face, flipping him backward where he hit the floor with a heavy thud. John kept kicking, stomach, legs, and when the butcher curled into a protective fetal position, the back and ribs. A fine line of crimson spattered the display glass of the meat counter.

The boy stared at his father being beaten, then locked eyes with Okie. The boy's eyes were filled with helpless hatred. If he'd been a few years older he'd have been on John with a baseball bat and a heart raging for vengeance.

John finally stopped and backed away. Stefanik was still breathing.

Then he went behind the counter, rang open the register, and scooped out all the bills. "I'll be back for the rest, and you better have it in American fucking money." He jammed the wad of Canadian cash into his jacket pocket.

Stefanik lay on the floor, groaning, blood running from his nose and mouth. John stepped over him as he came out from behind the counter and stalked out the door, approaching the car in no particular hurry. Okie followed him, his legs feeling like limp, raw meat.

As they drove off, he just stared out the windshield, his mouth too dry to speak.

John turned around and drove back toward the border. "Spit it out. Jesus Christ, it's like talking to a wall!" His face was pale, and his hands were trembling worse than before.

When Okie could gather enough spit to talk, he said, "What the hell was that?" He couldn't get the sounds of those kicks out of his head, or the look in that boy's eyes.

"Business," John said. "My old man sent me over here to send a message. Grooming me for the family business, you know." He gave a wan, humorless smile.

"I thought your old man owned a taxi company."

"He does. The Italian American Society threw him a huge bash at the Statler Hotel last year, gave him an award. Fanciest thing I ever saw."

"But he's a gangster?"

John shrugged. "It ain't that simple, like in the movies. Do I look like Edward G. Robinson to you?"

Okie snickered, in spite of himself. "You packing a gat?" He tried to make it sound like Edward G. Robinson but was closer to Bugs Bunny.

"There's one in the glove box for emergencies."

Okie checked. Sure enough, there was a cloth bundle around what looked like a revolver. "Jesus Christ, John! You brought a gun to Canada!"

"They never check."

"How could I not know this?"

"You? Fuck me, Okie, *I* just found out last year! But it's way more complicated than the movies. It goes all the way back to the Old Country. It's family, you know? Blood ties. My dad was born in Sicily, my uncles, some of my cousins. I'm first-generation American. But I'm Italian, too. It's in my blood."

"I guess I knew that, but..." Okie had never really thought about it. John's words sounded like his father talking.

John flexed his fingers around the steering wheel. "If you need a job, you can always ask me. I could throw you a bone anytime. You're the kinda guy knows how to keep his mouth shut. You should play poker."

"Thanks," Okie said, but if it involved immigrant shopkeepers who welshed on their gambling debts, he wasn't interested.

"So how about we put this behind us, drive up to Niagara Falls, find us some dames, have some beers."

Okie said, "Let's do it." And then he drank enough that he didn't remember the rest of the night. He was pretty sure there weren't any dames involved.

❁❁❁

It was days before the sick feeling in Okie's gut subsided. He spent the time walking around the neighborhoods he had known when he was a little boy. He understood them better now, noticed things with a more grown-up eye. They were filled with hard-working people, struggling people, God-fearing people. Like the butcher from Fort Erie.

One day, he passed two leathery, middle-aged men on the sidewalk. They smelled of sweat, coal, and hot iron. Before they left earshot, he heard one of them complaining. "These fucking kids today. None of 'em wants to work. Lazy bums all of 'em. Why, we got three slots open, can't find anybody to fill 'em."

Okie turned and called after them. "Hey!" After a few tries, he got their attention, and they turned grudgingly to regard him with skepticism and disdain. "Where do you work?" he asked. "I'm looking for a job."

The older one's jaw was grizzled with a salt-and-pepper stubble. Several toothless gaps showed between his teeth. "C.F. & I."

The other one looked Okie up and down, then scoffed. "You look like some college boy."

Okie squared on them. "I need a job."

The older one's voice sounded like he gargled wet cement. "Oh, do ya now? Like I said, C.F. & I. Ask for Sully."

They turned and ambled on, trading quiet disparagements about the younger generation.

Colorado Fuel and Iron had been one of Buffalo's chief steel mills for decades. Learning that kind of trade was a new idea for him, but it was honest work, and it paid reasonably well. But what gave him an evil grin was that he knew Emmett would hate the idea. From his youth, he remembered steelworkers as an insular bunch, bonded to each other by the hard, dirty work and the dangers associated with it. His mom's cousin Jake had been a steelworker, and his wife had made him change clothes in the basement and hose off with cold water every day when he came home. But oftentimes, rather than going home, those rugged steelworkers filled corner bars and pubs after the whistle blew.

Did Okie have it in him to be a steelworker? Was that part of the path God had in mind for him? It would be good to work with his hands for a while, to get dirty.

"What the hell," he said with a shrug, and the next morning he went down to Colorado Fuel & Iron and asked for Sully.

The name "Sully" proved to be short for Sullivan, a fortyish man with a barrel chest, meaty slabs for arms, and a walrus-red mustache. Tiny burn scars pocked his hands and face. He chewed a cigar stub and looked through Okie like he was tissue paper. After one look at the name on Okie's application, he said, "You Emmett Hansen's kid?"

Okie gritted his teeth and nodded. "Yes, sir."

"What the hell you doing here?"

"I need a job, sir."

Sully grunted and shrugged. He knew of the South Buffalo McGillicuddys, too.

Much to Okie's astonishment, he walked out of Sully's office with a job. Whether it was because workers were in short supply or because of his parentage, Okie didn't know, but he started work the next day. They gave him a company coverall and swept him up into some of the hardest grunt work he had ever imagined, in an environment so hot it was like the seventh level of hell itself. He had never felt such blasts of lethal heat. Sweat soaked his clothes ten times over.

When he came home, Ann marched him straight to the bathroom where she made him strip and shower, then threatened to burn his clothes.

The fellow steelworkers who bothered to get to know him even a little called him College Boy or Professor. He endured their hazing and ribbing with the stoicism he'd learned in football. They were just putting him through his paces after all. Mostly they were just betting on when he would quit. They weren't about to waste their time on someone who wasn't going to stick around. Once you passed some invisible Rubicon, though, once you were one of them, you were bound as tight as brothers. The shift crews were like families—often squabbling and contentious, but still families.

One thing that amazed him was the men who had been there for decades, some of them pushing fifty years on the job. These were the Grand Old Sages of the Steel Mill. No one knew more than they did. They'd seen it all ten times and done it twice themselves, just to see. They had been through the labor wars, embittered by their exploitation even as they cleaved to the company that used up their lives like toilet paper. Retirement was a dirty word. They planned to work until they physically couldn't anymore.

Okie's first paycheck helped him understand why they did it. He worked twelve-hour shifts, listened to his fellow workers bitch about the mandatory overtime with one breath as they scrambled for it with the next.

In spite of the grungy, dingy, scorching environment, it was spectacular at times. Watching a hundred and twenty tons of white-hot steel flow and splash like water could take the breath away with its raw power. He could imagine a hundred-foot, yellow-hot beam as the sword of an angel, a thing of purity. Like the swords of medieval knights, each massive beam was a symbol of power and honor.

A speck of impurity could ruin a piece of steel, weaken it invisibly. In that way, it was like a human soul. Sin was that kind of impurity.

He saw different kinds of weakness all around him. The steelworkers were as rife with it as his fellow students had been. Drinking too much. Philandering. Empty boasting and grandiose lies. Greediness. Cruelty. Failing health or chronic illness and injuries. Some of them took it out on their wives, others in liquor-fueled fist fights. A handful were good, earnest, God-fearing men who simply wanted to take care of their families.

About a month after he started the job, in mid-May, he was leaving the apartment for work when he opened the door to find Emmett standing there. At the sight of Okie, Emmett's face went white. One trembling hand clutched a letter, on which Okie spotted Holy Cross purple.

X

***"BLESS ME, FATHER,** for I have sinned. It's been a week since my last confession. I killed my friend."*

"What? You're only ten."

"My dog, Crusader. My dad made me."

"Tell me what happened."

"Crusader got bitten by a rat. This giant rat came out of the storm sewer. Crusader went after it and killed it but it bit him really bad on the face. Then he started to act funny. He didn't seem like himself. And my dad..."

"What happened, my son?"

"He made me shoot Crusader."

"He was right to do so—"

"I don't care! He didn't want to be shot. As soon as Dad got out the gun, he has this pistol, and Crusader saw it and knew what it was, and he ran. Dad shot him. But he kind of missed. All this blood started pouring out of his face and..."

"It's all right, my son."

"No, it's not! Crusader crawled under the porch and hid. Dad couldn't reach him. He said it was cruel to let him suffer and die alone. I told him the cruel thing was shooting him in the first place. Then he slapped me, and told me to crawl under the porch and put

him out of his misery... Then I...thought about...how much pain... he must be in and I...crawled under there with all the spider webs and gunk and I...I...I put the gun up to his head, and he just looked at me, with blood pouring out of his nose and mouth, all bright red and...he was so scared...and I, I shot him just like I was ordered. And he died. And I'm never going to have a dog again."

❁❁❁

"You little *bastard*!" Emmett growled through clenched teeth. "After all the strings I pulled, everything I did for you! And you wipe your ass with it all!"

That utterance marked the most profanity Okie had ever heard his father utter in a single breath.

"Wipe that smile off your face, you little shit!" Emmett surged forward, letter foremost in a trembling fist.

Okie dodged to the side, and Emmett stumbled past into the house.

"I have to go to work," Okie said. "If you want to stand here and yell at the wall, feel free." He tried to slip past, out the door, but Emmett seized the shoulder of Okie's work coverall and spun him around.

A fount of white-hot lava boiled in Okie's gut, and he braced himself for what was coming.

"You think the world revolves around you?" Emmett said, his eyes like cold rivets.

Growing up, Okie had heard these words a hundred times, but they somehow had lost their power over him.

Emmett went on, "You're going back there and beg them to let you come back. I'll call Coach Anderson. He might be willing to reinstate your scholarship as a favor to me, but—"

"No."

"What did you say?"

"You heard me." Okie's voice quavered with the effort of restraint. Somehow, he could sense a moment coalescing around him, a nexus point, as if he were only witnessing something beyond his control. The Hand of God in action. He was, in fact, smiling, bemused, even as the heat of his own rage built like the interior of a blast furnace, as if he had split into two Okies who were only vaguely aware of each other.

"I said, wipe that goddamn smirk off your face before I permanently remove it!"

"Try it," Okie said.

Emmett's open palm snapped toward Okie's face—shockingly fast, like a major league pitching arm—but Okie caught the blow on his forearm. Then he counterpunched, hammering his knuckles squarely into Emmett's jaw. Pain exploded up his arm. Emmett staggered back, arms flailing, eyes staring vacantly. Okie followed him with a swing that missed. Emmett crashed into an end table, sending Ann's third-hand lamp crashing onto the floor, where it shattered. Emmett's foot flailed high, and he tumbled onto his shoulder.

Like a ruptured blast furnace filled with liquid steel, Okie's rage exploded out of him. He fell upon Emmett, hammering blows, few of which actually connected.

A shrill scream halted him in a mid-swing. A grocery bag crashed to the floor at Ann's feet and burst wide, spilling cans and apples in all directions. Shattered eggs splashed from a burst carton.

"What are you doing?" Ann screamed, choking out the words.

The horror and hurt on her face quenched his rage like an avalanche of icy guilt. His nose began to run, and his stomach turned queasy. He straightened and backed away from his father.

Ann snatched up an apple and flung it at her father, garbling furiously. It thudded into his shoulder and bounced high. She grabbed another and flung it at Okie's head like Mickey Mantle. It smacked him just above the ear and exploded into juicy chunks.

"What...is...wrong...with you?" She unleashed another barrage of apples, punctuating each word with a new missile. Holding up his hands to fend off the fusillade, Okie thought it best to depart before she got to the tin cans. Her eyes glittered with the kind of flames only an Irish heritage could muster. He paused, filled with remorse, trying to flex the stabbing pain out of his knuckles. "I'm sorry!" he said to her, and only her.

Emmett rolled and heaved to his feet, blinking unsteadily, blood trickling from a split lip. He opened his mouth to speak, but Ann cut him off.

"No! You do *not* come to *my* house and act like a schoolyard bully!" She turned on Okie. "If I had a firehose, I'd blast you both!" Her voice trembled with passionate rage, her chest heaving.

Okie began, "But he—"

"Shut up! I don't care what it's about! It's always the same with you two! I'm done with it!" In that moment, Okie saw his mother reborn, all kindness burned away by a banshee wail.

"I'm sorry," Okie said. "I'll get you a new lamp when I get paid. If I miss my bus, I'll be late for my shift."

Emmett said, "Don't you walk away from—"

"Stick it up your ass," Okie said. He stepped around Ann, thought better of trying to touch her, and hurried out.

Despite his remorse at causing Ann such pain, not to mention making such a mess of her apartment, Okie was still fuming when he reached the steel mill. The whistle blew, and the crews filed into the plant, trading places with the previous shift.

Okie had been at the plant long enough to know whose teasing of the New Guy was good-natured and whose was malicious. He managed to avoid the latter most of the time, but this was not such a day.

While bundling a stack of rebar, Okie heard someone say, "Whaddaya think is worse, fellas, being a spud-fucker or a herring-fucker?" There could be no doubt who the voice referred to, as Okie was the only one around with a mix of Irish and Scandinavian heritage.

He dropped his rebar and turned to see Gino Ferolo grinning at him without a trace of actual mirth, among three other middle-aged veterans. Gino had a harelip and a buzz cut, and his voice carried a perpetual bronchial rattle. The absence of intellect in his eyes formed a contemptible mix with his lack of humor or good nature. Rumor had it he was oddly well endowed.

Okie took a few steps toward Gino, tugging off his leather gloves. "You care to repeat that, Gino? Not sure I heard you. Something about sticking your dick in a cannoli? Is that the only thing that'll hold still for you? Or do you need a macaroni?"

The words registered in Gino's dull eyes, building into a flare of anger. "Why, you little turd!" He charged. He was four inches shorter than Okie but had the strength of a lifelong steelworker. If there was anything Okie knew how to do, however, it was shrug off a clumsy tackle. He sent Gino sprawling into the stack of rebar.

"What's the matter, you crusty old fuck?" Okie said. "Too many drinks before your shift?"

Hoots of amusement erupted around them.

Gino righted himself and stumbled to his feet. He charged again. This time his iron-claw hand went straight for Okie's crotch and clamped around his nuts like a vise. Aching pain exploded through Okie's body, and his vision went scarlet. His fists turned into hammers. He and Gino descended into a snarling knot of straining, gouging rage. He bit down hard on a thumb, tasting blood and feeling a crunch. His fist slammed into Gino's nose, and he felt a pop. The taste and scent of blood filled his senses. A fist pummeled his eye, exploding white-hot pain through his brain.

Then rough hands were dragging them apart. Okie was flung to the ground.

A single voice roared above the din. "*Knock it off!*" A stream of profanity followed that would have made a sailor nod with appreciation. "What the fuck is going on here?" It was Sully, standing over them, gripping the naked oaken haft of what would have been a sledgehammer.

Okie got to his feet, wiping blood from the cut above his eye, spitting it from his mouth.

Gino shrugged off three men holding him back. "Smart-ass fucking punk, that's what!"

Sully turned his steel-hard gaze on Okie. "What do you got to say, kid?"

"Nothing, sir," Okie said. There was no point in telling the truth. Gino's seniority would make him impervious to repercussions. All eyes were on him, some amused, some contemptuous, some curious. He spat another wad of blood on the ground toward Gino.

"Nothing, eh?" Sully growled. "Then go home. You're done for today." Then Sully moved in close enough that only Okie could hear. "This is your only strike. I oughta fire you right now."

"But—!"

"Get outta here. Come back tomorrow."

"You look like you went a couple rounds with Rocky Marciano," John said as he slid onto the barstool next to Okie. He was wearing a nicely tailored pinstripe suit, even at this hour of the day.

Okie fingered his swollen eye. "He got a lucky punch." He emptied his pint and signaled the bartender for another, and one for John.

They sat in a quiet, neighborhood bar called Brunner's Tavern, the kind frequented by barflies and disgruntled young steelworkers at 10:00 a.m.

"Looks like I'm a few behind," John said.

They hadn't seen each other since the night of the trip to Fort Erie. The immediate brutality of the violence that night seemed less shocking now.

"To what do I owe the pleasure of beer for breakfast?" John asked. "You sounded a little shaken up over the phone."

"Got in a fist fight at work. Almost got fired," Okie said with a sigh. Saying the words made it feel incredibly mundane, a cliche. Made him sound like a bum. The kind of thing losers did, not him. But then again, who was the college dropout in this conversation?

"Did you win?" John asked.

"I'd have murdered him."

John gave him a long, still sober look. "I'm guessing it's a little bigger than that."

"The money's good, that I can say. I got some dough in my pocket. But..." He sucked the foam off the fresh pint the bartender had just put before him. "Yeah, it feels bigger than some asshole flipping me grief. First, I got in a fight with my father this morning. He found out about Holy Cross. Came over to Ann's place looking for trouble. We ended up busting up her place. I feel bad about that. So, yeah, two fights in one day. Before noon, even."

"Rough day." John nodded in appreciation, then eyed Okie. "So what else is it?"

"I've been thinking about it since that night we...went to Fort Erie."

John straightened and squared his shoulders, walls closing behind his eyes.

Okie asked, "Do you like it?"

John shrugged. "No, but somebody's gotta do it. Family business."

Okie scowled into his beer. They sat in silence for a while, the levels in their pint glasses creeping toward the bottoms.

"Truth is," John said, "it don't sit well."

Okie glanced at the bartender, making sure he was out of earshot. "Yeah, I can't get that kid's face out of my head."

"I'm a lover, not a fighter, right?" John said.

"Right. And I'm not a steelworker. I mean, I can do the work. All it takes is muscle and some common sense. But I'll never fit in there, doesn't matter if I work there 'til I'm fifty. I'll never be one of them. It doesn't feel like who I am."

"It's something you're doing until you move on to the next thing."

Okie nodded.

"So, what's the next thing?"

Okie wanted to tell John about the Order of Malta, but he didn't dare. He hadn't heard a word from William Casey since that night in November. And he didn't dare try to contact Casey through normal channels, such as via the Law Department at New York University. Maybe Casey had forgotten about him or written him off altogether when he'd drummed himself out of Holy Cross. He said, "I feel like God has a plan for me, but I've lost my grip on it."

John chuckled. "Like trying to hold a cat by the tail."

"I like shooting. I'm good with a rifle. Some bits of college I liked, others I hated."

"You're good at sports."

"Not good enough to play pro. *Maybe* I could try out for the minor leagues, but that's something Emmett would have done. That bastard can go die in an outhouse fire."

The beer continued to flow, and the day passed into the afternoon. The bartender fired up a toaster oven and made some Italian sandwiches for various patrons. The scent of toasted hoagie bun and salami made a small dent in his buzz.

John slapped the bar. "My old man can take that gold ring and shove it up his ass," he said, slurring his consonants. Then he looked surprised that he'd said such a thing out loud.

Okie raised his glass and proclaimed, "To old men shoving things up their asses."

This evoked dirty looks from a couple of other barflies.

Okie said, "Don't you want to make your own path, not take the one that's been laid out for you?"

"Yeah," John said.

"To hell with the family business."

"Yeah!"

"It's time to do something drastic. A real change," Okie said. It was like he could hear a tiny voice from deep down speaking truth to him. "Break out of everything."

"Yeah. But how?"

Okie turned back to his beer, took the glass in both hands, and closed his eyes. *Give me a sign, Lord. Please.*

Just then the front door opened with a tinkle of bells, and a man in uniform came in, removing his garrison cap and folding it. Four golden chevrons on his olive-drab sleeve proclaimed him a staff sergeant in the Army. The soldier ordered a sandwich.

Okie stared, and a tingle went up and down his spine. The hairs on his arms rose with the touch of the Holy Spirit. Unlike the ROTC cadets, this man was the real thing.

The soldier looked about 30, trim and fit, with the eyes of a man who'd seen more than he wanted to. Service ribbons gleamed on the pressed front of his uniform. He caught Okie staring. "Can I help you, kid?"

Okie blinked. "Uh..." He back-slapped John's shoulder.

John said, "What?"

"Sorry, mister," Okie said to the soldier. "You just gave me an idea is all."

The soldier smiled, "Glad I could help. What was the idea?"

Okie looked at John, then thumbed toward the soldier.

Realization spread across John's face. "You want to *join the Army?*"

Okie's head swam as he nodded vigorously. He said to the soldier, "How do I join the Army?"

The soldier's grin widened. "You follow me back to the recruiting office around the corner after I get my sandwich."

❁❁❁

When Okie told Ann that night what he had done, she just stared at him with a worried expression. "But people get killed in the Army."

He gave her the whole spiel about serving his country, serving God, and serving his fellow man by helping stamp out the scourge of godless communism. The Korean War had ground to a halt, but who knew what was coming next? As he spoke the words, still half-drunk, they came with a rush of nervous excitement. Not only did it feel right in ways he couldn't put his finger on, but it was also the best idea he'd had for as long as he could remember. It would give his life the direction he'd been yearning for.

"When do you ship out?" she finally asked him with a sigh.

"I have to report to Fort Ord, California for boot camp on Friday."

"So soon!" She looked on the verge of tears.

He shrugged. "No point in putting it off." He took Ann's hand. "Sis, this feels right. This feels like God speaking to me."

She pulled her hand away. "You're leaving me alone with Dad."

"I'll write to you as often as I can."

"You're leaving me alone with Dad."

Okie waited in the cavernous hall of Buffalo's Central Terminal, oblivious of the stately structure's art deco grandeur. Morning sunlight streamed through the towering, arched windows, four stories high, splashing across polished parquet marble floors.

Throngs of people hustled toward their tracks, and the towering clock in the center of the hall ticked toward 9:07, when Okie's train for California would depart. He paced and stewed, craning his neck over the crowds for any sign of John. They had enlisted together and were set to leave together. If they didn't get on this train, they would be late to report to boot camp, AWOL before they even started.

On his last couple of days at the mill, he'd asked for advice around the handful of men he didn't despise. A couple of them had been in the Army, fought in the war. They were happy to regale him with long-winded tales of the rigors of boot camp—often fraught with dire warnings like *Never volunteer for anything or you'll end up cleaning latrines!* But boot camp didn't scare him. He was in excellent physical shape. In fact, he looked forward to the challenge. He wanted to see what he was made of, for real, not the make-believe world of sports.

But where the hell was John?

8:58

In two minutes, he would board the train by himself. John was his friend, but Okie wasn't about to get thrown in the stockade for missing a train.

Then John emerged from the crowd, and by the look on his face, Okie knew something was wrong. John looked sheepish, regretful.

"Where the hell have you been?" Okie said. He almost said, *Let's go,* but John wasn't carrying any luggage.

John stuffed his hands in his pockets. "Sorry, Okie. I'm not going with you. I want to, but..."

"You signed the papers. You could go to jail."

John's expression became pained, angry. "I told my father what we did, and he...well, he lost his mind. We went round and round, but he's a stubborn old bastard from the Old Country. Sicilian, through and through. He pulled some strings, no more enlistment papers."

Okie stared, stunned, hurt, a little betrayed, but the moment passed quickly. John's presence had only given Okie the courage in the moment to do what he wanted to do anyway. "It's all right. I'll write back and tell you all the fun you're missing." He stepped forward and held out his hand.

John met him and shook it. "You're a good egg, Okie. I'll make sure to keep all the girls warm while you're gone. Now beat it, you got a train to catch."

XI

***"BLESS ME, FATHER**, for I have sinned. It's been two days since my last confession..."*

"What is it, my son?"

"Sorry, it's hard to talk about. It's too private."

"Nothing is hidden from the eyes of the Lord, my son. He already knows. He simply awaits your confession."

"I...engaged in...premarital relations, Father. That's all. That's all I can say."

"This is very serious, my son. You don't sound very repentant."

"How can something so incredible be a sin, Father? I mean, she's just incredible. The most beautiful woman I've ever seen. And she likes *me! Me."*

"Is she Catholic?"

"I...I don't know. I'll ask her tonight. We have another date."

"Do you intend to have relations with her again? Fornication is a grave sin, my son, if it occurs outside the sacrament of marriage. If this is a woman you truly care about, you must control those urges. For your sake and hers."

"Yes, Father."

Okie stood at attention before his drill sergeant, a hairy, steel anvil of a man who made up for his lack of height with a discipline that made Emmett's look like amateur hour. Sergeant Rudwall was the kind of man who shaved twice a day because he couldn't abide a five o'clock shadow. He could throw himself face-down in a bog and come out with his cover still in place, shoes shined, and uniform still immaculately pressed.

Second Platoon, Bravo Company, stood at attention on the parade ground on a brilliant summer day at Fort Ord, having lost any awareness for day of the week, much less the date.

Sergeant Rudwall's iron-gray eyes blasted through Okie like full-metal-jacketed rounds—Okie's fellow soldiers were convinced their drill sergeant shed excess heat by ejecting profanity, rather than sweating—but there was a flicker of pride in the sergeant's eyes, too. He presented Okie a leather clamshell case and opened it before him.

Sergeant Rudwall's voice sounded like he gargled with hot asphalt and staples. "On behalf of Bravo Company, second platoon, I hereby present you with the Expert Marksman medal. Keep up the good shooting, son."

Okie stiffened and saluted. "Thank you, Sergeant." He accepted the medal, his chest swelling with pride. The firing range was his favorite part of basic training. He loved the stillness, the controlled breathing before squeezing the trigger, the focus of the mind, and the kick of the rifle as it launched the bullet downrange. With pistols, he discovered he could quickly grasp an individual weapon's unique personality, its tendencies, its trigger-pull weight, which allowed him to adjust his grip and aim to allow for tiny variations in the sights. It took him only a couple of rounds for any pistol to become his friend, and then he could put rounds wherever he wanted.

Sergeant Rudwall moved on to present the next marksmanship badge, but Okie was the only one in Bravo Company to receive Expert.

Boot camp had been a revelation. Okie found he loved the structure, the regimen, the discipline, and the challenge. Sure, he was in good physical condition—maybe the top five in his company—but there were a couple of others who ate twenty-mile hikes in full pack for breakfast and washed them down with an obstacle course. He had discovered muscles that could hurt in ways he'd never imagined, not even after the toughest football training camp. Encased in ill-fitting army boots, the blisters on his feet sprouted blisters.

Camp Ord had recently been promoted to Fort Ord and built up to host some seven thousand men. Only a year or two ago, nearly all the old structures of the World War II era had been demolished for new dormitories, concrete barracks, and administrative buildings. Most of the soldiers who trained at Fort Ord were bound for the occupation forces of Japan or for South Korea, where the cessation of the shooting still balanced on a knife's edge. The basic training barracks were called Hammerheads due to their asymmetric shape, all lined up in precise rows. The sound of marching boots and cadence chants filled the daytime air.

Across every challenge on the obstacle course, Rudwall harangued them at the top of his lungs. "There are Commies on every doorstep, you fuck-brained maggots! They're coming to fuck your sister and shoot your fucking balls off! Are you going to fucking stand for that?"

"No, Sergeant!"

"I'll bet you'll lay down and spread your ass cheeks for 'em!"

"*No, Sergeant!*"

"So what are you gonna fucking do about it?"

"Kill, Sergeant!"

"I can't hear you! Bunch of fucking mama's boys!"

"*Kill, Sergeant!*"

"Scarpo, you fucking wop, get over my obstacle! Get the *fuck* over my obstacle! Your squad is getting their guts blown across the wall! Fucking *move!*"

It was clear from his liberal use of ethnic slurs that he hated them all equally. After the obstacle course, they fell into formation, drenched in sweat and breathing hard, while Rudwall stalked back and forth before them. "I don't give a greasy shit if your mama was a spic, wop, mick, pollack, bohunk, coon, or cracker." Several of the troops stiffened at the mention of their mothers, and Rudwall's gaze flicked toward them with deadly accuracy and instant challenge. "Until graduation day, you all are equally maggots. But you are *my* fucking maggots. And by the Virgin Mary's glorious pussy, when I'm done with you, you will be United States fucking *soldiers.*"

It was profaning the Virgin Mary that set Okie's teeth on edge.

Rudwall's eyes were already sighted in on him. Okie new better than to react.

In hand-to-hand combat training, Rudwall hounded them. "You will *kill* Commies in the name of Uncle Sam! You will spit him with your fucking bayonet. If you ain't got a bayonet, you will stove in his skull with your boots. If you got no boots, you will throttle him with your bare hands. If your hands are gone, you will rip out his throat with your fucking teeth!"

"Kill or be killed! Never hesitate, Sergeant!"

And so it went. Sergeant Rudwall was so creatively profane, Okie often had to suppress a smile. Getting caught with one on his face, however, would draw the drill instructor's ire like a white phosphorus flare, with push-ups soon to follow.

"You will push the fucking world until *I'm* tired!"

Unlike most of his platoon, Okie understood Sergeant Rudwall. The bitching and griping were incessant whenever the sergeant was absent, but having grown up with Emmett, Okie found Rudwall's hard-nosed, no-bullshit demeanor familiar. He understood the purpose of breaking down young men and rebuilding them into something else, elements of a unit. Cogs in a machine. He observed it happening all around him with an odd feeling of remove. He understood the intentional hardship, the grueling physical training, the endless shit jobs like KP and latrine duty. He understood the ways they were being groomed to fight, to kill.

Something that made it all more bearable was the fact that Okie's career path had already been steered away from the infantry. He was already enrolled in the Army Language School. His cohorts there were a more bookish lot than he imagined a typical assortment of recruits. That did not mean, however, that the drill sergeants cut them any breaks. If anything, quite the opposite. Because their physical abilities were often lacking, they needed more physical training to build them up. Okie found himself to be an exception.

After two weeks of basic training, he'd made squad leader, and he held the position until graduation.

During the days, he drilled, marched, shot, ran, fought, and marched some more around the green hills and valleys of Fort Ord and the surrounding countryside. In the evenings, he attended intensive language classes a few miles away in Monterey at the Presidio, the site of an old Spanish fort on a hilltop on a jutting peninsula overlooking Monterey Bay.

Around Monterey, some of the old Spanish walls from the late 1700s remained, as well as the original Spanish mission, the San Carlos Cathedral. It really was a picturesque area, with palm trees, meticulously trimmed greenery, rugged coastline, sparkling bay, and Spanish architecture. He counted himself lucky that he got to enjoy the temperate California weather, instead of having to slog through boot camp in some sweltering, mosquito-ridden hell like Mississippi or Georgia.

First and foremost, in his language courses were Russian and its many dialects. Later he would study Romanian, Czech, Polish, German, French, and Spanish. French and Spanish would be greatly accelerated by his knowledge of Latin. He loved studying languages, enjoying the play of grammar and vocabulary. The more he learned of other languages, the more he realized how ridiculously complicated English was. He counted himself lucky to be a native speaker. At nights in his bunk, his mind would be a jumble of new words and unfamiliar conjugations, his dreams filled with a polyglot babble he could somehow understand.

His language instructors ultimately accelerated his program because the standard pace was holding him back. Adjusting his mouth and ear for strange and subtle pronunciations was the most challenging part, but he still far outpaced his fellow soldiers. Some of them dropped out. A couple of young men, both clearly at or beyond their breaking points, received dishonorable discharges, drummed out in disgrace. They couldn't hack the mental exhaustion stacked on top of the physical.

Graduation from basic training was the proudest day of his life, more so than high school, more so than receiving his scholarship to Holy Cross. For the first time in his life, he'd accomplished something worthwhile, something that was his alone. It didn't belong to Emmett, had nothing to do with his father's renown or former prestige.

The day was made more special by Ann's presence in the audience. They'd exchanged letters every week or two, and she'd ridden three days on a Greyhound from Buffalo to Monterey to be there. It was her first real trip as an adult outside of Buffalo, and she'd been having a lovely time, despite the exhaustion. The truth was, she was happy to be away from their father.

"Being near him is like trying to breathe under a lead blanket," she said.

"If not for each other, we'd have both suffocated under it," Okie said.

After the ceremony, he had a few hours of leave, so they walked one mile down Franklin Street to 412 Pacific Street for dinner at Cademartori's restaurant in Casa Serrano, complete with wine, which he found he didn't like much. He'd prefer a Falstaff or two anytime.

"To my little brother," she said, raising her glass, "who's all grown up now."

He grinned as they clinked.

Over cannoli, she said, "I'm sure you're wondering about Niamh."

"Not really." He shrugged to help hide the lie, but the truth was, he still thought of her often, wondering how he might contrive to meet her again someday, wondering if she ever thought of him.

"Wow, I hate to say it, but you're just like Dad."

"Shut up," he said, and he wasn't playing.

"Seriously, the way you both just shut down, it's like talking to a wall. Do you actually have emotions in there?"

"Sure I do."

"Well, that's good, but maybe you could express them once in a while. When I tell you the woman you had a gargantuan crush on is about to get married next month, the least you can do is react."

Okie squeezed the stem of his wine glass, his heart sliding down around his ankles. "Good for her."

Ann studied him for a moment. "There are other fish in the sea, you know."

"Look at me," he said flippantly, "do I have time to go fishing?" The truth was, Honey had carpet-bombed any thoughts of Niamh, which all felt just juvenile now in the light of his vast sexual experience.

"I'm just saying—"

"Look, sis, the truth is, I found somebody else. Somebody who might be pretty special."

Her face brightened. "Finally! A peek behind the mask! Who is she?"

"I don't want to jinx it. We've only had a couple of dates. So, like I said, you don't need to worry about me."

"Of course I'm going to worry about you, you meathead. You're in the *Army,* where people shoot at you."

Over the weekend, they did some sightseeing along the coast, until Ann had to take a bus back east and Okie had to report to language school full time on Monday, the 229th Military Intelligence Battalion at the Presidio in Monterey. When he saw her off at the bus depot, she said, "I am so proud of you. Promise me you'll be careful."

"I will," he said with a grin.

They hugged, and she got on the bus. He waited until the bus departed, waving until she was out of sight.

Okie was used to being in the top of every language class, always scoring the highest in listening, reading, and speaking. It turned him into a pariah among his less talented peers, but he wasn't there to make friends. He was there to fight communism and defend his country, likely destined for Army Intelligence somewhere in Europe. And he had never forgotten his last encounter with William Casey and the mysterious oath he had given to the Order of Malta. He could never discount the possibility that unseen gears were being greased for him. It made him aloof from his peers. He fancied himself a young great white shark among sardines.

That is, until the first day of German class.

Okie had been studying basic German on the side for a few days in anticipation of class, wanting to get a jump on the material, and it was always a good way to impress the teachers, nearly all of whom were native speakers of their own languages. Immersion was such an important teaching tool that it was rare to hear English spoken anywhere in the Presidio.

To open the class, a short, portly, balding man in a three-piece suit, with a bushy beard and a little black cap atop his head, cleared his throat and introduced himself in German as Dr. Janusz Plotkin. All their instructors were civilians, but this dapper fellow in his tailored suit stood out like the epitome of class in this room full of Army green.

While Okie was still realizing that had just met his first Jew, another student responded in perfect German. "It is a great pleasure to meet you, Herr Doktor."

The soldier who had spoken Okie recognized from around the Presidio and Fort Ord, but they'd never had the occasion to meet, as they were in different companies and classes. The soldier then proceeded to address Dr. Plotkin in Yiddish, which sounded a great deal like German, and then what Okie guessed was Hebrew. The soldier and the instructor conversed for a couple of minutes. Okie's impression of the conversation, gleaned from body language and context, was that Dr. Plotkin was pleased by the soldier's fluency with both Yiddish and Hebrew, and was asking if the soldier was Jewish, to which the soldier responded in the negative and continued with saying his Hebrew was not very good.

"What is your name, Private?" Dr. Plotkin asked in German.

"Donald Fell, Herr Doktor."

When Okie's turn came, he responded with the rudimentary vocabulary he possessed, but then added some Polish—he'd picked up enough Polish in his Slavic language courses that he could make basic conversation—guessing that perhaps with the given name of Janusz, Dr. Plotkin was a Polish Jew who'd escaped the Holocaust, or maybe had Polish connections. His guess proved correct, as Dr. Plotkin responded, "Your Polish is excellent."

"Thank you, sir. I still have much to learn."

Dr. Plotkin gave him a beneficent grin. "And you will, in my hands. What is your name, my boy?"

"Emmett Hansen Jr." The name felt wrong on his lips, but this was not the place for nicknames.

Then Dr. Plotkin moved on, Okie caught Donald Fell's gaze, and they exchanged flashes of respect.

The rest of the morning session was a painful morass of stumbling utterances from the less proficient students, and endless repetition of basic words and phrases.

In the mess hall at lunch, Okie introduced himself to Donald Fell. Don was sandy-haired and roughly Okie's height, lean and physically hardened by basic training.

"Okie Hansen," he said, offering his hand.

Fell shook it with a firm, long-fingered grip. "Don Fell. I thought you said your name's Emmett."

"That's my father's name. Everyone calls me Okie."

"Where did that name come from? You don't have an Oklahoma accent."

"No idea."

Their gazes held, and in Don Fell's, Okie saw a sharp intellect and a mischievous glint.

Sitting together with their mess trays of Presidio slop, which was marginally superior to Fort Ord slop, they exchanged small talk and bits of personal history. While Okie had been immersed in Slavic languages, Don was neck-deep in romance languages.

On breaks they traded Pall Malls. Okie soon discovered that Don's garrulous nature attracted circles of friendly acquaintances, and he found himself engaged in more conversations with other young soldiers than at any point previously. But with Don serving as a social linchpin, Okie didn't mind the interaction. Some of the men he actually grew to like, despite their non-Catholic upbringing and inferior intellects.

It was a warm night in July when they got their first weekend pass, and going out for beers was a given. But then Don said, "Let's think a little bigger. I'm sick to death of Monterey. Let's head up to Frisco."

"How? Bus? We'll burn up our whole leave just getting there."

Don waggled his eyebrows. "I know a guy in town. Translated some papers for him. He said he'd let me borrow his car." The way he said the last word suggested a greater meaning.

"Sign me up."

"See, I knew you were easy."

"What kind of car?"

Don waggled his eyebrows again. "Wait 'til you see this thing."

The car in question proved to be the sleekest vehicle Okie had ever seen. Out front of the barracks where Okie was waiting in his Holy Cross sweatshirt and pleated trousers, Army buzz cut carefully coiffed, Don pulled up in a snow-white dream with a yellow stallion emblem on the nose.

Don leaned out the driver's window and grinned. "Pick up your jaw before you step on your tongue."

"Where did you get this?" Okie said, still gaping.

"I told you. I know a guy. Did some work for him. Now get in before we're swarmed by peasants."

It was true. Every eyeball within range was fixed upon them.

Okie got in. The car's sheer elegance was akin to John Montana's silver and black Bentley, but more stylish.

Don petted the dashboard while the engine purred. "Ferrari 410 Superamerica."

Okie whistled, then made a grandiose gesture. "Onward, Jeeves. Beer and women await."

"Fuck you, you're Jeeves."

"I'm not the one driving."

Don slid the stick shift into gear. "I guess Jeeves *is* the smart one." Then he punched the gas and sprayed gravel in a rooster tail behind them.

The Ferrari drove like the dream it appeared to be and made the hundred-twenty-mile trip up the coast to San Francisco much shorter. Or it could have been Don's daredevil driving. All Okie could do was hold on and laugh with the thrill. The speedometer dipped under ninety only occasionally.

As the California coast swept behind them and the sun splashed a brilliant path across the Pacific, Okie asked, "Where did you say you got this car?"

"A guy I did some translation work for."

"He's not like, a local or mobster or something, is he?"

Don shrugged. "I didn't get that impression. Said his name was Bill. Never gave me a last name. Paid me in cash."

"What kind of documents?"

Don winked at him. "I'm not at liberty to say."

"Yeah, and keep your eyes on the road."

They arrived in San Francisco at dusk, dodging streetcars in the steep streets, whistling at young girls on the sidewalks, and savoring every moment. They crossed the Golden Gate Bridge, agog at the beauty of San Francisco Bay with its tiara of sparkling lights along the shoreline. They were princes of the world, looking to sow some wild oats.

Outside a neighborhood bar in Sausalito, they spotted some Army uniforms and paused to ask, "Excuse us, Sergeant, but where's the best place to find some women around here?"

Holding a beer and smoking a cigar, the leathery sergeant eyed them for a moment, appreciating the splendor of their conveyance. "You boys Army?"

"Yes, sir, up from Monterey on a weekend pass."

"A little late in the evening unless you're looking for the wrong kind of company. But there's a dance at the music hall tomorrow night. The band plays that rock'n'roll shit, but you little wetnoses might like it."

Okie saluted him and said, "Thank you, esteemed Sergeant."

The sergeant grunted and turned back to his buddies.

They decided to stay in Sausalito for the night, guessing it might be cheaper than the big city across the bridge. So, they pulled into the Flamingo Motel to bunk for the night under a flashing, neon flamingo ten feet high.

❁❁❁

As Okie and Don cruised the streets looking for the dance, they followed their ears. The skitter and throb of drums and the reverberating twang of guitars echoed through the seaside streets of downtown Sausalito. Seagulls dipped and squawked on the cool sea breeze. The sidewalks were filled with young men and women, more civilians of the female persuasion than Okie had seen in one place since leaving Holy Cross.

Don gripped Okie's arm. "The women, Okie..."

"I know!"

"We have hit the motherlode!"

"I *know!*"

Not only were there nubile, fresh-faced goddesses in skirts and bobby socks as far as the eye could see, Don and Okie were driving the single most spectacular car in a hundred miles.

"In the military parlance," Okie said, "this is definitely a target-rich environment."

He and Don had already split a six-pack of Olympia—these west-coast heathens didn't seem to grasp the magnificence of Falstaff—so they were already buzzing.

They paused at a stop sign and let two girls cross the street in front of them.

Okie slapped Don on the chest and clutched his sweater. "Do you—?"

"Yes!" Don croaked.

They were two of the most beautiful girls Okie had ever seen, like models, dressed in slim-fitting skirts that didn't even reach the knee, high heels, trim cotton blouses with little silk scarves around their necks.

The girls paused to appreciate the car, then surveyed its occupants. One of them—with short curls of rich, golden blonde, high, full cheekbones, heart-shaped face, crystal-blue eyes, and plump red lips—met his gaze. Then she gave her friend a little tap on the forearm.

Don leaned out the window. "Can I offer you ladies a ride?"

"Where you headed?" said the other girl, a brunette with longer hair, longer legs, dark eyes, and elegant cheekbones.

"Adventure," Don said. "But we're stopping at the dance first."

The girls laughed at that.

Okie found himself leaning out the window. He couldn't take his eyes off the blonde. "Uh, I'm Okie." His voice sounded like a croak, and his tongue felt thick.

"And we're going that way," the blonde said, pointing toward the echoes of music. "Are you?"

"Is adventure that way?" Don asked.

"That depends," said the brunette.

"On what?" Don said.

"If I told you, it wouldn't be adventure, would it?"

The two girls moved out of the street, their heads tilting together, whispering. The blonde glanced back, and Okie would have sworn she looked straight at him.

Okie licked his lips and swallowed hard, his heart thudding against his ribs like a thoroughbred at the starting gate. "Target acquired."

XII

***"BLESS ME FATHER** for I have sinned. No, wait. Bless me, Father, for I'm about to sin."*

❁❁❁

The eight-piece band played a passable if overly orchestrated rendition of Bill Haley and the Comets while Okie and Don searched the crowd for the two girls in the dim, smoky haze. The dance floor was full, and the side tables were crowded. The air smelled of a mélange of perfumes, aftershaves, and cigarette smoke, with a tang of liquor here and there.

In a lull between songs, Okie said to Don, "I think there are more people here than live in this whole town."

"Looks like this place is famous."

Along the sidelines, little gaggles of girls awaited dance partners, but Okie had a specific target in mind. Until she shot him down, no one else would do.

Don was less picky and soon swept a pretty brunette into a smooth rendition of Frank Sinatra's "Learning the Blues."

Up and down the sidelines, Okie wound his away around the perimeter of the dancing couples, searching.

And then, like the sun emerging from behind a cloud, the crowd near the bar parted, and there she was, holding a cocktail glass. His heart kicked against his rib cage as it seemed to swell within him.

She spotted him, too, their eyes met, and she gave him a little grin. His feet were rooted in concrete, but then he thought, what the hell did he have to be afraid of? He'd faced Sergeant Rudwall and lived. It was time to be smooth like his old hero, James Bond. He squared his shoulders and angled in.

"Hi, I'm Okie."

"That's what you said," she replied, taking a sip of her drink, but her little smile suggested she was just teasing him, not brushing him off. The big blue eyes looking up into his drew him in like whirlpools.

"Uh, would you like to dance?"

She held up her drink. "Sorry, my hands are full."

"Oh." He deflated in an instant, started to turn away, then paused. No, he couldn't give up yet. Not with this girl who had just walked straight out of his dreams. "Mind if I get one, too? We could dance the next one." He and Don had primed with a couple of beers on the way over here.

She considered this.

In the space he blurted, "Are you here with anybody?"

"You saw her."

"Yeah, but I meant—"

She laughed, a rich, musical sound. "I know. No, I'm not here with a date."

"My friend and I are—"

"Up from Monterey," she said.

He blinked. "How'd you know?"

"You have the whiff of the Army about you." She winked.

"Well, you got me there," he said. "It's the haircut, isn't it."

She glanced at his Holy Cross sweatshirt. "Officer?"

"No, I work for a living," Okie said, reciting every enlisted man's mantra.

"Thought you might be a college boy."

"I went to Holy Cross, played football." A stab of regret. "Didn't work out."

She shrugged, and her lips kissed the rim of her glass, and all he could think about was kissing them. "Where did two soldiers get such an amazing car?"

"We stole it from Mussolini."

She laughed again. "You're not old enough to be a vet."

"I was the toughest ten-year-old you ever saw." She laughed again, turning toward him, looking up into his eyes, holding his gaze.

"But how could you reach the pedals?"

It was his turn to laugh. "Touché." Their eyes met again. "Tell me. What is the story of the most beautiful girl in this place?" As soon as the words left his lips, he couldn't believe he'd said them.

She laughed again, not in an amused or genuine way, but as if she heard that kind of line many times a day. Strike one.

"Let me guess," he said. "You're an international magazine model who sidelines as a Catholic school teacher."

This time she laughed for real. "Bingo on one, but swing-and-a-miss, I'm not Catholic."

He indicated the tiny gold cross she wore around her neck, peeking in and out of visibility in the unbuttoned cleft of her blouse.

"I grew up Lutheran, from a long line of Scandinavian Protestants."

"At some point back through history, our people probably fought on opposite sides of the Thirty Years' War."

"You got me, I have no idea what that is, but I'm sure you're right." She eyed him for a moment, considering further, then downed her drink—a vodka-melon by the look and smell of it—and said, "One dance."

She set the glass of ice on a nearby table and offered her hand. Okie's heart pounded and his eyes misted over, giving her heart-shaped face a soft focus in his vision like a movie starlet's. He took her silky fingers in his and led her to the dance floor, where the band was already in the middle of "Dance with Me Henry."

He'd learned to dance at Holy Cross. He wasn't good at it, but he could get by with a slow jitterbug to this song.

The way her body moved, her athletic grace, transfixed him. The bounce of her hair, the blush of her cheek. The way he kept stepping into her delicate perfume. But it was not cheap, high-school or college-girl perfume. It had a sophistication that he could recognize if not name. Her scent alone intoxicated him.

But after the first couple of twirls, the song ended.

"Well, thanks," she said, turning to the sidelines.

But he held on to her hand. "Oh, come on. That wasn't even a whole dance. How about we do the first half of the next one, *then* we can stop." He managed a tone that bespoke confidence, rather than desperation.

She laughed and turned back toward him. Suddenly he felt like a rookie who'd just made his first base hit in the major leagues.

But then the next song was "Unchained Melody," and the other dancers moved into close embrace.

He held back. "Look, uh, if you—"

"It's okay," she said, and stepped closer to him, lifting her arms to his shoulders. "First half of the song, right?" she said with a smile.

He put a hand on her slim waist, taking her hand in his other one, and they danced. His mind went into orbit on an atomic rocket. The only conscious thought he could manage was *Don't screw it up,* over and over. She danced with a supple confidence that captivated him, and he avoided the schoolboy urge to admire her breasts. But then they brushed against his ribs as she danced subtly closer, and their soft warmth turned his mouth into a desert.

By the end of the song, their thighs were brushing together, her soft hair against his chin, and he breathed her in like life itself.

When the song ended, she said, "I should go find my friend." But she didn't step away.

He nodded. "Me too." He stepped back, reluctantly, fighting it with every muscle fiber.

Then she laughed and pointed.

Okie turned to look. Don was already dancing with her friend, and both were looking at them.

"Well, I guess that's it then," she said with a chuckle. "My name is Rae. But everyone calls me Honey." With her rich, honey-gold hair, he couldn't imagine a more perfect name.

The four of them soon found their way outside as the band took a break. They exchanged small talk. Honey and her friend Lois were stewardesses for TWA, and San Francisco was one end of their route. The girls shared a rapport verging on telepathy, it seemed, as they exchanged knowing glances and finished each other's sentences.

Lois was thinner than Honey but no less beautiful, a crane and a swan. But they shared the same kind of charisma that quickly defeated Okie's awkwardness. Don brought to bear his own brand of wry charm that encouraged Okie to join the engagement, like coaxing an uncertain horse onto the racetrack. Before long, they were trading flirtatious banter in salvos that left all of them laughing at each other's audacity.

Then Lois said, "Well, you both have failed utterly. Let's go, Honey."

Okie stiffened. "What! What did we say?"

Honey said, "You haven't given us a ride in that Ferrari."

"An oversight easily rectified," Don said, offering Lois his arm. Okie followed Don's lead and offered his arm to Honey. As she slid her arm through his, his heart skipped again. He laid his hand over hers for a moment.

Earlier, they had parked the Ferrari a couple of blocks away on one of Sausalito's narrow, steeply graded streets, and soon they were speeding through the coastal hills overlooking San Francisco.

Don turned on the radio, and there was Frank Sinatra singing "Learning the Blues" again.

In the backseat with Honey, Okie said, "The band did this pretty well."

"Yeah, but I know Frank Sinatra," Honey said.

Okie stared at her. "No way."

Honey said, "I work first-class all the time. Who do you think flies first-class?"

Okie appreciated Frank Sinatra. "What's he like?"

"Very charming. And a little handsy."

"Aren't they all?" Lois said with a laugh.

Okie's ears warmed, and he was suddenly conscious of how close he was sitting to Honey. He edged away, not wishing to be considered one of those guys who took liberties.

She gave him a little smile and edged back.

A goofy grin spread across his lips. He put his arm around her, and she snuggled closer.

Just then, Don punched the gas, and the Ferrari responded like a fleet-footed stallion, charging along the road through the Marin Headlands, hugging its curves. The girls whooped and squealed, punching their fists in the air.

"Faster!" Honey yelled.

Don obliged. The engine roared. The tires squealed. The wind rushed over them. Okie braced himself against Don's seat and held on to Honey, and she to him.

They zipped past what looked like a former bunker and artillery battery, then moments later, Don slammed on the brakes, lurching all of them around inside the car. Amid a cloud of dust, he pulled off the road and skidded to a halt on a graveled sidebar overlooking the bay.

"Will you look at that?" Don said in wonder.

The moon cast a trail of silver coins across the expanse of the bay, hanging like an aloof eye over the glittering tapestry of San

Francisco. The elegant curves of the Golden Gate Bridge stretched across the distance, peppered with headlights.

They all bailed out of the car. The shoreline sat several hundred feet below them, down a rocky slope covered in scrub.

"Oh, it's just gorgeous!" Honey said.

"Skinny dipping, anyone?" Don said, pointing toward a dirt path that looked like it led down to the water.

Okie stiffened, worried that Don had just overplayed their hand, but Lois and Honey just laughed.

"You first," Lois said. "We'll just watch."

Okie had no interest in the girls seeing what that notoriously chilly water would do to certain parts of him.

"If only we had some way to keep warm," Don said.

The girls glanced at one another.

"Say," Honey said, "you know what? We have some friends having a party tonight. They're swell guys. It might be fun to introduce you."

Okie felt a jab of resistance. Taking the girls into a place where there might be competition didn't sound like a good idea. In that moment, he felt his James Bond confidence slipping away, like sand through his fingers. Don seemed to hesitate for the same reason.

But then again, tonight, Okie was James fucking Bond, former center for Holy Cross, Expert Marksman. He was a goddamn Knight of Malta. "Sure, why not?" he said.

As if reading his thoughts, Honey eyed him with a bit of surprise.

He slapped Don on the shoulder. "No matter what happens, we'll still be the most interesting guys these girls met tonight."

The girls traded little smiles.

Don gave an appreciative nod.

To hide his rush of satisfaction, Okie turned toward the water and breathed deep, looking out over the dazzling seascape, feeling the Hand of God at work.

Twenty minutes later, Don pulled the Ferrari up against a vine-covered retaining wall abutting a narrow side street on the steep hillside overlooking the Sausalito shoreline at the edge of town.

As soon as they got out of the car, Okie could hear music playing nearby, just audible above the susurrous wind. The streets in this part of town were steep and crooked, often little more than one-lane switchbacks held in place by old stone retaining walls, populated by ancient, windswept trees and meticulously trimmed shrubberies. The Ferrari gleamed in the moonlight. A couple of cars, one a brand-new red Thunderbird and the other a yellow Corvette convertible, stood parked near a tiny, one-car garage, beside which a narrow brick stairway led up the hillside.

Lois and Honey led them toward the cars and the music grew louder, filtering down the stairs. "Sh-Boom" by the Chords. Life could be a dream indeed.

"Is this a 'Who Has the Sweetest Wheels' party?" Don asked.

"We'll still win," Okie said, elbowing him as they approached the gleaming machines.

The girls traded eyerolls.

A third car was parked on the concrete pad before the garage, a beige Studebaker sedan several years old.

The stairs wended onto a landing before a three-story house that appeared to be built partially into the hillside. Above them, a patio balcony on the second story was bathed in light from within. Another veranda circled half of the smaller third story, almost like the balcony of a turret. He'd never seen a house like this one.

"Wow," he breathed, pausing to admire it.

Honey hooked his arm. "Wait 'til you see the inside."

Lois knocked, and a moment later, the door opened to reveal a tall, dark-haired man in short pants and a striped tennis shirt. His tanned, athletic build stood an inch taller than Okie. At the sight of the girls, his broad smile filled with recognition, registering a moment of surprise at the sight of Okie and Don, but he didn't hesitate to invite them all inside. In a spacious living room furnished with a stylish sofa and some smaller chairs, the decor was chic, modern, straight out of a magazine.

The girls introduced the man as Kirby. Kirby gave both of them a firm handshake. "Party's just getting started." To the girls he said, "Everybody is upstairs. Bill is outside smoking a cigar with some new guy." Okie detected the scent of a barbecue grill wafting down some stairs. The music switched to Dean Martin singing "That's Amoré."

"You got Dean Martin himself upstairs?" Okie said. The music was so clear and lifelike, it did indeed sound like there was a live band.

Kirby grinned. "That would be the hi-fi."

Okie whistled. He had heard that such things existed but had never seen one. Honey and Lois had some well-to-do friends. Honey gave him an amused eyebrow raise, as if to say *told ya.*

Kirby led them up a narrow staircase to a dining room and kitchen area. An island full of food—potato salad, coleslaw, potato chips, a Jell-O mold, liquor bottles, and soft drinks—separated the kitchen from the dining room table and chairs. They found three more men in their twenties or early thirties holding beers and cocktails, and two women as well, both almost as beautiful as Honey and Lois.

"Beer is on ice in the bathtub," Kirby said.

With the exception of Kirby, the men were more on the physically nondescript side, but they carried themselves with no less confidence or athleticism. Any or all of them could be current or former military. But these weren't knuckle-draggers. Sharp intelligence filled their eyes.

Introductions were made around the room. The scent of barbecue, along with the tang of cigar smoke, wafted through open patio doors to an area of the balcony they couldn't see from below, nestled against the hillside.

Along the wall, a real-live hi-fi system with a great big speaker spun a stack of queued 45s. The whole apparatus looked like something out of a science fiction serial.

"Want me to make you a drink?" Honey asked him.

"Sure, I'd love one," Okie said.

"What do you like?" she asked.

He preferred Falstaff beer above all else, but what the hell, maybe he could branch out. "I am in your capable hands."

She turned away with a thoughtful look and perused the liquor assortment. "You look like an Old Fashioned kind of guy."

"Well, I guess with some things I—"

"No, silly!" she laughed. "It's a cocktail."

"Oh, sure! I knew that," Okie said, but he clearly hadn't. How many strikes did he have left? This girl seemed suddenly far more worldly than him. And how could she not be, jetting across the world daily. Was she a "beau in every port" kind of girl?

Lois went and hugged the other two women, and the three of them began to chatter as if they saw each other every other week. Could they be stewardesses, too? They were surely built for it, with the same kind of meticulously coiffed elegance. They were not much older than him, but they had been around the world.

Okie and Don eyed the four other men, who eyed them back, measuring them in ways that made Okie uncomfortable.

Kirby tried to break the ice. "You boys in the service?"

"Is it that obvious?" Don said. "Seems like everybody's got us pegged tonight."

Kirby shrugged. "It's not a big leap."

Just then, a solidly built man with backswept, steel-gray hair came through the patio doors holding a cigar and a tumbler of amber liquid. He had a square jaw, cleft chin, square shoulders, and piercing gray eyes, eyes full of more triumphs and tragedies than Okie could imagine, painting histories in the lines of his face, histories that were still unfolding.

"Bill!" Don exclaimed. "What are you doing here?"

The man didn't look surprised at Don's presence, then he cracked a grin like Okie had seen only on the faces of grizzled officers and veteran NCOs, men who were routinely shot at. "Nice to see you, Donald. Are you bringing my car back so soon?"

XIII

***"BLESS ME, FATHER,** for I have sinned. My last confession was at least a week ago. I'm not sure where to start. Life has been so great lately. But..."*

"Something is bothering you, my son."

"It's like it's all...too good to be true. Something happened recently. I can't go into detail, but... Have you had a moment where your entire world changed? All at once, like scales falling from your eyes."

"You're talking about an epiphany."

"I had one of those before, when I realized my father was having an affair, and it was awful. But this time, there was this moment of wonder where I met...where I learned about... Sorry, I can't give any details. On top of meeting this swell girl, it all added up to a night that was so amazing, I can't help but think it's too good to be true, like the Devil is at work somewhere."

"We must temper our joy with a mind toward our immortal souls."

"I think my sin is pride. All night long, I felt like I'd been somehow anointed. It was hard not to let it go to my head. There's a fine line between confidence and arrogance."

"Very true. Always remember you're an instrument of God."

❂❂❂

No one else present was much over the age of 30, so this man stood out like a weathered dock piling in a freshly painted picket fence.

The man fixed his gaze on Okie, sizing him up with a familiarity that made Okie squirm inside his own skin. He stuck the cigar in his teeth and offered Okie his hand. "Call me Bill. Wild Bill to my friends."

"Emmett Hansen Jr." Again, somehow this didn't feel like a nickname situation. And Wild Bill didn't look "wild" at all. "But my friends call me Okie."

Bill's handshake was pure sinewy strength, unexpected from such liver-spotted hands. "Are we friends, Mr. Hansen?"

Okie opened his mouth but couldn't muster a response.

A hint of amusement sparkled beneath the challenge.

"You can call me Okie if you want, sir." A moment of awe washed over him, the moment of recognition that he'd encountered someone like he'd never met before. Most disconcerting was the sense that this man already knew him.

"We're keeping it informal, aren't we?" Bill said. "It's not as if we're standing in front of some damn fool congressional committee."

Laughter rippled around the room.

Don was still agape. "But... I don't get it. What are you doing here?"

Bill slapped Don on the shoulder. "Relax, Donald. You haven't put any scratches on the car, have you?"

Don stiffened and swallowed. "No, sir! Never!"

"Enjoy the party. I can't stay long. I have to get back to San Francisco."

Honey came forward and kissed him lightly on the cheek. "Hiya, Bill."

"A vision as always, my dear," Bill said. "I wasn't expecting to see you tonight."

"Well, you know," she said, glancing at Okie. "That's just how things work out sometimes."

Okie suddenly felt like the only person in the room who hadn't the slightest clue what the hell was going on, like he'd just stumbled into a thick spider web in a dark basement.

"If you'll pardon me," Bill said, "there are more beautiful women to be greeted." Then he approached Lois and the other two women.

Okie and Don exchanged glances, both infused with *What the hell?*

Don shrugged and shook his head.

Honey's fingers brushed down Okie's arm, across his hand, sending electricity straight into his brain. "An Old Fashioned, was it?"

Okie swallowed hard and nodded, feeling the eyes of the other men on him, some of them tinged with envy or jealousy, others with curiosity. Kirby seemed to be enjoying Okie's and Don's discomfiture.

Then another man came in carrying a tray of barbecued steaks and burgers. "Let's eat!"

The sight of them turned Okie's confusion to hunger. It had been many hours since he and Don had eaten, and the last time he'd had a steak was boot-camp graduation weekend. The men encircled the island of food and fell to like wolves.

Okie and Don hung back until Honey put in Okie's hand a tumbler of amber liquid on the rocks, complete with a twist of orange peel. She said, "Don't be shy. It's a party." She raised a martini glass full of something sparkling with a wedge of lime.

Over plates of food, the men sat casually at the chrome and Formica dinner table. Honey sat beside Okie and dug into a hearty steak liberally dashed with Worcestershire sauce. He couldn't help but smile at her gusto. She caught his glance and said with her mouth full, "What? You never saw a girl who likes her steak?"

"I appreciate a girl who likes her steak," he said. Then he raised his fork with a chunk of medium-rare beef on it. "My compliments to the chef."

He and Honey clinked forks.

The man who'd carried in the tray saluted him, and Okie again wondered if he was military. His hair was slightly longer than Army regulation.

Don looked around. "Where did Bill go?"

Lois approached the table with a small plate of potato salad. "He left."

A bookish man named Andrew spoke with a mouthful of burger. "He does that a lot."

Don put down his knife and fork and echoed exactly what Okie was feeling, "Is anyone going to tell me what the hell is going on?"

"Isn't it obvious?" Kirby said. He let the moment hang, then grinned. "It's a party."

Chuckles circled the table. Don's cheeks reddened. He apparently didn't like being caught half a step behind any more than Okie did.

But then Lois whispered something in Don's ear, and he leaned into her cheek, her lips lingering, and his discomfort evaporated, at least for the moment.

The conversation fell to sports, with favorite teams ranging from Kansas City to Chicago to New York, mostly football and baseball. The bookish man, Andrew, didn't seem to know or care about such things. Kirby teased him about not knowing the difference between baseball and badminton. Andrew had the pinched look of a guy who loved math more than people, but he took the ribbing in stride and retorted with, "This from a guy who doesn't know the difference between a substitution cipher and a transposition cipher."

"Yeah, okay, egghead," said a muscular man named Raymond. "Let's just eat, drink, and be merry."

Andrew smiled. "As long we all remember the rest of that little phrase."

More chuckles. They raised glasses in a toast.

Okie combed his memory. *Eat, drink, and be merry, for tomorrow we die.* He couldn't help but wish someone would fill in some blanks for him, because he had the distinct sense that asking questions wouldn't do it. So, he decided simply to keep his eyes and ears open. Honey circulated around the room, falling in with the women at one point.

He couldn't help but try to eavesdrop Honey regaling the other women with a story.

"...So then Frankie says to me, 'Have I raped you?' So I says, 'No, but the night is young.'"

This raised a chorus of knowing laughter.

"Such a ladykiller, that guy," one of the women said.

"So, what happened?" said another.

Honey glanced toward Okie, then lowered her voice to the women, "If I told you, I'd have to kill you."

Lois slugged her on the arm, and the women laughed together again.

As the night went on, the drinks continued to flow, the music played, conversation shifted in waves and clusters, and Honey took Okie's hand. "Come on, let me show you the top floor. You'll flip your lid."

The liquor was doing its work, giving him a pleasant buzz, but letting him keep his feet steady.

She led him up a narrow back stairway to a short hallway with a bathroom on one side and a bedroom on the other. It was all incredibly cozy. The sight of the bedroom made his stomach flip over, and when she led him inside, it did a subsequent double backflip.

"Whose house is this?" he asked, spotting a man's duffel bag atop the dresser.

The double bed looked comfortable, perfect for laying her back upon it and covering her mouth with kisses.

"Bill's, I think," she said. "None of us really live here."

But she squeezed his hand and led him across the room to the French doors filled with silver luminescence.

Beyond them was a moonlight-soaked balcony that overlooked the bay. A breeze on the verge of chilly raised gooseflesh on his arms, or maybe it was the beautiful girl who abruptly huddled against him.

"Isn't it so beautiful?" she asked, looking out over the treetops and hillside toward the water a couple of hundred feet below. "This is my favorite place in the house."

"Mine, too," he said. He snaked both arms around her waist and squeezed her back against him, pressing their warmth together, smelling her hair. Her hands clasped his. Standing there with this goddess in his arms, looking out over the moon-dappled bay with the lights of San Francisco glittering in the distance, was the happiest moment of his life.

But then another moment replaced that one as she turned and looked up into his eyes, her gaze flicking to his lips, and then there were no more questions. He kissed her, and the jolt of feeling her lips against his curled his toes and energized his arms to pull her tight against him. She melded to him and snaked an arm around his neck, stroking the back of his head, his ear. Her breath was hot and tasted of gin and lime, her lips eager. Her tongue flicked against his, and suddenly his blood roared through his veins straight to his crotch. He loosened his grip before she could feel it swelling against her, his face flushed, his skin tingling from crown to heel.

For several minutes they kissed, their lips exploring different configurations and pressures, their tongues meeting, probing. He brushed his lips up her exquisitely scented neck, luxuriating in the softness of her hair. With soft sighs, she pressed herself against him. Before he knew it, his hands were roving over her soft contours, seeking the warm flesh beneath. Never once did he encounter anything but eagerness.

Her lips drew him back inside. Toward the bed.

His groin throbbed with incredible sensation. His heartbeat pumped in his ears. The liquor had peeled away all conscious inhibitions, turning him into a creature of instinct. His hands slid down over her hips and clutched her firm buttocks, squeezing her closer to him. She could feel his hardness now, and he pressed it against her with a need like he'd never experienced before.

She drew him back onto the bed. Her hands clutched his back, his hip, questing for his belt buckle.

He drew back enough to fumble through the buttons of her blouse. She grinned lasciviously at him, giggling like a kid headed for an unsupervised cookie jar.

Dear God, she was beautiful, one of the finest of God's creations. She belonged in a Renaissance painting of a Madonna.

Her exposed bra wiped away such conscious thoughts again, and his vision was lost in the marble swells of her breasts. Then he realized he had no idea how to take it off. But then her hand cupped his hard-on and he forgot about that. She squeezed and stroked him through his trousers, and on the third stroke, his eyes rolled back, and an exquisite pulse of pleasure rose in him, like an outbound wave, and suddenly his underwear was hot and wet with wasted seed. His body spasmed with a pleasure he had never known, not even all those times he had fornicated himself. His body momentarily went weak as a soggy dishcloth. She pulled him down and kissed him again.

Her hand paused. She seemed to know exactly what happened. "It's okay. It happens. Especially if it's been a while for you."

He didn't answer.

Her hand rose to her lips. "Oh my God, it's your—"

"My first time."

Several emotions he couldn't parse flickered behind her eyes, but they ended in a warm smile. "Oh, boy! Playtime." She rolled him onto his back, and he was still too stunned to resist.

She stood above him and stripped off her blouse and bra. He could only stare at the apples of her breasts with their erect pink nipples. Just as quickly, she shucked her skirt, hose, and underwear, and stood naked above him except for her silk scarf. Her honey-colored mound of pubic hair caught the moonlight spilling through the window, and words failed him yet again. Her supple stomach and alabaster skin gleamed, the soft indentation of her belly button.

Then she yanked off his shoes and socks, finished unbuckling his belt, and peeled off his trousers and underwear all once, leaving his manhood exposed, still softening, soaked in his own over-enthusiasm.

She crawled on top of him, straddling him, and his manhood could feel her moist heat, so close, but she went for his sweatshirt, peeling it up over his head with his assistance. When he could admire her again, she was clearly admiring him back.

"You are one beautiful man, Okie."

He couldn't protest being called 'beautiful' because his tongue was still tied in knots.

She lowered herself and began to grind her lips over him. Miraculously, all glory to God, he began to stiffen again.

"See, I was pretty sure we weren't finished," she gasped, eyes half-lidded, twisting her nipples in her fingers.

"Never," he croaked.

His hands slid up her silky thighs and pulled her against him. The rush of pleasure rose again, and his sphere of attention diminished to one place, one thing, with a deft tuck from her fingers, he slid inside her, engulfed in pulsating heat. Her eyes closed, her lips parted, biting the bottom one, her breaths turning to gasps and sighs of pleasure. Her rhythm started off slow, sliding up and down his shaft, but quickly began to pick up speed, and he felt another orgasm rising, toes curling, rising like magma from deep within, until a sudden clenching spasm inside her squeezed him so exquisitely he exploded into her. She gasped and cried out in ecstasy. He might have yelled; he couldn't be sure.

But then she collapsed atop his chest, flushed and sheened with sweat, body heaving with the convulsions of her own pleasure.

A minute passed as Okie lay there stunned and spent, stroking her hair with one hand, her back with the other.

She kissed him again, long and soft and tireless. "Pretty good for a rookie."

He swallowed hard. "For my first season in the majors, I'm going for home run champ."

A long moment passed, and she rolled off him and snuggled into the crook of his arm. Meanwhile he tried to stave off thoughts of how he had just committed a mortal sin. How could something so explosive, something that felt so perfect, so miraculous, be cause for damning his immortal soul to hell? Was it too soon for guilt? Too late?

"You look like a man with a lot on his mind."

"Just reveling in the moment." Amid the morass of Catholic guilt, his mind swirled with questions, and he wanted to ask them all at once, and at the same time bare his deepest heart to her. If she could look at that and not run away screaming, she was the one.

She kissed him again, then got up and grabbed a man's bathrobe that was far too big for her from a hook behind the door, which he just noticed was still open.

"You suppose anyone downstairs heard?" he asked, suddenly self-conscious.

She shrugged. "Wouldn't be the first time somebody got laid up here. Be right back." Then she crossed the hallway into the bathroom and closed the door, leaving him with his thoughts. He hung his legs over the side of the bed, still awash in the afterglow. Questions were re-emerging from the fog of pleasure, however.

What he'd just done was surely a sin. He certainly didn't want children right now, but he'd engaged in the act of procreation. And what about missionary position? It had been strongly suggested that missionary position was the only proper sexual method for good Catholic boys and girls. *Married* boys and girls. Guilt crept into his gut like a black, tarry serpent.

And what kind of place was this? She was clearly more experienced than him, and while he appreciated her expertise and gentle understanding with his former-rookie status, more questions were roiling all around him, and not all of them about her.

Her return, though, redirected his attention in the most startling right turn. She grinned and spread her robe wide, striking a pose. An alabaster goddess in moonlight.

He breathed, "Good Lord, you'd blow Marilyn out of the water."

"And you could be the next Gary Cooper."

"Then we could make movies together."

"Or at least sweet music."

This time, she shut the door, then let the robe slide down her back, and she came to him again. This time, she used her mouth to coax him back to erection, and then he eased her back onto the bed and entered her. He lasted much longer, able to explore different sensations, different rhythms, different angles of approach, pushing toward an ever-higher pinnacle before her own climax kicked him over the edge into oblivion.

Later, in the half-conscious hours before dawn, they talked. He told her about football and Holy Cross, his father, his language studies in Monterey, maintaining military security, of course. In six different languages, he told her how beautiful she was. She told him about sitting in Frank Sinatra's lap on a flight to Cuba, about modeling for Bergdorf Goodman ads, about being on a postage stamp with three other TWA stewardesses. He had to admit to a twinge of jealousy about the thought of her sitting in Frank Sinatra's lap.

"Tony Bennett, too. And Sammy Davis Jr. He's a lovely man, but I didn't sit in his lap."

"Is sitting in laps standard protocol for TWA?"

"Goes with the job. Ask Peter Lawford. I see those fellas all the time. Sometimes they even take us out for drinks after a long flight." She said this with a twinkle in her eye. "But I *love* it, though. All the traveling, the places I've seen. I feel awful lucky most of the time."

"You've had quite a life."

"And I ain't giving it up any time soon," she said, playfully but no less firmly, and he couldn't help but notice the immediate placement of that boundary line.

As the moon sank, they drowsed, limbs entwined, until a knock came on the door. "Hey, Okie, you in there?" It was Don.

Okie propped himself up on his elbows. "Yeah."

"Gotta go, buddy. Reveille is in three hours."

"All right, give me a minute." Then he rolled over and looked down at Honey. "When can I see you again?"

"Maybe next week," she said. "I'll be in the air, here there and everywhere, until next Monday."

"Can I call you?"

"What do you want to call me?" she said with a smirk.

He bit back several compliments that sounded overblown even in his sex-addled mind.

She took a pen and slip of paper from her clutch and said, "I'll be at this number in Oklahoma City. Back in California, Monday next." She wrote a phone number on the slip of paper from her purse, and he cradled it in his hands.

After dressing, they paused for another passionate kiss.

"You had better call me," she said, putting a finger on his chin.

"You had better answer."

From outside the door came, "Time's ticking, buddy!"

It was going to be a long week.

XIV

***"BLESS ME, FATHER,** for I have sinned. It's been more than two days since my last confession. I've never experienced anything like this before. It's making me nuts. I met this girl, and she's just swell. Beautiful and smart. But her job puts her in these...situations where men can stare at her, touch her. She even sits in their laps sometimes. She says it's part of the job."*

"Is this the girl you had relations with?"

"Yes."

"Perhaps her moral fiber is lacking. Are you sure this is the girl for you? Is she a practicing Catholic?"

"I don't know. It's all so soon. But she's been a model and travels all over the world."

"What you're describing sounds very much like jealousy."

"Yeah. Is it a sin?"

"Jealousy is a human failing, and can cause much suffering, but it's not a sin unless it leads you away from God. We can become too concerned with our own wants, rather than with serving God. This young woman sounds very immersed in worldly affairs, in the affairs of the flesh."

"You got that right."

Okie was right. The next week was utter hell.

He couldn't concentrate on his language studies. He kept imagining all the moon-eyed romantic things he would say to her in all the languages he spoke, imagined them running away together to the French Riviera or a similar exotic locale. Thoughts of her consumed him. He fornicated himself daily over thoughts of her, sometimes multiple times. He also found that he walked around the post and the halls of the Presidio with more strut in his step.

But all this was after the drive back to San Francisco in the wee hours of Monday morning, when Okie and Don wrangled the many disturbing questions the previous night had raised, beside the fact that they'd both gotten laid—Don and Lois in a downstairs bedroom.

Chief among the questions was: who the hell was Bill? According to the paperwork in the glove box, the Ferrari was registered to a "John Smith" with an address in San Francisco. Don's only contact information for Bill was a phone number, and when they tried to call it the next day during midday mess hall, there was no answer.

Okie's impressions of the men and women at the party were that they were all acquainted, but not necessarily friends, although some were. Innocuous comments here and there gave the impression that some of them had dated or were erstwhile or occasional lovers. He had seen enough similar behavior with various football players at off-campus parties to recognize it. The women were more cliquish, and he suspected all of them were international stewardesses. They all shared that kind of beauty and practiced poise and elegance.

But it was also clear that everyone at the party was *intended* to know each other. The whole thing felt purposeful. Preordained. Did that mean his meeting Honey had been planned? But how? Why? How could a chance meeting on a Sausalito street on some random weekend be planned, except by God himself? Something had passed between Honey and Bill, however, a relationship that was not fatherly or even of a sugar-daddy nature. And none of them seemed to own the house where the party took place. Yet they all were perfectly at home there, like it was a clubhouse. It all felt very transient. It made both him and Don feel like they'd somehow been set up, but the punchline had not yet been delivered.

God forbid, could Honey be some sort of prostitute? The very thought made him ill. But if so, wouldn't she have asked him for money?

Could all this be related to the Order of Malta? He doubted an ancient chivalric order would espouse sex parties. But if it were, did he dare ask Don about it? William Casey had sworn Okie to the utmost secrecy. His instincts told him...they might be related. Or maybe it was just the most palatable scenario. Was Honey a hooker or a con artist? Neither possibility made him feel good. And yet, in the moment, he'd felt totally at ease with her. Making love to her had been the most natural thing in the world, even as the guilt for his sinfulness joined the sick stew percolating inside him.

He and Don discussed hiring a private eye to investigate whether they were being scammed, but that would be expensive, and Okie needed to ask Honey directly. He needed to ask his questions and see her face.

These thoughts and their endless variations kept him from focusing on class, kept him awake in his bunk, gave him a feeling of unease that he had never experienced, even living with Emmett. His father's awfulness had been a known quantity, even if Okie never knew when it might erupt. This situation was like knowing there was a lion out there in the tall grass, watching, and not knowing when or even if it might attack.

He tried twice, once on Tuesday and once on Thursday, to call the number Honey had given him, but there was no answer. He couldn't even leave a message. He had no address for her, no other way to reach her.

Being smitten and embroiled in strange goings-on at the same time made a bitter stew that settled into his stomach and burbled.

In the meantime, though, he racked his brain for what to do for their first real date. Having so deeply experienced her holiest of holies, he couldn't very well ask her to go for milkshakes and a movie. Not this girl, who'd sat in the laps of Frank Sinatra and Tony Bennett and routinely jetted around the world and modeled for Bergdorf Goodman.

Unless all those were lies.

And then back into the heinous internal spiral.

To save himself from this heinous internal spiral, he started asking around. One day in the mess hall, an NCO at the next table overheard him lamenting his lack of date ideas to Don.

"Take her to Carmel Valley," Sergeant Lamarr said. "I took my wife there when we got engaged. There's a swell little resort called Los Laureles. It's an old ranch that goes all the way back to when

California was still Mexico. The old dame who runs the place is really gracious. And there's a swimming pool."

This sounded absolutely perfect. Okie thanked him, and immediately put the idea into action. He called Los Laureles Lodge to check the availability of rooms and chafed at every moment until he could get Honey on the line.

On Monday, a week later, someone finally answered his call, and his heart doubled its rhythm as it leaped into his throat.

He heard a hopeful, "Hello?" Honey's voice.

But then the operator interposed. "A collect call from Okie Hansen in Monterey, California. Will you accept the charges?"

"Yes, of course."

"Hello? Honey?"

"Hey! Hello!" She sounded legitimately excited. His heart kicked still faster.

He struggled to not explode from the things he was feeling, from trying not to say something stupid and sound like a dunce. "Hey! It's so great to hear your voice." He resisted telling her how many times he'd tried to call. Twenty? But he took a deep breath. *Be like James Bond.*

"You, too," she said, and he believed her, and it was like the soothing balm on a chafed soul.

He wanted to just talk for hours, but the collect charges would be astronomical, so he cut to the chase. "When will you be back?"

"I'll be back in California tomorrow."

"I can pick you up somewhere—"

"No, I'll meet you."

"Meet me in Carmel Valley."

"Carmel Valley? What's in Carmel Valley?"

He told her about Los Laureles Lodge and that he'd booked a room. That wasn't entirely true, but he knew there were rooms available.

"Ooo, that sounds like a lovely romantic getaway," she said. The excitement in her voice gave him fresh tingles.

"So you'll come?" he said, trying to hide his breathlessness.

"I'll be there."

He must have made a gesture of pure rapture because he garnered some amused looks from nearby soldiers. The barracks telephone was in a small hallway near the entrance.

"Okay, swell. Uh, what time can you be there?"

She thought for a moment. "How about 8:30?"

"Swell."

"Swell."

"Great!"

"Great!"

"Okay, uh, 'bye. See you tomorrow night."

"'Bye, Okie," Honey said, and she sounded like Marilyn Monroe, Lauren Bacall, and Rita Hayworth all rolled into one.

The moment he hung up, hoots went up from the four men who'd overheard. He waved them off, trying to hide his blush.

Now, however, he had two major problems. How to get himself to Carmel Valley, a picturesque little town about fifteen miles from Monterey, and getting a day or two of leave on such short notice. He didn't want to go AWOL for this girl, but in the state he was in, he probably would if he had to.

❂❂❂

Solving both problems proved disturbingly easy. Okie called Bill's number and was shocked to hear a scratchy male voice answer the phone. Don leaned against the wall right next to him, curious about the outcome.

"Uh, I'm calling for Bill."

"Speaking. What can I do for you, Okie?"

"How'd you know it was me?" A tingle went down Okie's spine.

"Call it an educated guess."

"Well, sir, it's just that... You've been so good to Don and me, letting us use the Ferrari and everything, I'd like to borrow it myself." He felt like a teenager asking his old man to borrow the car.

"To what purpose?"

"Well, sir, I've got a date with Honey tomorrow night. I'd like to drive it to Carmel Valley."

"A date with Honey, eh? I suppose that would be fine."

Okie's heart leaped. "Thank you, sir! Thank you. I promise, there won't be so much as a bug on the windshield."

"Fine, fine. No doubt you have your leave arranged?"

He swallowed hard.

Bill apparently took the pause as a negative. "Don't worry about it, son. How's a couple of days of leave time sound? Take your time."

Okie could hardly believe it. "Uh, that would be great—sir!"

"You treat her right, Okie. She's a good girl."

"Of course, sir! But...the leave time—"

"I'll take care of that."

"You can do that? How?"

"Let's table that conversation for now. Look for a call from me next week. There's something I want to discuss with you."

"Yes, sir! Looking forward to it, sir!" Why did he sound like he was talking to a general?

The line clicked, and Okie stood there holding the receiver, dumbfounded. He looked at Don.

Don looked at him. "Well?"

"I don't know what just happened, but he's letting me take the car, *and* get this. He said he would arrange a couple of days of leave time." And again, even after such an overwhelmingly positive outcome to the phone call, he felt off-balance, knocked onto his back foot, kept in the dark.

After a moment of gaping, unspoken questions swirling between them, Don's eyes brightened, and he snapped his fingers. "I know who he is." Then he looked around for potential eavesdroppers. "Let's go outside."

They went out into the open air, another glorious California afternoon. Still wary of extra ears, Don said, "At the party he called himself 'Wild Bill,' right?"

Okie nodded.

"Bill Donovan is a two-star, or was, back during the war. He was all over the Nuremberg trials. I remember hearing his name all over the radio back then."

"Now that you mention it..." The name was ringing bells for Okie, too, but it wasn't just from newsreels and radio broadcasts. "Okay, so if this guy is *that* Wild Bill, what does he want with us?"

Don shrugged and took an extra-long drag from his Lucky Strike. "Translators maybe?"

❁❁❁

Bill was as good as his word. Okie's leave papers were already approved in his CO's office when he went to put in his request. The way the secretary looked at him with a kind of curious suspicion made him feel like a cog in some unseen machinery. But he didn't dwell on it, because the most beautiful girl in the world was meeting him in Carmel Valley.

He picked up the Ferrari, made the drive, and checked into the hotel by 6:00 p.m. with a bouquet of long-stemmed red roses in hand.

Carmel Valley proved to be little more than a loose conglomeration of vineyards and ranchos amid greenish-brown hills, with a gas station, grocery store, and a couple of restaurants, one of them a greasy spoon and the other somewhat nicer. He spotted a couple of shiny new Cadillacs and some gated drives—suggesting affluence lurking among the picturesque hills—as he familiarized himself with the town, which took him all of about fifteen minutes.

Los Laureles Lodge was as picturesque as the area, a historic Mexican rancho modernized with a pool and a small restaurant. Extensive stables stretched into the scrubby trees, and the air was redolent with the aromas of hay and horses. The proprietress introduced herself as Mrs. Phelps, a gracious, steel-haired woman still vibrant enough to be at home in English riding boots, and he hesitated when she asked him how many guests would be staying.

"Uh, just me and my uh, wife. She'll be coming later."

Mrs. Phelps didn't bat an eye as she handed him a room key. "Kitchen is open until ten."

He counted the minutes until Honey was supposed to arrive, but when 8:30 came, and then went, he began to pace the room, then the grounds, checking his Heuer "Baby" chronograph incessantly, chewing on all the uncertainties. Had she been delayed? Could she find the place? Every flicker of headlights from outside brought him to the window, a flare of hope, then disappointment.

It was 9:17 when a taxi pulled into the drive, and his heart thundered. When she got out, a gush of elation dashed through him. He gaped at her. She wore a sleeveless, leopard-print cocktail dress that made her look like a movie star.

She struck a pose. "You like it?"

He made an incoherent noise and nodded fervently.

"It's an Oscar de la Renta. Got it after a photo shoot."

After regathering his senses, he hurried down to help her with her bag, and she said, "I'm sorry to be late. My last flight from London was delayed, and it was hard to find a taxi."

"Doesn't matter, you're here," he said. He stepped up to the taxi driver and handed him a twenty-dollar bill.

The driver's eyes bulged. "Hey, thanks, buddy!"

She gave him a flash of mild annoyance. "You didn't have to do that."

"It's the gentlemanly thing to do."

She put a hand on her hip. "Is it, now?" Then her face softened. "I suppose you do owe me for the collect call." She winked.

"How much was it?"

"A dollar ten."

He whistled. "I hope you're worth it."

She laughed. "I hope *you're* worth it."

He carried her bag and led her to their room.

Inside closed doors, he couldn't resist her exquisite scent, pulling her close and kissing her, and she molded to him with warm eagerness.

But after a moment, she drew back. "I'm starving. Are you starving?"

"Do you mean for food?"

She laughed.

"Actually, yeah," he said, his voice husky.

"They got any grub around here?"

"Kitchen is open until ten," he croaked, trying to rein in the throbbing stiffness in his trousers.

"Good." Then she kissed him again. "You're going to need to keep up your strength."

❁❁❁

After a delicious porterhouse steak dinner and cocktails, they retired to their room, and the passion flared like stoked coals. In the midst of a hot kiss that had part of him straining against his pants, ready to explode, she pulled away abruptly. She grabbed her purse and pulled out a small, silvery tin with a reddish-pink logo.

"Is something wrong?"

She grinned and held out the tin. "No glove, no love."

He looked at his hands, confused. "Gloves, why?" It wasn't cold outside.

She laughed, and his ears heated.

Then it hit like an entire locker room full of linebackers. "Oh, rubbers." He'd heard about them, but never saw one before. He turned away, his face flushing, his hard-on shrinking, his chest tightening.

She reached for him, her face softening, her hand closing on his.

"I can't," he said.

"Why not?"

"It's a sin." He released her hand.

"So is sex outside of marriage, right? And yet, here we are." She raised an eyebrow skeptically, clearly holding back things she wanted to say.

His mouth worked, but he couldn't arrange words with it. All he could think about was how much he wanted her, how the light caught her smooth cheek, how her scent intoxicated him, rich and musky.

"But we didn't have to do this before." But even as he spoke the words, he thought he sounded like a whiny little kid, and he looked away, abashed.

"It was safer then."

The machinery of his inexperienced brain chugged and ground its gears. "Oh, you're talking about the rhythm method."

"If that's what you good Catholic boys call it, yes. I was just off my period last time."

He didn't know why that mattered. The mysteries of feminine biology were beyond him. "I could pull out." He'd also heard that was an option, although he wasn't sure he could manage it in time.

She shook her head. "That doesn't always work. Just ask...a good friend of mine." She pointed the little tin toward his face. "Look, buster. You can spoil this if you want to, but I came here for a lovely romantic weekend." She waved the tin between her fingers and winked with a playful smile. "Besides, all you have to do is confess your sins, right?"

How forcefully had it been driven into him in catechism classes, by his teachers at Canisius, by the faculty at Holy Cross? Sexual relations were for procreation, not recreation. You rolled the dice and took the miracles God gave you. He had already led a life of profound sin, mortal sins of lust and wrath.

What was one more? And she was right. He'd go to confession the second he returned to Monterey.

He took her in his arms, and the embers quickly rekindled. She showed him how to put the rubber on, and they made love, and then again. Words were few, but their sweaty bodies spoke volumes. He wasn't sure he could manage four times in one night, but Honey's beauty and enthusiasm opened wells of energy he didn't know he possessed. And her little tin held six condoms. He'd no idea that sex could be performed in so many places and ways that weren't in a bed or missionary style. By dawn, they were so spent they slept until noon, dozing in languorous afterglow, and all worries over using birth control had been stuffed into a very small tin in the back of his mind.

They went horseback riding in the hills that afternoon, guided by one of Mrs. Phelps' stable hands, then swimming in the saltwater of the swimming pool. Honey was absolutely spectacular in a bathing suit, as if she'd stepped out of a pinup. But the saltwater was such an oddity that Honey asked a passing cleaning lady about it. The woman's name was Rosa. "*La jefa* likes swimming in the ocean," said Rosa, a portly woman with a single thick, dark eyebrow, much like Frida Kahlo, eyes sparkling with warmth.

As Okie and Honey lay drying in the warmth of the sun, Okie told her about Buffalo, and Emmett. And then, his mother.

Hearing his voice crack, Honey said, "She must have been a special lady."

"She was." And he just sat with the memory of her for a while.

Then he asked her, "What do you want out of life?"

She thought about this for a moment. "Have fun. Do work that's meaningful. Travel. So, you might say I'm doing exactly what I want out of life right now." She smiled and squeezed his hand. "And what about you, Deep Thinker?"

"Be of service. I met a guy once who really brought that home for me. I want to serve God and country. I mean, that's why I'm in the Army."

She patted his hand and pulled away to reach for her drink. "Very patriotic of you. Admirable."

"You think so?"

"A lot of men are greedy, selfish morons that give no thought to their fellow man. Devoting yourself to a life of service is rare."

He turned toward her and gave her a Clark Cable smile. "Is it... sexy?"

She laughed and slugged him. Then she said, "Very."

His heart fluttered and soared.

He eventually asked her about where she was from—the Chicago area—and then her family—she was an only child from a family she called "fairly well-to-do but boring beyond words." That was why she became a stewardess. In their conversation, however, he soon noticed a pattern. He wanted to know more about her, wanted to know everything, but all her responses were vague, abstract, and when he tried to probe deeper, she deflected the conversation back to him. Because he wanted her to know him just as deeply, he was happy to go on at length. But then it became a game of cat and mouse.

At one point, Honey said, "So you got the Ferrari."

"Seemed like Bill was expecting my call."

"Bill's a smart guy."

"His last name wouldn't be Donovan, would it?"

She gave him a little smile, but he couldn't penetrate her sunglasses.

"How do you know him?" he asked.

"He should explain that to you himself."

"I don't get all this."

"All what? We're both here in this beautiful place, having such a marvelous time. Why worry? Let's just enjoy this. Please." She held out her hand for him to take it, and he did. So, he clammed up and just held her hand.

Then she asked him. "So, what happened last night?"

"Uh, do I need to explain it? You were there," he said with a snort of laughter.

"No, I mean when I...got the rubbers out. You just shut down." She snapped her fingers. "Like a wall came down. I'm sorry it's such a touchy subject."

He shrugged.

"You're doing it again."

"I can't help it. It's how I was raised, I suppose."

"Staunch Catholic. Constant shame and tenacious guilt."

He nodded.

"We'll have to cure you of that," she said.

He bristled momentarily, until her musical chuckle defused his alarm. "What I mean is, you're so much more handsome when you take the mask off."

"You think I'm handsome?"

"Did I say that? I don't remember saying that."

They laughed together and held hands as the sun dipped lower.

In the early evening glow, they prepared to go back inside when Rosa ventured by again, Honey asked her, "Where do the kids go to...you know."

Rosa grinned and blushed, glancing back and forth between them. "Lover's Point they go."

Honey winked at Okie, then looked at Rosa. "So how do we get there?"

On Rosa's directions, they ventured up a narrow dirt road among vineyards and low-growing oaks to a hilltop overlooking the scattered lights of the town. They parked a respectful distance from the Packard already sitting up there. Then they spread a blanket on the ground and made buck-naked love under the stars—Honey wanted to do it on the hood of the Ferrari, but he was afraid of denting the sheet metal—then they opened a chilled bottle of chardonnay from a local vintner and munched on sandwiches, grapes, and cheese Mrs. Phelps had prepared for them. He lay there wondering where his inhibitions had gone.

"Mmm, this wine is excellent," she said.

He agreed it was fine, but he still preferred a cold Falstaff.

As he lay there under the stars with Honey nestled in the crook of his arm, he couldn't imagine a more perfect moment, as if God himself had constructed this perfection, this angel, just for him. All the Catholic guilt he had felt about fornication evaporated in an instant. A month ago, he'd never have dreamed he would lie outside naked as the day he was born. His childish notions about what love was evaporated like their sweat in the night air. This was what men and women were designed to do, a divine act. A sacrament.

In that moment, he knew. He loved her. But even in his profound ignorance about the ways of women, he knew he could not tell her that. He just let the warmth of that knowledge seep into him, all the way to his bones.

All other questions be damned.

XV

***"BLESS ME, FATHER,** for I have sinned. Yesterday I met my first certified Nazi, and I wanted to kill him. I mean, there he was, a real, live war criminal. Why they didn't execute him at Nuremberg, I don't know."*

"Perhaps this man is part of God's plan. But it is not a sin to fight, to take life, in a war. The forces of evil must be stopped."

"All I could think about was how easy it would be to strangle him right there. He's an old man now, after all, and prison wasn't kind to him. I could have shot him in the head and walked away. But those weren't my orders. And we're not at war with Germany anymore. So would it have been murder?"

"The Lord makes special cases of monsters."

As it turned out, Okie couldn't restrain himself for long. A few days after parting, they managed a phone call, and as the moment approached when they had to hang up, he said it.

"I love you."

The line went quiet, and he would have given anything to see her face in that moment.

"Sorry, that just popped out," he said, his heart sinking. What should he have expected to happen?

"You're so sweet, Okie," she said finally. "I'll be back tomorrow. How about some beach time? That one by Sausalito. The gang is having a party. Lois says to bring Don."

"I'll see what I can do. I'll see you then." He tried to sound as chipper as he could but didn't quite get there.

Nevertheless, the next day, a bright Sunday afternoon at the end of July, he and Don drove to Stinson Beach, across the peninsula from Sausalito.

With the Ferrari slicing through the wind, Don asked him, "What's up with you? You look like someone just kicked you in the gut. Is it Honey? I thought you just had a great couple of days with her."

"She's got me twisted up is all," Okie said, looking out the window.

With a raised eyebrow, Don held up a little finger and gestured wrapping something around it.

Okie slugged him on the shoulder.

"So, while you've been busy getting laid this week and neglecting class," Don said, "I've been doing some snooping about our mutual benefactor. We should read the papers more; we'd have caught on a lot sooner." His voice carried momentous weight.

"Come on, Hitchcock, spill it."

"Buddy, I don't even know where to start. I went to the library and started scanning newspapers going back forty years, then I started asking around Fort Ord. As soon as I saw his picture in the paper, I felt like such an idiot I didn't put two and two together sooner." Then he sighed. "Donovan, William J., a.k.a. 'Wild Bill.' A decorated colonel in World War I. Major general in World War II. Three Purple Hearts, Silver Star, Distinguished Service Cross. He was offered the Medal of Honor, but refused it, saying it 'belonged to the boys resting under white crosses.'"

Okie whistled. "That explains a lot."

Don laughed manically. "I'm just getting started. U.S. Attorney for western New York State, with some high-profile cases during Prohibition. And—you're gonna love this—he's a good Irish Catholic boy from Buffalo, maybe his people are from your neighborhood—anyway, he ran for Governor of New York in '32. And how about Assistant Attorney General of the *United Fucking States*."

Okie gaped. "What the *fuck* is he doing hanging out with us?"

"Oh, I'm not done, Mr. Potty Mouth." Don's voice rose in pitch. "He was one of the prosecutors at fucking Nuremberg, but let me back up a second. This offers some alarming possibilities for answering your question. He singlehandedly founded the OSS during the war."

"The espionage service."

"The same. You're familiar with the Central Intelligence Agency?"

"You're shitting me."

"His name is all over the place in the papers when they were putting together the National Security Act. He and a few other guys retooled the OSS into the CI fucking A."

Okie ran his fingers through his hair in growing alarm, with an undercurrent of intrigue. "So the setup that's been raising the short hairs...?"

"We're onto something."

"Or something is onto us."

Once Okie's mind got past the wonder of having stumbled into the orbit of a man like Wild Bill Donovan, it whirled with the dizzying possibilities. The thought of having some secret government eye focused directly on him made his skin crawl. How did Honey fit into this? Since Donovan was a Catholic, might the Order of Malta be involved?

When he and Don parked the Ferrari along the road near Stinson Beach and walked out over the dunes, they spotted a party already in progress.

Honey and Lois bounced across the sand toward them—wearing bikinis. Okie almost choked and his face turned red as he gaped at Honey's effusive approach, but when she threw her arms around him and kissed him, all of that drowned in an ocean of heat and relief.

"Did you forget your clothes?" he asked.

She twirled, and for the first time, his eyes devoured her astonishing beauty in the full light of day. He had never before seen a garment, outside of *Playboy* magazine, that concealed nothing. "Do you like it?" she said. "I got it in Paris."

"You're going to get arrested," he said, not entirely joking.

But she laughed and took his hand and led him toward the party, where blankets were laid on the sand, scattered with picnic baskets and some ultra-modern collapsible chairs made of aluminum tubing and fabric webbing.

Don and Lois were still enjoying a reunion, tongue-wrestling style, as Okie greeted Kirby, Andrew, and the others. There were unfamiliar faces who seemed to be part of the crowd, two men in their thirties and their wives, who looked more like civilians, carrying the softness of a comfortable married life. The two women regarded Honey and Lois with ill-concealed disdain, wasting few opportunities to steer their husbands' fields of vision elsewhere.

But Okie's interest lay only in correcting what he'd come to regard as his catastrophic malfunction on the phone yesterday. Honey noticed his reticence quickly, and her lips went into an adorable pout of sympathy. A decision flashed in her eyes, and she snaked a hand behind his neck and pulled his ear to her warm lips. Her hot whisper set every nerve ending aflame. "I love you, too, Okie."

And just like that, he came alive again, and the party became a party. He and Don shared "thumbs-up" glances, and the exultant joy within him flowed free, barely leaving any room for thoughts of why these men and women might know each other.

That day was the happiest of Okie's life, as echoes of *I love you, too* echoed in his memory, and every touch he and Honey shared was pure electricity, every breath of seaside air pure bliss, every sunbeam pure rapture.

After sunset, the party moved to the house in Sausalito, where the cupboards, refrigerator, and liquor supply were fully stocked. The women started cooking, and the men went outside to smoke and drink.

Out on the terrace with Honey out of sight and earshot, Kirby approached Okie with a congratulatory eyebrow raise and elbow to the ribs. After what Don had told Okie about Bill on the drive, Okie's perceptions of this group of people changed. Nearly to a man, they were amiable, friendly, prone to outbursts of bravado, but they revealed almost nothing of themselves. What they shared was a deep and sincere patriotism and an innate self-confidence. Whatever their specialty, they knew they were among the best at it. What was more, they asked for few details about Okie and Don, other than shallow everyday things like sports and current events. Conversation sometimes ventured into politics, thoughts about Eisenhower or McCarthy's anti-Communist witch hunts.

Okie felt no surprise when Bill Donovan appeared among the group as if he'd been present all along. Okie shook his hand vigorously, saying, "I had no idea who you were, Mr. Donovan, I'm sorry—"

Donovan raised a hand. "Think nothing of it, son. Before you head back to Monterey tomorrow, meet me at the house in San Francisco."

"The address on the car registration?"

Donovan nodded. "Come in through the garage." He circulated for a while, then departed.

After he left, Honey gave Okie a look of pride and pleasure. When she kissed him, she said, "I'm so happy I found you." Then they retreated to the upstairs bedroom and made love. In the afterglow, he felt like a puzzle piece settling into a place that had been prepared for him. By God? Or by Bill Donovan? His head spun with such thoughts long after Honey's breaths had subsided into sleep against his chest.

The next morning, he and Don took Honey and Lois to the airport, amid bittersweet goodbyes and a sense of shared, unspoken secrets.

The address on the car registration proved to be a nondescript but sizable residence among others on an unremarkable San Francisco street. A street-level garage led up into the well-appointed house infused with the kind of masculine decor one might expect from a man of Donovan's stature. But like the house in Sausalito, it didn't exactly feel lived in.

Donovan offered him a cup of coffee, which Okie happily accepted. He had gotten little sleep and was feeling both drained and elated at the same time. They sat on leather chairs in the living room, with a wide picture window overlooking the street below.

"I'll get right to it," Donovan said. "I know you have a lot of questions. Do you know who I am?"

"I found out yesterday, sir. Don did some poking around."

"Exactly why I'm interested in him. He has a sleuth's nose. But you, Okie, let's talk about you. Expert marksman medals. By the time you graduate from ALS, you'll be fluent in six important languages. Have you given much thought to your career?"

"I figured Army Intelligence is where I was headed. Most of my classmates are."

"You seem like a go-getter. I'm looking for go-getters. But then we have forfeiting a full ride scholarship to Holy Cross. You could have been an officer in Army Intelligence, instead of an enlisted man. Tell me about that."

Okie had had some time to think about this. "I don't regret it. Holy Cross was my father's plan for me, although it took me a while to figure that out. I'm not interested in anyone else's plans for me."

"Some men need to be their own man first, is that right?"

Okie nodded. "Can I ask you a question, sir?"

Donovan tipped his head in the affirmative.

"You're from Buffalo?"

Another nod.

"Are you any relation to the Donovans in South Buffalo? My mother is, was, a McGillicuddy. We lived there until I was twelve. I went to grade school with several Donovans."

Donovan gave him a thin smile, a tweak of his lips. "South Buffalo is indeed a small town, as it were."

"You didn't go to Canisius, did you?" Because that would be too weird.

"St. Joseph's." Another Catholic prep school, in the Tonawanda area farther north.

Then Okie had a realization that sickened him. Donovan was just the kind of Buffalo upper crust that Emmett loved to rub elbows with. If this setup was all Emmett's doing, he was going to throw up. "You don't...know my father, do you?"

"I know of him, but we have never been introduced."

The sick feeling diminished. Donovan was a South Buffalo Irish Catholic boy made good, really good. Okie sat up straighter. Donovan's fatherly demeanor was putting him at ease, but there was no softness. This man was an old warrior who now fought battles on a grander scale, with his mind rather than guns, even though guns were still an option.

Donovan's mien became businesslike. "A friend of mine brought you to my attention, Okie. William Casey."

Okie stiffened and his eyes bulged. "I knew it!"

Donovan raised an eyebrow.

"Sorry for the outburst, sir. I'm all ears..." He let his voice trail off in the glow of his epiphany. Several puzzle pieces fell into place all at once.

"We're here today so that we can discuss your future. As I said, I'm looking for go-getters, but of a particular flavor, one might say. In your case, you're a skilled marksman who speaks several languages, and you have a world-class poker face. You're a hard one to read."

"I guess I get that from my father," Okie said wryly.

"It's a priceless skill in this business. Anyway, when it was time for the OSS to evolve, I stepped out of the light, but I've been actively building the foundations of its successor ever since. Such foundations are made from the right people."

Okie tingled with excitement, as if the eye of God Himself were focused for the moment on only him.

"If you say yes, I will ask much of you, but you're a man with a lot to offer. Let me ask you this. Are you a man of faith?"

"Absolutely, sir."

"Do you love your country as much as you love your own life?"

"Absolutely, sir." His chest swelled with the yearning to prove it to anyone, especially this man.

Donovan leaned forward, elbows on his knees, put his coffee cup on the table, and folded his hands. "You would remain in the Army as your cover, following orders when they come your way, but you would also be working directly for me and Allen Dulles. When you graduate from ALS, you'll be shipped to Berlin for a special project. Your commanding officers will be apprised of your special status, but they'll be given no details of its nature. All of this will of course be classified top secret. You are free to decline, in which case you'll continue with your Army career like any other enlisted man. But if you're considering accepting my offer, know this: I want nothing less than one hundred percent commitment. I will accept nothing less. The intelligence game is a chess match with the highest possible stakes, played by men and women who must remain in the shadows." He gestured to an elegant, walnut-and-maple-wood chess set atop a nearby table. "Do you play?"

"I used to play with my sister sometimes, but she wasn't very good."

"Shall we have a match?"

Okie considered, realizing this would be another test. He nodded his assent. They took their places on the matching chairs.

Over the next hour, Donovan bested him soundly, but Okie felt like he'd put up a good fight. As they replaced the pieces in their starting positions, Donovan said, "You need to learn to think a few more moves ahead. If you can do that, you'll be a formidable player. Now, do I have your interest?"

"Yes, sir!" Okie had never said anything so profoundly true. "So, you want me to be a spy."

"'Spies' work for the other side," Donovan said.

XVI

***"BLESS ME, FATHER,** for I have sinned. It's been...a week since my last confession. My sin is that it has been so long."*

"Are you sure that is all?"

"The trouble is, I can't talk about it. Any of it. Even with God."

Okie saw Honey again the following Saturday, but she was only going to be in San Francisco for one night. She had to fly out early the next morning. They went dancing, had a marvelous dinner, and retreated to a modest hotel. He had looked into staying places like the Intercontinental and the Fairmont, worried that he wanted to keep upping the ante to impress this girl who seemed so inexplicably in love with him, but he found himself financially embarrassed, especially considering what he'd just bought. He was just a private in the Army, after all. Honey never gave the slightest indication that she was disappointed, however.

In the twilight of their second bout of lovemaking, Honey asked, "So how did your meeting with Bill go?"

A dozen thoughts of secrecy and equivocation flashed through his mind.

"It's okay to tell me," she said. "I work for him, too."

The strangeness of hearing her admit it gave him pause. "It went well."

She rolled over and threw her arm around him. "Oh, that's so marvelous!"

"How did you meet him?" Okie asked.

She laughed and rolled back, memories playing in her eyes there in the dark. "It was on a flight to London. I was working first class, and it was the first time I met Frank Sinatra. Frankie was flirting with me like crazy, which was fun, because geez, it's Frank Sinatra!"

Jealousy stabbed into Okie's gut and twisted like a cold knife. She sounded so familiar with "Frankie." Had they had a fling?

"Anyway," she went on, "I noticed this old guy watching me. That's nothing new, but it was strange this time, because there wasn't any sort of dirty-old-man feeling in it. But I did feel like he was sizing me up. No man had ever looked at me in quite that way before. Calculating. You know that look now yourself."

"Yeah."

"So we land in London, and I'm walking to my cab outside the airport when this guy stops me. He says, 'Miss, I'd like a few minutes of your time.' I tell him I'm really tired, it's the end of a long shift and I need to get some beauty sleep. I keep looking for the dirty-old-man feeling, but it ain't there. I mean, he would hardly be the first guy that week to proposition me."

"That often?" Okie asked.

"Sometimes even for money. I swear, men! What do I look like, some kinda whore? It's disgusting. So, I'm looking for a sense he's trying to proposition me so I can shoot him down, but it was like he read my mind. He says, 'Please don't get the wrong impression. My intentions are pure.' He has that cultured way of speaking, you know.

"So I say, 'What, for some kind of modeling thing?'

"'No, not really. Forgive me, but no, although I *am* considering you for a job.'

"'I have a job,' I tell him.

"'Not like this one. It would require you to keep this job. Do you enjoy being a stewardess?'

"I tell him, yeah, it's the bee's knees. He tells me how he was watching me handle Frankie back on the plane, that I have this kind of natural charisma—"

"He's very perceptive," Okie said.

"Aww, you're so sweet, darling." She kissed him and went on. "He says I can make a lot of money and serve my country at the same time. So that of course got my attention. He takes me for a little walk, tells me about how he'd like me to make some introductions for him. He wants to meet people like Frankie, but he can't spend all his time flying around in first class, so he'd like me to cozy up to guys like Frankie and the other celebrities I see flying back and forth across the pond. And then I give them Bill's card, a special private phone number, and tell Bill about them. What happens after that, I don't know, but what I imagine happens is that Bill tries to get them to work for him in some way. I asked him, why guys like Frankie, and he says that celebrities can find themselves in places other people can't. We need eyes and ears behind the Iron Curtain. I mean, they're trying to get Bob Hope to perform in Moscow, and wouldn't that be something?"

"It sure would."

"Now let's get some beauty sleep, darling. I have to be at the airport at six a.m."

He kissed her forehead and let her drift off toward sleep. There was something he had to know, but couldn't bring himself to ask it, fearing it would ruin the moment. And that was, had their romance been a setup? Had she been sent to recruit him? But he couldn't ask these things because there was another question that was turning his insides to jelly and keeping him from succumbing to sleep himself.

When the alarm clock jangled in the wee hours before dawn, they showered together in preparation for Honey's departure. He waited until she was dressed and packed, sitting there on the bed, clutching the small case between his hands, praying for strength and guidance.

Her suitcase stood open nearby on the bed, and he noticed the interior pocket that held a weight with a distinctive outline. She was still in the bathroom, with the door cracked open, humming to herself. He reached into the pocket and pulled out a Beretta 418, a palm-sized, .25 caliber semi-automatic. Next to it was a string-tie envelope thick with contents—documents, cash? He tucked the pistol back into its concealment, wondering what sorts of missions she performed beyond recruitment.

Moments later, the bathroom door opened and she struck a glamorous pose, backlit by the bathroom lights, a stunning figure in her TWA uniform, with her delicate scarf, perfectly pinned hat and coiffure, and angelic face. But she saw the questions burning behind his tongue. "What is it?"

He held out the black felt box, now warm from his grip, and opened it, revealing the gleaming gold band. "Honey, I..." Then he felt a rush of strength that could only have come from God. The things he had just seen made him even more certain of his next words. He straightened. "I love you. Will you marry me?"

She dropped her clutch with a gasp, clapped both hands to her face.

He had imagined a dozen different joyful acceptances, but none of them encompassed the shock on her face. His courage faltered. "I couldn't afford a diamond. Maybe someday, and for the wedding for sure, but—"

She stepped forward and laid a hand on his wrist. "Oh, Okie! It's just so sudden."

"Well, yeah—"

"I mean, *really* sudden. We've only known each other for what, three weeks?"

"I've never been so sure about anything in my life." The little felt case was getting heavy, becoming an anvil.

"Oh, Okie. Oh, my God. I love you, I *do!* You're a swell guy, but..."

He felt his entire universe crumbling about him, his knees turning to water. He'd woken up one morning this week with the possibility fully formed in his mind. He wanted to marry Honey. There was no other woman for him in this world. And he knew as surely as he knew there was a God. But now, his certainty faltered at the stricken expression on her face. *Father in heaven, send me strength.* And suddenly his courage returned. He stepped closer to her, lifted her chin to look at up at him. "I know it's sudden. Way too sudden for most people. But we're not most people. Honey, be my wife."

The moment hung between them for a thousand thundering heartbeats as she searched his eyes for the answer.

Then she stepped away, her gaze falling to the floor. "I'm sorry, Okie. I have to think about it."

He closed the case and put it back in his pocket, feeling an invisible belt cinch his lungs tight. "We should go then."

She closed her suitcase and picked up her clutch. He grabbed their suitcases. They rode to the airport in stifling silence. She dabbed at the tears glistening in her eyes. He clenched his teeth hard on the emotions roiling inside, too fast and furious to identify. All he could do was his best to restrain them until the storm passed.

"I'll be back on Saturday," she said as they got out of the car. Her face was a tossing surf of conflicting emotions, and to him it all looked like sadness tinged with panic.

His heart cracked.

"I'll be here."

"We'll talk when I get back."

He nodded.

They hugged, and kissed, and then they said goodbye. He stood there watching her go long after he'd lost sight of her.

After leaving Honey at the airport, he went to early Mass to pray for her to say yes. He didn't need guidance—strength maybe, courage, but not guidance. His mind was free of any doubts about marrying her. The sacrament of marriage was the only way to make things right with God, in any case. Even if she wanted to get married, would she agree to that? Even if she said yes, would there be time to arrange a wedding Mass? He was supposed to graduate from ALS in about five weeks. Hopefully he would get enough leave before shipping out to Europe.

He thought it best not to call her that week. He didn't want to pressure her, even though his own internal pressure threatened to burst him like a big, messy balloon. Maybe she would miss him. Would she miss him?

He tried to distract himself from such bottomless spirals by throwing himself into his studies. It turned out that Don and Lois were in full fling, too, and they never talked about what Donovan may or may not have arranged with them. But it felt like they had all been admitted into a very exclusive secret club.

After Okie had accepted Donovan's offer, Donovan had spent the next hour going through the rules and the consequences for breaking them, which were dismissal, prosecution, and imprisonment, all of which were meant to protect both agents and the agency from forces that would terminate them without compunction.

"For example," Donovan had said, "this conversation never happened. We were never here. The same will be true for certain aspects of your life henceforth."

As the conversation progressed, Okie felt like he'd just jumped into very deep water without a life vest. What did he know about the espionage game? Only what he'd read in a couple of James Bond novels. *Moonraker* had come out earlier this year, but he hadn't had time to read it. He'd asked Donovan if there was any sort of training program.

"We're still working that out," Donovan had said.

But Okie was too excited to care.

They had parted with Donovan saying, "I'll be in touch." Okie took this to mean that life should continue as normal until he was given a mission.

On Friday morning of that week, Don showed up to class looking like a hobo, unshaven and bleary-eyed, and he wouldn't meet Okie's glance.

Okie cornered him in the mess hall. "You look like Satan's armpit. Where did you go last night?"

Don tried to edge away with a hangdog expression. "Party in Sausalito."

Okie felt a stab of confusion tinged with feeling left out. But he knew being "left out" would be par for the course in the compartmentalized information of the intelligence world. "I hadn't heard about it."

Don nodded and shrugged, clearly restraining some information.

Okie said, "All right, buddy, come clean. Unless it's classified, I guess."

"It's not really—"

"Then come on!"

"Honey was there."

"...Shit."

"But you're not joined at the hip, right?" Don sounded like he was trying to encourage Okie to brush it off, even though he wasn't sure of himself.

"Yeah, but...she could have told me she would be in town. Was she...?"

"Having a good time, yes. Was she with anybody else? No."

"Did she mention me?"

Don shook his head. "That was a little strange, I thought at the time. When I asked her where you were, she just shrugged and said, 'Don't you know?'"

Okie felt his mess tray slipping from his fingers, but he caught it without spilling anything. "I need to sit down."

They sat at a table.

Okie said, "I asked her to marry me last weekend."

Don's red-rimmed eyes bulged. "No shit!"

"She told me she had to think about it. It was too sudden. And she's right. But I've never been so sure of anything in my life."

"If it's any comfort, I didn't see her leave with anybody else."

Okie put his forehead on his hands, considered drowning himself in mashed potatoes and gravy.

Growing evermore frantic, he ran to the barracks and called her number, but there was no answer. He tried again. A third time.

For the rest of the day and most of the next his powers of concentration evaporated, and he just lay in his bunk staring at the ceiling, trying to ignore the sick churning in his gut, his mind endlessly rehashing every moment they had been together for some hope, some sign of what she might do. It was all so maddeningly self-contradictory.

He came back to the barracks from studying on Saturday afternoon to find a note on his footlocker.

From Honey, pick her up at SF airport tonite 8:00

This was it. The moment of truth.

He took the last bus to San Francisco that afternoon and arrived at the airport in time to wait for her. The only thing that could calm him was closing his eyes and praying.

One way or another, tonight would change his life forever. It was like meeting a train barreling toward a crossing and wondering if he could beat it.

From the airport terminal's crowds, she emerged like the sun from behind clouds. His stomach flipped like a half-done pancake. He spotted her first and got a look at her expression. It was stony, unreadable. This girl could play poker with the best of them. Then she saw him, and her face... He couldn't read it.

She came toward him with her bag in both hands, bumping it with her knees.

"Hi," he croaked.

"Hi," she said, still holding her bag between them, her body stiff, restrained.

He stood frozen before her.

"Okie, I... Damn it, Okie. I don't even know where to start."

"Start with 'yes' or 'no.'"

"It's not that simple."

"Yes, it is."

"I took a couple of days off and went to see my family. My father is furious that you didn't ask his permission. But my mother, she was so happy for me. I'm sure they both want a man to 'save' me from my jet-setting lifestyle and turn me into a respectable woman and have a herd of grandchildren. Since I'm an only child, that's my sole purpose in life."

"You were in Sausalito two nights ago."

She looked away and nodded. "I guessed Don would tell you. I was only in town for a few hours, and I needed to blow off some steam." Then her eyes met his with steel behind them. "You don't own me."

He raised his hands. "Never said I did."

"Yeah, well, that's a thing guys think. You have some fun with them and they think you belong to them. But here's the thing, I *love* what I do. I don't want to give it up. Not yet anyway, until I get too old, and the airline puts me out to pasture."

"You won't have to! I mean, we're both working for Bill now, plus there's the Army. I'm probably going to Europe in a couple of months. All I know is, I love you, Honey. There's no other woman in this world for me."

Her eyes glimmered. "I love you, too! I do."

"You think I'll be some sort of ball and chain?" he said.

"No! But—"

"It's your fun-loving soul that I fell for. I wouldn't dream of changing that. Plus, Bill might get upset that I stole one of his best men." He cracked a half-smile.

She put a hand on her hip and raised her chin. "He might."

"Look," he said, his voice cracking. "I know it was sudden. Hell, maybe it was a record. But you're the best thing that's ever happened to me. And I'll wait for you to figure it out—"

"You big dummy! Can't you tell?"

"Sorry, I—"

"Yes, for God's sake! I want to marry you, Okie."

Then she dropped her bag and came to him, and the rest of the world went away.

❁❁❁

The next few weeks disappeared in a whirlwind as they shared the news and started preparations.

The following night, amid burgers, silver fizzes and milk punch, they broke the news with their friends at the house in Sausalito. The sad part was that Honey had to leave early Monday morning and would have no time off for two weeks. They wouldn't see each other for almost as long as they'd been dating, which was a strange thought.

First, Okie called Ann and told her the news. Ann went over the moon with happiness for him and promised to throw a shower if he would bring Honey to Buffalo. Next, he called his father, his heart thudding. The last time he'd seen his father was the fist fight in Ann's living room.

He was surprised that his father answered the phone on a Monday afternoon.

"Okie, is that you?" Emmett sounded legitimately happy.

"Yes, it's me."

"Are you well?"

Okie caught himself rubbing the Heuer chronograph on his wrist. "I'm fine. I'm calling to let you know that I'm getting married. I'm engaged. We haven't set a date yet but—"

"Is she Catholic?"

Okie stiffened. "No, we haven't talked about that yet. Maybe she'll convert."

"So tell me about my future daughter-in-law."

"She's a..." He trailed off. He couldn't very well say she was an agent for the CIA. "She's a stewardess for TWA, travels all over the world."

"As long as she converts, everything should be fine," Emmett said, as if he were discussing a business proposition.

Okie said, "I'll let you know when we have a date."

"Congratulations, son."

Then they hung up, leaving Okie feeling like he'd just stepped into a surreal, Hieronymus Bosch world haunted by half-seen demons punishing a sinful humanity free of moral restraints.

The next two weeks were the longest of his life. When they finally saw each other again at the end of August, he gave her an Akoya pearl solitaire necklace that he'd spent two paychecks on. He was rewarded with enough glee and lovemaking to tide him over for the next week of absence.

"It's been utter hell not being able to reach you," he said. "Where've you been?"

She gave him a wry smile. "If I told you, I'd probably have to kill you."

After graduating from Army Language School on September 22, he and Don both received their orders—report to Bad Aibling Station in Bavaria to work for Army Intelligence at the end of October. Okie and Honey wanted to be married by then, so there would be no time for Honey to go through catechism and become a Catholic. Nevertheless, he wanted a Catholic officiant at the wedding. He wrote to Cornelius McGillicuddy and explained the situation, asking him to officiate outside of usual Church protocol.

He took a bus to Illinois to meet Honey in Elmhurst, a wealthy suburb of Chicago, where he would meet her family for the first time. Honey offered to buy him a flight, but he couldn't take money from her. He told her he liked the bus.

When Honey had said her family was well-to-do, he hadn't quite grasped the blueness of their blood. They lived in a mansion amid servants, gardens, and walled grounds, with a tennis court, swimming pool, and a nineteenth-century carriage house that had been converted into a guest house. Her father's family had gotten rich in the Chicago stockyards in the 1890s.

Honey's parents greeted him with a cautious skepticism that quickly turned sour when the subject of religion came up. They were staunch Lutherans after all, a founding family of Elmhurst College. When they found out he was only an enlisted man in the Army *and* a Catholic, her mother's initial enthusiasm evaporated, and the sudden chill in the room froze Okie's bones. Her father looked like he wanted to drive Okie off the property with a cattle prod. Okie reluctantly told them who his father was, which alleviated some of their disappointment—he also earned a few sympathy points for having lost his mother so young—but they made it clear that they had expected more of their daughter's marital choice.

The irony that her parents were so deeply disappointed in their daughter—a jet-setting model and CIA operative who hobnobbed with international celebrities—was too thick to cut.

Nevertheless, they managed to get through it all with the agreement to have the ceremony in their Fox Lake home garden, with all expenses paid.

Having a Catholic priest perform the ceremony was a vitriolic sticking point until Okie framed it as a "compromise." "We could just get married next year in a Catholic church. Of course, Honey would have to convert. In the meantime, she'll be moving in with me in Germany," Okie had said, praying they wouldn't call his bluff. He wasn't sure *he'd* have felt okay living in sin with her, however much penance he had to do with all the sin they'd been committing. The negotiation took a couple of hours of back and forth, during which her father stormed off repeatedly, only to be brought back by Honey's mother, Ruby, who ultimately bore her disappointment with grace and acceptance.

He breathed a huge sigh of relief when they finally got out of there and headed to Buffalo to introduce Honey to Ann and Emmett and whatever McGillicuddy relatives he could wrangle into a knot. John would flip his lid.

On the plane to Buffalo, Okie told her, "It's no wonder you had to get the hell out of there."

"And go far, far away," she said with an earnest sigh.

Ann greeted Honey like a long-lost sister, and the two of them seemed to hit it off, a huge relief after the bone-crushing tension of Elmhurst. Ann threw together a linen shower with several McGillicuddy cousins. Emmett was surprisingly cordial with Honey and behaved as if his and Okie's last encounter had never happened. Okie's expectation of John's reaction had been accurate, and he asked John to be his best man, "as long as you don't try to steal her," Okie added.

"That dame has eyes just for you, pal," John said, after he'd picked up his jaw.

The days passed in wedding preparations as they went back and forth between Chicago and Buffalo.

Okie received a phone call at Emmett's house that Cornelius acquiesced to Okie's request to perform the ceremony, on the promise that as soon as possible they would be married before God in a proper sacramental Mass. It was good to hear his cousin's voice again, and it warmed his heart to be joined by family to the woman of his dreams.

Father Cornelius McGillicuddy married them on Saturday, October 15, 1955, on a pleasant, sunny afternoon on the Fox Lake estate. Don and Lois flew from California. Lois was the maid of honor, with Ann the only bridesmaid. Don was Okie's groomsman. The ceremony was a cultured affair dripping with hothouse flowers, champagne, hors d'oeuvres, and tension. Okie found the caviar disgusting—"fish eggs, are you kidding?"—but Honey loved it. John Montana Sr. was in attendance, as well as a few dignitaries from Emmett's Buffalo orbit and the handful of McGillicuddy relatives who could afford the trip. Most of them were agog at the affluence on display. No doubt that for years to come it would be the subject of evermore exaggerated stories in McGillicuddy circles. If there was anything that every McGillicuddy could do well, it was a tell a story.

A twelve-piece big band provided the reception entertainment, and he and Honey danced away to their Niagara Falls honeymoon on strains of "Moonlight Serenade."

"Ah, how oft we read or hear of
Boys we almost stand in fear of!
For example, take these stories
Of two youths, named Max and Moritz,
Who, instead of early turning
Their young minds to useful learning,
Often leered with horrid features
At their lessons and their teachers."

-*Max and Moritz: A Story of Seven Boyish Pranks*
written and illustrated by Wilhelm Busch (1865)

XVII

"IM NAMEN DES VATERS und des Sohnes und des Heiligen Geistes. Mein letztes Geständnis war vor einem Monat. In Demut und Reue bekenne ich meine Sünden."

"Your German is very good, my son."

"Danke schön, Vater. *I'm not sure what sort of sin this is, but I feel bad about it, so it must be something. My wife and I just rented a two-story flat with our friends Don and Lois. They live upstairs, we live downstairs, and we share the kitchen and bathroom. It's a cozy, little place, but kind of old. It somehow survived the war, both wars, you know?"*

"Such places still exist."

"Yeah. Well, we were very naughty. It was our first Christmas here, and I'd just gotten back from some martial arts training, so we had a party, just the four of us. Let me say that German beer is much stronger than American beer. We were all blitzed. We went out and found a Christmas tree, cut it down, and brought it home, but it was too tall. It was at least twelve feet high, maybe fifteen, took all four of us to drag it home. But we're all too sloshed to realize how big it actually was. So we cram it through the front door, but there's just no way to stand it up. It's all pretty fuzzy, but the next thing I remember, we're cutting a hole in the ceiling. Lo and behold, it now

fits perfectly, a perfect Christmas tree for the upper and lower floors. We decorated the top and the bottom. The landlord is going to be furious, though..."

❁❁❁

Nestled among the picturesque Bavarian Alps, among their snow-capped peaks and verdant fields, lay Bad Aibling Station, a.k.a. the 18th United States Army Security Agency Field Station, perhaps the largest listening post in Europe, tracking and intercepting communications throughout the continent. The white radomes resembled geodesic marbles clustered around several innocuous single-story structures and a modest-sized aircraft hangar, but the true workings of the station lay below ground.

It fell to intelligence operatives like Okie and Don to help translate and decipher the dizzying profusion of radio and telephone intelligence from all around Europe. Much of what they had to translate was communications gleaned from the Berlin Tunnel, a top-secret tunnel stretching underneath the Berlin Wall some 450 meters into Soviet-controlled territory, where operatives from the Army Security Agency and the CIA tapped into sensitive telephone lines. The conversations most often sounded mind-numbingly inane on the surface, but those were sometimes most likely to be conveying coded messages.

Okie and Don spent most of their time in the hangar, a section of which had been sectioned off into desks and worktables. Amid the bustle of Bad Aibling Station, Okie felt like a cog in a machine, just an enlisted grunt fresh from stateside, and for the most part was treated as something roughly equivalent to pond scum or used axle grease. It was not challenging work, just mundane transcription and translation, frightfully boring most of the time. Nevertheless, all of it had to be analyzed and reanalyzed for possible nuggets of actionable intelligence. What was exciting was hearing about the movements of Soviet and East German forces. The fate of the world balanced on a knife's edge that *no one* back home could see. Full-scale thermonuclear war could break out at any moment.

Okie, Don, and their fellow intelligence grunts often blew off steam at Schloss Maxlrain, a.k.a. the "Castle Brewery," a sixteenth-century castle with a steeply sloped roof and a four-story tower at each corner of the main building. The *schloss* lay about five kilometers north of Bad Aibling Station, amid the lush, idyllic Bavarian countryside, complete with a beautiful garden and a restaurant. The beer made Okie feel like he could see heaven from there, and the knackwurst with mustard and sauerkraut was the fare of kaisers.

And then there was Honey. Married life with Honey was pure bliss. With her work schedule and his duty assignments, they were apart enough to miss each other, and together enough to make it up in the most torrid way possible.

When he discovered that she kept a "go bag" tucked under the bed his admiration for her turned to wonder.

"You mean you don't have one?" she said only half playfully. "It's time to get with the program, buster."

She pulled out a stylish piece of luggage about the size of a bowling bag, unzipped it, and laid everything out on the bed, regarding him with a hand on her hip. Three U.S. passports, the Beretta semi-automatic he'd seen in her suitcase, a ka-bar, the M3 fighting knife, a bundle of maps, four packages of hosiery of various colors, a first-aid kit, a compass, a small set of binoculars, flashlight, and modest bundles of U.S. dollars, British pounds sterling, West German deutschmarks, French francs, Spanish pesetas, Italian lire, and Soviet rubles.

"It's not as much money as it looks like," she said with a chuckle.

"Impressive anyway," he said with a smile.

"You never know when we might have to bolt."

She was right, so he put his own bag together, but his also included a set of rosary beads. They also created contingency plans for where and how to find each other in the case of a catastrophe, and their plans went several layers deep for how to get out of the country, out of Europe, back to America, by land, air, or sea.

Okie reveled in the sense of purpose all of this gave him. He felt exceptionally blessed to be living this life, to have a beautiful wife, good friends in Don and Lois, and most importantly, a *purpose.*

It was an evening in mid-December that changed everything, when Honey returned to the flat they shared with Don and Lois. Okie came home from the station expecting her return and carrying a handful of flowers from the local hothouse, anticipating a night of frenzied lovemaking, but the moment he saw her face, he knew something was wrong. She gave him a warm hug and a kiss, but there was something half-hearted in her smile, a secret ghost.

To his query about something being wrong, he felt the strength drain from her limbs all at once, and she sank into the closest chair.

She clasped her hands between her knees as if to stop them shaking, and her eyes were glistening. Her mouth worked as if mustering some steam to produce words. "I… I was chatting up Frankie on the flight to Havana a couple of days ago. He had a show at the Tropicana. But then I…threw up."

"You threw up on Frank Sinatra?"

"I made it to the toilet, but—" She still looked pale.

"Are you feeling okay? Are you sick? Food poisoning?"

She shook her head and looked at him like he was a complete fool. "As soon as I had a break between shifts, I…went to the doctor."

He knelt before her and took her hands in his. "Are you all right?"

"I'm…" She took a deep shuddering breath and let it out. "Congratulations, Daddy."

Her words took a moment to land, and he blinked. But then a rush hit him like a warm blast of propeller-wash. "Really?"

She nodded, tears in her eyes, but strangely they weren't tears of joy.

"But how?" They used condoms most of the time, except for a few moments that were too hot and heavy, or Honey's supply had been depleted.

She gave him a helpless, forlorn shrug.

He stood and drew her up with him. "That is the best thing I've heard since the day you said, 'I do.'"

She clung to him but wouldn't look at his face. "You really think so?"

"God has blessed us. When is the baby due?"

"July, they said."

"Oh, Honey." He squeezed her and kissed her head and smelled her hair, trying to wrap his mind around this seismic shift in their wonderful little world. His knees went weak.

Eventually they kissed, and the passion flared as it always did, and they compounded and compressed all these emotions into physical ecstasy. But afterward, she lay staring at the ancient wooden beams that supported the high ceiling, tears trickling toward her ears, interrupting his whirling reverie of all the ways their lives would soon change, all the things he imagined their children might become. He hadn't expected God to bless their family with children so soon, and the wonder of it was still settling in.

Honey's distress was plain, however.

When he asked her what was wrong, she said, "Nothing. I'm just happy is all." But it was a lie.

She put on a good face when they broke the news to Don and Lois, but he caught a shadow flickering across Lois's face as she paused to study Honey's. When the two women hugged, something passed between them that he couldn't grasp.

It wasn't until she returned from her next rotation that he was able to get it out of her. She gave him a tearful, stricken look. "How could I tell you the truth? You were so happy."

"The truth about what? I want you to be happy, too!"

"I *love* my life, Okie. I love traveling. I loved being a model. I love...doing what we do. Do you understand what I'm giving up?"

"Well, sure, but—"

"No, you don't!" Her vehemence pushed him back half a step. "Do you know what pregnancy does to a woman's body? I'll start showing soon. I'll probably lose my job at TWA. I will no longer be a TWA Angel. Bill will probably fire me. He wouldn't put a pregnant operative in harm's way. And somebody will have to raise this child, and that falls to the mother. You'll get to go off and keep your life, but mine is *over!* Can you see that?"

The enormity of it started to take hold. "Well, yeah, but it's only natural that it's the mother's job to raise the baby. That's the way it's always been. The Bible says—"

"*Fuck* the Bible!"

He stiffened and his cheeks grew hot. "Children are blessings from God, Honey. You need to remember that." He had assumed that motherhood was something that she, as a woman, had been prepared for since puberty, something she'd always wanted, deep down. It was God's way of things, as sure as the sunrise. It was the woman's purpose to bear children and care for them.

"Don't give me that shit!" she said. "You need to remember, *I* recruited *you.*" She gave him a glare so fiery and haunted it put him back a step. "You don't know the half of the things I've done! It's not just recruiting!" She spun and began to pace, leaving him with the screaming question of what the hell else she had done.

Then she sighed heavily and slumped into herself, her voice cracking with sobs. "All the things you love about me will be gone."

He leaped to her side, babbling about how this could only make him love her more. This seemed to assuage her pain and quell the deluge of sobbing tears.

Hours of back and forth followed, fraught with fears and hard realities. Okie tried over and over to curb her malaise with hopes and dreams for this child, but without significant success. He tried distracting her from the pain of the moment by tossing in innocuous questions about her exploits, but she remained tight-lipped about this. He would be gone soon, for a while—he didn't know how long—so at least she would have Lois for support. Don and Lois were studious about using birth control for just these kinds of selfish reasons, but he still felt condoms were an affront to God. It didn't matter that they weren't "ready to have children." It was something Okie kept silent about, and he couldn't very well tell her in this moment that he was happy his seed had found its way to a miracle.

Eventually he had to tell her that in two days he'd be away for two weeks but couldn't tell her it was for CIA training. His Army chain of command was more than a little chapped about clandestine services running roughshod over their duty roster, but henceforth the Army would be just his cover. He could already feel the ground of his world shifting beneath his feet.

Everything he knew was about to change. He could see that much. He just couldn't see the results.

❂❂❂

"Have you heard of the Monuments Men?" Donovan asked, leaning across his desk.

Okie nodded. "My father claimed to know some of them, but never said who. They were searching for all the art that the Nazis looted all across Europe."

"They still are."

Okie raised an eyebrow. "What does it have to do with being a sniper?" He brushed a dry leaf from his camouflage trousers. An hour ago, he'd been hiding in a tree, picking off sniper targets, but "Wild Bill" had called him in for a meeting. His face still bore the dark, oil-paint smudges. His muscles were still knotted from the punishing bout of hand-to-hand combat training yesterday, which had taken his Army training and cranked up the brutality to levels of "dirty" fighting Okie hadn't known existed. Eye gouging, throat punching, nostril ripping, biting, kicking, clawing. Points of vulnerability on the human body. Improvised weapons. He had left the session exhausted, with an odd mix of horror and fascination. *Especially in Berlin,* the instructor told him, *be ready for anything. Double-crossing. Attacks out of nowhere. Someone might try to grab you right off the street, especially after dark.* He shook off the alarming concerns and tried to focus back on Donovan.

"Nothing, except perhaps a sharp eye. So you're aware that the Nazis looted the entirety of Europe. Untold thousands of artworks, everything they could get their hands on." Donovan shuddered. "And not just art. I... Well, let's just say one never forgets seeing a wooden crate the size of a steamer trunk filled to the brim with gold teeth."

The image of such a horrific thing sent a chill up Okie's neck. "How can I help, sir?"

Donovan sighed. "You and Mr. Fell make a superb team, and there's an ongoing effort to recover these stolen artworks. Ike wants the search to continue without hesitation. Rare books. Tapestries. Paintings. Sculptures. Priceless treasures of human history. Have you heard about the *Madonna of Bruges*?"

"The Michelangelo statue of Madonna and Child? I've seen old photos. When I get some leave time, I'd love to travel to Belgium and see it."

"Are you aware that the Nazis stole it in 1944 as they fled the Allied advance after D-Day?"

Okie shook his head.

"Its whereabouts were unknown, along with hundreds of other pieces. When the Allies got too close, the Nazis destroyed the art. They torched hundreds of works, leaving a trail of ashes behind them. The *Madonna of Bruges* was feared destroyed. We're talking about Michelangelo here. But only hours ahead of a Soviet column, it was discovered in an ore cart, wrapped in a mattress, in a salt mine near Altaussee. It's an incredible story all by itself."

"It sounds like it, sir."

"The Nazis cached their stolen loot all over Europe in places like salt mines, caves, catacombs. The Monuments Men were, are, on a quest to preserve human culture, in the face of the forces of evil that literally wanted to burn it to the ground so they could replace it with whatever Hitler's diseased mind could conjure. Thousands of priceless works have been recovered, but many thousands more are still lost. Recovery efforts are ongoing."

As Donovan spoke, Okie noticed that the hale heartiness Donovan had displayed a few months back had diminished. The strength of intellect was still behind the eyes, but he looked pale, drawn.

Donovan went on, "One of the most important works that's still missing is Raphael's *Portrait of a Young Man*."

Okie's memory shot back to the print of *The Transfiguration* by Raphael that still hung in Emmett's study at home. The thought that an important Raphael painting was among those stolen made it seem more real and immediate.

"Its last known location was in the hands of the Nazi governor of Poland, a man named Hans Frank. He was sitting on a whole trove of looted art, but when he was arrested, this painting was not to be found. He was executed as a war criminal in '46." Donovan pushed a thick manila folder across the desk. "This is everything we know about this particular work."

"Are there any thoughts on where to start looking? This feels like a needle in the proverbial haystack."

"It is. Would you care to indulge me in a personal theory?"

"Sure thing."

"Our mutually esteemed Vatican Bank laundered money for Hitler for years, until it became too much of a political hot potato. We know, but we can't prove, that a great number of looted works found their way into Vatican vaults in the chaos after the war. I'm sure the Vatican would argue that they're protecting them. We know that Pope Pius XII made an agreement with Hitler and Mussolini to look the other way in exchange for their promises not to sack the Holy See. Even nowadays, the Vatican trades in religious art. Since the war, the Vatican's been trying to wash its dirty hands, or at least hide them."

Okie squirmed. Talking about the Vatican, and indirectly, the Pope, as if they were simple constructs in the mortal world, rather than the voice of God Himself on Earth, made Okie's guts twist with discomfort. How could such a holy organization soil itself by associating with war crimes and looted art?

"You have a relative working in the Vatican now, don't you? A cousin?" Donovan asked, clearly already knowing the answer.

Okie nodded, frowning, as this all felt like something of a hard turn. Because he was in the middle of sniper training, he envisioned that he'd soon be placed somewhere along the borders of the Iron Curtain. The dividing line between East and West Germany, as well as the border between West Germany and Czechoslovakia, had become clearly defined with fences, minefields, patrols, and signs warning approaching personnel. Snipers lined both sides of every border between East and West. The Soviet bloc shot people trying to escape to freedom. CIA snipers shot spies trying to sneak back *into* the East, as it was assumed that no one but a spy would be trying to sneak *into* the land of Soviet horrors.

Okie was a crack shot with a high-powered rifle, and his Expert Marksman Badge in basic training had landed him in CIA sniper school. Thus far, his longest shot to be judged a successful kill was 984 yards. It was a stationary target, but still a tremendous accomplishment. It represented the Finger of Death with a half-mile reach.

But now they were talking about stolen Nazi art, his cousin Cornelius, and disparaging the holiness of the Church.

"Does all this make you uncomfortable, son?"

Okie nodded.

"You're a good Catholic boy, Okie. I can see that. But you must keep in the mind that the Catholic Church is not just a spiritual organization, but a political one. It's had almost two millennia to practice walking that line. You'll be surprised to know that the Catholic Church sanctioned the genocide of over two hundred thousand Serbs during the war. Serbs as an ethnic group are mostly Eastern Orthodox. The fascist Croat regime, one of Hitler's puppet governments, was mostly Catholic. It legitimized its extermination of Serbs, Jews, gypsies, and others by getting the quiet sanction of the Vatican. Hell, a Franciscan friar ran one of the worst extermination camps. That camp alone killed over a hundred thousand, and the archbishop of Sarajevo gave it all his blessing."

"I... I can't believe it." Parts of him were screaming *Then they must have deserved it!* But that was exactly the kind of thinking that led everyday Germans to look away from the atrocities committed on their very doorsteps. Nevertheless, he had sworn an oath to the Order of Malta to protect the Church. What did it mean to "protect" an organization capable of such things?

"You'll have a hard time finding anyone who speaks English to talk about it, but, son, I can tell you firsthand. I interrogated some of these bastards at Nuremberg. You can bet the Serbs aren't going to forgive and forget what happened. Someday there will be hell to pay in Eastern Europe."

"Why are you telling me all this?"

"You're a good man but used to seeing the world like it's a movie. Black hats and white hats. You're entering a world of grays and complicated shadows, and as we've been teaching you these last few weeks, there are a million ways to make someone's life a living hell, without killing them."

"Anything can be used as a lever to exert pressure, right, sir?"

"We can make them feel like death is a mercy."

Okie nodded. In between thousands of rounds at the firing range that turned his shoulder into a mass of bruises and uncomfortable hours of hiding in the cold Virginia countryside, peering through a high-power scope, waiting for a "target" to appear, he spent time in the classroom as well, learning the basics of clandestine warfare and the espionage game.

Donovan continued, "You'll find yourself at times having to work with some detestable people, in the name of national security. This world is complicated, and few things are exactly as they seem."

"May I ask a question, sir?"

"You may speak freely."

"Why me for this kind of mission? I'm not an investigator."

"I mentioned a personal theory, and here it is. There is one major lead that remains untapped, for political reasons. I think Raphael's *Portrait of a Young Man* found its way into the Vatican vaults. Cornelius McGillicuddy might be able to ask sensitive questions or have access to certain records. The Vatican will move heaven and earth to keep its dirty laundry hidden. Now, we're not interested in airing any Vatican laundry. We just want the painting to be recovered. If it mysteriously reappears in a warehouse somewhere, so much the better."

XVIII

"Many commit the same crime with a different result.
One bears a cross for his crime; another a crown."
-Juvenal

***"BLESS ME, FATHER,** for I have sinned. It's been ten days since my last confession... I have abstained from taking communion. Lord, I am not worthy."*

"Go on, my son."

"Sorry, Father, I... I can't tell you about it... It was justified... Self-defense, but..."

"Are you still there, my son?"

1956

"It's good to see you, Okie," Father Cornelius McGillicuddy said with a warm smile and a handshake. "And so far from home!"

"This Roman sunshine is a welcome change from Bavaria in January," Okie said, returning the gesture.

It was a beautiful morning, temperature in the fifties, the sky a cerulean blue, strips of cloud tinged with pink by the morning sun, stretching over ancient streets where Caesars once walked. The cafe along the cobbled, narrow street of Borgo Pio, only a few blocks from Vatican City, sported red-and-white checked tablecloths, and the strongest scent of coffee Okie had ever encountered. He'd heard tales of Italian-style coffee—*espresso*, they called it—strong enough to stand a spoon in it, but this was his first opportunity to give it a try. His flight, a military transport, had arrived before dawn. A good jolt of Lavazza would help clear out the cobwebs.

"I was surprised to hear you were coming to Rome," Cornelius said.

"I'm excited to be here, but unfortunately it's business, not vacation." In his briefcase was the Monuments Men file on the Raphael painting. He had spent a couple of days studying it, sensing the fervor with which earlier investigators had followed every lead. Sadly, with each passing year, the trail grew colder.

Raphael's *Portrait of a Young Man* was painted probably in 1513 or 1514 and was considered by many to be the most important work of art to have been stolen during the war. Along with Leonardo da Vinci's *Lady with an Ermine* and Rembrandt's *Landscape with the Good Samaritan*, it was stolen from the Prince Czartoryski Museum in Kraków. When the Nazis invaded Poland in 1939, the three paintings (known as LRR for Leonardo, Raphael, Rembrandt) were walled up in an outbuilding of an aristocratic villa in the small town of Sieniawa. However, the cache was discovered by the Gestapo, who delivered the paintings to the Nazi governor of Poland, Hans Frank, who decorated his residence in Kraków with them.

According to Nazi shipping documents and interviews, they later were moved to the Führer's own collection in Linz. Hitler believed that Catholic-commissioned works of art contained coded maps to Christian treasures or *Arma Christi,* the "weapons of Christ." The Nazi Horde of stolen artworks was part of their supernatural beliefs, which they associated with the Holy Grail and the Ark of the Covenant. In August 1944, the Leonardo and the Rembrandt were moved to Hans Frank's headquarters in Sichów. The Raphael was not mentioned in this transfer.

Alongside the file in Okie's briefcase was a report to Congress detailing the Monuments Men's—and Women's—investigations, dated a couple of years ago. It was strange to read about such exciting discoveries and heartbreaking losses written in such dry, academic prose. They needed better writers. Nevertheless, the Nazis had cached their loot all over Europe, abandoning it, sometimes destroying it, as they were forced to retreat from the Allied advance. The maps were dotted with handwritten marks identifying these caches. Many of the key witnesses, unfortunately, were now dead. The recovered art was worth untold millions of dollars, some of it belonging to Jewish families who had been exterminated in the camps. The ownership of those works was a legal quagmire crossing numerous national borders. The titanic scope of the project would require decades to resolve, if it ever was. The most likely outcome was that whoever had them would get to keep them, or they'd be donated to various museums like the Metropolitan Museum of Art in New York, which served as the effort's de facto headquarters.

But he was here to do a single job.

Cornelius drew him back into the moment. "Army Intelligence brings you to Rome?"

"It's a special project. But let's catch up first."

They spent the next hour discussing things like family news, married life, current events. Cornelius was delighted to hear that Honey was in a family way.

When Okie's espresso arrived in its tiny cup and he took his first sip, it hit his tongue like a lightning strike, sitting him straight up in his wrought-iron chair.

Riding the jolt, Okie gently steered the conversation to life in Vatican City, where Cornelius was a low-level aide to the Director of the Vatican Museum. Okie amplified his natural enthusiasm to reduce Cornelius's possible resistance to what was coming. He asked what he hoped were innocuous questions about the Vatican Museum's inner workings. When he sensed vagaries or hedging in Cornelius's responses, he knew he was approaching the limits of how far he could probe. The same blade cut both ways, and he soon saw a similar realization in Cornelius's gaze.

One realization Okie's research had given him was that the Vatican was as steeped in secrecy as the CIA. What disturbed him most was that his beloved Church had so many things to hide. How could God's work come with so much dirty laundry?

Cornelius finished his cream-filled *maritozzi* and said, "So tell me about this special project. It's the reason for your trip, after all."

Okie took a deep breath. "Have you heard about the Monuments Men?"

"Looted Nazi art. The Vatican Museum has been in contact with a number of those investigators. We've helped uncover a great many stolen works. Such an important project. A terrible crime what the Nazis did. Another among many, I suppose. Is this your new assignment?"

"I'm here to ask you a favor."

"I'm happy to entertain it."

Okie gave him a long look. "Do you know about the Raphael?"

Cornelius leaned forward, his eyes flickered as he searched his memory, then he shook his head.

Okie told him about the 450-year-old portrait, trying to gauge whether his cousin's interest was straightforward or a facade hiding something. After relating how the painting's trail was lost, he said, "The Vatican Museum has extensive vaults, right? Stuff going back centuries. You just basically told me as much."

"It's true," Cornelius conceded. "Some of it is uncatalogued, in need of study and identification."

Okie checked for possible eavesdroppers, then leaned closer. "Isn't it possible that some of that Nazi loot found its way into those vaults?"

Cornelius gave him a long look, then glanced around. "Publicly, they will say there's no possible way. But between us and the cobblestones... There was a lot of chaos after the war. The Vatican was landlocked inside a fascist country allied with the Axis. Italians are somewhat sheepish about Mussolini these days, but his sympathizers and former collaborators are still around. How do you go back to regular everyday life when your country has just had its behind soundly kicked? And the Vatican...well, it's the Holy See. The public face and the inner workings bear only passing resemblance to each other, much like the spiritual realm and the earthly realm. The Vatican must contend with both. During the war, there was an effort to remain neutral and protect artworks, provide a safe haven, but having no army, they couldn't antagonize the fascists. Nearly everything the Vatican possesses is religious art, but there are a few exceptions."

Much of what Cornelius was saying sounded rote, as if he were dancing around the real answer. "Let's entertain a hypothetical occurrence," Okie said. "Let's say in all that chaos, a famous painting or two might have found its way into Vatican vaults... Is that possible? Sitting in a crate or rolled up in some anonymous, uncatalogued tube? Hiding in plain sight?"

Cornelius nodded and leaned back. "Again, publicly, not possible. But realistically..." He shrugged.

"Would you be able to do some checking? All of this is strictly on the hush-hush. If the painting turns up—"

"If the painting turns up, it would be a sensation in the newspapers that the Holy See does *not* want."

"And it wouldn't have to be connected to the Vatican at all. It could be found behind a wall in some bombed-out warehouse, or whatever story we want to tell."

Cornelius wiped his mouth with a napkin, considering. "I'm only an aide, one rung above janitor. I don't have that kind of access."

"But I'll bet you work with people who do. Maybe a janitor has seen it." Okie gave him a little grin.

Cornelius met his grin with a chuckle.

It was a freezing night in Berlin, well below zero degrees Celsius. Much like languages, Okie had found it easier to just think in the metric system, rather than trying to translate metric into English units. He clutched his pea coat around him and lifted his collar. This was not one of Berlin's more boisterous neighborhoods, so the late hour, approaching 10:00 p.m., meant the streets were all but empty except for drunks stumbling home—and people like him. People who were up to something.

Thick icicles hung from windowsills, balconies, and eaves, lining the narrow, cobblestone streets like fangs glittering in feeble streetlights. Piles of glimmering snow lay scattered on the streets and walks. The air smelled of wood smoke and bitter chill, reminding him of winters in Buffalo.

Stalin was gone, but his cult of personality remained. Nikita Khrushchev had shocked the communist world with negative comments about Stalin's worst atrocities, but he was still a Soviet hardliner. Europe was crawling with Soviet Bloc spies engaged in a secret war with the CIA, MI6, and other Western intelligence agencies. Nowhere in the world was this clandestine war hotter than the streets of Berlin. With its own operating airport, Berlin was also a pipeline for people desperate to flee to the West. The Soviets knew it and were trying to staunch that hemorrhage in every way they could, short of open war.

The Soviets were making it harder and harder, Okie had heard, for people to move around within Berlin. Everyone was on edge worrying about who was spying on whom. There were fears that the Soviets would erect some sort of barrier, similar to their attempt to blockade the Western sectors back in '48 and '49. Many people lived in one zone and worked or had family in another. East Germany was evolving into a true Soviet satellite state, Khrushchev's foothold in Western Europe. The Allies, it seemed, could never agree on much with respect to how to administer their respective zones, so the city was a mess, a tiny sliver of flailing democracy in danger of being swallowed by increasing Soviet aggression.

But the Allies had just formally ended the occupation back in May. The Federal Republic of Germany would have to stand on its own—with the backing of NATO, however. West Germany was a full-fledged member of the Western World. Everywhere were remembrances of the war and, if one looked closely, how it was still going on, but the adversaries had changed. German reunification was a dead issue.

Much like the strange fraternity that frequented the Sausalito house—which Okie now knew to be a CIA safe house and transit location—the agents walking the halls of CIA headquarters in Langley, Virginia, formed a strange group. Okie's presence made him part of that club, however incongruous it still felt. How long, he wondered, before he felt like part of that fraternity? All the way up to Director Allen Dulles and Wild Bill Donovan, still working behind the scenes, they were all making up the international espionage game as they went, a game with no rules, building upon techniques and technology developed during the war, but constantly improving with cutting-edge advancements in radio, electronics, and photography. It was a game of moves and countermoves played against a clever, implacable, adaptable adversary. Some of those agents had harrowing stories to tell, made all the more incredible by the matter-of-fact way they told them, as if a hair's breadth escape was like an afternoon raking leaves. The names of those who didn't make it home were muttered with reverence, if they were ever spoken of at all.

The glimpses Okie received of this deadly clandestine world filled him with endless excitement. This was what he was meant to be doing, set on this path by the Hand of the Almighty.

Okie went on a courier run from Bad Aibling to retrieve some documents from the U.S. Mission Berlin, a sort of de facto embassy, even though the official embassy was situated in the new capital in Bonn. He had flown into Berlin on a Douglas C-47 Skytrain in the wee hours of this morning, a short hop from Bavaria.

The U.S. Mission was in a building amid the complex of the former Luftwaffe headquarters, under the command of the U.S. Army. Some of the buildings still bore great concrete eagles at the corners, although the swastikas had been chiseled away. To avoid the appearance that this was an official embassy, the complex was guarded by U.S. Army military police, rather than U.S. Marines.

On this cold winter night, on his first real mission, Okie felt *alive,* with vigilance pumping through his veins. His blood thrummed with the desire to prove himself, to measure himself against the forces of evil. God's Templar knight.

Statistics were hard to come by, but many people went missing on the streets of Berlin. Scuttlebutt was that the Stasi, the East German secret police, were most active after dark, often sneaking into West-controlled sectors to kidnap people, including Americans suspected of espionage. Between the Stasi and the KGB, Okie had received dire warnings to watch himself after dark.

Inside the briefcase that contained his courier packet had been a small note:

Meet me at Max und Marlene Bierhaus, near Bornholmer Strasse at 10. Got something for you.

Kirby

Okie well remembered the tall, athletic man who'd first welcomed them into the house in Sausalito. He still didn't know Kirby's full name, but this had to be "company business."

Bornholmer Strasse was a major thoroughfare that led toward East Berlin. At this time of night, checkpoints would be most vigilant, so he was glad he wouldn't have to deal with them. The Max und Marlene Bierhaus lay just on the western side of the border. The streets of Berlin were a patchwork of old and new construction as the city had been rebuilt after being bombed to rubble. Some obliterated buildings had been cleared and the land converted to parks. You couldn't swing a dead cat in Berlin without hitting a peace memorial or war monument.

The streetlights cast Okie's shadow out ahead of him. Maybe this pub would have some food. He hadn't eaten since this morning. A plate of sauerkraut, sausage, and potatoes would set his taste buds into a lively polka. According to the street map he'd memorized, he was about a block from the bierhaus when he turned down a narrow street. One of the streetlights was out, and only a couple of feeble lights brightened the apartment windows above. He could hear a faint radio broadcast somewhere—Édith Piaf, "Non, Je ne regrette rien," he thought—and the luscious scent of *sauerbraten* wafted on the night air, making his stomach roar.

As he passed a decrepit Opel Blitz truck older than he was, a sense of alarm threw his heart into his throat. Could he have subconsciously heard the scuff of a shoe or the whisper of clothing? He didn't know, but the knife blade caught the starlight as it stabbed toward his kidney.

He dodged and spun, arms flailing, and the knife hissed past. It wasn't just a knife. It was a combat knife, like a Marine's kabar. There was no time to go for his .22-caliber Iver-Johnson in its shoulder holster before the knife was whishing back toward him. The attacker lunged and tackled Okie against the side of the truck, driving him down against the wheel and fender, the impact dislodging icicles from the running board. The assailant's gray woolen cap cast his face in shadow, but his teeth caught the light like the knife blade as it stabbed toward Okie's throat. It could have been the attacker's weight or Okie's thundering heart that made it impossible to breathe, but his ears roared with the surge of blood in his veins. The man was strong, compact like a wrestler, and his breath smelled of mint toothpaste.

Okie caught the knife wrist with his left hand, and they struggled for it. Okie tried to bring his right hand to bear, but he'd been shoved partially into the wheel well and a torn edge of rusty sheet metal snagged his coat sleeve. He tried to bring his legs into the fight, but his assailant had jammed a knee into Okie's belly, driving the breath out of him.

The knife point pressed toward his throat, inexorably.

With the last moments of his life hanging from the point of that blade, Okie heaved like an offensive lineman, and his right sleeve came loose with a ripping sound.

His hand clasped around something cold and slick, as thick as a fat carrot.

The icicle snapped free in his grip.

With another desperate heave, he freed his arm, hooked his thumb over the broken end, and stabbed the point of the icicle straight into his assailant's throat. He felt the point snap off against the man's coat collar, but the man made a horrid choking nose. The hand holding the knife weakened for a split second, then redoubled its strength as a hot blast of desperate breath hit Okie in the face. The man's other hand flailed for the icicle but missed as Okie drove the blunted point into the man's Adam's apple. There was a wet, muffled crack. The man's eyes bulged, and his body stiffened. Okie shoved him up, giving himself room to draw back the icicle for a final stab. Straight into the man's eye.

The point went deep with a crunching, crackling noise.

The icicle snapped off in Okie's hand as the man convulsed backward, clutching at it, his other eye bulging, making a sound like *muh-mmuh-mmuuh*. The man flopped onto his back. Two inches of broken icicle protruded from one ruined eye socket. Okie flung himself to his feet, gasping.

The man's left hand clutched at the sky spasmodically. The kabar fell from twitching fingers.

With the heel of his shoe, Okie jammed the icicle two inches deeper into the man's skull. Dark blood bloomed around the ice, steaming.

The man spasmed once more, then subsided, his foot twitching like a beheaded chicken's.

Okie reeled to the side, gagging. After a few deep breaths, he got control of his gorge. His entire body trembled like an electric current flowed through him. His knees drained of strength, and his hands trembled. The crystals in the piles of snow were so beautiful. His mouth was dry as paper.

Somewhere along the street he heard a window open.

He ran.

Keeping to the shadows, gasping as loud as a freight train with every step, his heartbeat louder than his footsteps.

Moments later, he came upon a circular sign, painted with the cartoonish image of a stout tavern keeper and his wife, hanging above an old tavern door. Yellow-orange light spilled through two diamond-paned windows. *Max und Marlene.*

He straightened himself, wiped his eyes and mouth with the back of his hand, took a deep breath and went inside, trembling so badly he could hardly stand.

The wash of warm air carried the smells of beer and wood smoke. A surprising number of eyes turned his way momentarily, then turned away to study him without watching. Fourteen male patrons at scattered tables, all of them older than him, plus a buxom young barmaid toweling out a beer stein. A large fire crackled on the hearth at the back of the room. Kirby was not present.

His mind flashed through a thousand thoughts like *Do they know? Can they see? Do I have blood on me? Are they going to call the police?* His legs were still jelly.

Then he noticed something cold dripping from his knuckles. Water.

He still clutched the broken icicle.

He palmed the icicle up his sleeve, then crossed the room toward the fireplace. Smiling at the pretty blonde barmaid, he said, "*Es ist tolles Badewetter, ja?*" *Great beach weather, isn't it?*

She chuckled with an exaggerated eyebrow raise. "*Oh, ja, es ist Kaiserwetter.*" *Weather fit for an emperor.*

He knelt before the fireplace, nonchalantly placing his murder weapon on the hearth, where it proceeded to disappear.

For a time, he simply knelt and breathed and waited for his guts to stop wringing themselves like dirty laundry.

Finally, a voice at his shoulder muttered in American English, "How long are you going to sit there with your back to the room in a place like this?"

PART II

Fīat jūstitia ruat cælum

"Let justice be done though the heavens fall."

XIX

***"BLESS ME, FATHER**, for I have sinned. It's been two days since my last confession. I'm having trouble sleeping lately. I was...attacked last week. I haven't even told my wife this. The man's face... haunts me, and I didn't even see it clearly. It's like when I shut my eyes, my brain tries to fill in this awful blank space with demons. I keep dreaming about pieces of the experience, rethinking what I could have done, rehashing it over and over, and all I want is to be able to think of something else, anything else, when my mind goes quiet...*

"Like I said, I haven't even told my wife about this. But I need to talk to God about it."

"He is listening through your prayers, my son. Your soul yearns for confession."

"I don't know who he was, or what he wanted, he never said a word, but... I signed up to be a soldier. For God. For my country. Worrying about it like this... It's not right. This kind of weakness is for other men.

"O my God, I am heartily sorry for having offended Thee, and I detest all my sins because of thy just punishments, but most of all because they offend Thee, my God, who art all good and deserving of all my love."

❂❂❂

Okie jumped up and spun, tensed to fight again.

Kirby regarded him, then his expression went serious and alarmed. He glanced around the pub. "Did something happen?"

There were too many ears to hear, and the way Okie's stomach was churning told him they were indeed listening. He shook his head.

"Let's have a seat," Kirby said.

Okie scanned the room for empty tables, and there were only a handful. All the others were occupied by pairs of men. No women, save the barmaid. Not entirely unusual, but something niggled at the back of his mind. They took a seat in about the center of the room, Kirby sitting with his back to the wall. Okie's gaze kept returning to the front door, expecting the *Polizei* to come charging in looking for him.

The barmaid brought them two full mugs of frothy lager ambrosia, and before she left, he ordered a couple of pickled sausages to quell the hunger he'd had until a few minutes ago. His mouth was still desert dry. He took a long pull. With his empty stomach, the strong German beer was going to smack him like Joe DiMaggio swinging for the upper deck.

The barmaid swayed back to her place behind the bar, and Kirby leaned in. "Whatever happened, don't tell me about it, but I'm guessing it relates to why I asked you here in the first place."

"Trying to get me killed?" Okie said, suddenly angry for reasons he couldn't pin down. Had Kirby set him up as a target? Could he trust anyone in this game?

"The opposite, actually," Kirby said. "But you're new in Berlin. There's a lot you don't know. Have you heard of this place before?" He gestured around him.

Okie shook his head again.

Kirby spoke slowly, carefully, choosing his words. "Berlin after dark is the Wild West. Look around. Tell me what you see."

Okie's training at Langley had taught him to look beneath the surface, peel back the obvious. Traveling around Europe had shown him that a person's nationality or ethnic heritage related to facial structure. America was a melting pot where ethnic lines were blurred, but Europe, less so. Germans looked like Germans, French people looked French, and so forth. There was no mistaking these faces. Among the faces gathered in Max und Marlene Bierhaus were aquiline British noses—not surprising, since this was a Western-controlled sector—German faces, and the stolid, blockish look of...two Slavic faces. He focused his ears on them and caught the unmistakable lilt of Russian.

"You see it, don't you," Kirby said.

Okie nodded.

Kirby made little indications with his head. "Those two over there are MI6. Those two are KGB. I suspect the barmaid is Stasi, but the jury's still out on that one."

Okie hissed, "What the hell have you gotten me into?"

"Relax, kid," Kirby said. "Those of us in the business have found it useful to have a place where we can...talk. It's a sort of gentlemen's agreement. Inside the pub is neutral territory. It's not an *open* secret, but if you spend any time in Berlin..." He shrugged and sipped his beer. Okie got the sense that Kirby was taking in the room at all times, and had deftly positioned himself to do so, using innocuous scanning techniques that Okie had learned in Langley, using his peripheral vision to remain constantly alert without appearing to be so. It was time to start using those skills, and part of that process was awareness of his own biases. He had written off the barmaid as one like any other, but when he started paying attention, he realized how skillfully she too was taking in the whole room. Indeed, everyone in the place was doing the same thing, except for the old man who appeared to be passed out forehead-down on the bar. But was it just a ruse? Could he be simply listening to everything around him?

As Okie concentrated, focusing his situational awareness, his heart rate evened out, and the jelly-like trembling in his limbs subsided. The table at which he and Kirby were seated was equidistant from the front door and a back door that led past the fireplace and presumably into the alley. The tables were thick, heavy wood that might stop a pistol bullet. A set of antlers above the mantel could be used as a weapon. So could the wrought iron poker. Or a nice, heavy beer mug for that matter, stout enough to crack a skull. He was surrounded by weapons, even beyond the fact that everyone in the place was likely to be packing.

Okie and Kirby drank their beers, playing a quiet game of observation. The *Polizei* never came, although he thought he heard a siren at one point. A few patrons came and went. Some of them joined other groups or dispersed. Once Okie knew what to look for, he couldn't look away. He felt like he was sitting at the edge of a chessboard, a piece waiting to be moved.

As closing time came, Kirby suggested they walk together until they reached a safer area, to which Okie happily agreed.

When he paid his tab, the lovely barmaid smiled and winked with a flicker of amusement.

Back in his hotel room, the events of the night played and replayed endlessly in his mind, plaguing him with questions and what ifs. The smell of the man's breath. The knife blade catching the light. The wet crunch of the man's ocular bone against the thrust of the icicle. Was his attacker man a mugger? An enemy agent? Had Okie been a planned target or a random encounter?

The lack of indication was what gnawed at him. He didn't know who his enemy was. The Russians and East Germans of course, but who knew for sure? He had to get comfortable with the uncertainty. There would no doubt be more times like this when there were things he just couldn't know. It was an uncertain world, and he and Honey were bringing a child into it. Soviet bombers could rain atomic fury onto Western Europe at a moment's notice.

He hadn't seen Honey in almost a week. She was just starting to show and would probably be sidelined soon by the airline. No one wanted to see a stewardess with a baby bump. She was going to chafe at that, but that was a woman's job, wasn't it? Chosen by God to bring the miracle of life into the world and nurture it. A sacred duty. Would Honey be a good mother? Would he be a good father? Or would he visit the same kind of horrors upon his children that

Emmett had? He prayed that he wouldn't, that the cycle would be broken, but part of him wondered if it was inevitable.

In the dark of the wee hours, he boarded a transport back to Bad Aibling, exhausted from the lack of sleep, and passed out against the fuselage, dreaming of Khrushchev coming at him with a knife. With ease he swatted the knife away and gleefully crushed the man's skull with his bare hands.

❁❁❁

It was February in Bad Aibling when a tall, athletic sergeant approached him in the cavernous hangar where Okie and Don did most of their translation work.

The sergeant introduced himself as Joe Olberding, and he had to be at least six foot five. "I hear you can play basketball."

"Where'd you hear that?" Okie asked, curious.

"Word gets around."

"I played in high school. I got a football scholarship to Holy Cross, couldn't do both."

"You're a college boy? What're you doing as an enlisted man?" He had a Midwestern accent with some elongated O's, Minnesota or North Dakota maybe.

"I guess I preferred to work for a living."

Olberding laughed. "You heard of Big Blue?"

"Yeah, does anyone not read *Stars and Stripes?*" The Army Security Agency basketball team made the newspaper all the time, nearly undefeated as they traveled around Europe playing other armed forces teams, but also teams from Italy, France, Holland, Germany, and elsewhere. "You recruiting?"

"We're recruiting. Tryouts are Saturday at Herzo."

Herzo Base was a military airfield near Nuremberg, seized by the U.S. Army during the war, now home to the Army Security Agency, the signals intelligence branch of the Army, under which Okie and Don ostensibly worked. How many of his colleagues were also CIA was a subject of speculation. Besides intelligence gathering, it was also responsible for electronic countermeasures and securing Army communications. Its unofficial slogan was, "In God we trust. All others, we monitor." Okie considered himself luckier than those poor slobs stuck listening to Morse code for eight or nine hours a day. He'd heard them say they went to sleep with their heads full of *dash-dot-dash-dot*.

Nuremberg was a bit of a trek, about two hundred kilometers north, but playing organized basketball again sounded like a lot of fun. He'd get to see a lot more of Europe and the leave time that came along with traveling would relieve some of his daily tedium.

The ASA Big Blue was one of those programs meant to spread peace, goodwill, and American values around a continent that was still bombed out in many areas. It was a morale booster for the troops as well. The unrelenting tension with the Soviets took its toll on the men doing the work. There were so many minor "incidents" about which the American public was blissfully unaware that everyone felt like war could erupt at any moment.

Okie looked squarely into Olberding's gray eyes and said, "I'll be there."

❁❁❁

The jealousy in Honey's face was plain when he told her about it. She had been grounded by TWA three weeks ago, and it galled her, even though she tried to put on a brave, "happy expectant mother" face. She'd taken up crochet with some other Army wives and was working diligently on baby clothes, even though she'd scrapped several early efforts. The related subjects of nurseries and cribs and new paint for their flat kept coming up. For a couple of weeks, he and Don had been working in their off-hours to repair the Christmas-tree hole in the floor and ceiling between their flats.

Honey's weird nesting behavior was made more bearable by an unexpected surge in her libido. He initially questioned making love while she was pregnant, but the Army doctor in Munich assured him it was fine. They were having more relations now than their first weeks of courtship.

She pouted about the basketball for a good long time, then finally said, "I suppose it's just like more Company business. It's not like you can ever tell me where you're going anyway." Then she kissed him and said, "Just make sure to bring me presents."

His tryout at Herzo Base near Nuremberg went well, and they invited him onto the team the same day. With a couple of weeks of practice, he'd be up to speed and ready to play the upcoming tournament in Brussels.

The ASA Big Blue team was a mix of officers, all of whom had played college ball, and enlisted men like Okie, who had experience and a talent for it, or else stood as tall as a Dutch windmill. The coach was a hard-charging captain by the name of Jerry

Choate, a West Point graduate with a blue-blooded Boston accent and a Matterhorn-sized stick up his ass. Nevertheless, Okie found himself having a great time playing basketball again. His skills were undiminished, and it was a different experience playing with grown men rather than high school ball. They were tougher, stronger, and his teammates were all ASA soldiers, which brought with it its own brand of esprit-de-corps that he found himself enjoying tremendously. Outside of foreign earshot, they jokingly called themselves "spooks and spies." Some of them had above-top-secret security clearance.

The United States' anti-Communist propaganda machine was full steam ahead, striving to prove the superiority of Western civilization. The government hoped that showcasing American culture worldwide would win ideological allies in the Cold War, and they had enlisted sports and several of the arts as weapons in this struggle. The Brubeck Quartet was touring Europe, and there was even talk that it would visit Poland, taking American jazz right to Khrushchev's doorstep. For several years, the State Department—and quietly, the CIA—had been funding modern artists like Jackson Pollock. Modern art in particular represented the liberalism, individualism, dynamic activity, and creative risk possible in a free society, even as the Soviets decried the United States as a "culturally barren, capitalist wasteland."

Big Blue finished the tournament in Brussels undefeated, having beaten teams from all over Western Europe. Honey was happy to accompany him to Nuremberg for practice days, enjoying the chance to get out of Bad Aibling, which was a small, parochial town. Now that she was grounded, her only social circle was other

Army wives, which she found less invigorating than jetting back and forth across the Atlantic. Meanwhile, her belly swelled along with the amplitude of her mood swings.

He did his best to help her, but there were days when she simply would not be consoled at the "blimp" she was becoming. The daggers her eyes occasionally shot at him for having done this to her were best avoided with more work and basketball.

On some basketball trips, he would have to steal away to serve as a courier or contact point for foreign nationals sneaking back and forth behind the Iron Curtain. The basketball team was the perfect pretense for some very unsportsmanlike activities. And he was certain he wasn't the only member of the team who stole away for extracurricular activities. No one asked, and no one told. Compartmentalized information was how they all protected one another. That was the nature of the game.

April in Bavaria was simply stunning. Crisp air and crystal-clear skies brought the snow-capped Alps into breathtaking relief, and there were days when Okie felt the presence of God in the sheer spectacle. The lush countryside awakened with spring, a multitude of greens re-emerging from winter slumber. It was the kind of beauty he wished he had the ability to paint.

His work on the Monuments Men project, coupled with basketball travels, gave him the opportunity to visit several art museums around Europe. Since Donovan had tasked him with recovering the lost Raphael painting, along with whatever other lost objects he could find, it behooved him to learn more about fine art. He could often find an hour or two before or after a game or an intelligence operation to visit the world's most renowned artworks. In them, especially in the religious art, he sometimes sensed God's hand guiding the artist with divine inspiration, like the words of the Holy Bible itself. Not all of it, but some of it was evidence of God's majesty, like the Alps in spring.

Okie and Don were working late-night shifts as rain drummed the metal roof of their hangar in Bad Aibling. It was about 0215 when a cry rose from the NSA guy's office, echoing through the cavernous space. "Well, the bastards finally found it!"

From their adjacent desks, Okie and Don looked at each other. The NSA guy's primary task was working with intelligence gleaned from the Berlin Tunnel. The murmuring buzz of speculation went around the room.

"Did everybody get out okay?" someone yelled back.

CIA agents and ASA soldiers had manned the tunnel continuously for the last eleven months, along with their British counterparts, sifting through thousands of tapped telephone conversations and teleprinter signals passing through the East German sector. Okie didn't know anyone personally who worked in the tunnel, but there were people in Bad Aibling who did.

The question hung in the air, unanswered, and eventually the murmurs and work resumed. Either they would be told what happened, or they wouldn't. That was the way of things.

Hours later, as the sun was coming up, they received a briefing that American agents at a nearby observation post had seen forty to fifty East Germans excavating directly above the tunnel and that

Soviet officers were now on the scene. Fortunately, all American personnel had been evacuated in plenty of time, having destroyed everything behind them.

"I guess that means we'll be looking for a job," Okie said to Don.

"Oh, don't worry, there's plenty of work to go around," said Lieutenant Atkinson, Okie's ostensible CO as he approached the desks where they worked. "Follow me, Hansen."

Okie followed the lieutenant into Captain Harris's office, which had a door. Lieutenant Atkinson ushered him inside, then closed the door behind them.

Okie stood at attention before Captain Harris, who looked up from behind his desk, a man who was bookish for the Army, with thick-rimmed square glasses that magnified his penetrating stare. Harris hadn't been happy to discover he was sharing two of his men with other operations, but there was little he could do about it. Eventually he had seemed to warm to the idea. Since he seemed to have sufficient security clearance, he got whiffs of the things Okie and Don were doing. He also knew that Okie had significant special training that went somewhat beyond what the Army had given him.

They saluted each other.

"At ease," Captain Harris said. Then he turned to Lieutenant Atkinson, a man about Okie's age. "Lieutenant, you may go."

The lieutenant saluted, turned, and departed.

Captain Harris pushed a manila envelope across the desk. "You heard about Berlin."

"Yes, sir," Okie said.

"The Russkies are having a field day. It's a propaganda frenzy, and we have to let them have it. We cleaned house before they got in—heard them coming—so they're not getting anything important." Harris spoke with a Maine lilt to his vowels. "But we're not going to let them have it all for free. One of the last messages we decoded mentioned that their clean-up operation would have sniper cover. A little payback is in order. A black eye, so to speak. Pack your counter-sniper gear. There's a plane fueling up to take you to Berlin."

XX

*"**BLESS ME, FATHER**, for I have sinned. It's been three weeks since my last confession, and I... I don't know what to do. I've been doing a lot of traveling, all over the world, and I feel evil all around me. The world is being swallowed up by the Devil, and he's using godless communism as a tool. So many evil bastards running loose, and all of them worthy only of death. Some of them a long, painful, excruciating demise."*

"It is for the Lord to judge such things, not you. You must—"

"But sometimes it's my job to judge such things! I've dealt with Nazi war criminals, common thugs, and Communist revolutionaries. Do I let this person live or die? I follow orders, and some of them... I've done...questionable things. Things normal people back home wouldn't believe."

"With penitence in your heart, the Lord will forgive you. You must open your heart to him. The Lord put you on this path, my son. And if your heart remains pure—"

"How can anything remain pure in this world? I think about the things my daughter will have to live with, and it just makes me sick. I need to keep secrets from my family to protect them. It feels like all the good things in the world are being swallowed up by this juggernaut and I can't stop it."

On the plane to Berlin, Okie studied the contents of the envelope he'd been given, which contained dossiers on several East German and Soviet snipers, including known and likely kills, personal histories, and favorite tactics.

In the back seat with him, concealed in a specially modified cello case, was his Springfield M1903, a bolt-action .30-06 model that had been in service for over fifty years. The Army and Marine Corps had moved on to the semi-automatic M1 Garand, like the ones he'd first learned to shoot at Holy Cross, but snipers still prized the Springfield's accuracy. It had fought two world wars, after all. This was the same rifle he'd been assigned at sniper training in Virginia, and it had been fitted with a cutting-edge, experimental scope, nitrogen-filled to prevent fogging, adjustable up to x15.2 magnification, handmade by a Swiss watchmaker-turned-optics-master. Okie had fired thousands of rounds through this weapon, both suppressed and unsuppressed, and knew how to compensate for the suppressor's presence. Initially, he had thought the suppressor would reduce muzzle velocity and thus, effective range, but that was not the case. He preferred using the suppressor to minimize announcement of his presence. He'd made "kills" reliably at 1,300 yards. Someday perhaps the armed and clandestine services would have more developed sniper training programs, but his had amounted to long-range target shooting under the personal guidance of master marksmen from World War II and Korea, mixed with ad hoc fieldcraft.

After their meeting at Max und Marlene Bierhaus, Kirby had taken him under his wing to teach him some urban tradecraft on the streets of Berlin. Today would be his first attempt to utilize those skills on his own. He was going into the field to face an unknown number of enemy snipers in an unofficial war. If something happened to him, Honey would have to raise their unborn child alone, and she would likely never know the truth of his demise.

The plane landed in Berlin before many people were having breakfast on this Sunday morning. The first thing he did when he hit the ground was check the current weather report and compare it to the location where he'd been assigned to create his sniper nest, a room on the top floor of an apartment block in the American sector, one with a clear view of the tunnel excavation site eight hundred yards away in the Soviet sector. The Company had been using the room to surveil the area with telescopes for months. A warmth-sucking drizzle fell from a gray sky, expected to continue intermittently all day. Wind northeast at ten knots, expected to remain consistent throughout the day. Welcome to spring in Berlin.

The thudding of his heart came and went, growing stronger as the "taxi" drove him to the location. The driver was a Company asset whom Okie would never see again. Nevertheless, he tried to appear nonchalant in his civilian attire, carrying his deadly cello case. He felt like a gangster on his way to a hit. The knowledge that he'd be facing trained snipers lodged a chill sliver in his heart. Soviet marksmen, even women, had been renowned since the war, when they'd fended off the Nazis in the Battle of Stalingrad. Their Mosin-Nagant rifles were easily equivalent to the Spring M1903, and some said, superior.

Would he ever see Honey again? Would he ever see his child's face?

No. Not helpful. That way lay madness and death.

Focus on the mission.

When the car eased to a stop outside the apartment block, he wrestled the cello case out with him. It was a new building, utilitarian and devoid of character, doubtless replacing the bombed-out destruction of the war. Then he walked on leaden legs toward the lift.

He emerged on the ninth floor and walked down the hallway toward the corner flat with a window that looked straight down the thoroughfare toward the Soviet sector. He knocked on the door with the prearranged cadence.

"Who's there?" said a familiar voice in German.

"Wilhelm Schwartzkopf."

The door opened to reveal Kirby, binoculars dangling from one hand. Pleased surprise registered on his face. "So they sent you."

"They sent me," Okie said, stepping inside. He surveyed the unlit room. Cot, table, two chairs, spartan kitchenette. On the table, set back about six feet from the window rested a powerful telescope on a tripod.

"Ready for your audition, I see," Kirby said.

"I think we're past the audition stage," Okie said, laying down his cello case. "What are they up to?"

"Digging like angry gophers."

"Russians?"

"Some, including Colonel Nikolai Gusev, KGB Signals Regiment. He comes and goes."

"Alas, he's not going to be the target today. I'm hunting snipers only, something to keep them guessing. Spot any?"

"Nothing yet, but it's only been daylight for an hour."

Okie unsnapped the clamshell case, then lifted the velvet-lined false bottom to reveal the sniper rifle.

Kirby returned to the window. "There are, however, a few likely spots. I've been watching them, but no sign of occupancy just yet."

In the dim light, Okie withdrew the rifle from its nest of silk and velvet, checked the action, and screwed on the suppressor. Its weight changed the rifle's balance, making it somewhat front-heavy, but the bipod eliminated that drawback.

"Gonna need your table," Okie said.

Kirby took down the telescope, allowing room for Okie to rest the rifle there. He would leave the window closed until he was ready to take a shot. Enemy snipers would be trained to look for sight anomalies, an incongruous spot of color, anything out of place, like open windows on a chilly day like this—or the glint of a lens.

"A little before 0100 hours," Kirby said, "several groups started digging along the east side of Schöenefelder Allee, maybe forty or fifty men at three-foot intervals, right above the wire-tap chamber."

"Did they know it was there?"

"Unknown."

"You been here all night?"

"Going on eighteen hours."

"Where's your relief?"

Kirby shrugged. "Unknown." He tried to sound blasé about it, but didn't quite succeed, considering one of their people would now be considered *missing.* "A little after 0200, they broke into the tap chamber. Then a Soviet captain showed up. An hour later, Colonel Gusev. Have you heard any tapes from the tap chamber mic?"

Okie shook his head and settled himself behind the Springfield and removed the lens caps. Then he bent over and peered through the eyepiece. "The biggest question in my mind is, did they, in fact, know what they were digging for? Or was this an accident?"

"There have been faults on several connecting phone lines for about a month. A couple of them are direct lines to high-ranking Soviet officers. Everything is as old as sin. Some of those lines could be original telegraph wires. We've been dodging East German Post and Telegraph technicians for two weeks. They *could* have been just looking for the junction."

"You don't sound convinced."

Kirby shrugged again. "Time will tell."

Okie slid a five-round clip down into the magazine and chambered a round. Then he settled behind his eyepiece and began to scan the area until he could bring into focus the bustling activity of East German soldiers around the excavation machines chewing up pavement and earth. At this range, he could see their faces clearly. The street had been cordoned off in all directions, with nary a civilian in sight. Among the East German uniforms, he spotted Soviets as well. It did indeed resemble a hornets' nest.

He spent several minutes methodically familiarizing himself with the limits of his sight picture, the field of view he had available through the apartment window, adjusting his placement by fractions of an inch, fractions of a degree. The area around the excavations was wide open, giving him a beautiful field of fire—if his possible targets were near the excavations. But they weren't. Shooting Soviet KGB in broad daylight would be an act of war. Covert snipers, on the other hand... Any enemy snipers would most likely be deployed several hundred yards beyond the excavation. The wide-open space was one reason this location had been chosen for the tunnel. Traffic noise would muffle the sounds of excavation, complete with the placement of steel support beams to hold up under the passage of Soviet tanks on the road above. There was no structure near the tap chamber to house someone who might otherwise overhear.

Once he had memorized the view, he superimposed an imaginary map of the weather. The wind was significant at 9-10 knots, but nearly parallel to any shot he might take. Then he began a methodical scan for any sight anomalies that might indicate an enemy sniper position—anything out of place. The glint of a lens or gun barrel, a head-and-shoulders silhouette, an open window where none should be.

He and Kirby settled into silence, eyes attached to eyepieces.

This was the hard part. Remaining still for hours at a time in awkward physical positions was incredibly difficult. His neck knotted up. His eyes burned. The rifle stock grew warm against his cheek. His back ached. Parts of him fell asleep until he massaged them awake again, but his eye remained behind the eyepiece. The human eye naturally scanned top-down, left-to-right, but one of his instructors, a leathery Marine recon gunnery sergeant and veteran of Iwo Jima had taught him to do it in the opposite direction, right-to-left, low-to-high. "You'll see things," Sergeant Spitz had said.

Kirby had rightfully identified four potential sniper nests a few hundred yards beyond the excavation, but Okie soon spotted six more, some of them hidden by the natural landscape, others by buildings. Height was always an advantage in the sniper game, but for that simple reason, ground-based locations must not be overlooked. It was too easy to focus on crow's nests and roofs and water towers, when a counter-sniper could easily be drawing a reticle onto your forehead from a basement window.

His mouth was so dry he couldn't speak, but at least he'd managed to rein in his galloping heartbeat. Now it was simply a game of cat and mouse—but with the most lethal of consequences. Patience was a sniper's greatest weapon, more important even than his choice of killing instrument.

It was three in the afternoon when he caught an out-of-place glint in the corner of his sight picture.

On the roof of an apartment block almost as tall as this one stood a ramshackle chicken coop. Within the chicken coop, set about two yards back from the coop's wire-mesh front, was a plywood partition that looked a little too clean, a little too new. In the middle of the partition, a horizontal slit, just tall and wide enough to accommodate a rifle and offer sufficient field of view to someone behind it. At this range, just under a mile, the slit looked thinner than a human hair.

It had not been there an hour ago.

"Possible target," Okie murmured.

Kirby perked up like he'd been stabbed with a cattle prod, but he made no sudden movements, which might draw the enemy sniper's attention.

Okie made some mental calculations based on the perceived height of the chicken coop, the magnification of his scope and the marks on his reticle. "Range, sixteen fifty. Chicken coop on the roof of the third apartment block from the north." He didn't take his eye from the slit—the firing port.

Kirby peered through his telescope, which was x42 magnification. "Got it."

Okie described the firing port. "Got anything behind that?"

Kirby didn't answer, adjusting the telescope with a feather-light touch. "Bingo. We have a gun barrel."

"Dimension of the firing port?"

After a pause to extrapolate from nearby features, Kirby said, "Approximately sixteen inches by eight inches."

With those dimensions, Okie could calculate how to adjust his shot. He would have to shoot *through* the plywood, extrapolating the shooter's location.

He could see the dull gleam of the gun barrel's tip now, a smudged pinpoint. Impossible to say whether it was pointed at him yet. But he had no doubt it soon would be. Time was running out. He had to take the shot and get under cover. His mission's rules of engagement had told him to engage any sniper he deemed a threat. Perfectly vague—and perfectly actionable.

The suppressor would keep the sound to around the level of a pneumatic hose coupler releasing, including the sonic boom of the round as it exited the barrel. It would travel faster than sound to its target. Whether it hit or missed, no one on the ground would know it had passed overhead.

Focusing his attention on the firing port, he imagined the position of the sniper behind it, the location of his head.

"Taking the shot." He would only get one. If he missed, he would immediately become a target himself. Then it would be a matter of time. Would the shooter pack up and take cover or would he immediately go on the offensive?

He slowed his breathing, thumbed off the safety mechanism on the rear of the bolt, and slid his finger into the trigger guard, never once shifting the reticle from his target. He imagined the shooter's body inside the chicken coop's interior space, imagined his head behind the scope, adjusted for gravitational bullet-drop, then windage. Then he adjusted again for the Coriolis effect, the rotation of the Earth, which at this latitude and bearing from the target meant the target would drop and shift to the right to meet the descending bullet between the time it left the barrel and the time it arrived at the target. The point of impact would deflect high and to the right by a few inches.

The trigger of his Springfield had been modified to a hair-trigger. All it took was the lightest of squeezes, less than a pound of force.

And then...

The rifle bucked. He held the scope's sight picture on his target. He would be too far away to see a bullet hole in the wood.

One second. Two…

The muzzle of a rifle barrel slid abruptly two inches farther into view, as if bumped.

Peering through the telescope, Kirby said, "Shooter down."

And then Okie could breathe again.

❁❁❁

That night, on the plane back to Bad Aibling, his cello case resting beside him against the fuselage of the Air Force transport, Okie's elation at that incredible shot began to diminish under the pressure of exhaustion and...something else. His eyes felt full of sand.

The moment his eyes would slide shut, begging for sleep, the image of the enemy sniper's rifle barrel sagging would kick into his mind with the sensation of a rifle stock against his shoulder.

He had ended a man's life. Unlike the man he'd killed with an icicle, up close and personal, Okie hadn't even seen his target. But his instincts told him the shot had been a success. He and Kirby had watched the protruding rifle barrel for over two hours, and it hadn't moved.

Who was he? An East German soldier? A Soviet spy? Did he have a wife? A child? Parents who loved him? He shook off such thoughts.

With a slightly varied confluence of circumstances, it might have been the enemy sniper who spotted Okie first, or Kirby. Would he have taken the shot? What had his orders been? Okie's had been to send a message. He had done that. No one who had heard the shot would likely recognize what it was. The dead sniper would not have heard the shot at all. One moment, alive, peering through his scope, oblivious to the approach of a supersonic projectile, and the next—taking the elevator to hell. Like all godless Commies. One less of them made the world a better place, after all.

But if he was so sure it had been a righteous kill, why couldn't he sleep?

XXI

"BLESS ME, FATHER, *for I have sinned. It's been two days since my last confession. I'm having second thoughts about fatherhood."*

"The Lord tells us to be fruitful and multiply. Anything else is selfishness."

"Yes, Father. But Mary was such a difficult baby. My wife doesn't want to go through that again, and I…don't blame her. But, I want a son. Someone to carry on the family name. Someone to remove the stains."

"What stains?"

"My father's. And…mine."

"Your father's sins are not yours to bear. And yours have been washed away by your confession."

"I…don't know. But regardless, having another child would be difficult."

"People have been raising more than one child for a very long time."

"No, I mean…conceiving another child."

"Is everything all right between you and your wife? She should submit to your wishes."

July in Venice was a sweltering sweat bomb, at least indoors on basketball courts, where sea breezes couldn't reach. Okie was in Venice with Big Blue to play against the Italian national team, when an urgent message from Don arrived in the locker room at halftime.

Still sheened in sweat from a vigorous first half, he read the message over again and felt the earth shift under his feet.

At the quizzical glare from Captain Choate, Okie replied, "It's my wife. She's at the hospital in Munich. She just had a baby. A little girl."

A cheer went up around the locker room, along with lamentations about the dearth of celebratory cigars.

The message made no mention about whether Honey was okay, but after a moment of worry, he settled himself with the knowledge that were she not, Don would have told him as much. He spared a moment to pray for her and thank the Almighty.

"Fellas," he said, still not quite believing it, "I'm a father."

There was much slapping on the back, and when he returned to the court, his feet had grown wings. He scored sixteen more points, for a total of twenty-three, and led the team in rebounds with ten offensive boards.

They had another game in Florence in a couple of days, but Captain Choate sent him on the next flight to Munich.

When he arrived at the Army Hospital in Munich at three in the morning, he rushed through the halls frantically searching for the maternity ward. At this time of night, he'd had no opportunity to secure flowers or any other gifts for Honey.

He found Honey's room first and rushed to her side. She looked exhausted, so disheveled he hardly recognized her.

He couldn't remember what he said as she opened her eyes except, "I'm here." And she hugged him and kissed him and said with a half-teasing smile, "You're lucky you weren't here, buster. You might not have survived it."

"Where is she?"

A passing nurse noticed his presence, and she came in to ask if he'd like to see the baby.

"Now that's a dumb question!" he said.

Honey swung her legs out of bed, moving gingerly, her face pale. "We'll go together."

"Want me to carry you?" he said.

She shook her head, but gripped his arm. They baby-stepped toward the maternity ward, as Honey half-dazedly related how the labor had come upon her, and Don and Lois had brought her to Munich. She'd sent them back to their hotel room.

The nurse finally ushered them into the room where only a single crib was occupied. His heart was hammering his ribs like a bass drum, and he found himself giggling like a schoolboy. The nurse scooped the swaddled bundle out of the bed with an indulgent smile.

"She's a gorgeous little thing," she said as she put the infant in Okie's arms.

Staring down into her little red face with her thick swatch of dark hair, he felt a moment of vertigo. As her azure eyes peeked open and closed again, her little fingers brushing her cheek, his first thought was *She doesn't look like me at all.*

Echoes of Honey were evident, but Okie saw nothing of himself. Then that moment of startled dismay passed in a wave of gratitude. "Let's call her Mary, after my mother."

Honey sighed and leaned her head against him. "That's a good name." She brushed Mary's cheek with her finger. "Hello, Mary. This is your daddy." She glanced at Okie—with a flicker of strange apprehension—then covered it with a teary smile.

❁❁❁

A few weeks later, when it came time to finally go home after a long workday, Okie said to Don, "How about lunch at the *schloss*?" Meaning Schloss Maxlrain, the bierhaus castle a few kilometers north of Bad Aibling. "I could go for a beer and sausages."

"What's the matter, afraid to go home?" Don said with a smirk, but the look on Okie's face must have told him his remark had hit too close to the mark. The mischievous grin faded. In the upstairs flat, he and Lois had no doubt heard a great many of Mary's endless crying jags. Okie's experience with the term "colicky baby" had reached beleaguered depths. All was not well in the Hansen household.

"All right," Don said, "let's go. Lois is over the Atlantic right now anyway."

So, over beer, bratwurst and apple strudel, Okie vented. He hadn't planned to, but once he got going, it all seemed to pick up speed with the telling. Honey was drinking a lot, constantly complaining about how she'd been grounded and couldn't wait to get back in the air. When Okie asked her who would take care of Mary, she answered with a venomous, "a fucking nanny, how about that?" Okie wasn't opposed to getting a nanny if it would keep Honey happy, but they couldn't afford it until Honey was back in the air, so it was a catch-22. He worried about her health, because her hair and eyes had lost their luster. She had bags under her eyes most of the time, which was no wonder, given how little sleep they were both getting. Okie was able to spell her a little, as he worked overnight shifts lately, giving her a chance to sleep during the day. It seemed their entire lives had shrunk to the size of an infant, and the very idea inflamed Honey so profoundly, growing into an issue so fraught with resentment that neither of them dared to bring it up. What was worse, Okie could feel her resentment growing with every trip he took without her, every mission, every basketball game. He had stopped asking her to come along. Neither of them could endure the shame of an inconsolable infant in public. The last time they had tried to go out to dinner as a family on a Sunday afternoon in Munich after a post-natal check-up, Mary had launched into a wailing fit that lasted two solid hours, and by the time they got home, Honey all but collapsed with weeping. As soon as they got off the train, Mary fell silent as if flipping off a light switch, fast asleep. Okie couldn't envision any further family outings anytime soon, and it saddened him. He and Honey hadn't had relations in two months, and the previous time hadn't been good for either of them. Honey had lain there stiff as a board, looking at the wall the whole time.

When he asked her what was wrong, she said with the iciness unique to women, "Just doing my duty, husband."

This infuriated him to the point he got dressed and went for a walk in the middle of the night. At least Bad Aibling wasn't Berlin;

he was somewhat less likely to find himself at knife point in a dark alley.

Don provided a sympathetic ear, and had little advice to offer except, "Hang in there. People have been having babies for a very long time. All this has to pass."

"When I hear a baby crying in public, it makes me want to break something."

"She'll grow out of it. She's healthy otherwise, right?"

"The doctor says so."

"Like Churchill said, 'When you're going through hell, keep going.'"

He prayed for strength for himself and Honey, and for his daughter to simply shut the hell up for a while.

❂❂❂

In August, Honey finally got a call, and Okie hadn't seen her so happy in months. "Oh, my God, I hope I can still fit in my uniform!"

Okie was pretty sure she'd been wearing it around the house occasionally when he wasn't home. Two months after Mary was born, Honey's body had returned to its former glory, plus a little extra curvature.

"It's too goddamn tight in the chest!" she complained. She had recently decided to wean the child. That decision fell into the amorphous mystery realm of Women Things, which excluded him with profound force. But the decision hadn't done any favors for Mary's colicky disposition or increased the number of hours of sleep anyone could get at a stretch.

"Stop cursing around the baby," he said reflexively, prompting her to flash him an angry look.

"Why do you care? You were off playing fucking basketball!" It came out of her like a slap to the face, and the hatred in her eyes was like a punch in the gut.

His own anger flared in response, but he bit down on a defensive retort. His fists clenched. If she'd been a man, he'd have punched her across the room. He kept his voice as even as he could. "Don't you have a plane to catch?"

"Tell me I'm beautiful," she growled like a lioness about to pounce, "or so help me—"

"Well, of course you are!" he sputtered, and it was true. She looked as fabulous as ever, maybe more so with her eyes flashing with fire.

"Make me believe you!" she snapped.

His mouth worked but nothing came out.

Finally, she just scoffed, grabbed her suitcase, and stormed out. "See you next week." She paused, hand on the door. "Maybe." Then she slammed it behind her.

XXII

"PERDÓNEME PADRE PORQUE he pecado. Han pasado tres días desde mi última confesión. *Please pardon my Spanish, Father. I have only been in your country a few days."*

"Proceed, my son. Your Spanish is very Castilian."

"I have been unfaithful to my wife, in my heart. I gave in to lust for a moment. I was...traveling to meet some men. A business trip, you might say. And there was a woman there, a waitress. I've seldom seen a woman more beautiful than my wife, but this one... It was her eyes. They were the eyes of a succubus. I couldn't get away from them. I think she was a jinetera. *She came to me and... I was drunk... I let her... I wanted to do more."*

"Do you repent your sin, my son?"

"Por estos y todos los pecados de mi pasado yo me arrepiento ante ti, oh Señor Jesucristo."

The entrance to Spandau Prison looked like a miniature medieval castle of red brick, complete with crenelations, two cylindrical towers flanking an imposing front gate of heavy, iron-bound wood. Beyond this gatehouse lay the four-story prison blocks and attendant grounds.

Okie waited at the gate to the outer fence, smoking a Lucky Strike and pondering the fact that this was a lot of prison for only five inmates. Even so, it could never be large enough to contain the atrocities these men had enacted or endorsed. These were the five most infamous prison inmates in the world—the last of the Nuremberg war criminals. After today only four would remain within: Walther Funk, Albert Speer, Baldur von Schirach, and Rudolf Hess.

It was a crisp afternoon on the last day of September, skies hanging leaden gray.

Okie eyed the Soviet guards at the wooden gate, and they eyed him back. They no doubt knew who he was here for. He memorized their faces in case he encountered them at Max und Marlene Bierhaus or elsewhere in West Berlin.

It was the Soviets' turn in the rotation of guards administering Spandau Prison. Since the war, it had been conscripted by the Four Powers to house Nazi war criminals, and American, British, French, and Soviet guards rotated through on a monthly basis. Because the prison was situated in the former British sector of West Berlin, the Soviets had vociferously demanded to keep their place in its administration. Everyone in the intelligence services suspected it had become a toehold for the KGB in West Berlin.

Okie's gut roiled at what he'd been ordered to do. His fists clenched in his pockets. He took deep breaths and focused on taking in every detail.

The bleakness of the prison's imposing edifice chilled him. The smokestack of the incinerator, visible from where he stood, hearkened to thoughts of how many Jewish bodies and souls had gone up just such a cylinder. Built by the Prussian Army as a military prison in the 1870s, Spandau Prison had been used by the Nazis as a proto-concentration camp before the war.

Nevertheless, orders were orders. He didn't have to like them, but he had to trust that there was a plan in place. Just as God suffered such men as Adolf Hitler, Josef Stalin, and their fellow mass murderers to exist. There had to be a plan. There *had* to be.

Was the man he was waiting for the worst of them? That question was like having a popularity contest among the Lords of Hell.

Karl Dönitz was the only man besides Adolf Hitler himself to bear the title of Führer. Before his death, Hitler had anointed Grand Admiral Karl Dönitz, commander of the German U-boat fleet, as his chosen successor. After Hitler's death, Dönitz assumed the office and held power for twenty-three days, until he finally surrendered to the Allies. A number of American Admirals, Chester Nimitz chief among them, had appealed to the Nuremberg tribunal for leniency, arguing that Dönitz was simply a brilliant, honorable officer doing his duty during wartime. Dönitz repeatedly asserted no knowledge of Hitler's Final Solution of the Jewish Question.

No doubt Donovan had thoughts on this if Okie ever had the opportunity to inquire about it. Wild Bill's health was failing, Okie had heard, and he was falling into semi-retirement from his intelligence roles.

But the fact that Okie was here, ten years later to the day, made him wonder how much Donovan had been involved with the fact that Dönitz had not been sentenced to execution then, like so many of the others. Had Donovan been playing a long chess game?

Photographers and reporters from the Western press clustered outside the prison fence. He kept his back to them, innocuously hugging the wall of the cobbled courtyard.

Then, unceremoniously, one of the heavy double-doors opened, and a man stepped outside. He paused and looked up at the steel-gray sky. An old man with receding, steel-gray hair, dressed in a tailored, well-pressed, gray suit, coat draped over one arm. He placed a fedora atop his head.

The Soviet guards rolled back the outer gate of painted iron bars to admit a black limousine, which rolled onto the cobbles and stopped about twenty paces from where Okie stood. Karl Dönitz, the Last Führer, crossed the courtyard toward the limousine.

Okie intercepted him at the car door.

Dönitz spotted him coming, and his eyes narrowed. He was a thin man with an expansive forehead, prominent nose, but it was his eyes that caught Okie's gaze. They were the eyes of a lizard, but far more calculating, bereft of humanity or compassion. He was said to be a brilliant strategist and naval tactician, architect of the German Navy's U-boat predation on Allied shipping. But now he was an old man. What had ten years in this place done to him? Had it softened his Nazi beliefs?

"Good day, Herr Dönitz," Okie said in German with a little bow of greeting. The first job of any handler was to develop and build rapport with his subject, no matter how distasteful. *"Welcome back into the world."*

Dönitz returned the bow perfunctorily. *"You are my...American benefactor?"*

Okie handed him a business card, which bore only a Berlin phone number and mailing address. *"Frederich Branding, at your service."*

Dönitz laughed derisively but accepted the card and pocketed it. *"Are you not a bit young to be CIA?"*

Okie ignored the jab. "Your wife is waiting for you at the apartment we arranged for you." He opened the limousine door. "I'll be in touch."

"I should hope so." The Last Führer straightened his coat, eyes like razors of anticipation. "There remains much work to be done."

Weeks later, autumn had descended on Berlin, leaving the trees looking like gnarled black claws reaching into the moonlit sky. Okie tapped the driver on the shoulder and pointed through the partially fogged windscreen. "That car. The blue Volkswagen Beetle."

The pale-gray front of the Deutsches Theater gleamed in footlights, as the cream of Berlin's culturati spilled from the open doors in long coats and long gloves, gowns and gold, pearls and pompadours. Cars and taxis came and went.

A few car lengths ahead, the owner of a West German import company, a portly, fiftyish man with porkchop sideburns and a shiny pate, held the passenger door open for a buxom blonde-from-a-bottle, who minced on high heels from curb to car. Hans Schneider, owner of Dunkler Adler Importunernehmen, ostensibly a buyer of American and British arms.

Even from this distance, Okie recognized the woman from her photo in the dossier. Yelena Solovyova. KGB honey pot. Ostensibly Herr Schneider's secretary. Yet another middle-aged businessman fucking his secretary. Except that this secretary was funneling intelligence back to the KGB. Herr Schneider's contacts among the occupation forces and local industry were extensive. He was practically a German version of Emmett. He'd managed to get through the war distributing munitions to the Wehrmacht, in spite of some Jewish ties deep in the woodpile. Various operatives had been investigating his background and activities for some time, and now the final solution had fallen to Okie.

Herr Schneider climbed in the driver's side and started the engine. In silhouette through the tiny rear window, Okie saw her lean close to kiss him. He could see the man shudder with pleasure at the touch of her ruby-red lips.

No doubt they were off to the next leg of their illicit liaison. Bold of Herr Schneider to parade his mistress in public, but his wife and family in Geneva were far away.

As the Beetle pulled out into the traffic of Schumannstrasse, Okie's driver put the "taxi" in gear and pulled out a few car lengths behind the Beetle.

The Beetle wended its way through the streets, while he considered Yelena Solovyova. She was as alluring in person as her photo had suggested. Magnificent lips, voluptuous curves, strong, cleft chin, and dark, smoky eyes. The epitome of the "honey pot" spy, a female spy whose chief assets were her feminine charms and willingness to use them to gather intelligence or subvert her target's loyalties. Had Honey ever used her charms like Yelena Solovyova?

Hell, she'd used her charms on *him*. Initially, *he* had been a mission. But that was different, and he couldn't let his mind wander too far down that road.

At this time of night, traffic was light, and they were able to follow the car easily. Recognizing where the Beetle was likely headed, Okie told his driver to hang back a little farther. And then, as expected, the Beetle's headlights went out as it pulled into a secluded park.

Okie's driver had been on operations like this before. He knew the drill. He drove past the parked Beetle, giving Okie the chance to ascertain that its occupants were already rounding first base and heading for second. A block away, the driver rounded a corner and stopped, releasing Okie into the shadows.

Okie circled the Beetle at a wide berth, letting the darkness cling to him, then cut through the park's green spaces to approach the car from the rear.

On this chilly night in late October, the windows were fogged. The car was rocking rhythmically, and the woman's cries of passion were as clear as they were overdone. She urged her mark on with throaty moans.

The Ruger .22 semi-automatic weighed down Okie's peacoat. He'd had the coat's interior pocket strengthened and modified to be six inches deeper to accommodate the suppressed pistol. Superficially the Ruger resembled the infamous German Luger, but this model was introduced by Sturm, Ruger & Co., a Connecticut-based arms manufacturer, after the war. It was sturdy, reliable, and had a ten-round magazine. His was wrapped in ladies' hose to catch the ejected brass.

They had laid down the front seats and she was riding him like a cowboy, gown hiked up, head thrown back. His naked, knobby knees were just visible beyond her grinding buttocks, his fish-belly-white legs disappearing into gartered black socks.

He shot her twice in the head through the side window. Pop-pop. Two tiny holes.

Glass shattered and fell in a crystalline cascade.

Her head snapped to the side and she collapsed atop her lover, limp as a slab of beef.

A .22 bullet was powerful enough to enter a skull easily, but not strong enough to exit, so it simply bounced around through her brain for a few milliseconds before its energy was spent.

Before Herr Schneider could scream, Okie stepped up to the shattered window, poked the muzzle of the suppressor through it, and shot him twice in the face.

Then he slipped the pistol back into his peacoat. Those four shots had made less noise than a passing car. Then he opened the car door, pulled out a penlight, and searched them. To make it look like a robbery, he took everything—jewelry, watches, wallet, purse, including a search of the glove box and boot for any intelligence. He would go through everything at leisure later.

Then he quietly closed everything back up again and walked off through the park, briskly but not hurriedly, toward where his car was waiting.

Perhaps by morning the corpses would be found. Like most such killings in Berlin, this story wouldn't make the papers. Herr Schneider's disappearance would soon be noticed, but in this case, the family would be quite happy to help the Company keep the circumstances of his demise out of the papers.

"Do you play baseball?" Fidel Castro asked, flicking ashes from his cigar and leaning back in his chair.

Okie nodded. "When I was in high school. My father played professionally." The street-side bar where they sat was unoccupied by any other patrons.

The two men in olive-drab fatigues measured him, both wearing somewhat scraggly dark beards. Looking his full six foot three, even sitting down, Castro wore an olive-green cap, and his Argentinian friend, a black beret.

"That cannot have been long ago. You look very young," said the Argentinian in Spanish. The dossier had said this man, Ernesto "Che" Guevara, shorter than Okie at about five foot nine, was a medical doctor, and the intelligence in his smoldering eyes was plain. He did not offer to shake hands but regarded this American with unconcealed distrust.

Across the cobbled street, a great roar rose from Plaza de Toros. The three-story high arena's exterior blazed with color like a yellow and crimson bullseye in the center of Merida, Yucatan. Crowds thronged the streets of this quaint resort city a few miles from the Gulf on this November day. The tropical evening was still warm, but he caught the scent of blood and shit wafting over the arena's ten-foot adjoining wall of the enclosure where the bulls were kept before the fights, and where they were dragged afterwards.

Okie spotted a couple of men across the street—bodyguards. Castro and Guevara were hunted men. Cuban *presidenté* Fulgencio Batista had put prices on their heads after the failed insurrection that prompted their flight to Mexico, where the leftist-leaning government tolerated their presence.

"Looks can be deceiving," Okie said, clearing his throat. He had been sent here, he suspected, because of his youthfulness. He would be perceived as less threatening, perhaps even callow.

He settled himself in the chair across from them and folded his hands, elbows on the table. He opened his mouth to speak, but then a waitress emerged from the bar wearing a scarlet dress with more cleavage than Okie had ever seen at one time, acres of it, topped with the kind of dark, smoky eyes that could make a man murder his best friend.

Castro said to her, "*Tres agave mojitos por favor, Hermosa.*"

Okie couldn't take his eyes off her as she walked away. He blinked and shook himself to dispel the enchantment.

Guevara spoke in Spanish, his voice dripping with scorn. "Our imperialist friend likes the Latin girls, eh?" It was the first time Okie had ever heard the Argentinian accent, which sounded more like that of Spain, or even Italian, than the predominant Mexico City one, although the accent of Yucatan was also different in many ways. "Perhaps you're here for some *concha.*" Okie deducted what Guevara meant by the use of *shell* in this context.

Castro said to his friend in Spanish, "Let's not be rude to our American friend. We must hear what he has to say. He has come a long way." He turned to Okie and said in English, "Have you ever seen bullfight?"

Okie shook his head.

"A terrible cruelty," Castro said in Spanish, "rightfully outlawed in my country since we threw off Spanish rule."

"Blood and circuses," Guevara spat.

Okie said, "Isn't the phrase 'bread and circuses'?" He'd first heard the term at Holy Cross while studying classical poetry. It came from the Roman poet Juvenal who wrote a satire about the kind of superficial appeasement that kept the masses distracted and docile.

"I have read Juvenal," Guevara growled. "Behind such facades, nothing ever changes." The way he said the words sounded like change was already in motion, driven by the force of his will.

That was what Okie was here to suss out.

"The bull is a noble creature, fighting its tormentors to its last breath," Guevara said.

Castro raised a fresh *fuma,* and an olive-clad bodyguard appeared as if from thin air to offer a light from a battered Zippo. He said to Okie, "You must forgive my friend. He tends toward the over-dramatic." Castro offered Okie a hand-rolled *gran panetela* with a pigtail cap. Okie wondered if this particular cigar had been hand-rolled by Castro's friend, Eduardo Rivera Irizarri, the master cigar-maker. The dossier on Castro and his connections back in Cuba was *very* thorough.

Just then the waitress returned with a tray of Mexican *mojitos*, and Okie just stared. She caught his glance and winked as she departed again.

In her absence, Okie regathered his composure, raised his glass. "To new friends."

Castro raised his glass and drank. Guevara did not. That one bore as much watching as Castro, perhaps more, because according to the dossier, Guevara was an avowed Communist. Castro, on the other hand, as the son of a wealthy sugar cane plantation owner, could go either way. An educated man, a lawyer, Castro had once run for office, but lost.

Fulgencio Batista was a corrupt, tyrant bastard to be sure, but American business interests loved him. He kept the casinos and resorts open, and the sheer volume of cash flowing through the playgrounds of Havana staggered the imagination.

Before Okie had left Bad Aibling, Honey had enthused about how much fun was to be had in Havana. *But not too much fun!* she'd told him pointedly.

Unfortunately, most of that cash was funneled straight into the pockets of the Italian Mafia, but Okie was not here to ask those kinds of questions. He was here to determine on which side of the fence Castro was likely to land—democracy or communism—if he actually managed to depose Fulgencio Batista.

"Do you play baseball?" Okie asked Castro.

"I played a great deal at university. On one of my visits to the United States, I considered playing professionally. But there was too much injustice happening in my country for me to stand aside. Baseball is the most democratic of sports. It requires only a stick, a glove, and a ball."

Guevara said, "Nine men must work together as a well-oiled machine. *Si uno falla, todos fallan.*"

Right now, they were just two hothead revolutionaries with no army to back them up, rebels without a war, like zealous but helpless beatniks railing at the sky, but Okie could already sense why they might be truly dangerous if they ever got an army behind them. There was a charisma about them, one cool, one hot, that Okie had seen in a few of the best military officers, the captains of football teams. Guevara carried an air of revolutionary zeal. He would burn down the entire world if only the proletariat could rise from the ashes. Castro burned with a kind of democratic idealism and intelligence Okie recognized in himself. These were not Third World thugs. He was having difficulty deciding which of the two was more dangerous.

His dislike for Guevara, however, had already lodged so deep he was considering tailing Guevara back to whatever squalid jungle hideout he slept in—and shooting him. Castro, on the other hand, might yet be salvaged and brought onto the side of God and capitalism. He considered shooting them both right here, but he was sure those two hard-eyed bodyguards were packing. In addition, he hadn't been sent here to kill them. His was an evaluation mission.

He looked squarely at Castro. "The way I heard it, you could have played for the Yankees."

He'd been right in his assessment that Castro had a big ego. Castro's little smile told him this bit of flattery had struck home.

To the rise and fall of the crowd noise in the open-air arena across the street, they drank and pretended they were all old college buddies. Okie pretended to greater inebriation than he felt. He titrated his alcohol consumption carefully, except for a couple of shots of *mezcal*. Eventually Guevara warmed up enough that he actually cracked a smile or two. By nightfall, the bullfights were over, and the crowd dispersed through the streets, a riot of color amid a continuing festival atmosphere.

Soon he found the beautiful Mexican goddess sliding onto his lap. Soon after that, she no doubt sensed part of him had enthusiastically risen to meet her. The longer she squirmed against it, maybe a little too enthusiastically, the more he ached to have her. He drank in her scent of roses and coconut and tried not to immerse himself in the spectacular view not inches from his face. He was forced to consider how many history-changing events had hinged on sex or the promise thereof, how many empires from time immemorial had risen and fallen in the pursuit of *concha.*

Eventually, Castro pointed straight into Okie's face. "You tell your superiors back in Washington this. Our revolution will be committed to American-style democracy. When the time comes, you back our play. When Batista's head is hanging above the doors of the presidential palace, we will remember our friends."

Guevara's face soured at this, but he said nothing.

"All we want," Castro went on, "is to throw off Batista's yoke and chase your Italian Mafia back to Miami. Havana is drowning in foreign vice."

"Your people deserve to live free," Okie said, clinking beer bottles.

"To accomplish that, we need weapons, supplies, transport, air support," Guevara snapped, almost sneering. "Will your capitalist overlords supply this?"

"I will convey your message," Okie said. "That is why I'm here."

Just then a teenage boy, about 14 or 15 came running up carrying a Polaroid camera. He looked hopeful. "Your photograph, *señores*?"

Okie couldn't have asked for better proof of his mission. "Sure, kid." He scooted Hermosa from his lap with a little tickle, evoking a playful squeal.

She said, "*Un momento!*" Then she ran inside and returned carrying a huge straw sombrero, which she placed firmly on his head, then stroked his cheek. "You are so handsome, *papi.*"

The young photographer arranged them before a well-painted mural depicting a beachside *cerveza* stand. While the waitress looked on, the three men threw their arms around each other's shoulders, and the boy snapped the photo. He pulled it out and peeled off the protective film, flapping the photo. Then he gave an apologetic smile. "*Solo un dolar?*"

A whole dollar was practically highway robbery, but Okie admired the kid's gumption and pulled a George Washington out of his wallet.

The boy's eyes glowed with pleasure as he took it and scampered off in search of other marks. He could probably feed his family for a week on that dollar. Okie took a moment to admire the photo before tucking it in his pocket.

He handed the sombrero back to Hermosa. As she accepted it with one hand, she pulled him down to kiss him on the cheek with the other. "You are so handsome, *papi.*" Her breath was hot against his ear.

On his next trip to the toilet, he accepted a blow-job from her in the alley out back, the best compromise he could manage between his immortal soul and his sinful flesh. As he spilled his seed into her mouth, he told himself this could go no further. Once for his country was enough. Fortunately, Mexico was such a Catholic country, there was a church confessional on almost every street corner. He'd have some penance to do this week.

"Fuck me, *papi*," she begged him, but there was a fearful desperation in her voice that suggested he might not survive the encounter. He imagined thugs bursting in at his most vulnerable moment to rob him of dollars and blood. On the other hand, she could be working for Castro and Guevara, with the aim to compromise him somehow.

He shrugged her off and returned to the table to find Castro and Guevara gone. But no matter, he'd gotten what he came for.

XXIII

*"**BLESS ME, FATHER,** for I have sinned. It has been two days since my last confession."*

"Proceed, my son."

"I...I feel guilty by association. What kind of sin is that?"

"A man is responsible for only his own sins. We cannot be responsible for someone else's actions."

"But what if we know about awful things they've done?"

"Perhaps there is culpability for one who has suspicions but keeps quiet about them. For instance, if a woman was cheating on her husband, and the husband suspects but says nothing. He is responsible for his wife's spiritual well-being. Or if a man dates a woman who is a fornicator. She might seduce him into such harmful, distasteful activities—"

"This is more serious than that, Father. I have been ordered to associate with criminals of the worst sort. War criminals. Lust mongers. Dope dealers. Mass murderers. Could their evil somehow rub off on me?"

"Only if you fail to stop them from doing more evil."

"That's what I was afraid of. The Lord will have to forgive me for that."

"For what, specifically?"

"I can't tell you. I'm sorry. But God knows. I have to allow or even abet all sorts of crimes of morality, all in the name of stopping a greater evil. The things I've seen. The things I've done..."

"Perhaps it's time to reconsider your line of work."

"Maybe that's my sin. I love it too much."

1957

"I'm getting discharged from the Army," Okie said, bouncing Mary on his knee at their tiny kitchen table. He'd sent the nanny home when he'd returned from the post this afternoon. With both he and Honey working again, the nanny was overburdening their paychecks, but as soon as Honey got the word she was back on flight status, she'd been ecstatic.

The toddler slobbered and burbled and grinned at him with her crooked smile, four little teeth like porcelain nubbins in her pink gums attacking her plump knuckles. His little angel, at least in one of her rare quiet moments, like this one. His blue-eyed cherub.

Honey dropped her flight bag with a sigh of exhaustion, still in her uniform. She made no motion to kiss her daughter or her husband, stoking the heat of buried resentments. "I need a bath."

She went into the bathroom, flipped on the light, started running water in the tub. Then her voice came out, "So does that mean we can get out of this godforsaken country?"

"I thought you liked Germany."

"It's time to move on, get a bigger place."

She was talking about Mary, he knew. The endless, sleepless nights of screaming had turned all the neighbors against them, and left Honey with only a shadow of her former vivacity. Their tiny apartment, redolent with the odor of dirty diapers and regurgitated milk, had turned into a pressure cooker, even though Honey was back flying for TWA. She'd weaned the baby about a month ago, couldn't take the teeth, she said, didn't want her nipples turning to leather.

Through the open bathroom door, he heard her slip into the tub. "So why are they discharging you? There's another whole year on your enlistment." The swirl of water echoed out with wisps of steam.

"They want me back stateside. Company office in Buffalo."

"You're fucking kidding me."

He covered Mary's ears. "Language!"

Mary giggled and drooled at him. He gave her a crust of buttered bread to chew on, afraid of another outburst of distemper.

"Buffalo!" Honey exclaimed.

"I think they want me to have some...downtime. Now that the tunnel is gone, it's not a useful cover anymore."

He had never told her about the people he'd shot in Berlin, the faces that still haunted his sleep.

It could be that his face was becoming too well known among Berlin's clandestine circles. Two nights ago, he'd been followed by at least two men after delivering a packet to Herr Dönitz at his Berlin flat. Okie's instincts had screamed at him that he was being hunted, and he managed to give them the slip. Given who he'd just visited, he suspected his stalkers were Mossad. The Israeli intelligence service was doggedly hunting Nazis who'd escaped justice after the war. Okie could hardly call Herr Dönitz a "former" Nazi—the man had not shown an ounce of regret, or even renounced his association with the Third Reich. He believed himself a patriot doing his duty for the Fatherland, to this day.

"But why Buffalo?" Honey said, sloshing the water. "It's cold in Buffalo."

Okie released a bit of the steam trapped in his chest. "Aren't you going to say hello to your daughter?"

Honey scoffed, "I'm sure there will be plenty of time to get reacquainted about three a.m." Her face drained of hope.

Okie had not stood on this stretch of curb since he'd left Holy Cross.

"Are you sure you're all right?" Honey asked him.

"I'm fine," he said. But was he? Given the number of people he'd taken out since then, he shouldn't be afraid of his father anymore. Nevertheless, his mouth was paper-dry, and his heart thudded like a rabbit's warning.

Hanging on his arm, Mary tugged at her lemon-yellow dress, her dark curls tied into two wispy pigtails, unsure what to make of this new wardrobe development.

Honey had insisted they go shopping for new clothes the moment they landed in New York. "I'm not about to take my daughter to meet her grandfather looking like a ragamuffin." Of course, there was also a lovely new black polka-dot dress suitable for

Audrey Hepburn in the offing for Honey. It had brightened her mood considerably.

Mary started to fuss, until Okie realized he was clenching her plump thigh. He loosened his grip, and the fussing ceased.

"We don't have to do this," Honey said. "You don't owe him anything."

Back in their Bad Aibling flat, they had had a few talks about Emmett, comparing their fathers' litany of sins.

"Sounds like a fine, upstanding citizen," Honey had said with distaste. "But mine is no better. You'll have a hard time finding a bigger hypocrite in the Chicago area. If you have enough money, no one will question anything you do."

Okie's gaze traced the outline of the North Bailey Avenue Amherst house where his mother died, where Emmett had burned their family to the ground. It was just a house now, and it belonged to someone else.

He still felt strange wearing civilian clothes. Until leaving Germany, his life had been a succession of uniforms. First, altar boy robes. Then Canisius. Then Holy Cross. Then the steel mill. Then the Army. But now it was time to shed all visible affiliations and look like any average Joe. The Company preferred nondescript operatives. Even when he wasn't on a mission, his job was to blend in. It was a skill he actively practiced.

He took a deep breath and licked his lips, trying to gather enough spit to talk. "Let's get this over with."

One of his orders had been to acquire a plausible cover while operating out of the Company office in Buffalo. Watson Safety Equipment might be able to provide such a cover. It depended on whether his father was interested in rebuilding bridges. Okie wasn't, but this might be an expeditious method of acquiring a cover.

They climbed the steps onto the porch and knocked on the door. Okie had called ahead on this warm Saturday afternoon. It was summer, and Emmett liked golf to cultivate his relationships.

Honey squeezed Okie's free hand as if to lend him strength. He looked at it, and gave her a wan smile, an acknowledgment of the show of affection, a rare event lately. But did she really care, or was she simply very skilled at playing the part of the dutiful wife?

A shadow appeared behind the window, and the door opened to reveal Emmett, dressed as if he'd just come home from the office. His expression became the kind of charming smile Okie hadn't seen in years—the kind reserved for clients and business associates. Abruptly, Okie felt like a potential business client.

Emmett stepped aside. "Please, come in, come in."

They stepped into the foyer, and suddenly Okie was a teenager again. His mother's scent lingered as if she were in the kitchen even now, preparing to bake cookies. But then he heard movement in the kitchen, the rustle of activity. He froze to listen. Could no one else hear that? Who else could be here? His stomach began to seethe. If that were Marge in there, he might very well kill them both right now. Emotion clogged his throat, and he swallowed it as best he could before he spoke. "Pops, I'd like to introduce your granddaughter, Mary. Mary, this is your grandfather."

The one-year-old eyed the older man skeptically.

Emmett took her fingers gently and shook her hand. She tolerated this for a moment, then pulled them away. He turned to

Honey, "And you, my dear, are as beautiful as ever. What a gorgeous dress."

Honey turned on her well-practiced charm. "Aw, thanks! This old thing?" She fluffed the skirt, then leaned up to air-kiss his cheek.

"I can't tell you how pleased I am to hear you're back in Buffalo," Emmett said, leading them into the parlor. The room looked exactly as Okie had last seen it. A sofa and coffee table by the window. Two chairs before the fireplace. All the same decor that his mother had picked out.

A stout gray-haired woman in a maid's uniform, with ankles that looked like thighs, came out of the kitchen carrying a tray laden with tea and cookies. "Put them on the coffee table, Elsa," Emmett said.

Tension released simultaneously from every muscle in Okie's body, the kind of tension when he knew he was either the hunter or the hunted. He collected himself enough to not drop Mary and managed to raise an eyebrow. "You have a maid?"

Emmett shrugged. "It's not as if I know how to cook."

A biting question paused behind Okie's lips. *So, where's Marge?* But now was not a politic time to rip open old wounds.

Elsa set the tray down and gave Mary a yellow-toothed smile. "Oh, aren't you just cute as a button!" she beamed in a Scandinavian accent.

Okie sat with his family on the sofa while Emmett pulled his customary, wing-backed chair closer.

"How does it feel to be back on American soil?" Emmett asked.

"Like I never left." Okie had been back and forth to American soil several times in the last year for training in Virginia.

Honey smiled. "I've been on American soil three times this week."

"Of course. No doubt you are quite the jetsetter." Emmett turned to Okie. "It seems you've successfully kept the Red Menace at bay. No doubt you cannot talk about any of it."

"I could tell you stories that would curl your hair, but they'd probably arrest me for that." *At the very least.*

Honey chimed in, "Buffalo is so beautiful this time of year. Everything is so green."

"I doubt it much compares to Bavaria," Emmett said.

"Well, Bavaria is in a league of its own," Honey said. "But there are too many former Nazis around."

Emmett's almost imperceptible wince caught Okie's eye. What had he reacted to? Whatever it was, it disappeared behind a sheen of polished urbanity. "No doubt they know enough these days to keep their mouths shut."

"For the most part," Okie said, "but there are a few fascist rags circulating around Berlin."

"Communists on one side, fascists on the other," Honey said.

Emmett raised an eyebrow. "Do you take an interest in politics, my dear?"

"Got to," Honey said. "Part of my job."

"Oh, really?"

"You hear all sorts of things in an airplane," she said with a mysterious curl of her lips.

For a while, they chatted about Watson and various goings-on around Buffalo. Okie asked after the Montanas, whom Emmett said were quite well.

"I'll have to give John a call soon," Okie said.

As the list of safe subjects drained away like the sands of an hourglass, Okie sensed the time was coming to ask what he'd come here to ask. And then Emmett broached the subject for him. "So now that you're out of the Army, what do you have on the board for gainful employment?"

It was time to don the guise of the man who could consort with war criminals, thugs, and spies, another skill he actively practiced. "I have a favor to ask, Pops—"

"You need a job."

Okie nodded. "I need a job."

"I happen to be looking for a new floor manager."

Okie stared at him for a moment with the sudden feeling that this was too easy. "Really?" If he'd been expecting anything at all, it was janitor.

"You're a man now. You have a family to support. We can't very well leave the bread-winning to your wife. She should stay home to take care of the baby in any case."

Honey's smile faltered, then was quickly spackled back on.

"Of course," Okie said. "We'd love that."

"Besides, no doubt the Lord will soon bless you with more children," Emmett went on.

"No doubt," Okie said, patting Honey's knee, feeling her stiffen at the assumptions passing back and forth between the men. He and Honey had had relations all of twice since Mary was born.

"So when can you start?" Emmett asked.

It was all happening so fast, Okie hardly knew how to answer. "Uh, how about Monday?"

❁❁❁

John Montana Jr. clapped Okie's hand in a fierce handshake. "Look at what the cat crapped out!"

"Aren't you a sight for blind people!" Okie said with a grin. "Perfect face for radio."

There in the entryway of Valentinelli's Ristorante in downtown Buffalo, they looked each other up and down. John was dressed in a tailored, pin-stripe suit, Okie in a white shirt and dark tie.

"Looks like married life is keeping you on your toes," John said. "'Cept for that pot belly you're growing. All that German beer and sausage."

Okie laughed, even though he knew he was in the best shape of his life, somewhat more muscular than he'd been the last time he and John had played basketball together. "You look more like your old man than ever. Thought I was in the wrong place."

John's grin faltered at that, telling Okie the old tensions were still there. His memory flashed back to the butcher bleeding on the floor while his kid watched. After the things he himself had seen—and done—it didn't seem so shocking now.

But the air smelled of garlic, fresh bread, and marinara. Crisp, checked tablecloths adorned the tables and waiters in starched white shirts circulated among the well-heeled patrons.

John gestured. "I got us a table in the back." He led Okie past the bar through a pair of French doors into a spacious private dining room.

A beautiful, dark-haired waitress beamed a smile at them. "Good evening, Mr. Montana. May I bring you a bottle of wine, on the house, of course?"

"Sure, Rosella. The 1955 Riserva Ducale Oro. Say hi to your pop for me."

"Of course," she said, her smile faltering for a moment before she departed, leaving a wake of vanilla and roses.

Okie moved toward the seat facing the entrance and found both his hand and John's falling on the chair at the same time.

Their eyes met, and John released the chair first. "Be my guest."

Okie sat. This was the perfect point to survey entrance and egress points while assessing potential weapons and defenses, which he did in a split second. Not that he was expecting any sort of attack, but ever since that first night in Max und Marlene Bierhaus, it was something he did automatically. His back was now always against a load-bearing masonry wall.

"So, you're back in Buffalo," John said, easing back in his chair. "For good?"

Okie shrugged. "For a while."

"Got tired of killing Commies, eh?"

Okie looked away. The truth was, there was nothing more thrilling than the intelligence game. "Army decided it was done with me."

"And how's the wife?"

"She's great. Beautiful as ever."

"And you got yourself a little girl, I hear."

"Yeah, just over a year now."

"Need a job?"

Okie chuckled. "Got people need leaned on?" He meant it to sound light-hearted, but a shadow crossed John's face.

"I don't know what you're talking about."

"Sorry. Didn't mean to offend you."

"Think nothing of it."

Just then, Rosella returned with the best bottle of chianti from the cellar, which she opened and poured for them. Okie noticed an extra button had been undone in her white blouse, and that she bent further in front of them than necessary. A small, gold crucifix dangled between beautiful mounds of olive-skinned bounty. She also wore a skirt with dark stockings and black, patent leather shoes. He watched John admiring her and tried to discern whether any sort of relations was in progress or on the horizon.

"The usual?" she asked John.

"Yeah, lasagna for me."

"Is it good here?" Okie asked.

"Best in town," John said.

"Then lasagna for me, too." He'd eaten some spectacular lasagna last time he'd been in Rome. Ordering it here in Buffalo felt somehow provincial now, but he'd take John at his word.

John patted Rosella on the ass as she went away, eliciting no reaction from her.

Okie raised an eyebrow. "Nice girl."

"I tip well," John said.

"So, no steady girl for you?" Okie asked.

"I ain't got time to settle down," John said.

"Got your eye on this one?"

"She'd make a great Miss Saturday Night. But enough about her."

"How's your old man?" Okie asked.

"Same as he ever was. Yours?"

"Bastard actually offered me a job."

"You take it?"

Okie shrugged. "Mama needs a new pair of shoes."

John laughed, but there was no mirth it, more a tone of *Well, you got what you bargained for.*

"So what did I miss while I was gone?"

John shrugged. "Nothing changes in this town. Truth is, I'm bored outta my mind. This town's only so big, you know? But that's life, am I right? Gotta take over the family business. Blood is blood."

Okie held up his wine glass. "*Salute.*"

"*Salute,*" John said, clinking glasses.

Rosella returned with a basket of fresh bread and a bowl of salad, and over the next two hours, Okie watched John shower her with charm. He wondered how much she knew about the Montana family. John Sr. was a pillar of the Buffalo business community, but after what Okie had seen John Jr. do that night across the river, he knew all that cultured respectability to be a facade. As dinner progressed, he couldn't help but notice John's boyish cheer had been replaced by a hard, gritty edge. Could John see the same in him? He guessed by the scrutiny in John's eye that his friend was asking the same kinds of questions.

What he came away from the meal feeling was that the gulf between him and his old friend had widened, rather than been bridged. Beneath John's pinstriped suit, beneath his skin, beneath his charm, were scars he would carry with him forever. They lived in different worlds now, and neither could be allowed to peek into the other. They were funhouse mirror distortions of their former selves.

Okie could count the people who knew the truth of his current life on one hand, and even Honey didn't know everything. Don was still in Europe. The Sausalito gang were simply acquaintances who'd found themselves at a node in Wild Bill Donovan's covert web.

As Okie and John parted ways outside, telling each other and themselves they would do this again soon, Okie had seldom felt more alone.

XXIV

"BLESS ME, FATHER, *for I have sinned. It's been—"*

"Hello, Okie."

"Mr. Casey?"

"I trust you and your family are well and thriving in God's service."

"Of course, sir! But what are you doing here?*"*

"I'm here to let you know that your service to the Order has been exemplary, my boy. We have watched your progress with great interest."

"I...I don't know what to say, sir."

"Then say, 'thank you.' Doors have been opened for you. You're aware of that, I'm sure."

"I am very aware, sir. I'm just never sure which doors or why."

"That is as intended. No doubt it hasn't always been easy."

"Some things have been...very difficult."

"But you've always come through. Your skein has many winding threads. More will be asked of you. Perhaps things even more difficult."

"I understand, sir."

"You don't yet, not fully, but your loyalty is appreciated. You must trust, though, that it all is in the highest service to God and the Church."

"I'll remember, sir."

❁❁❁

Okie waited in the hallway, morning paper in hand, for Marge Hall, the home-wrecking harpy to vacate Emmett's office. In the months since Okie had started working at Watson Safety Equipment, he and Marge had come to an uneasy détente. He'd never spoken of his revulsion for her—hiding his inner life was a well-cultivated skill by now—but she was too cunning not to have sensed it. The truth was, he could count the number of words they'd exchanged on his fingers and toes.

He'd heard that Gerhardt, her oldest son, had graduated from Holy Cross and gone to work at Hall Industries, her family's company. But she still worked for Emmett, ostensibly as his secretary. Her duties and authority comprised far more than that, however.

What was strange was that Okie had never once witnessed a moment of true affection between them. When he and Honey were dating, she had slathered him with affection, but these two were like weathered boulders resting near one another, but somehow content. Nevertheless, it was also clear that they knew each other incredibly well, often seeming to know what the other wanted or was thinking at any given moment. It didn't make him hate her any less. It just mystified him. If they were fornicating like teenage bunnies—nauseating as the thought was—that at least he could understand, if not condone. Somewhat wiser now in the ways of the world than the angry teenager he had been, Okie tried to make an analytical study of their relationship. The only way he could look at her and not want to put a .22 bullet in her brain as she was walking home on a given night, was to treat her dispassionately as he might an enemy agent, someone to be surveilled.

The newspaper felt hot in his hand, because the moment he'd read the article over his lunch break, something had clicked, and he needed to confirm it.

The sound of the molding machines and pneumatic presses in the cavernous factory echoed through the walls, made the floor vibrate. As floor manager, he was a supervising supervisor, the one to whom the assembly and quality control foremen reported. Most days there was little for him to do, because Emmett managed to hire good people, and the company treated them well. Most of the men directly underneath him had been there for years. The roughest friction came at the fact that he was one of the youngest people in the building. But it was here that his...training came in handy. After the things he'd seen and done, he feared no one. A couple of times, early on, he'd had to face down men who steamed through the world fueled by belligerence and bluster. But he could shatter those facades quickly by imagining a few of the excruciating or lethal things he knew how to do to them. Bullies could instantly recognize the more dangerous dog in the fight. They went away with their tails between their legs. There were others to whom he related easily, the war veterans, either World War II or Korea. He was a former enlisted man like they were.

As a result, no one messed with him. The production floor ran smoothly, and Watson Safety Equipment made money.

A few looked at him askance when he returned from unexplained absences. Odder still, Emmett never once asked him about it. On weekends and evenings, he occasionally checked in at the

Company office in Buffalo. When he was to be sent on a mission, they called, and he went. Since Honey was still flying, they saved some nanny costs by having Ann babysit on her days off. She had been delighted to have Okie and Honey back in town and had a knack for soothing Mary's colic.

In the six months since returning stateside, Okie had traveled to four countries, mostly acting as a courier for people he'd rather shoot than speak to, such as Karl Dönitz, and now, most recently, Klaus Barbie, the Nazi known as the Butcher of Lyon, who was now hiding out in Bolivia to evade the French death sentence for his war crimes. Nevertheless, U.S. counterintelligence had recruited Barbie back in '47 to take advantage of the anti-Communist spy network the Nazis had woven in the run-up to the war. He had seldom seen evil so personified as in the eyes of Klaus Barbie, and it had been his job to trade envelopes and depart. Thankfully, their meeting had been brief. Throughout the journey home, Okie had been plagued by thoughts of how such a man could possibly be part of God's plan.

The office door opened, and Marge emerged carrying a sheaf of invoices. Spotting Okie, she paused, lifting her hatchet chin in acknowledgment of his presence, then turned down the hall toward her own office.

Okie walked into Emmett's office and closed the door. Before Emmett could speak, he tossed the newspaper onto the desk. In huge type, the headline blazed: *UPSTATE RAID COLLARS 62 MAFIA LEADERS.*

"How long have you known the Montanas were mobsters?" Okie asked. It was not an accusation, but a simple question.

Emmett's only reaction was an eyebrow raised in a face that otherwise resembled marble. He stared at the headline as if trying to absorb the huge letters one by one.

The article described a meeting of over a hundred mob Mafia leaders attending some sort of crime congress near the tiny town of Apalachin, which lay along the Pennsylvania state line about halfway between Buffalo and New York City. It must have been a chaotic scene, with local, state, and federal authorities swooping down on a lavish country estate at the end of a dead-end road, corralling almost a hundred brand new Cadillacs, mobsters and their henchmen fleeing through the woods like scattering rats. To think a bad check written for lunch at the local diner set things in motion.

John Montana Sr. had been one of those arrested. Okie had read the list of names three times, looking for John Jr. but there was no mention of him.

Emmett met his gaze with cool flint. "You sound as if you've known for quite some time."

Damn the man for deflecting a direct question. "I saw John shake a guy down once, but I thought it was just a minor-league thing. How close are you with the old man? Is he some sort of boss? You scratch each other's backs?"

"My relationships are none of your concern. John Sr. is a respected Buffalo businessman—"

"And a gangster, apparently! Not just a small-time hood."

Emmett shrugged. "He has a number of aboveboard ventures ongoing. He'd hardly be the first community leader with skeletons in his closet."

"Yeah, fresh ones!" Okie said. How could Emmett be so sanguine about this? Then again, Okie could hardly judge anyone for having skeletons in the closet. He took a deep breath and let it out. "I want to know, Pops. How much do you know? How big is he? This won't go any further than this room, but I don't want to be surprised if the feds come swooping down on us, too." If that happened, he could kiss his security clearance goodbye, and maybe Honey's, too. She'd never forgive him for that. Then he really would be just some average shmoe, outcast from a life he loved, a life that felt important, meaningful, ordained.

There were other questions, too, like whether John Jr. was now in the authorities' crosshairs. On one hand, he didn't want to see any harm come to his longtime friend, but on the other hand, John had made a bed and was sleeping in it, however uneasily.

What Okie was having trouble absorbing was the scope of the bust. Over a hundred mobsters had been present at the meeting in Apalachin. A hundred. It was not a lodge convention full of underlings. He knew most cities had some element of organized crime, but this was huge. Were they all connected? John C. Montana's stature in the Buffalo community, as well as greater New York State, could not be underestimated. He'd run for U.S. Congress, been a city councilman, and he was a mover and shaker in the state Republican party. Hell, he was friends with Vice President Nixon.

Emmett looked him squarely in the eye. "There are no criminal enterprises associated with Watson Safety Equipment."

Okie chewed on Emmett's phrasing, eyes narrowing. "You know I'm not asking about just Watson."

"You should get back to work, son. I'm sure this will all blow over. Just because it's in the paper doesn't mean it's true."

Okie heard Mary crying as he climbed the stairs to their apartment. The hoarseness in the baby's voice suggested she'd been crying for a while. He sighed, then quickened his step. Honey was supposed to be home today, a day off before flying to La Guardia then London.

He entered to find Mary sitting in the middle of the living room floor, her face red and soaked with tears and snot. As he scooped her up—she reeked of filthy diaper—he spotted Honey sitting at the kitchen table, staring into an almost empty bottle of vodka he didn't recognize. Her bleary eyes glanced toward him like those of a fish spotting movement outside its bowl.

"What the hell are you doing?" he yelled, as he tried to bounce Mary on his arm, feeling the child's diarrhea soak through his jacket sleeve. Blood pounded in his ears, and his mouth went dry. He stormed across the room to the kitchen and stood over her. Mary screamed and screamed.

Honey looked up with half-lidded, bloodshot eyes. "Oh, good. You're home." But in her voice was only sarcasm.

"How long has she been crying?"

Honey shrugged. "A thousand years or so."

"What the devil is wrong with you!"

She laughed, a bitter, despairing sound. "Dean Martin is supposed to be on that flight to London tomorrow. How can I schmooze him reeking of baby shit?"

That was when he spotted the mustard-brown stain down the front of her new dress. The stain had been there long enough to dry around the edges.

He slapped her across the face. "Snap out of it!"

She sprawled from the chair.

Mary's wail shrilled toward the ultrasonic.

The bleariness in Honey's eyes evaporated in the fire of shock as she cupped her cheek. As she struggled to her feet, the shock shifted to outrage. After a long moment, she composed herself enough to spin and stalk toward the bedroom. She slammed the door hard enough to shake the windows.

He took half a step toward the door, preparing to kick it down, when Mary gathered another lungful for a fresh, ragged fusillade.

He signed again and took her to the bathroom, where he placed her in the tub, ran some warm water, and began to strip her. She had runny yellow shit all the way up between her shoulder blades, even in her hair.

"Oh, my girl," he said, trying to soothe her. He did everything he could think of, wiping her nose and tears, stroking her cheek and hair.

It took him half an hour to get both of them cleaned up. A warm soapy bath seemed to settle her down, and she finally subsided into quiet wonder, playing with soap bubbles while he watched from where he sat on the toilet lid, clutching his hands into fists, still feeling the slap against his palm. It had been a good one. Solid. Honey would have a bruise tomorrow, and he couldn't decide how he felt about that.

All his suppressed frustrations with Honey over the last year or more—her dislike of motherhood, the lack of marital relations between them, the evaporation of their romance—had boiled up in him like a bottle of shaken soda, and Mary had popped the top.

He let Mary play in the water until it got cold, then he bundled her up in a towel, dressed her in her flannel pajamas, and sat with her in his lap on the couch in the glow of the television, *The Thin Man.* Mary fell asleep against his chest, and he let himself descend into the weariness.

A shadow falling across him snapped him awake. He reached for a gun that wasn't there.

Honey stood over him, arms crossed, her face limned by the white static on the television screen. Her eyes caught enough of the light for him to see the cold fire in them. "If you ever have a mind to hit me again, you need to remember one thing." Her voice was as cold as a switchblade. "You know who *I* work for, too. And I know where you sleep."

XXV

***"BLESS ME, FATHER,** for I have sinned. It's been one day since my last confession. I have...greatly misjudged my father. I don't even know where to start. I have done him a great injustice..."*

"In what way, my son? With God's forgiveness, perhaps He will move your father to forgive you."

"I can't say exactly, except that I wish I had known many things much sooner. I feel like such a fool."

Tinsel and garland festooned the break room of Watson Safety Equipment, and the smell of roast beef and roasted potatoes filled the air, mixed with a dozen different aftershaves and the hint of cigarette smoke. The punch bowl glistened with bright red effervescence. The cacophony born of a score of conversations boisterous and subdued filled the space and spilled out into the hallway.

Okie manned the ice chest full of beer, popping tops for employees and guarding another ice chest full of champagne, awaiting the moment to start opening bottles.

The crowd of workers lined up for the catered food, and the air thrummed with a pleasant congeniality. Ann had made several batches of Christmas cookies, the plates of which had been quickly ravaged as if by hyenas. Okie was actually having a good time. Except for the way Marge was clinging to Emmett as if they were newlyweds. Her uncharacteristic, snaggle-toothed smile looked out of place in her hatchet face. She and Emmett never showed affection openly, especially at work, even though their relationship was an open secret, but tonight she practically hung on him. Had something changed?

Okie washed away the distaste with a steady stream of Falstaff and turned his field of vision elsewhere.

Standing on a chair, Emmett gave his obligatory speech, thanking his employees for their hard work to give Watson Safety Equipment its best year ever, eliciting a rousing cheer. Okie punctuated the moment with the pop of a champagne cork, which struck a light fixture and caromed into the punchbowl. Amid the resulting laughter, he began to pour the champagne into paper cups. None of the working-class Joes and the handful of Janes were likely to care that the Dom Perignon was served in paper cups. They would be happy for the gesture. One of the things Emmett did well as a leader was to offer perks to his employees that built loyalty worth more than a dollar value. Real Dom Perignon, which few of them had likely tasted before, was a perfect example. Some might say it was casting pearls before swine, and they wouldn't be entirely incorrect, but it was still an appreciated gesture. The Christmas bonuses no doubt also helped.

One of the foremen stepped in next to Okie to open bottles while Okie poured. As he distributed champagne, Emmett went on to talk about hopes and plans for the next year. During the speech, Marge looked distracted, kept glancing toward the door.

At one point, Emmett gently admonished everyone to wait for the toast. After finishing his speech to a round of applause, he approached Okie and took two cups of champagne, but as he turned away, Okie saw something that made him stare, made him take a long moment to wonder if he had just seen what he thought he saw.

As Emmett took one of the cups, fine, white powder had fallen from his carefully cupped fingers into the champagne. Okie fixed his attention on the cup. Had that been real? Yes, because Emmett was gently swirling both cups almost imperceptibly. The sleight of hand had been superb.

The doctored cup he handed to Marge, who accepted it with glowing eyes and a blush in her cheek.

A voice snapped Okie out of his stunned immobility. "Hey, keep pouring, kid." It was one of the janitors impatiently awaiting his allotment.

Okie flashed him an apologetic smile and returned to pouring.

Marge cupped her champagne in both hands, beaming.

But then one of the faces he least expected to see appeared before him.

"Gerhardt!" Okie said, unable to mask his surprise.

"Okie," Gerhard Hall said, his face a chiseled Aryan bust. The military buzz cut made him look older than he was, and his cold blue eyes flickered with amusement at Okie's discomfiture. He took up one of the paper cups and regarded it. "Classy."

Okie bit back a fiery *Go fuck yourself,* smiled instead. "What are you doing here?"

"I'm on leave for Christmas." The German accent Gerhardt had had in high school was almost gone.

"So you're in the military."

"Oh, you haven't heard? Got my Second Lieutenant bar in June."

Okie nodded but couldn't bring himself to offer congratulations. "Air Force?"

"How'd you know?"

"You seem like the type." The implication was that the Air Force was the cushiest of the armed forces.

"I hear you're out of the Army."

"May."

"Being a grunt didn't agree with you?"

Okie felt no need to be goaded, so he handed a cup of champagne to the man next to Gerhardt.

"Another cup of champagne, Private," Gerhardt said with a half-sneer and an authoritative tone. "That's an order."

Okie met his gaze, pricked at numerous levels. But he wouldn't let Gerhardt see that his jab had landed. He gave Gerhardt his best smiling mask and offered another cup, behind which he envisioned jamming an icicle through Gerhardt's eye socket.

Gerhardt's sneer faltered, and he moved on.

With all the champagne distributed, Emmett raised his paper chalice. "A toast! To all of you! Merry Christmas!"

"Merry Christmas!" rose in chorus around the room.

Marge downed her champagne.

Over the next twenty minutes, Okie watched her eyes begin to droop, her voice to slur, as she lavished praise and affection on her son. She beamed with pride, and Gerhardt lapped it up like a hog at the swill trough. Okie studied Emmett as well, who gave zero indication that anything was amiss, maintaining his habitual, tightly wound, staid demeanor. Marge began to lean on Emmett, cling to him, turning her bloodshot eyes up into his with unconcealed infatuation, and he allowed it. She murmured things up into Emmett's ear that Okie couldn't hear, her too-red, too-thick lipstick cracking like old paint on her thin, withered lips. Emmett listened but didn't react.

Positioning himself nearer to better hear their conversation, Okie chatted up other employees and tried to control his churning stomach. At one point he caught a snippet of Gerhardt telling a joke with the word "kike" in it. The men around him laughed, so he told another.

Okie wondered if the Air Force would care that one of their newly minted officers was an honest-to-God Nazi. He still remembered the disparaging things Gerhardt had said about Warren Spahn back in high school because of his "kike nose," and Warren wasn't even Jewish. The stench of associating with Nazis wasn't something Okie could easily wash off himself. After all, Klaus Barbie, the Butcher of Lyon, and Karl Dönitz, the Last Führer himself, were in the employ of the CIA, the former propping up anti-Communist autocrats in South America via ratlines—clandestine pathways for moving personnel and materiel across denied areas—and the latter feeding the CIA intelligence via Germany's old spy network and helping to repurpose a network of old SS escape routes to extract former Nazis from Europe. They funneled through the Bavarian city of Memmingen, then to Rome, then by sea to retreat colonies throughout the southern hemisphere.

Marge stumbled into Emmett and clung to him. "Perhaps you should take me home, *Liebchen*. It seems I've had too much to drink."

Emmett looked down into her eyes. "Of course, my dear. Let's go." There was a tone in his voice that might have suggested unspoken words: *before you embarrass us both.*

Still unsure of whether he had really seen Emmett slip his secretary a mickey, Okie had been watching her closely ever since. She had drunk only the one cup of champagne. How short of a step was it from adultery to rape? But why would Emmett need to drug a woman so obviously enamored of him? As distasteful as the idea of sex between them was, it seemed something that would be freely given, not taken.

Okie had learned to listen to his instincts, so when Emmett guided Marge to the coat rack, he knew he had to follow them.

Emmett said to Gerhardt, "I'm taking your mother home."

Gerhardt nodded acknowledgment. "I have an engagement with friends after this. I won't be home tonight." The younger brother, Karl, would still be away for the last two weeks of the semester at Holy Cross.

As Emmett helped Marge with her coat, Okie slipped out through another door and ran for his car, which was parked on the street. He waited for the two of them to stumble from the entrance toward Emmett's Buick. Silhouetted in the car, Marge flung herself against Emmett, but he gently pushed her away. She lolled against the passenger window, subsiding into sleep. The Buick pulled out of its parking place, and Okie started the car to follow them at a distance. He knew how to tail without being spotted, and he knew where Marge lived, just a couple of blocks from Emmett.

He parked a block away from Marge's house, got out, and hurried toward it, just in time to see Emmett wrangle her barely conscious form out of the car and support her as she stumbled toward the house. Okie clung to the shadows along hedges and naked trees, approaching with all the stealth at his disposal. Buffalo still awaited its first winter snow, which would have made him much easier to spot.

Marge's house was a plain, modest two-story, somewhat smaller than Emmett's Queen Anne in Amherst.

Okie paused below the hedge of the neighboring property, waiting for the front door to close. When it did, he hurried across the lawn and crept onto Marge's front porch, careful to keep his tread on the supporting studs to prevent creaking boards. He peeked through the front door's curtained glass in time to see Emmett helping Marge up the stairs to where her bedroom presumably lay.

When they had gone out of sight, a light came on upstairs. Okie could hear shuffling footsteps, sighs and half-coherent moans, and Emmett's quiet tones of reassurance. He wished for a way to peek through the second-floor windows, but the nearest tree was a tall, straight-trunked oak that offered no easy climb. Footsteps creaked back down the stairs.

Emmett.

Okie ducked aside and prepared to dart around the corner of the porch.

But Emmett didn't leave the house.

Instead, a light came on in a back room, beyond the foyer, next to the kitchen, where a sewing room might be.

Okie circled the house and crept toward the window, from which a column of dim lamplight spilled out between the curtains. To control his hammering heart, he breathed slowly and deeply. Then he peered through the crack between two heavy drapes.

About six feet away, Emmett sat at a roll-top desk, rifling through its drawers, examining files and loose papers. He pulled out a ledger and paged through it. The tilt of his head and a pause suggested he had spotted something of interest. His finger traced up and down columns. He turned the page, traced more columns, brow furrowed. Then he paused to search a couple more drawers but found one of them locked.

Then, as if it were the most natural thing in the world, Emmett Hansen, Buffalo's former athletic star and golden boy of business, pulled a set of lockpicks from his jacket and deftly unlocked the drawer.

Okie could hardly believe his eyes. *Emmett* had just picked a lock as if he'd been doing it his whole life.

Emmett opened the drawer, withdrew a stack of manila files, and began to sift through them. On most of them, Okie could see the Hall Industries logo. They looked like shipping manifests, invoices, bills of lading.

Then Emmett did something even more shocking. He spread several of them on the desktop, arranging them carefully. Then from the same breast pocket, he pulled out a tiny Minox slide-action camera, about six inches long and an inch in cross-section, stood over the paperwork, and started clicking photos.

A whispered expletive escaped Okie's lips before he could stop it. He clamped a hand over his mouth to prevent further outbursts.

It didn't seem Emmett had heard. For several minutes, he continued shuffling papers and snapping photos with a camera made for espionage. After he was finished with the file folders, he photographed several pages of the ledger as well. Then he carefully replaced everything and relocked the drawer. He reached for the switch of the desk lamp, and Okie ducked back, lest his silhouette be visible behind the drapes.

Soon, Emmett's footsteps moved through the house, climbing the stairs to the upper floor, then the creak of bedsprings.

For a long time, Okie stood there leaning against the wall, unable to make his legs move, his mind clutching at the earth-shattering significance of what he had just witnessed. Every fiber of his muscles wanted to burst in there and demand answers.

But that would raise too many dangerous questions, like why had Okie been following him? How had Okie recognized that something covert was happening? How did Okie have such advanced surveillance skills? It took a spook to recognize a spook.

Emmett was a spook. Okie's *father* was a spook. That could be the only explanation. But who was he working for? Whose side was he on? Undercover cop? FBI? CIA? And what was his mission? Why Marge Hall? Who was she really? Was she Emmett's mark? Had she been Emmett's mark *all these years*? His mind boggled at the possibilities. He couldn't imagine that golden boy Emmett Hansen would be working for the wrong side, so it was just a matter of who.

And then his mind began to churn through all the assumptions Okie had made since his mother had died, most of which were now likely false.

That was when his breath caught, and his eyes misted with tears. He stole away into the night before the dam of emotions could break loose.

❁❁❁

Throughout the drive back to the apartment, Okie kept muttering to himself.

"I *knew* it."

The storm of emotions knocked him into a tailspin. Anger, remorse, regret, wonder, all flashing by too fast to grasp.

His entire life had been a setup.

It was all connected. He could now see the entire chessboard clearly.

Emmett, Casey, Donovan, the Company, the Church—hell, maybe even the Mafia. He'd heard stories about how the OSS had enlisted the Sicilian Mafia to help infiltrate Italy during the war.

Doors had been opened for him by unseen hands, perhaps even as early as Canisius. Of course, he could have chosen not to go through them. Had he known that Emmett's hands were on any of them, he probably would have slammed them shut out of spite. He kept going back to Emmett's relationship with Marge Hall and its discovery on the day Okie's mother died. Could he forgive his father for fornicating with Marge Hall—if in fact he was—when Marge was either an asset, a mole, or a mark? That would take some time.

Suspicions roiled at every turn.

None of this made him love his father. Emmett was a cold, loveless man at the best of times. But in his own way, he had helped build his son's life into one that suited Okie in ways beyond the understanding of a teenage boy. Emmett *knew* his son better than Okie knew himself and had used his connections and influence to put Okie on this path.

It was a path he loved. He served God. He served his country. Everything else was superfluous.

Even Honey. Even Mary.

Nevertheless, appearances must be maintained. He and Honey appeared on the surface to be the typical young family, the darlings of popular conception about what a family was. He and Honey had roles to play. Emmett had a role to play. Likely, each of them had a role that shifted depending on the nature of the stage currently underfoot.

To the outsider, Emmett was the successful businessman, a captain of industry, a pillar of the Buffalo community, a former athletic golden boy, an upstanding Catholic. Okie was the breadwinner of America's brand of ideal family, going to the office every day, briefcase in hand, like his idealized peers. Honey played the role of the modern, forward-thinking career woman and devoted wife and mother. But *all* of it was a lie, a facade. Every outward detail. And it was a pack of lies that he and Honey had to cultivate. It was their job.

Okie didn't need to let Emmett know that he knew. Emmett *already* knew that Okie knew. Emmett had *always* known. And Okie had been kept in the dark for years. If not for a chance observation at the airport, he would be in the dark still.

But that was the way of the clandestine services. Every day, the stage underfoot was built upon suspicions, possibilities, mysteries, never quite solid enough for comfortable footing, leaving him and Honey constantly walking at tiptoe stance. Getting caught flatfooted in this business could mean an ignominious demise. How often had he awakened like a sprung bear trap to the sound of a dream bullet blasting through his skull?

How much anger, even rage, had Okie swallowed during all this time? He was only twenty-three—his mother had been gone eight years, a lifetime. At this moment, all that anguish felt like a profound waste. But without it, would he have been as driven to prove his father wrong at every turn? On the other hand, it wasn't his father he'd been fighting against; it was Emmett's *facade*. The real Emmett was a puppet master as adept as Bill Donovan or William F. Casey, always several steps ahead.

Donovan had told him once that chess was the perfect tool for teaching a person to think several moves ahead.

Tomorrow, he would challenge Emmett to a game of chess, and he had no doubt he would lose. It was time for him to learn from a grandmaster.

XXVI

***"BLESS ME, FATHER,** for I have sinned. It's been a week since my last confession. I've been...not myself lately. I've spoken sharply to my wife. I spanked Mary when I caught her trying to stick a nail into an electrical outlet. I regret these things. I haven't seen my only friend in months. He's off somewhere in Europe. My deepest fear is that I'll die friendless and alone."*

"The Lord is always with you. You will never be alone. Turn to Him."

"Yeah, well, He doesn't talk back. You can't go have a beer with God."

"Isaiah reminds us, 'Do not fear, do not be dismayed. For I am your God. I will strengthen you and help you; I will uphold you with my righteous right hand.'"

"I try, Father. I pray every day. But there's so much on my mind, I don't even know where to start. I want a son, but my wife doesn't want any more children. I have done things that...keep me up at night. I feel right with God for them, but...I haven't been sleeping. And my wife and I, things have settled down, but some days we're like strangers, especially when one of us comes home from a job. At least Mary is sleeping through the night now. Honey is in better shape now that she's getting more sleep."

"But not you?"

"Not me."

❁❁❁

1958

Okie looked at the typed note, then at the return address on the envelope, then at Honey, who stirred a saucepan of marinara.

He sat at the kitchen table with the rest of today's mail resting nearby.

Mary sat in her highchair, giggling and slapping at a little plate of buttered spaghetti, snatching up a fistful of noodles and thrusting them into her mouth.

"Well," Honey said, "what does it say?"

Okie cleared his throat.

"*My dear Mr. and Mrs. Hansen,*

I hope this letter finds you well in all respects. I am writing to thank you for your service and sacrifice. It has been my great pleasure to guide you thus far in what have been performances commensurate with your immense talents and dedication.

The time has come for me to step away. There is only so much I can do from a hospital bed, after all.

I am sure you will continue your duties with the same dedication and skill that brought you to my attention. May you both continue long and illustrious careers.

Respectfully,

Bill"

Honey stared out the kitchen window, a tear glistening at the corner of her eye. "Last time I saw him, he looked..."

"Frail," Okie said. The vitality of the old general he'd met in Sausalito had diminished significantly over the last couple of years.

She nodded. “At one point, he seemed a little confused, like he'd forgotten why I was there. But he hid it quickly, and then the meeting was over.”

A changing of the guard was coming. Donovan had never been a front man in the Company leadership. He'd been denied the directorship thanks to internecine political machinations but had worked behind the scenes for years, which is how he'd handpicked Honey, Okie, Don, Lois, and the whole Sausalito crew. Allen Dulles had been the director for several years, but there were others involved in the upper echelons of the covert operations shadows, not all of them specifically with the Company. The spheres of operation were muddy and blurred, sometimes by the necessities of the moment but mainly by interservice jealousy. The bureaucracy was fraught with people zealously guarding their own anthills.

As Okie contemplated unseen changes to the intelligence landscape underfoot, he saw more tears trickling down Honey's cheeks. Bill had been her mentor, her gateway into a world very few women were allowed to enter. Okie stood and approached her. She turned to hug him and cry quietly against his chest, and he held her.

Okie spent several days in Belgium, during which time he met three different assets at the World's Fair in Brussels—an East German colonel, a Ukrainian nuclear scientist seeking asylum in the United States, and a Czech industrialist with fingers in the munitions industry. Okie delivered packets of documents and cash and faded back into the crowds.

When Okie got home, he found Mary asleep and Honey exercising in the middle of the living room. He caught her in the middle of a set of jumping jacks. He took a moment to admire her as he set his suitcase on the floor, then took her in his arms and kissed her, which she returned not unwillingly.

"Did you have an interesting trip?" she asked.

He pulled her tighter, and she allowed it. "I missed you."

"Really?" she said, raising an eyebrow.

"Really," he said and kissed her again, and this time, the willingness flared.

They made love on the couch in a brief torrid explosion of desire. Afterward, as they sat naked, partially entwined and smoking Lucky Strikes, Honey gestured toward the kitchen table. "There's a letter for you from your cousin Cornelius. Arrived a couple of days ago."

He crossed the room and picked it up, opened it.

Dropped it.

Picked it up and read it again to make sure he'd read it correctly.

"What is it? Bad news?" she said behind him, concern growing.

His heart pumped faster, and his mouth went dry.

"C'mon, don't hold out on me," she said.

His eyes traced the little marks of fountain pen script. "He's inviting me to the Vatican..."

"Okay, that sounds swell, but—"

"To meet the Pope."

PART III

"What is past is prologue." -William Shakespeare, *The Tempest*

XXVII

***"BLESS ME, FATHER,** for I have sinned. It's been two days since my last confession. My sin is pride. I had a moment yesterday where it consumed me. You see, I've been invited to the Vatican for an audience with the Pope."*

"That is a great honor! Most priests never receive such an invitation."

"It's the opportunity of a lifetime. I leave for Rome in a few days. I was...I was sitting in the middle of Mass yesterday, and I had this moment where I felt chosen. It came to me like a wave, like a punch, and I was so utterly sure of it, sure of myself. And I looked around the church and saw all these people I see every week. And I was better than them. I get to meet the Holy Father. I felt God's Hand guiding my life. None of these people would ever do the things I'll do—the things I've done—their lives are small and weak. Helpless. It's right *for them to be in church. They're sinners. Of course, I'm a sinner, too, but...better than them. Disdain is the word I'm looking for. I have... held people's lives literally in my hands..."*

"That is indeed the sin of pride, my son. Malum in se.*"*

"Maybe a minute later, Mary started crying and wouldn't stop. My wife gave this look like, 'It's your turn.' So I took the baby outside, but she just screamed and screamed. After about ten minutes of this,

she let loose and just filled her diaper, then her dress and my sleeve, too. I said a few bad words and took her to the car to change her. Then it came to me, just as strong. A punch from the other direction, like the second of a one-two combination. There I was, the Chosen of God, with baby poop all over my arm."

"Children have a way of keeping us humble."

It was a sunny day in late September, approaching eighty degrees, when Okie touched down at Rome Ciampino Airport. Cornelius met him at the terminal, and after a cordial reunion they took a car to Vatican City.

His previous trips to Rome with Big Blue had been too short to enjoy the vastness of its history, but this time he wanted to take some of it in. It was as if he felt the Hand of God guiding him from one wonder to the next.

Cornelius took up the role of ad hoc tour guide. "This area we're passing through is called the Borgo district. It stretches east and west from the Tiber River to Vatican City. The name comes from the Gothic corruption of *borough*. Caligula built a circus here once, a racetrack for chariot races, as well as a space for executions. Emperor Nero expanded it. But it was here that Saint Peter was martyred on Nero's orders. Saint Peter requested to be crucified upside down as he did not feel worthy to be crucified in the same manner as Jesus Christ. It's much like a kind of antechamber to St. Peter's Square."

It was indeed a pretty neighborhood, with architecture stretching back hundreds of years. The cobbled streets were old and narrow, just wide enough for a car, cutting between four- to six-story buildings of tan, gray, and mustard yellow. Cafes, shops, and hotels dotted the streets at ground level. At the eastern extremity of the Borgo district stood the magnificent Castel Sant'Angelo, the Pope's fortified retreat in more turbulent times. Stretching straight as a spear shaft between Castel Sant'Angelo and St. Peter's Square was a broad thoroughfare, the Via della Conciliazione, which had been built by Mussolini in the late 1930s to symbolically connect the Vatican to the heart of the Italian capital. Just to the north, however, running roughly parallel to the Via della Conciliazione, was the Via dei Corridori, the Vatican Corridor, a crenelated fortification that stretched a half-mile along this street.

"This is the Passetto," Cornelius said, referring to the medieval fortification. "It was built in the thirteenth century as an escape route from the Palace to Castel Sant'Angelo. Pope Alexander VI used it to flee the invading French in 1492. But the wall goes back a few hundred more years." Cornelius was clearly enjoying the history lesson, giving it with the proper mix of enthusiasm and gravitas. "The most recent escape was in 1527 when Pope Clement VII escaped the mutiny of Charles V. Twenty thousand of his troops slaughtered the Swiss Guard and thousands of women and children on the steps of St. Peter's Basilica."

Okie was appreciating the history lesson, too, reminding him that the Catholic Church had a long, tumultuous history. If not for the grace of God, it might not have survived almost two thousand years of greedy monarchs, ambitious princes, and catastrophic wars. Rome itself had been sacked twice in the last nine hundred years, and five times before that by various Germanic tribes.

But the Church endured, in spite of it all.

"Ah, here is your hotel," Cornelius said. "I'm sure you're tired from the journey."

The driver stopped the car before a modest-looking facade upon which hung an overhead sign. *Hotel Bramante.*

Okie said, "That would be a great idea, but I'm not sure I'll sleep until I'm on the plane back home." He could still hardly believe this was real.

"You should probably look human for your audience tomorrow. Ten o'clock sharp. I'll come by to pick you up at eight. We can get breakfast. His Holiness does not grant many audiences these days. He's grown quite frail."

"Then how did you get me an audience?"

Cornelius gave an enigmatic smile. "Through channels. His Holiness saw fit to promote me recently. *Assistante Docente* of the Vatican Museum."

Okie grinned. "It just floors me that you *know* the Pope."

Cornelius laughed. "We're hardly on a first-name basis. His mind has been growing scattered lately. I think I was simply in the right place at the right time."

"Timing is everything," Okie said.

"And then, after that, we'll go to confession." Cornelius gave another enigmatic smile.

"Um, well, I was planning to, anyway. Who wouldn't go to confession in St. Peter's Basilica?" Then he eyed his cousin. "But I don't think that's entirely what you meant."

"You'll see."

❖❖❖

Since 1873, Hotel Bramante had displayed a charming brand of simple elegance. French doors from his room led to an interior garden courtyard. But before he got too comfortable, he did a security sweep of his room, checking locks and window latches and looking for bugs. No one but Honey and Cornelius knew he was coming to Rome, but if he'd learned nothing else it was to always be aware of the possibility of a tail. No doubt with the trail of successful missions he'd left behind him, he'd made enemies all across Europe.

After dark, he explored the streets around Borgo Pio, venturing toward the Vatican. It was a shockingly short distance to St. Peter's Square—a couple of football fields' distance—and the Basilica's beautiful dome rose like a monument worthy of God's majesty. It was only a couple of blocks to the forty-foot-high medieval fortifications surrounding Vatican City, and only two blocks more to the stunning spectacle of the Colonnade surrounding St. Peter's Square.

Footlights illuminated it all in stark drama. A mix of tourists and faithful still lingered in the *piazza,* interspersed with dark-robed clergy and nuns hustling about their business.

Atop the Colonnade stood well over a hundred larger-than-life marble statues of saints and popes.

A tingle shot through his body, became a rush, holding him in place at the mouth of the great oval, looking past the ancient Egyptian obelisk in the plaza's center, toward the magnificent Basilica, with its baroque Renaissance dome, itself bathed in floodlights. Spreading in both directions from the Basilica's facade was the oval colonnade that encircled St. Peter's Square. From above, the layout of the plaza resembled a giant keyhole, symbolic of the keys to the Church given to Saint Peter by Jesus.

Off to the right beyond the colonnade, a tall, blockish structure hove into view—the Apostolic Palace. On the top floor, a row of windows stood dark, except for the one on the far right. The Pope's personal chambers. Okie had studied maps of Vatican City before arriving. Off to the left was the *Braccio di Carlo Magna,* the "Charlemagne Wing."

The marble gazes of over a hundred statues pressed down upon him—saints, popes and even Jesus and the apostles—judging.

How much confession would it take to wipe the stains from his soul? How many more would he accrue?

Slowly crossing the expanse of the plaza, his feet got heavy and his breath short, until he lost all momentum and ground to a halt. Overwhelmed by beauty, drenched in history, bathed in the glory of God, he gazed up at the sky, saddened briefly that the city lights obscured the stars. His eyes misted, and the mist became tears streaking his cheeks. He didn't bother to wipe them away. He would wear them with honor before the very house of God.

When Cornelius arrived for breakfast at the hotel, Okie was too nervous to do anything but stare at the delectable-looking pastry before him. He'd barely slept, plagued by dreams of walking naked through the halls of the Vatican, amid stares and incredulous laughter, desperately seeking something he couldn't find and couldn't remember. When he finally gave up on sleep, he dressed in his best suit, polished his shoes five times, checked himself in the mirror over and over, arranged and rearranged every hair on his head with careful precision.

Meeting the Holy Father was the greatest honor a pious man could receive, even more so than meeting the president of the United States. The Pope answered directly to a higher power.

Cornelius did his best to calm Okie's nerves, but Okie was still practically vibrating out of his skin. His mind hovered in a strange dual state—half buzzing hyper-awareness, half dissociative fugue, as if he were temporarily inhabiting someone else's life where he dared not miss a single detail.

Nevertheless, the hour drew inexorably nearer, and Cornelius, with practiced familiarity, took Okie into St. Peter's Basilica through a special entrance, avoiding the crowds of pilgrims already streaming into the world's largest, most famous church. The hundred-thirty-foot facade dwarfed him, hammered him with awe. High atop the facade, with its ninety-foot Corinthian columns, the marble eyes of Christ and His Apostles gazed kindly down.

Okie and Cornelius passed into the Atrium and approached a door blocked by Swiss Guards in their striped uniforms, orange, black and purple. The Swiss Guards stood aside when Cornelius flashed a Vatican ID.

From there they passed into the nave, and Okie's strength of limb abandoned him. His legs could barely support his weight as the sense of awe hammered him harder. He became a flea, a speck, a mote before the vastness and grandeur of the basilica's interior.

Every square inch of it in every direction was more beautiful than anything he had ever conceived. The magnificence of it beggared his mind. The eye could not pass a sliver of view without being bedazzled by frescoes, mosaics, paintings, marble statues. It was as if two thousand years of history were happening all around him, all at once through the hands and souls of Renaissance master artists, funneling the divine into tangible reality.

He did not know how long he stood there slack-jawed, wide-eyed, splayed hand over his heart, blood rushing in his ears, his entire body tingling. How many normal-sized churches like his back in Buffalo could fit within this cavernous space? Twenty? Thirty?

Finally, Cornelius tugged at his elbow. "We mustn't be late."

Okie allowed himself to be led. "I could spend a week in here trying to take it all in."

"It takes longer than that."

Immediately to the right of the entrance gates from the Atrium stood the *Pietà,* Michelangelo's famous depiction, carved from a single large block of white marble, of Mary holding her dead son in her lap removed from the cross. Okie recognized it immediately. He had grown up with a miniature version on his mantelpiece. But comparing that cheap, tawdry copy to this was like comparing a flashlight to the sun. He stood there, rapt, transfixed. The Virgin Mary was so lifelike she could have stood up from her woeful seat. His eyes misted with tears and a lump caught in his throat. It was as if he were standing there with the beautiful Mary and her murdered son at the foot of the cross.

He blinked and roused himself to find Cornelius giving him a thoughtful smile. "After we're finished you can spend all the time you like with them."

The vastness of the interior of St. Peter's Basilica was difficult to grasp. The *Pietà* stood fifty yards away from where they had come in, and the far end of the interior, past the Papal Altar at the intersection of the floor plan's cross, was some two hundred yards away.

Cornelius led him past the *Pietà* and its crowd of onlookers, then down a tiny, secluded side passage, one that seemed to be made for people somewhat smaller than he was, and with just a few steps more, he found himself at the mouth of the Sistine Chapel.

"You'll have time to see it all later, I trust," Cornelius said, "but we must keep moving."

"Can I just live here?" Okie said. "I'd discard everything I own and camp out here as a penniless monk if I could just sit here and absorb all this art."

"I often have similar thoughts," Cornelius said, quickening his step. "I count myself incredibly blessed."

They were in a high-ceilinged, vaulted hallway, marble floors polished to mirror brightness. Frescoes, gilding, and bas reliefs adorned every square inch of wall and ceiling and arch and lintel, all of it steeped in Catholic symbolism, beauty so intense and intricate it was difficult to overcome the weight of overwhelming majesty. Angels and apostles, saints and cherubim, scenes of Christ's life and death and resurrection. Simply studying the art in a single hallway could be the work of a lifetime.

As two Swiss Guards fell in on either side of them, their escort into the Apostolic Palace, Okie's rubbery legs solidified. He could tell by the way these men moved that their role was not ceremonial. They were trained fighting men, brightly hued regalia notwithstanding. They looked like they'd stepped out of the seventeenth century, complete with pikes and swords.

The only sounds were their footsteps and the rustle of clothing. The only audible voices echoed as hushed murmurs as if unwilling to disturb the silence of these hallowed halls.

Through more vaulted hallways, they finally reached the interior gateway to the Apostolic Palace, the Pope's residence. They were met by a man dressed in the robes of a monsignor, with a crimson cap and a crucifix hanging around his neck from a long golden chain.

Cornelius leaned in and whispered something to the monsignor. The older man barely acknowledged Okie's presence, and Okie bristled slightly at the sense of being beneath this man's notice, just another task on his schedule for the day. Nevertheless, they fell in behind him, and he soon led them into another immaculately decorated room with wallpaper of golden brocade, topped by gorgeous frescoes. A crystal chandelier glimmered over their heads. There was no smallest part of this place that did not scream "*palace!*"

The Swiss Guards took positions on either side of the door.

The monsignor said in Italian-accented English, "His Holiness will join us momentarily."

Okie's heart thumped and thudded. He exchanged nervous glances with Cornelius, who tried to allay Okie's discomfiture with smiles of reassurance. Okie tried to occupy his eyes with taking in the room's frescoes. He checked his chronograph: 9:56. Minutes ticked by. No one spoke. He tried to gather enough spit to wet his desert-dry tongue. 10:04.

Cornelius had warned him that His Holiness had grown quite frail. He operated these days at a pace dictated by his physical limits. But then, at 10:14, Okie heard soft footsteps and swishing robes echoing down the hallway. The approach was so slow it seemed to be coming from a great distance.

And then the doorway was filled with men in black robes chased with gold and crimson, and then a man in dressed in snow-white robes tottered into view. Red velvet slippers decorated in gold braid with an embroidered gold cross near the toes peeked out from beneath the white robes. His raiment included a shawl of scarlet silk, a white cap, and a mantle embroidered with gold thread. Pope Pius XII looked like a man clinging to life with all the strength he possessed. Pale, paper-thin skin, narrow, sunken cheeks. He moved with a slow, careful step. Behind thick, circular lenses, his hooded eyes seated the guttering sparks of a failing intellect. Pope Pius XII was not a well man.

His handlers parted and one of them gestured for Okie to approach. Cornelius stepped aside with a bow and let Okie move forward.

The Pope extended his ring finger, and it was with strange wonderment that Okie took that old hand with its liver spots and gnarled blue veins, bent, and kissed the massive gold ring set with a large emerald circled by topazes and smaller emeralds. Okie knelt at the Pope's feet and bowed his head. A sour, medicinal smell crept into his nostrils.

The Pope's cold, dry hands cupped Okie's head beneficently, and then he spoke in Latin. "Bless this man, a soldier of Christ.

Grant him strength and wisdom as he protects the Church from the evils of the world. May God forgive his sins and grant eternal salvation in the name of the Father, and the Son, and the Holy Spirit. Amen. Rise, my son, and go forth, without hesitation, doing God's will."

A powerful rush shot through Okie. Every nerve ending buzzed with sensations he had never felt before, as if every hair stood on end.

Okie stood, towering over this hunched old man, but could not bring himself to meet the Pope's gaze.

"Know this, my son," the Pope said in Italian. "You are an instrument of the Lord."

Okie wiped tears with the back of his hand. "Thank you, Your Holiness." Did the Pope know who Okie was, what he had done?

And then the old man's vitality diminished as if spent, and he turned away and tottered out with his procession, leaving Okie to feel as if he had just been baptized anew, as if all his multitude of sins had been washed away in an instant. He was a new man, with carte blanche to do what was asked of him, knowing that no matter what he did henceforth, he would be forgiven for it. Eternal damnation transformed into everlasting absolution.

As he followed Cornelius out of the Papal Palace, Okie felt like he'd just been whacked by a dozen feather pillows—a little woozy but in a pleasant way.

"Are you all right?" Cornelius asked. "You look drunk."

Okie laughed. "That's how I feel." He paused and looked at his cousin. "Thank you for this."

Cornelius squeezed his shoulder and smiled. Then they walked on.

Past the Sistine Chapel again, back into the nave of St. Peter's. The crowds of pilgrims and tourists were thicker now. Had any of them ever experienced the majesty, the glory, of what he'd just felt? He walked half in a daze down the nave toward the intersection of the left and right transepts—the analog to the crossbar of a crucifix—where the Papal Altar stood beneath the ninety-foot-high bronze dome, the highest point of which stood fifteen stories above the marble floor. Cornelius led him down the left transept and around the periphery of where a Mass was being held with hundreds of congregants. The smell of incense filled the air, and strains of Latin chant echoed from golden vaults. A right turn brought them before a breathtaking masterpiece.

"The Monument to Pope Alexander VII," Cornelius murmured. "This is one of Bernini's late masterpieces. He was eighty when he finished it."

Between red marble columns stood an alcove, in which resided a curious scene in marble and bronze. Alexander VII in marble knelt in prayer over a gilded bronze image of a skeleton holding an hourglass, a depiction of Death. Alexander's figure rested atop a red marble shroud or drapery, surrounded by four mortal figures. The shroud decorated the frame of an ancient door.

"Where does that door lead?" Okie asked.

"Down to a crypt where many former popes are interred."

Scattered around the interior of the basilica were several confessional booths of dark, lustrous wood, each of them labeled to indicate the language of the confessor.

Just to the right of the monument stood such a confessional, this one labeled *GERMANICA*.

"Shall I hear your confession?" Cornelius said in an oddly mischievous tone.

Okie blinked and shrugged. "Uh, sure. Do I have to give it in German?"

Cornelius entered the confessional's middle chamber and closed the door behind him. Okie stepped into one of the two confessor booths and found himself in one like many others he'd been in, but this was by far the oldest. It had the usual ten-inch metal screen that separated the priest from the confessor. He opened his mouth to begin the standard litany—but then the partition between Okie and Cornelius swung aside, and his cousin stood there with a grin. "Come on," Cornelius said as he stepped out of sight, through the back of the booth where there should have been a marble wall.

Bewildered, Okie followed him, like stepping from one phone booth into another. But instead of a marble wall in the rear of the priest's alcove, there was a cramped stairwell of worn stone leading down into darkness.

XXVIII

***"BLESS ME, FATHER,** for I have sinned. It's been one day since my last confession. I am...having doubts..."*

"About what, my son?"

"About...a lot of things. Yesterday, I saw...something that makes me doubt. I... Is not the Pope infallible? Is he not the voice of God on Earth?"

"That is Church doctrine."

"Then why did the Catholic Church—this Pope—collude with the Nazis? Why is there a whole trove of stolen art right beneath our feet? Why hasn't it been given back to the rightful owners? Why—"

"In hoc signo vinces."

"You're right, Father. Please forgive my moment of doubt."

Ancient stones, worn smooth and uneven by the passage of countless hands and feet, led down into a passage as dark, dusty, and mysterious as any castle dungeon. A powerful thrill sent Okie's tongue against his palate, and his stomach flipped and tumbled. He suddenly felt like he stood in the midst of a Gothic movie.

"Is there a dungeon down there?" Okie asked.

Cornelius chuckled. "Come on." He gestured Okie to follow him.

Okie took it slow, letting his eyes adjust to the dim light filtering down. When they rounded the next revolution of the downward spiral, the light behind faded to leave them in blackness, and Okie was forced to feel his way down.

At one point, Cornelius said, "Watch your head."

The ceiling dropped so low Okie had to stoop, and he found himself getting disoriented because the walls narrowed then spread out again; the steps were of uneven height and different textures and materials, most of them chiseled stone or marble. A shaft of light spilled through a small aperture in the ceiling, making their going a little easier. The air was moist and earthy and cool. The deeper they went, the heavier the sense of antiquity, as if each step took them further back through the centuries. Soon a dim yellow glow emerged below, which proved to be a single, naked lightbulb hanging from a wire in the ceiling of a rough stone chamber, one wall of which was comprised of a stout bronze door that was green with age.

Cornelius knocked twice on the door. A face-sized viewport opened to reveal a guard in military-looking fatigues. Cornelius held up his Vatican ID. The viewport closed, and heavy keys rattled and clanked against the door. A heavy lock creaked and snapped. The door swung open on well-oiled hinges to reveal a long, earthen passageway.

The Swiss Guard stepped aside and stood at parade rest. Okie was quick to notice the man's sidearm. After they passed, the guard locked the door behind them.

Okie stood dumbstruck. One side of the passageway was a meticulously constructed brick wall, interspersed with doorways and windows. It looked like a buried city street.

Cornelius said, “St. Peter’s Basilica was built upon an older basilica by Emperor Constantine after he legalized Christianity, which in turn was built on an ancient Roman necropolis. But to prepare for construction, they had to level the ground. Rather than tearing down the necropolis, they filled it in. The original Roman basilica is at the level of the Grottoes, directly under the main floor upstairs. The current basilica was built on top of that.”

“Saint Peter himself was buried in that old necropolis?”

“Covertly, yes. That is tradition. He was martyred in the Square, which was Nero’s circus at that time. Peter’s followers took his body to the necropolis, which lay just outside the city limits on this hill.”

“So, Peter’s grave is down here?”

“Excavations are ongoing. We’re looking for Peter’s tomb.”

Underfoot were ancient flagstones carefully swept clean. They had been laid in a city with almost three thousand years of history. They had lain here for two millennia under fifty feet of earth, while the world went on, wars were fought, empires rose and fell.

It struck him then that there was more light than the few incandescent bulbs could provide. Light was filtering down from above.

“Daylight,” Okie said with surprise.

“Yes, there are grates built into the walls and floors above that bring in daylight all the way from outside.”

Cornelius led him down the subterranean street. The ceiling’s height varied, in one place stretching more than two stories above, earth that had been removed to reveal a two-story building almost fully intact, complete with a linteled front door. An ancient two-story building to house Roman dead—*beneath* St. Peter's Basilica.

They paused at the door of the house. Inside was a priest in his collar and soiled black trousers and shirt crouched under a tripod lamp, brushing at the earth obscuring the floor. What lay revealed was a mosaic in black and white of four horses pulling a chariot. The walls were of red brick, interspersed with white marble alcoves and more mosaics. The priest spotted Cornelius, gave a nod of acknowledgment, glanced once at Okie, then went back to his work.

Okie could feel the grit of the ancient walls and the uneven floor underfoot. He felt covered in death, an oddly curious feeling. Down here in the catacombs, he felt substantially deeper than "six feet under." It was a feeling he couldn't shake. The only sounds were their footsteps, and the footsteps of unseen others at work. The scent of dust mixed with mold and the faint whiff of decay. Suddenly he was very thirsty, parched, longing for a drink of water to moisten his tongue and throat.

Down the passageway Cornelius led him, some hundred yards of ancient city street. The houses looked almost lived in. He stared, rapt by how well-preserved the street appeared. In places, the brick walls were as erect as the day they were built. In other places, they were crumbling, pocked with age, or showing the marks of the chisel that carved them two thousand years ago. It was as if he had walked into another time, strolling through the literal roots of the Catholic Church.

"I must tell you," Cornelius said, "you can speak of this to no one. This excavation is of the utmost secrecy."

Okie nodded.

"It's only because you're a member of the Order that I was allowed to bring you down here. No one outside certain members of the Vatican Museum are allowed down here. We're going to be entering an area of the Vatican that doesn't appear on any map. Only a handful of priests know that it even exists."

"I understand."

"The Key Master will show us through the Vatican Museum Vaults."

At the far end of the necropolis excavation was another bronze door with its attendant guard, who allowed them to pass into the narrow tunnel beyond.

They were met by another priest, a middle-aged man with a stern demeanor. Hanging from the belt of his black cassock was a massive ring of ancient keys. He gave Okie a long, appraising look.

"Father Gerhart, this is Emmett Hansen," Cornelius said in Italian. "He's been given a special dispensation. Did you receive my memo?"

"I did. A pleasure to meet you, Mr. Hansen," Father Gerhart said in Italian.

"The pleasure is mine, Father," Okie said.

"You will both stay with me," Father Gerhart said. "You will not wander off. You will touch nothing. Do you understand?"

Okie said, "Yes, sir."

"Very well. Let us proceed."

The priest spun with an august swish of his cassock and led them through a disjointed connection of passageways, blocked off by another thick, bronze gate. The massive ring of keys, of a multitude of sizes and shapes, made him look like a medieval jailer. These he unhooked from his belt of golden rope, and he sorted out one longer than a hand and fitted it into the heavy lock. With a twist of the lock, he pushed open the aged gate to admit Okie and Cornelius. Then he locked it behind them and led them onward.

This narrow passage lacked the apertures for natural light, illuminated only by a few feeble incandescents. It was an arched brick tunnel perhaps forty paces long, which came to a junction and another bronze gate. The subterranean silence was unnerving, made Okie feel like there was someone behind him, even though he was bringing up the rear. Through this gate and down a few steps that didn't quite match up. Then they were in a passage that looked like newer architecture. The concrete floor was stained by age but far newer than the fitted flagstones of the necropolis.

With each bronze door, the passages descended, and their character shifted, until they entered a dark chamber where the echoes shifted into the distance.

The Key Master flipped a wall switch. A series of metallic *chunk* sounds spread in succession through the sprawling chamber as banks of buzzing fluorescent lights came alive. They were in a low-ceilinged chamber filled with arched brick support pillars. The space and walls were filled with endless stacks and shelves of cardboard tubes and wooden crates of innumerable sizes and shapes. The air was cool and comfortable with minimal humidity.

"May we take a walk through the vault?" Cornelius asked.

The Key Master nodded his assent. He hung back as Cornelius led the way, and Okie could feel the man's hawklike gaze on the back of his neck.

"What's in all of these crates?" Okie asked.

"*Objets d'art,*" Cornelius said.

"There are thousands of pieces here!" Okie blurted, sensing Father Gerhart stiffen behind him.

"Indeed," Cornelius said. "The Vatican Museum has one of the largest collections in the world."

Maybe the largest, Okie thought, glancing back at the glowering Key Master.

Many of the wooden crates were stamped or stenciled in German, mixed with numbers, addresses, shipping documents stapled to them.

Some of the works stood exposed. A white marble Roman bust nestled in a bed of straw. Religious paintings with a Renaissance feel and earlier, many renditions of Virgin and Child. There were others of more modern, French impressionist style. Could that one be a Monet? He was not well-versed enough to identify any artists. Still lifes. Landscapes. Sculptures in stone and metal. A six-foot stack of Persian rugs.

His gaze fell upon a stunningly beautiful painting of an impressionist landscape, about twenty by twenty-five inches, depicting a forest glade in which a band of frolicking children caught a shaft of sunlight among the boles. Even in the dim light, the painting's lush greens held his gaze, and the dancing children brought a giggle to the back of his throat.

The chamber stretched away into dim reaches. Not just thousands of pieces. Ten times that, a hundred. The sheer volume of art that the Vatican was literally sitting on made Okie's head swim. Why was it not on display? Shouldn't it be on exhibit?

The question came out of his mouth before he realized it.

Cornelius glanced carefully at Father Gerhart. "There simply is no place to put it all. There is only so much space in the Vatican Museum."

Okie opened his mouth to ask another question, but his mind seized the answer first.

This treasure trove of art was just that—treasure. The Vatican's true wealth, amassed over almost two millennia, could only be guessed at, and this secret storehouse represented a considerable chunk of that wealth. Artworks would be the perfect vehicle for storing and moving wealth that wasn't just currency. It was a commodity.

Cornelius leaned close and spoke quietly enough that the Key Master could not hear. "And much of this is of, shall we say, complicated provenance. Possession doesn't always confirm legitimate ownership."

Okie met his glance, and puzzle pieces fell into place.

They were surrounded by Nazi loot.

The rumors he'd heard among the Monuments Men investigators were true. The Vatican possessed untold millions of dollars in artwork stolen by the Nazis.

The queasiness in his belly twisted into a hard knot.

How many murdered Jews were represented by all this stolen art? Okie's sense of awe and wonder evaporated in a kind of heat he couldn't name.

Scattered around the outer walls were several gated alcoves. Art behind bars. Cornelius angled toward one, as if choosing at random. When they drew closer, he could see inside a wooden crate stenciled with the word *RAFFAELLO*. His heart leaped into greater speed again. Behind the crate stood a marble altar just large enough to support the framed oil painting resting thereupon. It stood about twenty-eight by twenty-two inches, depicting a handsome, fine-featured young man in a dark hat, white shirt, with a sable fur draped over his nearer shoulder.

He recognized it instantly from the photograph given to him by Wild Bill Donovan.

Raphael's *Portrait of a Young Man*.

He paused to take it in. The young man was so fine-featured, his hair so wavy and long he could have been mistaken for a woman, and he looked out from the painting with a wise kindness few possessed.

Father Gerhart cleared his throat, as if wishing to herd them onward. Cornelius glanced back and ambled on, as if this had not been his destination all along.

They made a loop through the chamber, taking in other gorgeous masterpieces, but Okie could hardly take his mind off the Raphael.

The Monuments Men were right, however much he'd been reluctant to believe it until now.

The Vatican had laundered art for the Nazis. It had taken in all this stolen art, possibly some of it after the Third Reich had fallen, knowing that it had been stolen. Had any effort been made to identify it, catalog it, or return it to its former owners? It didn't matter that many of those owners had been turned into ash on the wind.

They left Father Gerhart behind when they emerged into the subterranean levels of the Gallinaro Tower.

Cornelius was speaking again, but Okie was too shattered by the implications of what he'd just seen to keep his attention focused.

"Gallinaro Tower was built between 1578 and 1580 in four stages of progressive development. It was designed by the Bolognese architect, Ottaviano Mascherino, to house the Vatican Observatory, the 'Specola Astronomica Vaticana,' which was critical for astronomical observations and the Gregorian calendar reform..."

Ascending from the basement, on a gently graded ramp of white herringbone brick floors, they emerged on the mezzanine of the Sundial Room. The floor consisted of a marble meridian embedded in the floor extending across the floor in a north-south orientation.

Cornelius kept glancing at him, his voice shaky. "The noon sun could be measured while the anemoscope, affixed to the ceiling, would calculate the wind speed. There are the Pomarancio frescoes, by Nicolò Circignani, on the west and south walls. The ceiling is adorned with frescoes, by Matteino de Siena, known as the Allegories of the Seasons..."

Okie needed fresh air. His chest felt tight, as if a fat man was sitting on it. The beautiful frescoes all around him seemed to taunt him, sneer at him.

Finally, he stumbled into sunlight and fresh air in the gardens behind the Vatican Museum, amid palm trees and meticulously manicured hedges. He sank onto a marble bench and put his head in his hands.

"I can't believe it," was all he could manage to say.

"The past is a complicated thing," Cornelius said, looking into distant thoughts of his own, and that was all.

Okie sought some emotion in his cousin's face but couldn't penetrate the mask.

"What's going to happen to the Raphael?" Okie asked.

"It's scheduled to be shipped to South America. They have a buyer."

His thoughts flicked immediately to the Nazi monster hiding in Bolivia. "The buyer wouldn't happen to be Klaus Barbie, would it?"

Cornelius shook his head. "The buyer's name is confidential. The sale was brokered through a third party."

For a long time, Okie stared through the garden's greenery, but he saw only those soft brown eyes. "Thank you for showing me. I'll pass the word along. Maybe we'll find it after it gets to South America."

XXIX

***"BLESS ME, FATHER,** for I have sinned. It's been three days since my last confession. Last night, my wife and I had our first night out together in a long time. My sister agreed to babysit, so we went to a new picture I've been hearing about. It had Jack Lemmon and Tony Curtis and Marilyn Monroe."*

"I've heard of this one, a Billy Wilder picture. Some Like It Hot, *yes? It sounds positively pornographic. Cross-dressing, nudity, lascivious behavior."*

"Well, yeah. It was *pretty racy. I'd never seen Marilyn Monroe in a picture before. I've seen her in...magazines and such for years, but this is the first time I've seen her in a movie. The whole time she was on the screen, I...had irresistible lustful thoughts. Generally, I have lustful thoughts several times a day, but this was stronger. More intense. I...had dreams about her sexually dominating me, so intense I had to get up and...I have sinned in thought and flesh."*

"We must not immerse ourselves in the sins of Hollywood."

"There's just something about her."

Soon after Okie returned from Italy, Pope Pius XII retired to his villa in the hills and passed from the earth.

A few days after that, Okie was offered an expanded role in Company operations, but it required a move to Chicago. He found no resistance from Honey, as it would take her closer to her hometown of Elmhurst. Even though her relationship with her parents was strained, it was still "home."

For two years, Okie had been ostensibly employed by Watson, splitting time between his cover job and his real work in a nondescript office in downtown Buffalo, interspersed with overseas missions and training in Virginia. He kept up his sniper and tradecraft skills, although the Wild West of Berlin's back alleys was starting to feel like ancient history. He felt like he was spinning his wheels. So, this opportunity in the Chicago office excited him tremendously.

He walked into Emmett's office that same afternoon to give him the news. "I'm leaving. We're moving to Chicago."

Emmett gave him a long look with hints of sadness behind the wall, as if he were unsurprised. He knew where Okie was going. He took a deep breath and nodded slowly, steepling his fingers before his chin. "Get out while you can, son. Get out while you still have a soul." His gaze went distant even as it turned inward.

That ended the conversation.

They purchased a small house in Evanston, a suburb just north of downtown Chicago. This was all a great delight to Honey's parents, who had no other grandchildren. To their neighbors, Okie and Honey were the quintessential American family: hard-working breadwinner, beautiful young wife, perfect little child. When the neighbors asked what he did for a living, he told them simply, "I'm a consultant," then changed the subject.

1959

On January 11, just days after Fidel Castro seized control of Cuba, he appeared on *The Ed Sullivan Show*. Okie and Honey watched the show while Mary played with blocks on the living room floor.

In the lead-in to the interview Ed Sullivan said, "Somebody has said that freedom is everybody's business."

"Can you believe this?" Okie kept saying. Honey's gaze kept flicking between him and the grainy picture on the TV screen. He had never told Honey that he'd met Castro and Guevara—they didn't discuss their clandestine activities—but she could probably tell he was operating on information that went far beyond what the general public knew.

On New Year's Day, 1959, Castro's *revolución* had driven Fulgencio Batista from power. Castro and Guevara had launched the revolution from Mexico in November 1956, five months after Okie had met them in Yucatan. For over two years, they waged a guerrilla war through the hills, forests, and sugar cane fields of Cuba, an effort that was more lucky than skilled, from what Okie had read in internal Company analyses, but also fueled by Batista's continuing corruption and heavy-handedness. Castro's initial landing had been disastrous, leaving only twenty of his men alive to flee into the hills. But from that, they had built a movement.

And now, here was Fidel Castro, darling of the American media, bogeyman of the American conservative, on *The Ed Sullivan Show*. Sullivan had flown to Cuba to meet Castro a few days before. The interview was recorded at 2:00 a.m. local time, surrounded by bearded revolutionaries with guns.

Sullivan asked Castro to describe the horrors of the Batista regime.

"Thousands were tortured," Castro replied in English.

Sullivan said, "I'd like to ask you this, Fidel. In Latin American countries, over and over again, dictators have come along. They break the country, they have stolen the money, millions and millions of dollars, tortured and killed people. How do you propose to end that here in Cuba?"

Castro answered, "Very easy. Not permitting that any dictatorship come again to rule our country. You can be sure this will be the last dictator of Cuba, because now, we are going to improve our democratic institutions."

"The people of the United States have great admiration for you and your men, because you are in the real American tradition of a George Washington, of any band who started off as a small body, fought against a great nation and won. How do you feel about the United States?"

Castro's broken English was difficult to understand in the recording, and Okie leaned forward, elbows on his knees. "My feeling to the people of the United States is a feeling of sympathy because they are a very work hard. They have found that big nation working hard very much. It is a nation that belongs to the people of every world. The United States is one not race of people, they came from every part of the world. It is a nation that belongs to the world, to those who are persecuted. Those who could not leave their own country came to the United States, joined to the United States, and made it a big nation."

"We want you to like us, and we like you, you and Cuba," Sullivan said.

As Sullivan and Castro thanked each other for the interview, Sullivan handed him a folded piece of paper that Castro quickly read and tucked into his shirt pocket.

Honey saw it, too. "Ed just gave him a message."

Okie rubbed his chin. "He sure did. Is Sullivan working for us?"

"He was on the list, but if he is, it wasn't me. I never got the assignment."

In April, Castro came to the United States. At the invitation of the National Press Club, he gave a speech and took questions. Okie listened to the recording and noted that Castro seemed a bit more strident, a bit less conciliatory in the way he answered questions from the American press. He'd requested a meeting with President Eisenhower, but the request had been ignored.

His activities throughout his visit to the United States were in all the papers. In New York, he fed a tiger at the Bronx Zoo and gave a speech to thirty thousand people in Central Park. In Washington, he ate ice cream, signed autographs, and kissed babies up and down the National Mall, happy to practice his English with anyone who approached. In the Capitol, he met with the

Senate Foreign Relations Committee, declared his disinterest in nationalizing any foreign-held—i.e., U.S.-owned—property, and waved away questions about the Communists in his government. He wanted American-style democracy. When senators pressed him about firing squads, reported to have executed over five hundred people thus far, he insisted they were all "war criminals." He promised Cuba would have free elections within four years, and soon, a free press. The papers sang his praises, comparing him to the Founding Fathers. He was "larger than life," stirring passions of America's revolutionary past. Company sources in Cuba, however, reported that Communists were infiltrating every town and trade union. Okie figured this was Che Guevara at work.

For all five days Castro was in Washington, President Eisenhower was pointedly absent, playing golf in Augusta, Georgia. American corporate interests were sure Castro was going to shut down or steal their Cuban properties—the sugar industry, casinos, and others. He had already nationalized the American-owned Cuba Telephone Company.

Vice President Richard M. Nixon met with Castro for over two hours on a Sunday afternoon at his office inside the Capitol.

Castro had come out of that meeting less than enthusiastic and gone back to Cuba, all but giving the United States a great big middle finger. Batista had been a puppet of the American elite, and Nixon had demanded that Castro toe that line. Castro had no intention of following in Batista's footsteps. The intransigence of an idealist couldn't be underestimated.

An unconfirmed brief said that Raul Castro had sent an envoy to Moscow at the same time as Fidel's visit to the U.S.

So what game was Castro playing? Cuba had scarce resources besides sugar. It couldn't survive without aligning itself with a global power. The U.S. and the Soviet Union were the only significant players in the game. Whose side would he come down on?

Despite his celebrity status in the media, the winds in America shifted against Castro after his visit.

Then in November, Okie flew to Langley to attend a Company meeting with Director Allen Dulles, several other high-ranking leaders of the clandestine services, and several agents, including Don Fell, whom he hadn't seen since leaving Germany, plus Kirby and a couple of others from the Sausalito gang.

They all had a cordial reunion in the hallway outside the briefing room. "It's like old times all of a sudden," Don said as they all shook hands.

"Drinks later," Kirby said. Then he chucked Okie on the arm. "Shoot the ass off any gnats lately?"

Okie chuckled. "Unfortunately, no. Haven't spotted any Commie gnats."

Their happiness ended the moment the meeting started.

Director Dulles got up before the room full of men in suits and launched into it without preamble. Castro had turned full into embracing communism, and now actively courted the Soviet Union. Incensed at the possibility of having Communists on their very doorstep, the Eisenhower administration had drafted a plan to overthrow the Cuban government and tasked the Company with that mission, codenamed Operation Mongoose.

"In short," Dulles said, "we're going to kill Castro."

A ripple went around the room.

Dulles went on, "There's no one else in Castro's inner circle with the same mesmeric appeal. Without Fidel, they will collapse."

The Company would use every means at its disposal to accomplish this mission, including underworld contacts still extant in Cuba.

He means the Mafia, Okie thought. The Mafia owned, directly or indirectly, most of the casinos in Havana.

Over the next week, he and fellow operatives brainstormed ideas for assassination.

"With a good spotter," Kirby said, "Okie here could shoot him from Miami. Problem solved."

Okie wondered if he'd be sneaking into Cuba soon for just such an attempt.

Even the most outlandish ideas were on the table.

"Exploding cigar," someone said.

"Poisoned wetsuit. He loves scuba diving."

"Botulism in his food."

"Train Cuban exiles as counterrevolutionaries."

The methods and ramifications of every idea, no matter how outlandish, were discussed in detail. Turning one of Castro's inner circle. A commando squad infiltration. Hiring the Mafia to put out a hit. They hated Castro for the loss of their casinos, and they had close connections to the Cuban refugees who'd fled the revolution. Okie offered his connection to the Montana family as something that could be exploited, but someone said, "The Trafficante family in Tampa or the Chicago syndicate are better options. They have more Havana connections."

Over long, exhausting hours, proposals were drafted and submitted. Afterward, drinks were had. Okie found himself enjoying all this immensely. He could almost forget life's mundanities back home like an endlessly crying baby and her attendant bodily functions, or a hot-and-cold bedmate.

Then in the middle of these efforts, Director Dulles took Okie into his office, where every meeting was a closed-door meeting. Okie had never spoken with the Director before, so he tried to conceal his nervousness. He found himself standing at attention.

Dulles noticed this, and with a slight smile gestured him to sit. Okie sat.

"Allow me to compliment you on your work, Mr. Hansen," Dulles said.

"Thank you, sir."

"You show great promise."

"I do my best."

Dulles waved away further platitudes. "The vice president wants to meet you."

Okie stared. Blinked. "Did you...say the *vice president* wants to meet *me*?" It seemed odd. Nixon seemed somewhat outside the normal chain of command. The word was that he was going to run for president next year, and he had enough popularity nationwide that he could win. He seemed like a moral, upstanding, patriotic man. Okie liked the things Nixon had to say, and he admired the public debate Nixon had had with Khrushchev back in July about the merits of freedom versus communism at the American National Exhibition in Moscow, part of a cultural exchange between the U.S. and the U.S.S.R. Exhibitions included American art, fashion, cars, model homes and futuristic model kitchens. More than three million people visited the Sokolniki Park venue. They were calling it the "Kitchen Debate," because it had taken place in a model kitchen set up for the fair. For a brief period, within the faux walls of a modern American kitchen, the gloves had come off. America and the Soviet Union had sparred over whose system was superior—communism or capitalism. The U.S. media had had a field day.

"He asked me for files on a few promising agents. I sent them over. He asked for you."

Okie straightened, imagining Fidel Castro in the reticle of his sniper scope. "He's out of town at the moment, but it's on his agenda. Someone will reach out."

The only thing Okie told Honey about the trip to Washington was that Richard Nixon wanted to meet him based on President Eisenhower's recommendations.

She grinned, and he saw the real pride in her eyes. "*My* husband! My Big Boomah!" After that, they made love with an intensity that had been absent for a long time. She seemed imbued with fresh heat, a glow, a ripeness.

As they lay on the bed covered in sweat and afterglow, she rolled onto her side and looked at him, traced a finger that smelled of both of them across his chest. "I have something to tell you." She paused, as if uncertain, then said, "You're going to be a daddy again."

XXX

"BLESS ME, FATHER, *for I have sinned. It's been a week or so since my last confession. I have wished someone harm of the most extreme sort, even fantasized about it. She's one of the most vile individuals I've ever encountered, and I've met real-life former Gestapo. If anyone deserves the Sword of God, it is her."*

"It is not your place to make such judgments, my son."

"But isn't it? I have done terrible things in my country's name. Judge, jury, all that. But doing away with her would be a service to the human race. She's been working for my father since before my mother died. She and my father have been lovers for years, although probably not as hot and heavy as I once thought. Two weeks ago, she quit working for him, abruptly, because she had another plan in place.

"She took over her family's company in a sort of coup. She literally seized power away from her brothers in some way that hasn't been made public. If there were an entire family I would wish harm upon, it would be all of those closet Nazis, but this was extraordinary. I'm not sure how she did it, but it's made a big stir around town.

"Their company has been one of my father's minor competitors for the last few years. Within two weeks of taking over Hall Industries, she's stolen several of my father's major accounts. How? Inside

information. My father discovered that a number of files are missing from his offices. Without those accounts, it becomes an open question whether he has to start laying people off. I told him he should sue her ass off, but he says he has no proof. He knows things he's not telling me.

"I have to hand it to her, she's as slick and ruthless as they come. I'm angry because I should have seen it coming. Maybe I did, a long time ago, but then...I don't know. I guess I thought he had her under control. She was more dangerous than I realized. Even thinking about it now, I want her dead."

1960

In the early months of the year, Okie watched Operation Mongoose ramp up. Its name changed as fast and often as things were developing in Cuba.

From January to March, unmarked airplanes flown by counterrevolutionaries and supplied by the CIA dropped incendiary bombs on Cuban sugar cane fields, the country's chief resource.

In March, a French cargo ship, *La Coubre*, laden with arms for Castro's new regime mysteriously caught fire in Havana harbor, killing over a hundred crewmen and injuring three hundred more.

Also in March, President Eisenhower approved a CIA policy paper titled "A Program of Covert Action Against the Castro Regime," a paper Okie had seen in various drafts. The CIA plan put forward four courses of action: forming an opposition group in exile with rhetoric focused on restoring the revolution that Castro betrayed by turning to communism; setting up a radio station to broadcast anti-Castro programming into Cuba; creating a clandestine network within Cuba, working for the opposition in exile; and training a paramilitary force that would deploy into Cuba to train and organize resistance forces there. All of this was to be done with the utmost secrecy. There must be no whiff of U.S. involvement.

So, the CIA began training exiled Cuban nationals in Florida and Panama to spearhead an invasion to take down Castro. Okie couldn't help but wonder how three hundred disgruntled Cubans could keep their mouths shut. The fact that Castro announced as early as March that any invasion would be "fought to the death" raised worries that perhaps he already knew something was in the works, which raised questions of moles among the trainees.

In April, a fifty-kilowatt radio station was erected on Swan Island, a tiny, contested territory off the coast of Nicaragua, which the Company had used in its campaign to oust Guatemalan president Jacobo Árbenz back in the early 1950s.

Also in April, amid the endless flurry of communiques, analyses, and reports from Operation Mongoose, Honey gave birth to a son. They named him Emmett Hansen III.

On May 12, near the port city of Mariel, Cuban forces shot down a Piper Apache flown by an operative, Matthew Edward Duke, whom Okie had met during the planning sessions. The pilot was killed, further escalating the Company's direct involvement on the island.

In July, perhaps because of worries about loose lips among the trainees, the guerrilla training camps were moved to the Sierra Madre on the Pacific coast of Guatemala. Three Americans whom

Okie knew only as Bill, Bob, and Nick were in charge of training exile members in radio communications.

At what point did Okie pause to celebrate the fact that he had a son? He couldn't remember. He had been in Guatemala helping ferry materiel when Honey went into labor, and when he returned, Honey was already home from the hospital. He felt terrible about missing the birth, so he showered her with bouquets of flowers for a week after his return. His son—they started calling him "Trey"—was an angel compared to Mary's colicky temperament. Okie imagined he could see the innate intelligence in the infant's azure eyes. This kid was going to be too smart for his own good.

But the truth was, a new baby felt like the worst possible distraction from work that was important on a global scale. He didn't have time for diapers, spit-up, and incessant wailing.

A few weeks after Trey was born, on a Saturday afternoon, Okie and Honey flew the whole family to Buffalo to introduce Trey to Emmett. Mary was almost four now, and was quite capable of walking, but preferred that Daddy carry her.

"What a handsome lad!" Emmett said as the three of them looked down on the swaddled bundle with its pink face peeking out. "A chip off the old block."

"He's got my nose," Honey said.

"I big sister, Grampop," Mary said grinning.

"I see that, my dear," Emmett said warmly. "You have to help him grow up big and strong and carry on the family name."

Mary frowned a little, confused.

Emmett went on, "Now we'll have to see about getting him into Holy Cross."

Okie stiffened.

"Maybe he'll finish," Emmett said.

Honey flashed Okie a warning glance. "Oh, it's a little early for that, don't you think? I was thinking more like Northwestern University. Evanston is our hometown now. He looks like a scientist to me."

"A discussion for another time," Emmett said briskly, and then they sat in the living room and managed an hour of conversation without ripping off any further old scabs or compromising national security. Emmett fully deployed his businessman charm.

Okie asked about Marge's *coup d'etat* at Hall Industries but refrained from asking what she'd stolen from Watson and from using the profane descriptions that should be properly ascribed to her.

Emmett said, "We have forgiven each other."

Okie stared. "You must be joking." How many times had he envisioned putting two in her skull like that Soviet trollop in Berlin? But Buffalo was not Berlin.

"Leave it alone, Okie," Emmett said.

Okie acquiesced, for now, wondering if Emmett had been directed to stay in with her. Could Marge Hall possibly know Emmett was a Company man? Why was she so important that Emmett would be directed to patch things up with her? He couldn't sit on his questions any longer, however.

*

That night, after the kids had been put to sleep back in the hotel room and Honey's nightcap had been administered, Okie returned to Emmett's house.

Emmett was surprised to see him at the door.

"Something on your mind, son?" Emmett asked as he stepped aside.

"We need to talk," Okie said.

"Do we now?" Emmett stiffened almost imperceptibly.

"There are some things I know, and some things I don't," Okie said as he stepped inside. He glanced around to make sure they were alone.

"I've sent Elsa home."

Okie fidgeted, unsure of how this conversation should go, even though he'd considered several gambits. He and Emmett had never once had an open conversation man to man.

Emmett said, "Maybe it is time we came to an understanding. Would you like a drink?"

"Beer if you have it," Okie said. A Falstaff or seven might make this go easier—or it could lead to fisticuffs.

Emmett nodded and went into the kitchen, and Okie heard the refrigerator door, then two bottles being opened. Meanwhile Okie surveyed the living room, which hadn't changed an iota since he was a child. The same print of *The Last Supper* above the mantelpiece, the same miniature *Pietà*, which looked cheap and tawdry now that Okie had stood in the presence of the real thing.

Emmet came back and gestured Okie toward the worn sofa, while he assumed his customary chair.

Okie took the bottle of beer—Falstaff—and sat, taking a drink. He gripped the cold glass. Emmett crossed his legs and regarded him.

"That night you drugged Marge—"

"I've been given the go-ahead—"

They both spoke simultaneously, then stopped, staring at each other.

"Proceed, son."

Okie spoke haltingly, watching for any reaction. "That night you drugged Marge at the Christmas party. I saw you do it. I followed you back to her place."

Emmett's face registered a moment of surprise, but not displeasure. "And what did you see?"

"I saw enough. Plenty. So my question is, who are you working for? And why Marge Hall?"

"Let's just say we have some mutual friends."

"And their last names are Casey, Dulles, and Donovan?"

The corner of Emmett's mouth twitched upward and he folded his hands across his torso. "Among others."

Hearing confirmation of this settled him like the keystone of an arch. Okie stood and began to pace. He didn't know how to feel about this. Years of resentment warred with pride for everything he had achieved on his own. How much of it was really his own? Was the web too tangled to easily extricate the threads?

"I must admit, son, I had my doubts." Emmett sipped his beer. "After you flunked out of Holy Cross, that is. But you got back on track. You may not realize this, but some of your former classmates at Holy Cross now work for the Company."

"Really?"

"The Company is a family business, so to speak. As is the Order."

It felt absolutely surreal to hear someone else say the words. Okie had suspected so much for so long. He barked a laugh. "All that, and I've never been to a single club meeting."

"The real work is never decided at 'meetings.' It is both more and less organized than you might imagine. Suffice to say, the means are less important than the overarching goals. Those goals often exceed human lifetimes. The Order plays a very long game, longer even than the Company."

"'Family business,' huh?"

"I never knew Bill Donovan, but we knew of each other. When the OSS was dissolved, he made it his personal mission to reconstitute it with the best people he could find. Many of the Company's personnel from the very beginning were handpicked by him and a handful of others, including our mutual acquaintance, Mr. Casey. But I suspect you already knew this."

Okie nodded, breathing deeply, trying to assimilate all this. "So tell me about Marge. I have to know."

"The Hall family trafficks in stolen art."

"Nazi loot."

Emmett nodded, and Okie thought he discerned a trace of regret.

"Are you working with the Monuments Men?" Okie asked.

"I keep an eye on Marge's books and forward that information along. Once certain pieces reach their destinations, they are... recovered."

"So all this time..." Okie's voice trailed off. "Was this...even before Mom died?"

Emmett nodded. "It is how the Hall family made their fortune in this country. Marge is now the head of that operation."

"Holy shit, Pops." The next question he wanted to ask was whether Marge thought she was working Emmett, rather than the other way around, but that delved too close into the nature and origins of whatever physical relationship existed between them. Okie's stomach couldn't handle that thought. In a strange way, it made Emmett a kind of "honey pot" agent.

Okie sat down, took a drink, then got up to pace again. "Holy shit, Pops," was all he could say as he looked in amazement at the man across from him.

XXXI

WITH TWO SMALL CHILDREN in their small Evanston house, Okie spent even more time in his downtown Chicago office working as an independent consultant.

Honey was much quicker this time to shed the chains of infant motherhood. He came home one evening to find a homely young woman in his living room, holding Trey while she watched Walter Cronkite, who had just taken over as anchor on the CBS evening news from Douglas Edwards.

At the sight of this strange woman holding his son, his instincts flew into deadly alarm. He dropped his briefcase. "Who are you?"

She gave him a tentative smile and spoke with a slight French accent. "I am Lena, your new nanny."

"Where's Honey?"

Her eyes locked on him like a groundhog with a predator in sight, her smile fading. "She said she was going shopping."

He took a deep breath and tried to relax.

"Um, I made your dinner," she said.

His nose registered the delicious aroma of meatloaf and mashed potatoes. As his mouth began to water, he grunted with a nod. "Thank you." He stepped toward her and leaned over Trey, who was fast asleep with two fingers in his mouth. "Hey, there, champ."

"He's such a good baby," she said. "He's going to follow in Papa's footsteps someday."

For so long had Okie been nostril-deep in Operation Mongoose and new-infant exhaustion that he completely forgot about the invitation from Vice President Nixon that had never come.

It was a Tuesday afternoon in mid-July, just before 4:00 p.m., when the call came to his desk in his windowless office. This was a line that was routinely checked for taps, but it almost never rang.

He stared at the receiver for a moment before he picked it up.

"Emmett Hansen Jr.?" said a male voice, quick and businesslike.

"Speaking," Okie said. The name grated on him less these days.

"I am calling on behalf of Vice President Richard Nixon. He would like to request a meeting with you. You're in Chicago, right?"

The surge of emotions filled his chest, dried his mouth, and drowned his voice. If he hadn't heard such an invitation might be coming, he might not have believed the call was real.

"Sir?"

Okie cleared his throat. "Yes, I'm in Chicago."

"Is your wife available? The Second Lady would like to meet you both."

"Of course," he said, certain that Honey would leap at the chance to meet Richard and Pat Nixon.

"Very well, next Saturday, the twenty-third at the Blackstone Hotel. Six p.m. A car will be sent for you. Where shall I send it?"

In a flash of inspiration, Okie gave the name of a hotel he knew located downtown. Both he and Honey would enjoy getting out of the house, and a commute to downtown was a bit far, and this seemed the perfect opportunity for a bit of celebration.

Okie opened his mouth to say thank you, but the click cut him off.

Honey was as ecstatic as he imagined she would be, then she panicked. "What on earth am I going to *wear?*"

The following Friday evening, they ensconced themselves in their Morrison Hotel room for a night of lovemaking unburdened by the possibility of feedings or incessant squawking. It was a much-needed harbor of not-so-quiet pleasure in lives that had become increasingly chaotic.

During the day, while Honey went shopping for a new outfit, Okie found a barbershop for a fresh haircut, and decided to occupy himself for the day at the Art Institute of Chicago, which was located downtown less than a mile from the Blackstone Hotel.

Athwart the stately museum entrance, the bronze Lions of Michigan Avenue, green with age, struck stately poses of regal alertness. Inside the museum's cavernous galleries, Okie shuffled through centuries of mankind's greatest works of art, hands in pockets. Seeing the names of masters old and new that filled the halls, works ancient and modern, he was struck once again by how many such works he'd seen in a dark, dusty vault beneath the Sistine Chapel. How many of these pieces had been recovered from Nazi hordes? He knew that a few recovered pieces had been sent to the Art Institute of Chicago but couldn't remember which ones. Some of the paintings and sculptures gave him pause, drawing his feet to a halt before he realized it, touching him deeply for reasons he couldn't explain, much like Michelangelo's *Pietà.* In those, he could feel the hand of the master in the brush strokes or at the chisel. Others he could pass and feel nothing beyond a vague curiosity or an appreciation of the artist's skill—or mystification that the piece in question could be considered "art" at all, much less find itself in such a prestigious institution.

He found himself standing before a painting. He had already been here, on this spot, for at least a few minutes, so profoundly had it seized his attention, as if an ephemeral hand had just reached into his soul with a tuning fork and struck a resonance with everything he had ever felt in his entire life.

It hung just under three feet high and five feet wide. At first glance, it was just a simple scene depicting the front of a diner in the dead of night on an empty street. From a distance, the viewer looked through broad, glass picture-windows at the three customers, two men in suits and fedoras and a red-haired, hawk-nosed woman. The white-capped waiter groped for something behind the counter. All of them looked profoundly alone, their faces slack and unfocused, people without newspapers to hide behind. The lights within were stark, harsh, bleeding out on the deserted sidewalk.

A tear trickled down Okie's cheek. His arms had gone limp. He felt like a crumpled wad of sweaty paper. Every breath was a ragged sigh from a thickened throat.

Loneliness.

So vast and permeating it was as if no other emotion existed.

Nighthawks, the placard said. *Edward Hopper, 1942. Oil on canvas.*

The painting punched a hole in his soul like no piece of art he'd ever seen before, even at the Vatican, and spilled his heart out onto the floor.

Other museum visitors moved past him or paused for a moment to view the painting, but he ignored them, imprisoned in a desolate diner late at night with other lost souls. It was a long time before his legs wanted to move again.

❁❁❁

When he returned to the hotel to dress for dinner, he felt like a stranger in his own body, filled with an ache he couldn't name.

Honey returned, laden with shopping bags. She took one look at him and said, "What the hell happened to you?"

"I went to the museum."

"What kind of museum? Medieval torture?" She knew him too well.

Abruptly, he crossed the room and hugged her tight. She returned the embrace, confused, but it didn't assuage the ache inside of him. He didn't even care about how much financial damage her shopping bags represented.

"Are you going to tell me what happened?"

Releasing her, he said, "I saw a painting. Hit me pretty hard is all. Spoke to my soul."

She teased him gently. "Oh, look at you, the big softy."

"Pretty dumb, I know."

"What was the painting?"

"Some people in a diner." His words felt so inadequate they were laughable. He tried a few more sentences, then gave up. He couldn't explain it to her when he didn't understand it himself.

She listened with suppressed skepticism, then patted his cheek. "That's swell, Boomah, but we have to get dressed for dinner. We can't keep the vice president waiting."

Okie dressed in his best suit and let Honey fuss over him with a lint brush even though the suit was freshly cleaned and pressed.

Honey was stunning as ever in an Oscar de la Renta cocktail dress with knee-length hem, cinched waist, long sleeves, and Mandarin collar. The fabric was a bright brocade with red, green, blue, purple, and silver fading into darker waves, trimmed with gold ribbon and rhinestones. She looked like she belonged on a magazine cover, not in a kitchen mothering two children. Her makeup was perfect, her skin flawless.

A black Lincoln Continental limousine picked them up outside and drove them to the Blackstone Hotel, the "Hotel of Presidents." Nearly every American president of the twentieth century had stayed there, done business there. Richard M. Nixon had made it his headquarters in his preparation for the Republican National Convention in two days, at which he was expected to win the nomination for president in a shoo-in. When the limousine pulled up outside the Blackstone, Okie understood why it was the place of Astors, Rockefellers, and Vanderbilts. It was also a little notorious for being favored by mob bosses "Lucky" Luciano and Al Capone.

Built in 1910, it was a twenty-two-story rectangular edifice of granite, glazed terracotta, and red brick, with a grandeur suitable for heads of state, a monument to a gilded age and halls of power.

At the hotel entrance, they were hailed by a man in a suit. "Mr. and Mrs. Hansen?"

They approached him. "Uh, that's us," Okie said.

"Follow me, please."

The hotel lobby dripped with luxury. Ornate chandeliers, lush carpeting, polished marble, elaborately carved white ceilings, and pillars and walls sheathed in dark, gilded wood. The only building Okie had ever seen more lavishly decorated was the Vatican.

Honey squeezed his arm, biting her lip in excitement.

Their escort ushered them into a private dining room of shining white tablecloths and ornate hardwood chairs with cushions of scarlet velvet. “I’ll inform the vice president you’ve arrived,” the man said, then departed.

They waited ten minutes, then fifteen, then thirty. A waiter brought them drinks and canapes. Okie wondered if the waiting was a strategy calculated to make him sweat or if something important had come up. The man was the fucking *vice president*, after all, and six months from now could very well be president of the United States. Honey’s polished facade of beauty and charm emerged with impeccable self-control. Tonight, she would be on her game.

Finally, after thirty-three minutes, two dark-suited Secret Service agents entered the dining room and approached the table. Okie tried to make eye contact, one operative to another, but they avoided his gaze and took up positions near the table. The pressure of their alert scrutiny was palpable. A moment later, in walked Richard Nixon and his wife Pat.

The vice president looked just like in the newspapers, dark suit, dark tie, but in person there was a wolfish vitality about him, a dark-eyed intensity Okie had never seen before. His wife Pat walked with the easy confidence of the smartest woman in any room. Even at the age of almost fifty, she was a looker, with a perfect sandy-blonde coiffure and a stylish, black-trimmed white dress. She was almost as much a public figure as her husband. She had traveled with him to dozens of countries. Instead of teas and luncheons, however, she visited orphanages, hospitals, even a leper colony in Panama.

Nixon extended a hand. "Mr. Hansen, it's a pleasure to meet you. I've heard great things."

Okie's tongue was sandpaper as he shook hands. Nixon's hand was warm, dry, strong without needing to dominate. "Thank you, sir," he croaked. "The pleasure is all mine. I can't tell you what an honor it is to meet you. My father voted for you and Ike. Twice."

"We're both big fans," Honey said.

"Now aren't you just lovely," Pat said to Honey with a voice slightly roughened by smoking.

"I'm second loveliest in the room," Honey said. The women were like two swans appreciating and sizing each other up at the same time.

"That dress is just stunning," Pat said.

As Honey twirled with a beaming smile, she became a resplendent rainbow. "Oh, this old thing?"

The vice president unabashedly looked her up and down with raised eyebrows.

Pat said to Okie, "My husband tells me you're a young man to watch out for, a man of action and few words."

"I serve at the pleasure of the director, ma'am," Okie said.

"Good Catholic boy, Pat, you'll love him." Nixon gestured to the table. "Shall we? I'm famished."

They all sat and made small talk for a while, getting acquainted as if they were normal people.

Nixon ordered two bottles of 1959 Château Lafite Rothschild. Okie still wasn't a wine guy, but he would endure. "Don't worry, it's the real thing," Nixon said. "Sometimes I order cheaper stuff for guests and have the waiter cover the label with a cloth."

They all laughed politely. Okie and Honey traded *what the hell was that?* glances.

Digging for topics of easy conversation, Okie said, "Your campaign seems to be going well, sir." The papers were giving Nixon a slight edge over John F. Kennedy in the national polls.

Honey said to Pat, "What every man needs is an incredible woman behind him." When other people said such a thing, it might sound like flattery, but she said it with complete conviction.

Pat smiled, and the vice president leaned in and said, "That is a truth that goes back to the beginning of time. With Pat campaigning for me, I can't lose."

"If only I didn't despise and revile campaigning," Pat said wryly. Nevertheless, she seemed as comfortable in the halls of power as a shark in water.

Okie was still so amazed to find himself here, in this place, with these people, that he forgot to pick up his menu.

Nixon said, "You should order the broiled prime filet mignon. It's second only to Pat's secret meatloaf recipe that I adore."

His wife swatted his arm. "Oh, stop." Then she looked at Okie. "Don't let my husband railroad you, Mr. Hansen."

"You can call me 'Okie.' Everyone does."

"I didn't think you were from Oklahoma," Mrs. Nixon said.

"I'm not."

"Then where did the nickname come from?" Nixon said.

"I'm named after my father, but where 'Okie' comes from, I honestly have no idea."

Nixon absorbed this for a moment, then said, "You know that Pat is a nickname for her given name of Thelma, because she was born on the eve of St. Patrick's Day."

She smiled warmly at them. "You can call me Pat."

The wine arrived, and its perfume suffused the air around the table, fruity and rich. Nixon took a drink without preamble and smacked his lips with satisfaction. Okie gave the rich, red Bordeaux a swirl and sniff. He knew to do that much. Then tasted it. It was delicious, but he'd have been hard-pressed to describe why. No doubt it was very expensive and should be treated as such.

Pat pulled out a silver cigarette case. "Since we're giving away secrets already, you *must* keep this to yourself." The play in her voice smoothed over a serious admonition. The media had never mentioned that the Second Lady smoked.

"Oh, don't worry, Pat," Honey said, pulling out her pack of Pall Malls. She offered one to Okie, and the four of them filled the room with a smoky haze until the food arrived. Okie and Honey both ordered the filet mignon, and it was indeed divine.

In between the main course and a dessert of brandied cheesecake, Nixon said, "So let's get down to business, Okie. You're a man with unique talents. You're a sharpshooter with a real moral code, with loyalty and love of country. You speak more languages than most people have heard of. You're a fighting man with an analyst's mind. Your record is beyond exemplary. And you come recommended by men I admire and respect."

Okie's chest swelled at every word, and all he could do is listen and wonder, *What men?*

"What I would like is for you to join my presidential campaign as an 'analyst,' an 'advisor.'"

"Me, sir? An advisor? I don't know anything about politics. Zero."

"That's why we're here. You're a man on the outside. But politics is a business that gets people dirty, skews their vision. That's just the way it is. I need people around me I can trust. Can I trust you, Okie?"

"Absolutely, sir."

"Call me, 'Dick.'"

"Thank you...Dick."

"This business runs on the inside line, the secret handshake. A lot of those hands are dirty. Everybody has their own game they're playing. The stakes can be astronomical. This country is full of people trying to bring it down. Like, for instance, those goddamn protesters." Nixon's voice turned hard. For days, Chicago's streets had been thronged with protesters led by the Negro preacher, Reverend Martin Luther King Jr. Okie had seen photos in the papers of the seas of black faces and their signs. *Jim Crow must go! Voting Rights Now! March for Freedom!*

"Dick, language!" Pat said.

"You'd think she'd be used to it by now," Nixon said confidentially.

"Don't worry, Dick," Honey said with a musical laugh and a beaming smile. "We both swear like fucking sailors."

Pat gave a faux scandalized gasp, then smiled as she lit another cigarette.

"If you come to work for me," Nixon said, "I may have you manage the Reverend King matter going forward. We can't have these crooks getting in the way of democracy."

Okie nodded. The preacher's followers looked a rabble of unwashed radicals and militants.

Nixon went on, "Anyhow, you would report directly to me. Nothing in writing, ever. I can arrange this leeway with your superiors. We go way back. You'd still be on the Company payroll. Think of this as a side job. You do your regular work, but I call when I need you, and the work we do is strictly confidential." He glanced at Honey. "And you're Company, too, right, sweetheart? You know the score."

"I have no idea what you're talking about." She smiled and winked. "I'm just a silly little stewardess."

Okie glanced at Honey, who looked at him with a raised eyebrow. "Uh, that's a lot to take in, sir—uh, Dick. When would I start?"

Dick's dark eyes bored into him. "The convention starts on Monday. So, how about tomorrow?"

XXXII

***"BLESS ME, FATHER**, for I have sinned. It's been two months since my last confession. My sin is that I haven't been to Mass in two months. I have allowed too many worldly distractions. There's been the election, and...other matters. I've been out of the country..."*

"Have you kept the Lord in your heart?"

"Not as much as I should. I have this new job working for a very important man, and I enjoy it quite a bit. It's exhilarating. Maybe it's pride. I can't let it go to my head."

"What do you do for this man? Is he leading you away from the Lord?"

"Mostly I just...observe. Tell him what I see. It's like an extra job, on top of my regular job, which is currently going supersonic all by itself. I think about it all the time, though, this path that I'm on. I feel like the Hand of God Himself has put me on this path. How can I say no to the Lord's purpose?"

"We must trust that He has a purpose. For us, and for mankind. And you are part of that plan, perhaps playing a larger role than other people."

When they were back across town, Honey asked, "Why does a presidential candidate need a sharpshooter? He mentioned that specifically."

"Protection, I suppose," Okie said.

"He has the Secret Service for that."

Okie didn't have a response. He was still floating in semi-disbelief that he had just been hired as a personal advisor to the vice president of the United States. But his analytical brain kicked into gear. "It sounds like a more...offensive role."

Their eyes met, and the deeper meaning passed between them.

"Okay, let's back up," Okie said, pouring himself another glass of room service champagne. "American politicians don't go around assassinating their enemies."

Honey shrugged. "You mean like Lincoln? Garfield? McKinley?"

"Those were a long time ago."

"And we have *way* better weapons now. What's your farthest confirmed kill?"

He paced, downed his champagne, and wished for a can of beer instead. "Should I say I changed my mind? Tell him no?"

"I think it would be the quietest career suicide ever if you did. Besides, we both got a read on them. Pat is ambitious, fiercely behind her husband, willing to let him make hard calls. But it seems like her heart is in the right place. She's more famous than the First Lady at this point. Dick is ambitious, too, driven, probably ruthless."

"How ruthless?"

"That's the question isn't it. He might well ask you to put a bullet in Kennedy's head. What then?"

That was a good question. He paced some more. "That would depend on who the president is."

Honey leaned forward in her chair near the bed, raising an eyebrow, eyes smoldering with curiosity as if they'd just peeled back a layer neither of them knew was there.

Okie paced more, trying to parse the words he'd just uttered. Had he just agreed to become Richard Nixon's personal assassin? If so, did it matter whether or not Nixon was president?

He shook his head. He wasn't a hit man. "No. This isn't the Mafia. Dick is a good man." The truth was, all through dinner, Okie had felt like he'd met a rare man, the kind of man he could truly respect, and the number he'd met he could count on one hand.

Honey hit a cigarette. "He was grooming you pretty hard."

"What do you mean?"

"Just calling 'em like I see 'em."

Okie stiffened, suddenly feeling defensive. "I don't think it was like that at all." All through dinner, Dick had felt almost...fatherly. He knew she was right, and she had a razor-sharp eye for reading situations, probably better than his.

She took a long drag and let it out. "He's a politician, Boomah, a goddamn savvy one. It's his job to make you feel that way."

From the fringe of the arena stage in Chicago's International Amphitheater, Okie watched Dick deliver his acceptance speech for the Republican nomination.

"One hundred years ago, in this city, Abraham Lincoln was nominated for president of the United States. The problems which will confront our next president will be even greater than those that confronted him." The applause was deafening.

Okie was fascinated to watch all this happening from the inside. It was a tremendous thrill to be on the stage of history as it was happening. He followed Dick from state to state, always present, but always in the background, like the Secret Service security detail, but more unobtrusive. His job was to watch the people around Dick, keep his ears open. His training helped him blend into the woodwork, remain nondescript, keep his role vague. He and Dick rarely interacted when other people were present. Their conversations were always private, behind closed doors. Despite the secrecy, the conversations happening around him seemed very mundane, an endless series of minor fires to be extinguished as poll results came in and appearances were scheduled, speeches written. Not long after winning the Republican nomination, on the campaign trail in North Carolina, Dick injured his knee on a car door, and the subsequent infection cost him two weeks of campaigning, during which Kennedy retook the lead in the national polls.

Meanwhile, in August, Cuba nationalized a slew of U.S.-owned businesses: the Cuban Electricity Company, petroleum refineries, and thirty-six sugar factories. August was also the month that approval came down to enlist *mafiosi* to assassinate Castro. The Italian Mafia, particularly the Chicago syndicate and the Trafficante crime family out of Tampa, had been particularly damaged by the loss of their lucrative Cuban playgrounds, and they were looking to cash in their vendetta.

John F. Kennedy and Richard M. Nixon remained neck and neck all the way through the campaign season, right up to November 8. The election was going to be a squeaker, almost impossible to call, as this would be the first American election with fifty states participating. The electoral playing field was an entirely unfamiliar configuration.

Reverend Martin Luther King Jr. and baseball legend Jackie Robinson endorsed Nixon, as the Democratic party was the party of segregation in the South, and the marches for civil rights for black people showed no signs of abating. King said, "We are here to dramatize the significance of the civil rights issue. We feel that this is the most pressing moral issue facing our nation, and we are here to urge the Republican Party to come out with a strong, forthright civil rights plank in the platform." In October, King was sentenced to four months in jail for violating his probation, which he'd incurred for participating in an Atlanta sit-in. Nixon ignored King's pleas for help, even those of his wife, Coretta Scott King. The race was so close, Okie worried that this might cost Dick the black vote and swing the race. Kennedy, on the other hand, made a point of publicly denouncing King's incarceration and phoned Ernest Vandiver, governor of Georgia, requesting Reverend King's release, a request that was granted.

By the end of August, it was clear the Cuban guerrilla efforts alone would not be enough to unseat Fidel Castro. At every turn, Castro's security forces were neutralizing CIA-backed resistance cells in-country. His popular support within Cuba was still high. The Company's covert operations against him began to shift from guerrilla warfare and infiltration to an amphibious invasion. Okie saw plans for a force of at least 1,500 men to seize an area by sea and air assault to get a toehold on Cuban soil and expand from there. Kirby and a few others from the Sausalito gang were in Guatemala training disgruntled Cuban exiles.

The Republican Party threw its entire weight behind Nixon, with heavy hitters from across the country taking prominent positions in his campaign.

In September, the Cuban resistance fighters in Guatemala took on the name Brigade 2506, after the ID number of one of their members who fell to his death from a two-thousand-foot cliff on a training hike. Castro called the radio station on Swan Island a new aggression by North American imperialists. In a speech before the United Nations, he declared the U.S. had placed the radio station in the hands of war criminals. The Company attempted a drop of weapons and supplies to Cuban resistance forces, but the drop was seven miles off-target, landing straight in the hands of Castro's forces.

The first debate between Kennedy and Nixon, which took place on September 26 at WBBM-TV in Chicago, was the first presidential debate to be nationally televised. It was also broadcast nationwide on radio. In the studio, Okie watched the debate from the shadows off-stage.

Kennedy attacked Eisenhower's Cuba policy. "If you can't stand up to Castro, how can you be expected to stand up to Khrushchev?" Later he said, "We must attempt to strengthen the non-Batista democratic anti-Castro forces in exile, and in Cuba itself, who offer eventual hope of overthrowing Castro. Thus far these fighters for freedom have had virtually no support from our government."

Dick was, of course, fully aware of Operation Mongoose and its activities. He called Kennedy's position on Cuba "irresponsible" and "reckless." If the U.S. backed the Cuban exiles, he said, it would be condemned in the United Nations. "It would be an open invitation for Mr. Khrushchev to come into Latin America and to engage us in what would be a civil war and possibly even worse than that." Instead, Nixon proposed a quarantine of Cuba, a blockade.

In October, the Cuban government denounced the imminent invasion by the United States. They knew it was coming. They knew about the training camp in Guatemala. Later in October, a CIA operative in Cuba was executed by firing squad along with seven resistance fighters. Throughout the month, in retaliation for "U.S. aggression against Cuba," the Cuban government nationalized more than five hundred businesses: rum distillers, breweries, dairy products, soap, textiles, banks, and sugar manufacturers. CIA arms shipments to Guatemalan trainees and Cuban resistance fighters continued, even after a Honduran newspaper reported on the existence of the training camp.

So, Castro knew they were coming. All of Latin America knew. Every Cuban exile in Miami knew, and doubtless the Soviets as well. The biggest question on the invasion would be not if but when to pull the trigger.

Okie was in Nixon's campaign headquarters in the Ambassador Hotel in Los Angeles on November 8, along with campaign advisors, aides, even a couple of senators, when the voting results started coming in. It was a nail-biter. The tension in the room rivaled that at Bad Aibling the day the Soviets discovered the Berlin Tunnel, a day that could easily have turned the Cold War hot.

Every incoming phone call was an emotional lurch. Winning much of the east, Kennedy opened a big lead in the popular and electoral votes. In Nixon's campaign headquarters, the mood was grim, but with spasms of hope. Okie just felt queasy for much of the night. As returns came in from the rural and suburban Midwest and the western states, Nixon steadily closed the gap. Kennedy won Texas, but Nixon won California. *The New York Times* called it for Kennedy at midnight; there were still too many votes to be counted for Nixon to concede. At 3:00 a.m., he gave a speech that wasn't a concession, hinting that Kennedy may have won, but it was still too close to call.

Meanwhile, Dick fumed, glaring at the chalkboard with vote counts from Chicago. "Fucking Joe Kennedy, that son of a bitch. He's pulling strings with Daley. I fucking *had* Chicago. Every fucking poll! There's no way that little shit carried Chicago."

Nevertheless, to the mystification of all, John F. Kennedy carried Chicago by a hair's breadth, and thus, the state of Illinois. As soon as Illinois was called, Nixon flew into a rage, kicking over a chair and sweeping a stack of papers from a table. "They must have dug up half the fucking dead people in Illinois to go and vote! Sons of bitches!"

Illinois was enough to seal the electoral deal. Kennedy won the election with 49.71 percent of the popular vote. Nixon had 49.55 percent. It was the closest presidential election in U.S. history. Nixon carried the new state of Hawaii by 141 votes.

Dick gave his concession speech at 3:00 o'clock the following afternoon. He was stiff with tension, exhausted. "I could think of no worse example for nations abroad, who for the first time were trying to put free electoral procedures into effect, than that of the United States wrangling over the results of our presidential election, and even suggesting that the presidency itself could be stolen by thievery at the ballot box."

After what Okie had witnessed overnight, he could also hear the bitterness in Dick's voice. Dick believed fervently that the Kennedys had stolen the election. Between Lyndon Johnson's political machine in Texas and Mayor Richard Daley's in Chicago, they had eked out enough fake votes to turn the electoral tide.

Nixon sequestered himself to lick his wounds, and Okie went back to Evanston with an acid queasiness in his stomach that wouldn't go away. His faith in American democracy was all but shattered. All pretense of "government of the people, by the people, and for the people" lay in ashes. The Kennedy family were traitors to the American people, to democracy itself. And Richard M. Nixon, a man he respected and admired, had just been dealt a mortal blow by the daggers of hidden power.

In December, President Eisenhower met with the President-Elect to inform him of the plan to dethrone Castro. The invasion force would be ready in April. Company airplanes flew over Cuba dropping anti-Castro leaflets. Eisenhower placed a U.S. embargo on Cuban sugar. On New Year's Eve, Castro declared that if the U.S. intends to invade, it will have a real fight on its hands, saying that invasion forces will pay a heavier price than in the landings in Normandy and Okinawa.

Within the halls of Okie's windowless offices in Chicago, the Cuban situation continued at a slow boil. On the occasions he made it home to sleep in his bed, he began to have a recurring dream. He was sitting in a diner, late at night, surrounded by darkness, even at the brightly lit counter, and the waitress just ignored him; he kept trying to get her attention, to no avail. But then a dark figure appeared at the front door, dressed in trench coat and fedora straight out of a gangster movie, dragging a cello case, and somehow, he felt comforted, as if he'd been waiting for the figure all along.

A call came to Okie's office one afternoon in late December.

Okie was surprised to hear Dick's voice. "I need you to come to Washington and have a meeting. My house in Wesley Heights." He had had no contact with Dick since the days immediately following the election. No doubt the man had to recoup after a defeat like that, and Okie often wondered what Dick's next steps would be. He was too young, too driven, too power hungry, to stay out of politics for long.

"Of course," Okie said. "After everything that's happened...how are you?"

"I've been licking my wounds too long. It's time for some payback. But we need a plan, Okie. I'll be getting some boys together."

XXXIII

"BLESS ME, FATHER, *for I have sinned. It's been twelve hours since my last confession. Yesterday, I had...murderous thoughts."*

"Did you act on them?"

"Not yet."

"Do you intend to?"

1961

A January cold snap in Washington, D.C. dipped temperatures into the single digits, a bitter, brittle cold. A rime of refrozen snow and ice crackled underfoot as Okie approached the front door of the fieldstone Tudor home on Forest Lane Northwest in Wesley Heights, a quiet, recently built suburb a few miles northwest of downtown Washington. The house stood at the end of a narrow cul-de-sac, flanked on both sides by houses of great affluence. The abundance of trees and other greenery made the area feel as if it were carved directly from native forest. The sun dipped behind roofs and treetops, casting the cul-de-sac in shadow, banishing even the suggestion of warmth.

Okie heard the taxi drive away and pulled his collar around his neck, unable to ignore the biting chill.

Lights glowed in several windows. The three-story house before him sported a grand stone chimney and dormer windows in the roof. Lights glowed in two of the dormer windows. It was by far, by almost an order of magnitude, the largest house on the cul-de-sac. As he approached the front door, he was reminded of Schloss Maxlrain, back in Bavaria, but this edifice was much more somber.

A stout, middle-aged man in a black suit and bowtie opened the front door. "May I have your name, sir?"

"Emmett Hansen Jr. Okie."

The man stepped aside and ushered Okie within. "They are waiting for you in the study."

"I'm not late, am I?" Okie said with a sudden sinking feeling. He checked his chronograph.

The man didn't answer, just led him deeper into one of the most incredible houses he'd ever seen. *So this is how the rich and powerful live,* he thought. And then it occurred to him. Dick had a real, live *butler.* Okie suddenly wanted to start calling him "Mr. Nixon" again.

Light-oak hardwood everywhere, elegantly carved or milled. French doors. Grand open spaces. Parquet marble floors in one room, rich, dark walnut in another. Everything about the place felt steeped in power and authority. Dick currently held no public office, so who knew where he got the money to maintain such a place. Nevertheless, he remained a kingmaker in the Republican party, and planned to remain so.

The butler led him up a beautiful oak staircase, up one floor, then into the third—an elegantly finished attic space lined with bookshelves and filled with luxuriant chairs and sofas. The air smelled of cigar smoke, cigarette smoke, and expensive whiskey. "Mr. Hansen, sir."

Four middle-aged white men in suits rose from their seats. Dick crossed the room with an earnest expression and shook hands. "Glad you could make it, Okie, glad you could make it. Let's introduce you to everyone."

"Am I late?" Okie asked, suppressing a stammer and checking his chronograph again.

"No, no, you're right on time. Robert, meet Emmett Hansen Jr."

A beefy man in a tailored suit came forward, somewhere around forty years old. "Robert Abplanalp. Emmett Hansen...where do I know that name from..." He spoke with a suppressed Bronx accent. "The athlete. All-American fella from Holy Cross."

"He's my father, sir," Okie said.

Abplanalp's face brightened. "Well, no kiddin'! I remember hearing about him back in high school at Fordham Prep."

Okie had played football against Fordham University, and he recalled that the university also oversaw a preparatory high school. It seemed like a lifetime ago. What an angry twerp he'd been back then... Then he spotted the man's tie pin—gold and lacquer, about the size of a thumbnail, bearing a white cross with eight points on a red oval, centered beneath a golden cloak and crown.

Order of Malta.

Okie blinked and tried to conceal his astonishment. Then again, maybe he shouldn't have been surprised at all.

The other two men Okie recognized from Dick's campaign headquarters, but they'd never been introduced: the freshman U.S.

senator from Kentucky, Thruston Morton, chair of the Republican National Committee; Leonard Hall, a former congressman and former chair of the RNC, Dick's general campaign manager. Recognition glinted in their eyes as they shook his hand, and perhaps a bit of surprise. Okie was by far the youngest man in the room.

"This is part of the inner circle, Okie," Nixon said. "Nothing that's said here leaves this room."

"Of course," Okie said.

Nixon said, "Okie here is a very skilled intelligence operative. Did some ultra-classified work in Europe. One helluva sharpshooter. Loyal Republican. Good Catholic boy, Robert, you're gonna love him." Then he rubbed his hands together. "Let's get down to business, gentlemen. How do we make the fucking Kennedys suffer for stealing the election *and* boot them out in '64?"

For months, Okie kept abreast of Operation Mongoose, now called Operation Zapata, from his office in downtown Chicago.

The new president wasn't thrilled to discover that an invasion of Cuba was already almost underway. There were rumors that Kennedy would pull the plug on the project for fear of upsetting the Soviets, but that didn't happen. It could have been pressure from President Eisenhower, Director Dulles, and other high-ranking intelligence officials, railroading the new, young president. Eisenhower told him in no uncertain terms that it would be "the new administration's responsibility to do whatever is necessary to bring it to a successful conclusion." It could have been the momentum of effort already underway. It could have been unwillingness to squander years of effort and millions of dollars already spent, but ultimately Kennedy allowed the plan to crawl forward. The condition was that U.S. involvement be concealed at all costs.

Two air strikes against Cuban air bases would neutralize Cuba's meager air forces, protecting the main invasion force. For this, the CIA had provided World War II-era twin-engine medium bombers, B-26 Marauders repainted to look like Cuban Air Force. Once Cuban air support was out of commission, paratroopers would be dropped in advance of the amphibious assault to disrupt transportation and ground forces. To double the confusion, a small, decoy force would simultaneously land on Cuba's east coast.

The real landing point, however, would be the Bay of Pigs, a secluded swampy backwater on Cuba's southern coast. This main force of 1,400 men would come ashore against little resistance, then advance eighty miles straight north to Matanzas, a city on the northern coast some fifty-six miles east of Havana. Matanzas was one of Cuba's most culturally important and strategic cities, known as the "Venice of Cuba." Once there, they would set up a defensive position and expand their efforts. Since there would be no reinforcements from the U.S. or anywhere else, the entire plan hinged on the willingness of the Cuban people to rise up against Castro and join the invaders. Cuban exiles were waiting in Florida to return and establish a provisional government.

Meanwhile, Cuban forces were fortifying themselves with fresh shipments of arms and materiel from Czechoslovakia. Rumblings went through the halls of the CIA that the longer Castro was left in power, the stronger his position became. The pressure was on to act now, rather than later. Cracks full of conflicting opinions broke open in February and boiled among the CIA, the Joint Chiefs, and the Departments of State and Defense. The battle for the president's ear raged. Defense Secretary McNamara and the CIA were enthusiastic about the existing plan. The State Department took a somewhat cooler view, fearing grave political consequences both in the United Nations and across Latin America. The Joint Chiefs pointed out that a single airplane with a .50-caliber machine gun could sink the entire invasion force—surprise was paramount. Even within the CIA itself, once-enthusiastic support for the plan had cooled considerably as operational snafus accumulated.

In Miami and elsewhere, Cuban exiles, far from creating a united front, squabbled and schemed among themselves, jockeying for power in an imaginary new Cuba. Within Cuba, Castro's forces continued to round up counterrevolutionaries and spies, including Company operatives. Some were imprisoned, some executed, others escaped to successfully exfiltrate to the United States.

By late March, President Kennedy had soured on the whole thing. He expressly reserved the right to pull the plug right up until the last minute.

The plans shifted and changed. Competing plans floated up and down the halls of power. In early April, the Departments of State and Defense, the Joint Chiefs, and the CIA reached a compromise on the air plan, allowing the operation to move forward again. U.S. naval forces were given strict rules of engagement not to fire on Cuban forces. The necessity of avoiding any sign of U.S.

involvement was paramount—even more important than the success of the operation, it seemed.

That was when Okie was called to Langley. He packed up his things and left his family for the duration of what was to come, however long that might be. Initially he expected he might be called to provide sniper support if the invasion force could get a toehold, but when he arrived in Virginia, he was told that the Company needed every able body at headquarters. For the duration of the invasion, he'd serve as a "communications liaison," which was a fancy name for "message gofer." He'd listen to radio communications and relay messages and intelligence to the appropriate recipients, and occasionally serve as an analyst, having been one of the few operatives who had met Castro and Guevara personally.

Tension was high in every hallway and back room of CIA headquarters, fraught with grumbling about how the politicians were making it less and less likely the operation would succeed, implicitly laying the blame squarely on John F. Kennedy. Kirby and Raymond from the Sausalito gang had been in Guatemala for months and would be landing as advisors with Brigade 2506. Reports kept coming back from Guatemala that the invasion force was ready and raring to go, despite a revolt among the trainees. The entire 2nd and 3rd Battalions resigned. A dozen instigators were imprisoned, to be held until the operation was over.

He found himself reunited with Don, who'd recently been reassigned to Langley, and they spent their rare off-hours drinking beer in the closest bar and lamenting American beer's inferiority to Bavaria's. Together, they quietly discussed the growing malaise in the air at Langley, the sense of inevitable, impending doom.

Throughout the multitude of new introductions to operatives, analysts, and administrative staff, Okie started to chafe at his own name. "Okie" lacked gravitas, and occasionally led to him being taken less seriously than should be for a man who'd neutralized a Russian sniper at 1,600 yards, a man who'd actually met Castro and Guevara before the revolution. But he didn't know what else to call himself. The thought of calling himself "Emmett" still put a bitter taste in his mouth.

The hours and days ticked on, with the operation rushing forward, come hell or high water, notwithstanding the Kennedy administration's waffling. No one either for or against the invasion would be dissuaded from their fervent belief in its chances of success.

Honey called Okie excitedly one night in his hotel room. "Trey took his first step today!" she said. But Okie was mostly annoyed for having been distracted from thoughts of the operation, of being deprived of a few precious minutes of sleep. Or maybe it was the incessant build-up of frustrations in the halls of the CIA. She soon hung up in a bit of a huff and didn't call him again.

As soon as the operation's forces began to move, the missteps and frustrations began to stack, the sense of looming catastrophe heightened, all Okie could do was watch and listen and follow orders as it unfolded around him.

April 17 would be D-Day, but Kennedy was still waffling. On April 14, he inexplicably cut the strength of the planned air strikes in half, even though he'd already approved the plan. The invasion force had already sailed from Guatemala on five U.S.-built N-3 class freighters, along with numerous support craft and a dozen landing craft of various types, aiming for a nighttime landing in the Bay of Pigs.

On April 15, eight B-26s attempted to strike three air bases in Cuba to destroy Castro's air assets, but despite positive initial reports, the actual results were minimal. Nevertheless, to continue the sham, a bullet-riddled B-26 landed in Miami, with its pilot and crew claiming to have defected from Castro's forces. Castro decried the attack and publicly blamed the United States, immediately putting all his forces on high alert. Photographs of the attacking planes were distributed, which proved them to be of U.S. origin. The CIA-supplied planes had solid metal nose cones. The Cuban Air Force's planes had clear plastic ones.

As the failures and missteps continued to mount, Okie railed at his powerlessness. He wanted to be in the action. Give him a sniper nest in Havana and he could spot Fidel Castro. One shot, one kill. But being trapped at Langley often left him with the surreal sense that he was standing at the crux of history itself, watching it happen all around him in stunned silence.

Radio Swan began broadcasting bogus, cryptic messages to the Cuban populace, suggesting that an invasion was underway and that all secret revolutionaries should be activated, all of which was designed to confound Castro's security forces. "Alert! Alert! Look well at the rainbow. The fish will rise very soon. Chico is in the house. Visit him. The sky is blue. Place notice in the tree. The tree is green and brown. The letters arrived well. The letters are white. The fish will not take much time to rise. The fish is red."

The smaller diversionary force aborted its landing twice, claiming that their onshore friendly welcoming committee had not made the rendezvous.

Meanwhile, Cuban security forces rounded up one internal resistance cell after another, thousands of suspects, many of whom were Company attaches and advisors. Those that weren't summarily shot ended up imprisoned in deep, dark holes.

At midday on Sunday, April 16, Kennedy finally gave the authorization to go forward with the amphibious landing. The assault ships steamed toward Cuba for a Monday morning landing in the Bay of Pigs. While the ships were enroute however, at the recommendation of Secretary of State Rusk, Kennedy canceled the second air strike, fearing another failed strike and revealing U.S. involvement. In the halls of the CIA, howls of consternation and rage went up.

"He canceled their fucking air cover!"

"Those poor bastards are fucked. They're just fucked."

Over the course of the months and weeks leading up to the invasion, Okie grew increasingly tortured by oscillations between anger and despair. Watching the Kennedy administration betray all these carefully laid plans, all these men who'd put their lives on the line, incensed Okie in ways he couldn't easily control. Thoughts crept in, dark imaginings where he walked up to John F. Kennedy and put a bullet in his brain, and not just Jack Kennedy, but Bobby and all their toadies and enablers in the cabinet and in Congress. He wanted to clean house of the vermin infesting the U.S. government so that good, decent men like Dick could take their rightful places in the halls of power.

Air cover had been critical to the assault plan. The lack of it would leave the entire invasion force with its naked ass hanging in the wind, waiting to be shot to pieces by aircraft that should have been destroyed in the air strikes.

Okie and Don had friends on those ships.

When the Joint Chiefs learned of this impending catastrophe, they managed to dispatch two of the B-26s to provide air cover on the beachhead.

When the invasion force arrived at the remote Bay of Pigs, there were, of course, no docks or wharfs to tie up the ships. The landing was launched at 0100 hours. The seas were choppy, and the bay itself was more than eight hundred feet deep in places, so anchoring the ships was all but impossible. On top of all that, treacherous coral reefs made the landings a nightmare of navigation. Getting the troops loaded into the landing craft and ferried to shore proved time consuming and difficult.

And then, almost at once, they were spotted by a local militia patrol—almost as if Castro's forces knew this was coming—who immediately mobilized further defense forces and armed militias.

The assault force was expecting an unopposed landing in the middle of nowhere, but the Cuban forces hit them immediately.

Everyone in the war room at Langley was forced to listen in horror as the broken expostulations of Spanish came over the relayed radio channels.

Cuban airplanes, left intact by the failed air strike, strafed the ground forces and assault ships, sinking two escorts and destroying the meager B-26 air cover. Several other ships were badly damaged.

Mechanical trouble with one of the landing craft further hampered the operation, leaving troops stranded on the beach under fire. One of the freighters was sunk by a rocket attack from a Hawker Sea Fury, a World War II-era British fighter that had found its way into the patchwork Cuban Air Force—along with ten days' worth of food, ammunition, medical supplies, and gasoline. The explosion was immense.

"God Almighty, what the hell was that? Fidel got the A-bomb?" came an American voice over the radio.

"Naw," came another voice, "that was the damned *Rio Escondido* that blew."

Brigade 2506, more accustomed to mock boot-camp exercises than live fire, scattered into the swamp and jungle. Radio communications with individual units were a shambles because most of the troops were forced to wade or swim ashore, getting their radios wet.

At around midmorning, one of the merchant captains in charge of the support flotilla radioed CIA headquarters demanding air support. "If it doesn't come, we're putting back out to sea." The air support did not come, and he was good to his word. Several support ships disengaged and headed south to take cover under the umbrella of U.S. naval ships on station about fifty miles offshore.

Before daybreak, Brigade 2506 managed to regroup to take the village of Palpite and defended it for several hours, but, as the day ground toward nightfall, Cuban forces retook the town. By the end of the day, Brigade 2506 held two of the three access roads to the area and little else.

Cuba's handful of T-33 fighters, the first jets of post-WWII, were making mincemeat out of the B-26s, half of which had been downed. The CIA ordered another air strike on Cuba's landing fields by the B-26s to destroy the jet fighters, but the pilots couldn't find the targets.

In the morning, the Cuban Air Force napalmed the invasion force on Red Beach, wiping them out.

On the morning of April 18, Soviet Premier Nikita Khrushchev announced: "It is not a secret to anyone that the armed bands which invaded that country have been trained, equipped, and armed in the United States of America. The planes which bomb Cuban cities belong to the United States of America, the bombs they drop have been made available by the American Government. As to the Soviet Union, there should be no misunderstanding of our position. We shall render the Cuban people and the Government all necessary assistance in beating back the armed attack on Cuba. We are sincerely interested in a relaxation of international tension, but if others aggravate it, we shall reply in full measure."

In the war room at Langley, someone said, "Well, that's it then. We're done."

"No way will Kennedy go face-to-face with Khrushchev over this."

"That fucking pussy."

By afternoon, the writing was on the wall. Bobby Kennedy told a Senator, "The shit has hit the fan. The thing has turned sour in a way you wouldn't believe."

For Okie, it was like sitting in the locker room at halftime of a game that was long since lost. The malaise of defeat was palpable, as was his rage at the Kennedy administration for "fucking up the whole thing." The Cuban forces were stronger. There had been no popular uprising, despite all the expectations to the contrary. Their tactical position was feeble. Castro's tanks and air cover had ripped through the invasion forces, destroying morale. They kept begging for more air cover or artillery cover from the U.S. naval forces floating fifty miles offshore. But nothing came. The Cuban B-26 pilots, exhausted and beaten, refused to fly any more support missions. Two Alabamian CIA pilots took over and managed to inflict some real damage, but it was too little, too late.

That night, Admiral Arleigh Burke, Chief of Naval Operations for the Joint Chiefs, begged the president for "just two jets" to fly to Cuba and shoot down the entire Cuban Air Force. Kennedy refused.

By dawn of April 19, nine of the sixteen original B-26s had been shot down, including one piloted by Thomas "Pete" Ray, one of Okie's acquaintances from the Sausalito gang, and most of the other Marauders were no longer flightworthy.

"We need close air support *now!*"

"If I can't get a destroyer escort for this freighter full of ammunition, my Cuban crew is going to mutiny!"

"Two thousand militia are coming at us from the west!"

"You don't know how desperate our situation is. All we need is strong air protection. If not, we don't survive."

Later that morning, Okie overheard that someone spotted former vice president Nixon coming out of Director Allen Dulles' office. Okie's heart leaped at the chance to catch him. He managed to spot Dick stalking down a long hallway before he left the building. He didn't know if Dick would be willing to talk or even publicly acknowledge they were acquainted, but Okie hailed him, perhaps hoping for some sort of reassurance that all this time, money, effort, and lives had not been spent in vain. He wanted to know what the hell to *do.*

He was relieved when Dick paused long enough for Okie to catch up.

"Christ, Okie, when was the last time you slept?" Dick asked.

"Uh, maybe Saturday." It was now Wednesday. "What did the Director say, if you don't mind me asking?"

Dick's face flushed with barely controlled anger. "His exact words were, 'Everything is lost. The Cuban invasion is a total failure.' That simple."

By this time, Okie had a thorough understanding of failures' causes. "It was the Kennedys. All those pussies derailed the whole thing before those fellas hit the beach. Too many last-minute compromises."

Dick nodded. "That's what the Director told me, in so many words. Ike planned it, and Kennedy fucked it up. Well, fuck them. Their day will come. I'll be in touch, Okie." Then he spun and stalked off, his hard-soled wing tip shoes echoing down the hallway.

XXXIV

***"BLESS ME, FATHER,** for I have sinned. It's been two days since my last confession. For weeks, I've been swimming in wrath, and I don't know how to let it go.*

"So many people I know have died, all because of one man's stupidity and cowardice. They were good men. Some of them were friends of mine. I could have been one of them. They served their country, and...now they're gone. And for what? They had the rug yanked out from under them. They...they were betrayed."

"All things happen for a reason, my son."

"There has to be some payback. A failure like this can't be allowed to stand."

"That is not for you to judge, my son. The Lord works in mysterious ways. Justice comes to us all in the end."

"I'm not sure I believe that anymore."

Over the next day, roughly 20,000 Cuban troops advanced on Brigade 2506. Cuban airplanes commanded the skies. With the entire operation already lost, Kennedy finally authorized six unmarked fighter planes to take off from Nicaragua to help defend the beleaguered B-26s, but they arrived an hour late, confused by the time zone difference between Nicaragua and Cuba, and were all shot down.

"Am destroying all equipment and communications. I have nothing left to fight with. Am taking to the woods. I can't wait for you."

The Bay of Pigs was eighty miles from the rugged safety of the Escambray mountains, where Castro had managed to evade Batista's forces for two years. The invasion force had nowhere to run for safety.

A handful of exiles managed to escape back to sea, but almost 1,200 Brigade 2506 members surrendered and were imprisoned. With the exception of a small handful who managed to escape into the wilderness, the rest were killed. Most of the escapees were later rounded up.

In public, Kennedy ate crow, taking full responsibility for the operation and its failure. But privately he said, "I want to splinter the CIA into a thousand pieces and scatter it to the winds."

And in the halls of Company headquarters, the enmity was mutual. "Fuck him. Fuck that guy." It was a sentiment Okie deeply shared as he went back to Chicago, to Honey, to Mary and Trey. Everyone involved had lost someone, a friend, a respected colleague. They had sworn their lives to their country, and the president had pissed on them.

He'd missed his son's first birthday party. He felt a slight pang of guilt but assuaged it with the knowledge that the boy wouldn't remember his father's absence. Honey harangued him about this, but he quelled her with the promise to never do it again, even though he knew it to be a lie. If called upon for Church or Country, he knew he would abandon his family for his duty without a second thought. The way Honey glared at him said that she knew it, too. She might well do the same if the roles were reversed, and that incensed her even more.

The rumblings and aftershocks of the Bay of Pigs fiasco didn't die away; they increased. By autumn, the heads were rolling. Director Allen Dulles was forced to resign, along with Deputy Directors Cabell and Bissell. A multitude of other plans to depose Castro were concocted, including some by the Joint Chiefs for a full-on invasion of 60,000 U.S. troops.

But what they eventually settled on was assassination, by any means necessary. They enlisted the Chicago syndicate and the Trafficante mob out of Tampa to do the job, it didn't matter how. Poison. Bullet. Even exploding cigar. All options were open, and they had plenty of contacts still in Cuba, people for whom such work was an everyday task.

Okie was so far away from the action in his Chicago office, he felt lost, unmoored, wishing he could be back in Langley.

1962

It was May 19, and Okie stood on the floor of Madison Square Garden, surrounded by some fifteen thousand people, mostly show-business people, high-ranking Democrats, and rich donors, all there to wish Jack Kennedy a happy forty-fifth birthday. The President's Ball, it was called, and Okie was there simply to pay attention. To watch. To observe. It was easy to remain in the shadows tonight, as all eyes were on the stage in the center of the arena. Spotlights bathed the platform, spilling onto President Kennedy, who sat alone in the front row. The First Lady had apparently canceled her appearance at the last minute to instead ride her horse, Ninbrano, at the Loudon House Horse Show with her children, John and Caroline.

This was one of the more difficult operations Dick had ever tasked him with, because with the crowds and Secret Service presence, it was difficult to get close enough to the president to see or overhear anything of import. Okie couldn't understand it, but Kennedy was somehow wildly popular, especially with the media and the show-business glitterati.

The cream of American show business gathered to pay him homage. For Okie it was like strolling through a who's who of the rich, famous, and corrupt, and the entertainers who catered to them.

Peter Lawford, the president's brother-in-law and member of the infamous Rat Pack, served as emcee. Ella Fitzgerald, Peggy Lee, Jack Benny, Jimmy Durante, Henry Fonda, Harry Belafonte. Even playwright Arthur Miller, divorced last year from Marilyn Monroe, was in attendance. A Greek opera diva Okie had never heard of, Maria Callas, raked an aria across Okie's eardrums. Opera was not his kind of music. The others he enjoyed a great deal, which made it difficult to focus on the task at hand, which was: observe Kennedy and the people around him. These show-business types were just caricatures of actual people anyway, empty skins.

As he was not of the "official list," he was forced to circulate, always pretending to be returning to his seat, only to find it occupied.

With all eyes glued to the stage, however, it was easy to remain innocuous and nondescript. As the entertainers came and went on the central stage, he used a pair of opera glasses for closer looks at the Kennedy brothers and their hangers-on.

It was when Peter Lawford announced a particular name, that Okie froze and stared at the stage.

"Mr. President, Marilyn Monroe."

Okie's heart skipped a beat.

A wave of applause went up, and Jack Kennedy stared at the stage, eyes aglow. Okie's gaze flicked to nearby Bobby Kennedy's face; he wore a smug grin, full of himself, arms crossed.

Marilyn Monroe did not appear. Spotlights searched the stage for her, but in vain.

Lawford cleared his throat. "A woman about whom it truly may be said, she needs no introduction." He was clearly stalling. "Let me just say," then he glanced over his shoulder, "here she is."

Drums rolled.

No Marilyn Monroe.

Lawford cleared his throat again. "But I'll give her an introduction anyway, Mr. President, because in the history of show business, there is no one female who meant so much, who has done more..."

And then she appeared, like Aphrodite rising from a clamshell, wrapped in a white ermine stole, mincing toward the lectern like a geisha. A sensation spread through the crowd.

Lawford threw up his hands in exasperation, but Okie could only stare at her. The fur concealed her torso, but from the thighs down, her legs moved in a waterfall of glittering rhinestones that became stars themselves. She gave the audience a peek at what lay underneath the fur wrap, and it looked like she was naked.

Okie's entire field of vision shrank to this luminous goddess, swathed in sparkling stones as if they'd been glued onto her naked skin. A rush of gasps rippled through the crowd.

Kennedy's body went limp in his chair as if he'd been gobsmacked.

Lawford leaned into the microphone and put his arm around the starlet's naked shoulders. "Mr. President, the *late* Marilyn Monroe."

The audience laughed, but the laughter immediately rose into gasps as she swept the white stole from her shoulders, revealing what lay beneath. As they took it in, the gasps intensified. Everyone in the place thought at first that she really was naked. But no, she was in fact wearing a dress. It was made of flesh-tone silk, skin-tight, without a hint of bra or even panty lines.

In the air of the arena, Okie could almost smell the lust rising like a wave.

She looked nervous, uncertain, like a schoolgirl standing before her massive crush. Then she tapped the microphone, and just like that, she transformed. No more hesitant schoolgirl, but a luscious sexpot that could bring every man in the world to his knees. Okie felt her pull.

"Happy birthday, to youuu..." she sang, "Happy birthday...to youuu."

She glittered like a sky full of stars.

The more she sang, the more it was clear how truly smitten she was by John Kennedy. Nor could there be any doubt that her desire had been consummated.

Kennedy looked uncomfortable, squirming in his front-row seat. Nearby, little brother Bobby grinned like he'd just orchestrated a successful schoolyard prank.

When the Happy Birthday song was over, she segued into another verse:

"Thanks, Mr. President

For all the things you've done

The battles that you've won

The way you deal with U.S. Steel

And our problems by the ton

We thank you so much!"

Then she encouraged the audience to launch into a Happy Birthday sing-along with the band, while two burly chefs carried out a massive, six-tiered birthday cake on poles as if it were a medieval satrap on a palanquin. A host of candles blazed.

As Marilyn hustled off stage, she grinned and flushed like a schoolgirl who'd just climbed out her parents' window to meet her lover.

Kennedy climbed onto the stage with his politician's mask firmly in place and took his place at the wooden lectern. He leaned into the microphone and said, "I can now retire from politics, after having had 'Happy Birthday' sung to me in such a sweet, wholesome way."

The irony was not lost on the crowd, but they laughed along and applauded, thousands of heads tilting together to ask some version of "What the hell just happened?"

This certainly wasn't going to make the rumors about Kennedy and Marilyn go away. Okie felt awful for Jackie Kennedy. No wife deserved to have some slut make love to her husband on national television, in front of 66 million people, even one stupid enough to be married to a man like Jack Kennedy. On the arena floor, it was now Bobby Kennedy's turn to be red-faced, not with giddiness or embarrassment, but with jealousy. Like a moth circling a flame.

"Holy shit," Okie breathed. Bobby was fucking her, too.

"That was the most disgraceful thing I've ever seen," Dick said, stubbing out another cigarette. "To disrespect the First Lady like that." He shook his head and spoke with wry disgust. "How can Camelot survive?"

Okie sat smoking a Lucky Strike with a tumbler of 30-year-old scotch in his other hand. It was brilliant summer evening on the back patio of Dick's Wesley Heights home, looking out over the forested hillside that separated the development from other suburban enclaves. The air smelled of honeysuckle and fresh-cut grass.

"Thanks for coming, by the way," Dick said. "I realize it was a bit short notice, diverting your trip home from New York. I'm sure your kids miss you."

"They'll survive it," Okie said. He took another sip of the scotch, like a caramel drop roasted in a campfire, but with a bite. No doubt it was expensive.

"Where are we on this Cuba fiasco?"

"Still a fiasco, of course," Okie said. "No one knows their asshole from their elbow. And apparently Fidel has more lives than a cat." Several assassination attempts had already failed, each of them more ingenious or outlandish than the last, including the interior of a wetsuit slathered in contact poison.

"That dumb bastard is going to get us fucking nuked, while he's sticking his dick in Marilyn. Goddamn disgraceful."

Okie couldn't disagree. He'd already reported his impressions of the evening at Madison Square Garden, who he'd seen talking to whom, the backroom rumors he'd heard. Apparently, Marilyn's appearance at the event had been cooked up by Bobby as a kind of prank. The brothers were seen arguing at one of the after-parties, and the Secret Service confiscated all camera film that might contain a photo of Jack and Marilyn together.

"He's a stain on the presidency," Dick said. "I tell you, Okie, it keeps me up at night. Well, that and campaigning." He gave a dark chuckle.

Dick was running for the governorship of California, and the Republican primary was in a couple of weeks. He had only one remaining contender, the minority leader from the State Assembly, and the former vice president was a heavy favorite.

"But, seriously, Okie, you are my number one guy. If Jack Kennedy wins a second term, this country is finished. I need you to stab him in the heart. Not literally, of course, that would be treason. But he needs to know that he's on thin ice. He needs to *feel* it." Dick clenched a fist. "Think of all your dead friends. He needs to pay for leaving them with their balls hanging out, waiting to get shot off."

"What would you like me to do?" Okie asked matter-of-factly, as if he were a simple janitor asking which trash cans to dump.

Dick fixed him with a long, dark look, then looked away. "You're a smart guy, the smartest. I'm sure you'll think of something. Just make it good. Make it *big*. The kind of thing no one will ever forget."

XXXV

CURSUM PERFICIO
My journey ends here.
—inscribed on the tiles leading to the front door of
Marilyn Monroe's house

***"BLESS ME, FATHER,** for I have sinned. It's been a lifetime since my last confession."*

"That long?"

"A thousand lifetimes."

"Has something happened, my son?"

"How many people have a moment where everything has a before and after, and it's like you stepped into a different universe where everything is irrevocably changed and you weren't yourself anymore?"

"Do you mean like before the war and after the war?"

"More like before the Bomb and after the Bomb and you're the pilot of the Enola Gay. I have now broken nine of the ten commandments. I'm only twenty-six. I am not proud of my transgressions. I'll continue to confess and repent my venial sins. I have been asked to commit a mortal sin and violate the sixth commandment for God and country."

"My son, how have you found yourself in this dilemma?"

"A very powerful man needed me to defend his honor and collect his pound of flesh. I couldn't say no. Leviticus 24:19-21. 'A fracture for a fracture, an eye for an eye and a tooth for a tooth.'"

"Is it a righteous thing you were asked to do?"

"Let's just say the Chief of the Chowder and Marching Club needed my unique skill set."

"God the Father of mercies, through the death and resurrection of His Son, has reconciled the world to Himself and sent the Holy Spirit among us for the forgiveness of sins. Through the ministry of the Church, may God give you pardon and peace. I absolve you from your sins, in the name of the Father, and of the Son and of the Holy Spirit."

"O my God, I am heartily sorry for having offended Thee, and I detest all my sins, because of thy just punishments, but most of all because they offend Thee, my God, Who art all good and deserving of all my love. I firmly resolve, with the help of Thy grace, to sin no more and to avoid the near occasion of sin. Amen."

"In hoc signo vinces."

Okie parked the car several blocks away on South Carmelina Avenue. Don sat across from him, staring at the dashboard, his face a mask.

The house was situated at the end of a narrow, walled cul-de-sac called Fifth Helena Drive, one of a long series of cul-de-sacs that branched from South Carmelina.

It was a cool, comfortable August night, like most nights in Los Angeles.

He had been on missions like this before—quiet, get-in-get-out, fade-into-the-night affairs—but this was the first on American soil, and the first time the target was a woman, much less a celebrity.

He had enjoyed *Some Like It Hot* a great deal a few years back. Honey was a fan. She'd once said, "If that broad was smarter, she'd make the perfect spy. Any man on the planet would kill to get under her skirt." Having seen her in person, Okie had to admit there was something about her, a magnetism, a luminosity. That was the power she'd used to ensnare two Kennedy idiots. They should have been better Catholics. And there was a war going on in the hidden halls of power. In war, there were always civilian casualties. He couldn't bring himself to think of her as innocent. More likely, she was a tool of the Devil, the most beautiful tool imaginable, sculpted from men's deepest, most sinful desires.

He glanced at Don, who hadn't moved since Okie had shut off the engine of this nondescript Oldsmobile.

Don met his eye. "This doesn't feel right."

"You want to back out?" Okie glared at him. "*Now*?"

"I didn't say that. Orders are orders, I know that. But this feels dirty. More like a Mafia hit than anything about national security."

Okie kept his voice even, teeth clenched. "She's a fucking slut who deserves to die." And burn in hell. One less sinful hussy made the world a better place. At least, that's what he'd been telling himself. "She's a national embarrassment. That 'Happy Birthday' song? While Jackie was in Virginia with their kids?" He could almost feel Jackie Kennedy's shame as her husband was being seduced and serenaded by this trollop, at Madison Square Garden, no less.

"I know," Don said.

"And what about Kirby! And Miles! That sonofabitch left them to die on a fucking beach in Cuba. He's going to pay. And we're going to make him."

"That's the trouble. I'm not sure we're in the revenge business."

"Bullshit. How many enemy spies have had targets painted on their foreheads for exactly that reason? Kennedy is worse, because, as much as it makes me sick to say it, he's one of ours. And the Russians! Jesus Christ, you think he's got the balls to stand up to Khrushchev without *us* forcing him to have a spine? After tonight, he will know who ought never to be fucked with." Even as he said the words, his chest and throat tightened with rage. Tonight, he and Don would make history—and no one, *no one,* would ever know.

But *he* would know, and that was enough.

He grabbed his satchel from the seat between them. "You're either with us, or against us."

Then he got out of the car and quietly shut the door. Best not to draw any attention at all. As he started up the street toward Fifth Helena Drive, Don got out of the car and followed him.

It was a bright, moonlit night, and the low, pale walls along the street caught the light. He appreciated the lack of streetlights. They kept low and moved silently. Crickets sang on this quiet street just as loud as the LA traffic farther down the hillside. Somewhere nearby, a football-sized dog, the perfect size for a solid punt, barked at an open window like the world was coming to an end. A cigarette-roughened female voice yelled, "Muffy, get down from there! There's nothing out there." Okie caught the scent of a clove cigarette on the breeze.

When Okie and Don reached the end of the cul-de-sac, they found a chest-high gate, beyond which lay a lush green lawn surrounding a Spanish Colonial-style, single-story house. The half-acre grounds were meticulously landscaped. They rolled quickly over the gate and, avoiding the loop of driveway, circled around the hedge bordering the property toward the back. Bamboo grew sporadically alongside the hedge.

The house stood dark, except for a feeble lamplight coming through the glass-paned French doors toward the kidney-shaped pool. Those doors would be to her bedroom. In planning for this mission, he had studied the public records of the blueprints of the roughly 2,300-square-foot, three-bedroom hacienda. The guest house nearby was dark and empty with a stepladder standing outside the door over a bucket of paint, a bag of plaster, and a rolled-up drop cloth. There was a live-in housekeeper who kept up the place and did her best, some said, to keep the drug-addled starlet between the ditches.

She had moved in here six months ago.

As they circled the house, Okie peeked in windows, looking for any potentially unpleasant surprises.

Through the French patio doors, he could see the pale form of a naked woman draped across her bed like Venus in a Renaissance painting, platinum blonde, at least on top. A single white sheet draped her hip and legs. The bedside lamp was on. A telephone sat on the bed beside her. They watched her for at least two minutes, during which she didn't move a muscle.

He gestured at Don to move closer. They circled the pool onto the courtyard patio and knelt on either side of the patio doors, which stood ajar.

Standing only a few feet away from her naked, motionless form, her sheer beauty locked his gaze upon it. His eyes took her in, every inch of her, bathed in the light of the bedside lamp. Lying on her side, delicate pink nipples, the kind of curves that drove men insane with lust, a dark thatch of sin half-hidden between her legs. But her sleeping face, unadorned by makeup, her hair like a busted bale of faded silk, hardly resembled the face everyone in America knew so well, the one he'd seen in Madison Square Garden just three months ago. She hadn't been seen in public since that night. Here was just a lonely woman, desperate for attention and approval, thrice divorced, fending off middle-age with every weapon at her disposal, living alone in what she told herself was her dream, so steeped in immorality she had become a tool of evil, a plaything of lesser men.

The house looked barely lived in, almost empty of furniture and decor, which he thought a little strange. In the bedroom, her things lay mostly stacked against the walls. From within, through the window glass, he caught the sound of someone snoring like a buzz saw from another bedroom.

Okie glanced at Don, whose face had gone tight-lipped, eyes haunted.

Their eyes met, and in that moment, as it had happened on previous missions more dangerous than this one, their inner fortitude shored up each other's.

Okie eased open the patio door with his gloved hand and stepped inside, Don close behind him.

Beside her on the nightstand was a prescription bottle. By morning, the whole country would believe that this poor tortured starlet, this lust-mongering Jezebel, had committed suicide. It was like she'd just written her own suicide note.

Her breathing was heavy, deep.

Her arm stirred with a sigh, and they froze. As she subsided again into heavy breathing, he crossed the room and locked the bedroom door. The bedside prescription bottle of chloral hydrate sedative had already had its way with her, it seemed.

It was time to execute the plan.

She lay backwards on her bed, feet toward the wall. Okie carefully moved the phone to the nightstand while Don positioned himself at her head, gathering up handfuls of bed sheet.

Okie opened his satchel and withdrew the fountain syringe with its payload of quiet death. While he prepared the insertion tube and attached it to the bag, Don watched for signs that she would awaken, ready to clamp off any sound she might make. But she looked practically comatose. Earlier tonight, he had filled the fountain syringe with warm water, in which he had dissolved over sixty pentobarbital capsules and twenty chloral hydrate pills, enough barbiturate to kill twenty people.

The next part was where it might get loud, especially since he had never done this before, only read about it in a classified after-action report.

Don looked at him expectantly. He nodded.

Don jammed a wad of bed sheet between her parted lips and clamped his hand over her mouth.

Her eyes flew open. Her body convulsed. Even through the drug-addled haze, she recognized the presence of two men standing over her. Her arms flailed at Don, her legs kicking into the air at Okie, screaming into Don's gloved palm. Okie caught her legs, one in each arm, and in her weakened thrashing, found his head between her knees, up close and personal with the most desired *concha* on the planet.

In the span of less than an eyeblink, a succession of thoughts flashed through. Joe DiMaggio had been in there. Arthur Miller had been in there. John and Bobby Kennedy had been in there. How many others? The only other female sex he'd ever seen this close before was Honey's. His eyes lingered there. How much sin had been committed between these two creamy, petal-soft legs, those delicate, pink lips? After tonight, no one would ever be in there again. Except for the coroner.

After tonight, this storied orifice would be so much dead, cold meat.

He clutched her thighs and forced her haunches down onto the bed, then extricated himself and held her legs down. Don let her fists and forearms pummel him as he held her fast. Whatever sedative she had taken was consumed in a raging fire of adrenaline, it seemed. Her body bucked and thrashed, but her strength was no match for two trained killers.

"Flip her," he whispered.

He locked gazes with Don, counting down silently, then levering her onto her stomach.

Her breath gasped and sobbed, her eyes bulging with terror, and in between muffled screams she struggled to beg for her life. "Puh…! Pleeee….! Nuuh…!" Tears soaked her cheeks.

Don straddled her shoulders and sat on her, maintaining his grip over her mouth and gag. Okie straddled her calves and looked down upon her shapely, quivering buttocks and the glimpse of the delicate pink lips below them. With her sufficiently immobilized, he grabbed the fountain syringe, unrolled the tubing, and prepared to insert the enema pipe into her rectum. He had to be careful, gentle as possible. The coroner mustn't find any tearing. But in it went. Then he held the bag high and let it drain. Slowly, slowly, the bag shrank as the barbiturate concoction filled her colon and large intestine, where it would be absorbed into her bloodstream and leave no evidence of needle marks or injury. Maybe Dick had the LA coroner in his pocket already.

Minutes passed, and her struggles subsided. Okie could feel the muscles of her legs slackening under his weight. Her eyes slid closed forever.

When the bag hung empty, he yanked out the pipe and put it back in his satchel, but he did not get up, in case there was still fight left in her.

Fifteen minutes later, he checked her pulse at her neck. It was weak and fluttery, and her limbs had gone as a flaccid as raw steak.

He rose off her and gave Don the signal. The barbiturates had taken hold. She would never wake up again.

They arranged her on the bed as if she had simply fallen asleep. Then he noticed her clutching a scrap of paper in one hand—it had apparently been there all along. Her limp fingers let him examine it, and after a moment of realization and recognition, he put it back with a smile.

It was a number he knew well, one he'd memorized long ago as one critical to national security. The direct number into the White House, past the switchboard, into the residence and Oval Office.

He put the phone back on the bed beside her and put the receiver in her hand. In rigor mortis, her fingers would clamp around it.

The press would say she died trying to call the president. Let that be on that bastard's conscience.

Then he sprinkled some of her own chloral hydrate pills around the nightstand and left the bottle open.

It was done.

He stood over her for a long moment, then arranged the sheet over her buttocks a little more naturally. Artfully. There, that was better.

Then he noticed something.

The freight train of snoring in the other bedroom had fallen silent.

Time to go.

So they went, making sure to leave nothing they had brought with them—except their souls.

EPILOGUE

November 19, 1962

EMMETT HANSEN JR. sat in a booth of the corner diner on a cold, austere Chicago night. Winter had already moved in and started sending brittle winds across Lake Michigan through the canyons of downtown. The streets were deserted at this hour, bathed in the light of a crescent moon.

The only other people in the place were the beleaguered waitress behind the counter and the hairy fry-cook shuffling around in the kitchen. The waitress didn't look up from her paperback, *Franny and Zooey* by J.D. Salinger.

The diner's harsh fluorescent light spilled through the windows to illuminate the dark, urban streetscape outside, deserted as if there was no one else in the world. The clock on the wall read just after 4:00 a.m. Light bled onto the adjacent street corner, spilling from inside through the great picture windows. A haven against darkness's encroachment.

He sat with his hands clasped tightly on the Formica tabletop, squeezing them, trying to compress the burning pain in his stomach that had persisted since he'd returned from Los Angeles. He was too young to have an ulcer. Lady Macbeth's line haunted him: *Out, damned spot! Out, I say!* But he had far more blood on his hands than Lady Macbeth.

He had committed heinous acts in the name of God and Country. A country that hired former Nazis, and a Church that laundered Nazi hoards and quietly sanctioned genocide. Washington was swimming in corruption. The whole country was. So was the Vatican. Too many politicians were unworthy of life. Too many others were unworthy to lick Dick's wing tips. He was a knight sworn to uphold justice and to protect the weak and the innocent. But who was truly innocent? What was justice and who deserved it?

Discarded newspaper pages fluttered past the windows like autumn leaves in a zephyr. How little of the truth they actually told, like trying to view an elephant through a keyhole. The world's hidden machinations were too complicated for a newspaper article, too complicated for the American public to understand. It was better that they remain ignorant and docile. Let them swallow half-truths and worry about sports and *The Beverly Hillbillies.*

How had he come to this place, this valley of darkness where the shadow of death dogged his tracks? Behind him lay a path of indelible bricks, every one of which represented a choice, bricks in a path that felt paved just for him, laid out by the Hand of God Himself.

Years of hatred for Emmett.

Holy Cross.

The Montanas.

A fight in a steel mill.

The Order of Malta.

The Army.

Language school.

Bill Donovan and the Sausalito gang.

Honey.

Sniper training.

The Monuments Men.

War criminals.

The Vatican vaults.

Dick.

And now...

Removing any one of those bricks would have led him elsewhere, down a different path. He could still be working in a steel mill, or married to a different woman, or working some mind-numbing office job, oblivious to the hidden world that he now knew Emmett inhabited. Had he ever really had a choice? What bricks lay before him?

Follow the yellow brick road! His chuckle sounded manic, because he sure as shit was *not* in Oz.

"Oh, God, what have I done?" he said aloud, startling himself.

The waitress glanced at him, then returned to her book.

He had confessed his actions—using the vaguest possible terms—in the confessional booth several times since then, but the stain on his soul might well be indelible. How could he allow the words of what he'd done to touch the ears of anyone but God Himself? He couldn't trust even his parish priest with this knowledge.

He had crossed a line, and he'd dragged Don along with him. When they'd parted ways in LA, Okie had wondered if Don would ever speak to him again. Whenever Okie had killed before, he had been able to come to terms with those instances, except for the occasional nightmare and the sense of a callus hardening on his spirit.

But this...

He blinked away tears and swallowed a spasm of ragged bitterness, a magma-burst of emotion boiling from the core. He silently begged the Lord for guidance, for comfort, grasping for whatever rationalization could make sense of it.

Approaching the diner's door came a dark figure, a coat with the collar up. A broad-brimmed, beaver fedora to obscure his face. Besides, the man had one of the most famous faces in America. He became a shadow on the door glass, then pushed inside with the clink of a bell.

Dick crossed the scuffed, black-and-white parquet tiled floor, carrying a gold epi leather Louis Vuitton briefcase, and slid into the booth. Without a word of greeting, he pulled a Vertex file folder from the briefcase and slid it across the tabletop. A stack of black-and-white photos peeked out, the top one far enough to reveal a smooth, creamy calf and limp foot sprawled amid white sheets.

"You got the crime scene photos?" Okie asked incredulously, glancing at the waitress, who hadn't moved. He didn't need to look at them, but the dead woman's foot held his gaze.

"A keepsake for you. Like I told you, we didn't need to worry about the autopsy," Dick said quietly, leaning forward. "Noguchi, the deputy medical examiner, and I go way back. Say, I'm famished. You getting breakfast?"

Okie shook his head.

"Most important meal of the day." Dick turned back to the waitress and snapped his fingers. "Hey, honey. Some service over here."

She looked up as if emerging from a dream, then saw who had summoned her. Her eyes bulged.

She smoothed her soda uniform dress and preened herself as she hurried around the counter.

Okie tucked the foot back into its folder.

As she stopped beside the table, she seemed to be having trouble gathering words. Her garish red lipstick looked like wax on her withered lips. She was missing an incisor.

Dick said, "Bring me a bowl of cottage cheese." He looked at Okie again. "Anything for you?"

Okie shook his head again.

The waitress hurried away, unsteady, as if in a daze. She disappeared into the kitchen and began a whispered exchange with the cook. The cook made sounds of disbelief and peeked through the order window.

Okie said, "Has it had the effect you wanted?"

"No question." The suppressed glee on Dick's face was plain. "They're shitting their pants."

"Then it's over?"

"Far from it. They've done too much damage to this country. Fucking scum. In bed with the fucking mob."

Okie nodded and placed his hand on the hidden stack of photos. This was just the initial stab of the dagger. Next, he would twist it. "We could take them out. Start with Bobby."

"No, I want them to suffer first. The way he fucked up the Cuban situation. Jesus Christ." Dick rolled his eyes. "Khrushchev knows he's a pussy. Bad things are coming."

The waitress approached the table with eyes as big and white as the bowl of cottage cheese in her hands.

She set it down before Dick. "Here you are, sir. I just want you to know, me and Mort both voted for you."

"You forgot the ketchup."

She blinked and flinched as if slapped. "Sure thing, sir." She spun and ran back behind the counter to return with a bottle of ketchup. "Do you need anything else, sir?"

He waved her away.

She took a few hesitant steps back. "I'll be right over here if you need anything."

He slathered ketchup onto his cottage cheese, then as an afterthought called back to her. "A cup of coffee."

She brightened, basking in the glow of the Great Man's fleeting attention, before rushing back behind the counter. "Of course, sir!"

Dick dug his spoon into the bowl and stirred. The ketchup turned to blood-red streaks among the white curds. "Tomorrow we cancel DEFCON 2, and Khrushchev will remove all missiles from Cuba. The blockade of Cuba will end. We got lucky. If Kennedy wasn't such a pussy, Khrushchev wouldn't have had the balls to push us in the first place. I want you to move to Langley permanently. You'll be closer if I need you. I'll introduce you to the new director."

Okie allowed only a slight smile, but he felt like he'd just been called up to the major leagues. "I need a new name." He paused, surprised that he'd said it out loud. Ever since the Bay of Pigs fiasco, his discomfort with his lifelong nickname, originally attached to his father, had continued to grow. And now, "Okie" felt like a different person entirely. "Okie" didn't exist anymore, not really. There was still a face that looked like the man people called Okie—but it was thin as an eggshell. A blank porcelain mask. Perhaps the name "Okie" could still be used as a facade in his quiet, suburban cover life, but the true man was someone else entirely now.

"Like a codename," Dick said, wiping his mouth, nodding. He narrowed his eyes and regarded Okie for a moment. "You remind me of my friend's dog, Seamus. An Irish Wolfhound. A monster of a dog, size of a Shetland pony. You just knew it could kill anyone it wanted to, and Seamus knew it, too. But it was the most loyal dog I've ever seen."

The moment Dick said it, the sense of rightness struck immediately. An animal bred for killing wolves.

"The Wolfhound."

"Like Zorro, or the Lone Ranger," Dick said.

The Wolfhound nodded, letting it sink in. "*Ego sum*...'Wolfhound.'"

"We're going to do great things together," Dick said. "You stick with me. The man of thought who will not act is ineffective; the man of action who will not think is dangerous."

The Wolfhound leaned forward, widening his smile. "*In hoc signo vinces.*"

THE END

"We in this country, in this generation, are - by destiny rather than choice - the watchmen on the walls of world freedom. We ask, therefore, that we may be worthy of our power and responsibility, that we may exercise our strength with wisdom and restraint ... and that we may achieve in our time and for all time the ancient vision of "peace on earth, good will toward men." That must always be our goal, and the righteousness of our cause must always underlie our strength. For as was written long ago: "except the Lord keep the city, the watchman waketh but in vain."

-JFK

President Kennedy was on his way to deliver a speech at the Trade Mart in Dallas on Nov. 22, 1963, when he was assassinated. The speech he never delivered.

the ART of SPIES
A Novel
Robert E. O'Connell III

COMING 2023

THE ART OF SPIES: LAST JUDGEMENT

www.ingramcontent.com/pod-product-compliance
Lightning Source LLC
Chambersburg PA
CBHW020617310726
48979CB00008B/1521/J